The Altered Moon III

The Guarded World

By
James Alan McGettigan

This book is dedicated to the closest and dearest friends I've had in my life; Zack Leavitt, Mia Nicolacoudis, Audrey Rose, Jason Frank Jr, Jing Huntley, and Serena Lucatero. While some my strongest connections have dwindled, the names listed here have almost always proven themselves to be reliable, supportive, and highly empathetic individuals for two very different regions of my life thus far. Should the keepers of these names read this message, I hope you do so, knowing that my connection with you is one of the only reasons I've reached the point in my life that I have, today. In my experience, there are very few, genuine, good-hearted people in the world. And for the hearts that each of you bear, you are brilliant treasures, in a sea of empty chests.

The Author would like to add a trigger warning for all readers of this novel. As there are graphic and complex fight scenes between male and female characters. There is also a scene that involves sexual harassment between two of the characters, though, it is kept fairly brief.

Contents

I
Annihilation of the Blood Eyes
(Amat)

The pale light of Anua shone brightly on the Pa'Zihnra desert; cool winds picked up the red sands. I never visited it in person—it was a truly desolate place on Galiza. "Pa'Zihnra"—the word translated as "piercing fire," in Zetian. It got its name for the blinding burns a tiny grain of sand would inflict, if one found its way into your eye. The sands were glass-sharp, and could scrape away at your flesh if the winds whirled them fast enough, burning you from the inside out if they were caught under your skin.

I was momentarily distracted by the Goddess who shone in all her luminous beauty. Though I knew it was only a hologram, manifested from Y'Gǔtsa's Matrix Platform, her appearance still brought tears to my eyes. A line of Cho'Zai stood before me with their hands bound behind them; their bodies had been stripped, and their eyes exposed to the sands. Despite the strain in their eyes, I did not catch a single blink from any of their stares aimed right at me.

Reikag Vykin stood at my side, along with several dozen Alpha-trained Warvs at my back, all of us armored and protected from the burning sands. The Reikag held a thick stack of files he'd been gathering over recent months, detailed with treasonous records and activities carried out by the Cho'Zai who stood before me. I glanced at Blick. We shared a nod, and I approached the Cho'Zai.

"Cho'Zai"—I spoke loud enough for my voice to beckon across the sands—"you are all here because of what I and my most reliable assets have discovered about your activities under the former Diramal's administration. Fifty-two have faced court-martial for their actions in Y'Gǔtsa alone. Those of you present, as well as an additional 627 of you across the country, have been found to carry out orders so inhumane, that no punishment less than the one you are about to receive can be deemed just, in the eyes of Anua." I gazed and pointed up at her.

Blick came to my side and tossed the files before the Cho'Zai, their contents blowing and drifting across the sand dunes.

I trailed my gaze across each of their faces. Some of them were crying blood; their bodies were coated in tiny bleeding scrapes that swelled ever more by the second. But they didn't even shiver. I growled deeply, as I wanted so badly for them to strain and plead for my mercy.

"Murders, kidnappings, secret ops, torture of civilian personnel, corruption, the list goes on," I continued, taking my time with every word. "Under the new jurisdiction of this country, this behavior cannot go unpunished, regardless of its context. For these are crimes against humanity and your willingness to carry out said crimes demonstrate you are anything but. May Anua judge you justly."

Blick and I proceeded to leave the room. The line of Alphas approached the Cho'Zai and gunned them down. There were twenty-seven Cho'Zai in front of me, and it had taken me three months before I caved-in to the court's orders to carry out their sentences. It was my intention to prolong them until we'd scraped up every speck of dirt on each Cho'Zai within the base in case it might compel others into hiding with their former Diramal.

***

"Most of our active bases around Utopion have complied with your orders in finding Skivs and we've had an uptake in Alpha training from the Warvs that have willingly joined our forces, sir," said Blick, standing across from my desk in my office.

"What's the catch?" I asked.

"We're running out of rations to feed our kinsmen, sir. If we continue harboring people from outside the bases, at this rate we'll run out of food in less than four months."

I nodded.

"Did Olson report to you on the status of the buried starships? Has Rika come up with some way to reverse-engineer the sustenance interfaces within the ships' mess halls?" I asked.

I had assigned Olson to oversee the investigation and reinvigoration of the large starships that rested beneath our planet. From what he told me, they had found nearly eleven hundred.

After she successfully reverse-engineered the alien technology across our aerial crafts, I assigned Rika Rogen as head researcher on the investigation of the buried ships, working closely with Olson.

"No, but Rogen has made drastic progress on the ship's command interfaces and she has informed me that a launch is well underway."

"Good. Let the research team resolve what remains of that task. Put Rogen on ration duty. The countdown of our evac from Galiza is imminent but still out of reach at this point. It won't matter much if we can't keep ourselves well-nourished on our route to the Anobose system."

"Yessir."

"Is the mission to Giclon ready for take-off this afternoon?" I asked.

The doors to my office opened, and through them marched Zothra, with Xaizar and Voruke at his side. Blick turned from them to me and replied: "Yessir."

"Good, we'll conclude our business at a later date. Thank you, Vykin," I said.

"Sir," Blick said, as he turned and left my office.

I leaned back in my chair and stared into each of the Cho'Zai's eyes. Xaizar's were burning with rage, Voruke's were wide, filled with a bold confidence and Zothra's held a sense of betrayal; whether it was genuine or not, I couldn't say.

"Someone gonna say something, or did you all just come here to gawk at me?" I asked.

"You killed your own subjects!" Xaizar blurted.

I shot the Cho'Zai a stern stare, to which he seemed almost unfazed.

"Word has spread quickly of your actions from this morning, sir." Zothra spoke in a more reassuring tone, as he too gave Xaizar a silencing stare. "Given the nature of its exclusivity to our rank, we were merely curious if we, your best, should hold any concern for our well-being."

"That would depend on whether any of you are concealing anything that would be cause for concern," I replied.

"Of course not, sir." Zothra smiled. "It just seems a little extreme, don't you think? What you condemned those Cho'Zai to."

"Hardly," I replied.

3

An awkward silence fell over the room, more so for the three Cho'Zai. Something in their expressions suggested that were it not for the Alphas standing guard in my office, they might have tried to assault me.

"They were just following orders," Xaizar growled.

"Xaizar has a point," said Voruke. "It's easy for you to declare, from your perspective, Diramal, the actions of our fallen Cho'Zai as immoral and excessive." Voruke approached my desk, leaning over it. "But the same could be said for you and those that followed your command as Jinn-hid." I tilted my head up at Voruke. "You harbored Skivs in secret during the time of the former Diramal's administration. Until he sanctioned such actions, one could argue that you and those under your command were wasting precious space, resources, and rations throughout our bases in Utopion. Should those who carried out such treason be met with such justice?"

I squinted at Voruke.

"Harboring Skivs and taking up rations is nowhere near the same thing as killing, maiming, and conspiring against humanity. And I'll say, Cho'Zai Voruke, indirectly accusing your Diramal of treason isn't exactly the best way to avoid joining those he deems threatening," I replied.

"Oh, you're going to shoot me too now, are you?" Voruke asked.

I smiled.

"Currently contemplating the suggestion," I replied.

Zothra cleared his throat.

"We've not come to accuse you of anything, Diramal," said Zothra, directing his words at Voruke. The Cho'Zai pushed himself off my desk and found his place back at Zothra's side. "As we said, we're only concerned for ourselves and how you intend to proceed with others among our rank that have… ugly reputations?"

"Depending on their crimes, punishments may range to that of today's or a mere rank strip, imprisonment, and other mild consequences," I said.

Zothra saluted me with a smile.

"We thank you for your time, sir," said Zothra.

I returned the gesture.

"If there's nothing else, you are all dismissed," I said.

The three Cho'Zai saluted me and made their way out of my office. Sitting in silence, I considered my stance with the Cho'Zai as a whole.

Were I allowed more time by the courts, I might not have felt so pressured to act so soon. But there were too many Cho'Zai within the base who surely felt the same way as Voruke and Xaizar: threatened, if not concerned. I accessed the interface on my desk and made a few calls.

(Quavek)

I proceeded to listen in on Diramal Criptous after Zothra and the others exited the room. He contacted Jinn Ya'Que, the commanding officer of Qui'Jada, a base that rests on the way to Giclon from Y'Gǔtsa.

"Diramal," Ya'Que answered.

"Jinn Ya'Que, I have a request," Amat said.

"And what would that be, sir?" asked Ya'Que.

"I am launching a mission to Giclon today, but I'm going to be a few platoons short, four to be exact. On our way to the city, I'll require the aid of some of your own troops, preferably Alphas if you have some available." .

"Four platoons is a tall order to meet, Diramal. Not to mention, Y'Gǔtsa is one of the largest bases in the nation. Surely the number of troops you have readily assembled is adequate to take on whatever task you hope to achieve in Giclon?" said Ya'Que, in what appeared a passive-aggressive manner.

"Regardless, four platoons are what will be expected of you when I arrive at Qui'Jada, later today. That is an order," Amat said.

There was a resentful, suspicious pause from the Jinn.

"Very well, four platoons. I shall assemble what Alphas I can spare," replied Ya'Que.

"Good, I'll be seeing you shortly. Criptous out."

Hm, why would Criptous request additional troops for a mission he is already more than well-equipped to undertake?

I continued to observe as Amat made another call from his fizer.

"Reikag Vykin," Amat said.

I raised my eyebrows.

Mm, contacting the head of security?

"Criptous, sir?" Blick replied.

"Gather four platoons' worth of the Alphas; they're being reassigned to your command. You'll have a task here at the base that will require their skills while I'm away," I said.

"A task, sir?" asked Blick.

"The news of this morning's events didn't sit well with the best among the Cho'Zai. Based on the turnout of our… exchange after you left my office, they are clearly threatened by me. And if they can put the other Cho'Zai on edge, it could start a civil war within the base. So, as a preemptive act, I am ordering you and these four Alpha platoons to arrest all members of the Cho'Zai within the base until thorough background analysis and proper disciplinary action can be taken for each," I said.

Another moment of silence. The notion bewildered me.

"Is this task too heavy a burden for the Reikag to carry out, Vykin?" Amat pressed.

"No, sir. Just seems a lot for one day, is all."

"Traces of loyalty to the former Diramal among the Cho'Zai are still evident, Vykin. Such behavior cannot be taken lightly, as it is a potential threat to the safety and security of the human race."

"Yes, sir. I shall begin shortly after you depart," replied Blick.

Traitor, damn the humans! I thought to myself, as I cut the signal. *I need to warn the others of this.*

***

"He's going to do what?!" exclaimed Xaizar.

"Perhaps Criptous wouldn't feel the need for such drastic measures if the two of you knew how to bite down on your tongues," said Zothra.

"I was merely pointing out a simple flaw in the boy's logic," said Voruke.

"A point that served as a means to an end," I broke in. "Along with everything else that was said in that exchange. It was all for naught. All that matters is our next move."

"Well, we're not going to stand by and let it happen. More than half of our brethren will be sent to the slaughter, ourselves included. Leaving us with only one—"

"You should know, as much as the rest of us, Xaizar, that in the Diramal's absence, it is in Zothra's hands to decide these things," I said, cutting Xaizar short.

Xaizar scowled at me as Zothra contemplated a moment.

"We can't allow Amat and the humans to hold complete dominion over Y'Gůtsa. If we rebel, we lose all eyes and ears, not just here, but across all operating branches of the militia. Amat will outlaw the Cho'Zai, and we'll be shot on sight," said Zothra.

"It's already headed down that path for us," Xaizar said direly.

"Ah, but we still have our connections here and there, both within and outside this base," said Voruke. "If we play along with Amat's skepticism, many will die yes, but we might be able to spare *some* from their lethal fates. Reassign them to the Diramal's command in the waste."

"And if we rebel, we lose all of that. All monitorization, all our influence," said Zothra.

"What motive do we have in controlling what remains of the humans?" blurted Xaizar. "The Diramal's search has been ended and deemed faulty against Amat's impulsive behavior. We've narrowed the humans to—"

"It doesn't matter what we've done, or how you perceive the Diramal's pursuits, Xaizar. He is our leader and the strongest of all the Vix and Varx combined. To challenge him is to meet your own death. The only reason you're one of us is because he acknowledges your ability to get the others to fall in line, to a point. And that is what you will do. Spread the word; when Blick calls for the Alphas to apprehend us, we are all to *comply*," said Zothra.

(Amat)

Zothra, Blick, Shím, Quim, and Mae all stood at my side as we overlooked the hangar. The four platoons of Alphas had regrouped elsewhere in the base by that time, which Zothra promptly noted.

"The numbers seem a little light among the troops," said Zothra, sounding almost unsurprised.

"I've selected a number of our forces for reassignment," I replied. "Come, all of you, it's time."

7

Lara was among those I'd reassigned that day, as a precaution. With Blick leading what should have been a simple task, if anything had gone wrong, I wanted someone there to protect my mother and little sister.

As we approached the Fade Mae, Zothra, Shím, and I would be entering, I stopped to address Blick. Catching a glimpse of Zothra nodding sternly at someone, I turned my head to catch who it was and observed the Cho'Zai Xaizar leaning against a wall, arms crossed, irritated. The others walked past me to enter the Fade.

"Is everything alright?" asked Mae, placing her hand on my chest.

"It's fine," I said, expressing a reassuring smile. "I'll join you shortly."

Mae smiled back and headed inside as I stepped close to Blick.

"Something's up," I whispered. "Zothra just acknowledged Xaizar over there and the lesser Cho'Zai doesn't seem well spirited, given his expression. If there's a problem, refrain from telling me until I've returned."

"Xaizar is rash, but not entirely dull. I'll keep my wits about me as we gather the Cho'Zai, sir," replied Blick.

"I trust you will," I said, offering my hand. Blick took and shook it. "Be safe, my friend," I said.

It was the first time in a long time that I regarded Blick as such and I could see how he took it to heart. The muscles in his face relaxing as the weight of the compliment shifted Blick's mood. I turned and entered the Fade.

(Xaizar)

The final Fade flew out of the hangar… and it began. Blick had fled somewhere within the base, likely to some meeting point where the Alphas awaited him. They flooded Y'Gûtsa, leaving no stone unturned, no quarters unchecked.

I used my fizer and opened a channel to a group of Varx I had informed of the oncoming threat. Zothra had made a fair point earlier that day. I was good at getting others to fall in line… to do what *I* asked of them.

"Are you in position?" I asked.

"We are awaiting their arrival," said the Cho'Zai Drüfé, a Varx beneath his skinsuit.

"Good. When they rally us up, I'll find you and the others in the mix. If I can't, you know the signal to watch for," I said.

"Yes, sir," said Drüfé.

I closed the channel and remained in the hangar until a pair of armored Alphas found and held me there. Small groups of Alphas at a time had arrived with more Cho'Zai to join us. I shuffled within the group, staying at the front, before a particular Alpha. Our numbers were on par with one another—Alpha and Cho'Zai—if not, one might have held a slight upper hand over the other.

Many of the Cho'Zai were taken aback and upset by the circumstances, oblivious to what was about to happen. It struck me as odd that Blick hadn't put us straight into captivity, but it was fitting for what would occur next.

With all of us gathered in the hangar, Blick came out to address us. The Alphas had taken positions around the hangar, guns held at their sides. Perhaps the context of their former lives as Warvs explained the subtle pleasure each of them had on their faces at the sight of us. Herded up like lesser livestock.

"Cho'Zai, I'm sure you all have many questions at this present moment, and for a distant connection I have with each of you, I feel that some are owed an explanation," said Blick. "Due to past and present tensions in his relationship with certain members among your rank, Diramal Criptous has asked me to incarcerate each of you and that records of your previous operations be analyzed for acts deemed unjust and or corrupt—" An uproar began. Some laughed mockingly, others were outraged. "Carried out during the time frame of the previous administration."

I caught sight of Drüfé, and I gave him a nod to signal what would follow. The next instance he was gone. Spraying gunfire went off from three different Alphas and three more fell to their deaths, all in the same instance, as Drüfé and the others retaliated against the Alphas.

I pulled back at the forearm of my skinsuit, tearing it, and my true arm wiggled out, dripping in sludge. Raising my arm up high for all to see, I blurted, "Drakkar will consume the final Mai'Sahara!"

I altered time, just as the Alpha before me had as well. As she aimed her gun at me, I reached forward, grabbed the barrel of the weapon, and pushed its aim off to the side as her finger pulled the trigger. She ceased fire and I pushed it up against her snout. Her grip lessened enough for me to pry the weapon and gun her down. All of my brethren joined in the fight for our lives as it ensued around us.

(Log)

The boy and I have gotten along relatively well with one another these past few months. Likely because we've kept our distance from each other and taken our getting to know one another slowly. Warter still hasn't forgiven me fully, and I don't blame him for it. It's been three months since I lost my own parents, with their killer dead. His name and the resentment I hold for the Cho'Zai, damned to walk in the shadow of Anua, come up regularly in my mandatory meetings with my counselor. She's helped me to see it's for that reason I can't help Warter process his own pain, despite wanting to.

But then again, perhaps those wishes are more out of a sense of duty. While I am clear-minded and more responsible than I was a few months ago, I am neither happy nor sad, but numb with myself. It's as if I've been removing debris from a tunnel's entrance and there's one final stone keeping me from seeing the light of day, but I can't find its seeps in the dark.

The door rang, and I approached it, expecting Amat. He had come days before to tell me that the courts had forced his hand in carrying out the execution of several Cho'Zai who had been found guilty of various treasons and that none of them were Xaizar, unfortunately.

On the other side of the door was Kita.

Warter had taken a liking to her and she a notable liking to me. Nothing was said of it to me directly, but I suspected Amat had made her my designated watch guard, to some degree, given her lack of missions since my discharge from the med bay and how frequently she visited.

I was happy when Kita stopped by, since it was the only time I saw Warter's face light up. Kita stood with hands behind her back and her eyes calm, taking in my appearance.

"Kita," I said.

"Log," Kita replied.

"Come in."

I stepped aside and extended my arm into my quarters as Kita passed me.

"How are things?" Kita asked.

"Not much different from the last time you visited. Warter still keeps to himself," I replied.

Kita nodded.

"Have you tried reaching out to him more?" Kita asked.

"I can't, not yet. With Xaizar still so close and active, my mind can't quiet itself of the horrors he inflicted on me."

Kita paused as she selected her next words carefully.

"I wish I could say I understood what you are going through." Kita's tone was empathetic.

Looking deep into Kita's eyes, I replied: "No, you don't," in a way that said she would regret it if she did.

"Kita?" Warter said, peeking his head out of his room before Kita could reply.

Kita shifted her attention to the boy as they smiled at one another.

"Warter," Kita said, warmly. "It's so good to see you."

Warter walked up to Kita and embraced her.

"And you, Kita," Water replied.

"Are you doing well?"

Warter shrugged.

"Trying to. I'm still... fixing myself... from what I lost." Warter struggled to describe the process of mourning.

"So, you still write in the journal the Io-Pac gave you?" asked Kita. Warter nodded. "That's wonderful."

"Among other things. The other night he scared me almost half to death," I said and nodded toward Warter. "Screaming at the top of your lungs. I barged into your room to find you clawing and tearing apart the fabrics of your bed. At some point, we're gonna talk about that."

Warter turned his gaze from me. Kita frowned.

"I might be able to help with this," she said.

"That would be welcome, as always," I replied.

11

"Of course," Kita said. "Oh, I was going to say I haven't had any rations for the day. Would the two of you care to join me?"

I looked to Warter.

"What do you say, kid? You hungry?" I asked.

"Sure," replied Warter, almost as a whisper.

"Very well." I turned my attention to Kita. "I'll be just a moment; gonna go grab some ration cards."

"Oh, I'll cover it," said Kita.

I shook my head.

"No, it's alright. I may be temporarily removed from duty, but my cousin still provides me with some units here and there," I said.

Kita gave a half-smile as I turned away from her and started talking with Warter. Inside my room, I opened a drawer with almost a dozen ration cards in it. Grabbing two, I stopped myself as I slid the drawer closed. Pulling it back out slightly, I lifted the bottom and revealed my pistol. I carried it on me, in secret, every time we went out. No one else knew I possessed it, not even Amat. Despite having never used it, there was always a thought at the sight of it: *Today might be the day.*

I took the gun and hid it in my pants. Turning around, I noticed my closet was open slightly and on my way out, I shut it completely, hiding its contents. Kita's face lit up as I turned the corner and approached them.

"Right. Are we ready?" I asked.

"Yes, I think so."

"Warter?" I asked.

Warter nodded and proceeded out of my quarters. I followed him and Kita walked beside me. Warter intentionally stayed ahead of us. Any time we caught up to him, he picked up the pace.

"Hey, Warter, stay where I can see you, alright," I said.

Warter slowed down as he got the farthest from us he had ever been during that stroll—roughly fifty meters.

"A few months ago, I was losing my mind at the thought of raising the kid on my own. Now, I more often than not worry about *losing* him," I said.

"That's a good thing," said Kita. "After what he's been through, it's better to worry about him too much rather than too little."

I noted how she said, "After what he's been through," rather than "What you put him through," but I remained nonreactive. Kita's sympathy toward me, while nice at times, was not as greatly appreciated as she intended. It made me feel as though I wasn't being held accountable for my actions; that I wasn't enduring enough for the loss I'd imposed on Warter.

"Don't put it that way," I said.

"What?"

"The way you phrased Warter's circumstance. He is where he is because *I* put him there. If you're going to bring it up, say it how it is," I said.

"I didn't mean to put it like that—"

"I'm not innocent in this, any of it," I said.

"I don't think that you are." Kita spoke sternly.

I nodded, keeping my eyes on Warter.

"I don't deserve anyone's sympathy," I said.

Kita held a silence before replying.

"But the effort you're putting in to compensate for what you did to better yourself, I don't feel it should go unacknowledged. And I'm sorry if, in doing so, I remind you of any guilt you may be burdened with. That's not my intention," Kita replied.

"You're too kind to me, Kita," I said, staring at the ground. "It doesn't change the fact that Anua will likely shun me to her shadow, when my time finally comes…"

The rest of the walk was carried out in silence. I caught up with Warter in the ration line, paid for our "glop" of a meal, and found a table. A few columns up the way, I stopped in my tracks at the sight of a familiar face. Swiftly coming to Warter's side, I directed him away from Kaia. Unfortunately, she'd turned her head from her client just in time to catch a glimpse of me. A few columns over, we found a spot, isolated far enough from her.

"Everything alright?" Kita asked.

I glanced back to see if Kaia had followed us and refocused on Kita.

"Yes, why?" I asked.

"I… well, I noticed someone back there who seemed to recognize you, frowning when she noticed me."

I cupped my brow with my hand.

"Don't worry about it, she's just… an old acquaintance," I replied.

Kita's ears pricked up.

"Oh, come now, Log…" Kaia swung her leg beneath the table and dropped into the seat right beside me. "I thought we were a little more than that."

"I'm off, Kaia, you've got no business here," I said.

"Ohh, I know you had a rough patch a few months ago, and I can see you still have a little gloom in your eyes from it. But I got something that can make all that go away. Besides…" Kaia said, shifting her hand up my body, "It's been a while since you've given me a—"

I grasped Kaia's wrist firmly and grimaced. Warter had dropped his utensil and frowned at me. Kita clenched her fist and tightened her lips at Kaia.

"Never touch or come near me again. I am off it and I'm not getting sucked back into that void of *misery* again," I said, shoving Kaia's arm back.

Kaia took note of Kita's stern stare and gave a flaring smile in reply, squirming in her seat. She shifted her attention back to me, leaned in close, and whispered: "If you come with me now, I'll consider it a discount."

"Hey," Kita barked. "The Io-Pac doesn't want you here; go waste your breath somewhere else."

Kaia giggled aloud.

"The Io-Pac. As a Krollgrum, you should know Log's dear cousin stripped him of that rank after his little…" Kaia leaned in toward Kita. "*Incident.*"

"No doubt caused by the Diazep you sold to him…" Kita leaned in close toward Kaia. "Which any distribution, let alone possession of such material, is punishable by exile."

Kaia stared blankly at Kita and shrugged her face into the fur at the edge of her hood.

"Log, who's this weija?" Kaia asked. Kita's face turned pink as her eyes glinted with rage. "She your new—"

Blue lights lit up the room as a siren filled the air.

"What's wrong?" asked Warter.

"I don't know. Wrap up your ration, we're going back to—"

"Attention all occupants of Y'Gŭtsa, this is Jinn-hid Lara Criptous." Lara's voice blared out over the base intercom. "I've been informed by the Reikag that there has been an outbreak in the hangar. All occupants are to return to their quarters immediately. If you sight any Cho'Zai, proceed with extreme caution. Please lock yourselves in your quarters and do not exit them until the situation has been dealt with. Thank you."

I looked to Kita and then at Warter, took the boy by the arm, and started marching back to my quarters.

"Log, I can walk just fine on my own," Warter growled.

"We don't have time, Warter," I barked. "If there's even a chance that Xaizar or any other Cho'Zai has broken free of that hangar, I'll spend an eon in the shadow of Anua before I let them get within two steps of you." *And I'm gonna put an end to the nightmare he implanted in my mind.*

Kita followed me back to my quarters. I hardly noticed until we reached them. I placed Warter in his room, and Kita proceeded to follow me around my quarters.

"Kita, since you've decided to accompany me this far back to my quarters, you'll be watching Warter for me until I return," I said.

"Return?" Kita asked.

I entered Warter's room.

"Alright, Warter, no matter what happens, you stay right here with Kita. She's going to look after you," I said.

"Log, what are you planning?" Kita asked.

"You're going to join the fight," said Warter.

"You're not—"

"I am," I said, cutting Kita short. My focus remained on Warter. "I have to face him—"

"Log, you're under disciplinary action, under direct orders from your cousin…"

"It's the only way I can redeem myself for what I did to you and your family," I said, ignoring Kita.

Warter nodded as Kita continued to argue.

"I understand," said Warter.

15

"Kita." I raised my voice just enough to quiet her. I gently placed my hands on her shoulders and looked her dead in the eye. "I need to do this, and you can help by looking after the kid while I'm gone."

"How are you going to fight when you don't have access to a quantum suit?" asked Kita.

"Who said I didn't?" I asked, marching straight to my room. Kita followed me.

I proceeded to open my closet and unveiled a QS-25.

"How did you get access to one of those?"

"Well," I said, proceeding to throw my pistol on my bed.

"How did you get—"

"After demonstrating enough good behavior for about a month and a half"—I walked into my suit as the opening sealed around my rear— "Amat decided I'd grown responsible enough to be granted some level of security, for scenarios like this." I turned around and acknowledged the gun. "This thing, on the other hand, I've always had, for my own safekeeping."

I holstered the gun and proceeded to walk out of my quarters.

Halfway to the hangar, I had to be honest with myself. I wasn't prepared to face Xaizar. The trauma of that interrogation still lingered at the furthest point of my subconscious mind. The urge to keep Warter and the base safe was stronger, however. I had made an oath to Warter at the very least.

The hangar was as chaotic as I anticipated it to be. Coming through the doors, I was met with a Cho'Zai bearing a splice. I flicked one of my suit's claws out and unholstered my gun with the other hand. To stop the Cho'Zai's swing, I grabbed his forearm and dug my claws into his flesh. I raised my gun, and he lowered my aim. So I fired and landed a shot in his thigh. Kneeling, he rammed his head into my gut and knocked me back. With the air knocked out of my lungs, the Cho'Zai crawled, straddled me, punched me once, twice, and pressed his hands around my neck. I stretched and swung my claws at his neck. Even as he slowly bled to death, he exerted every fiber of his fading strength onto my throat.

I pushed the Cho'Zai aside and took in the pitch-black room. My particle sensors in the suit's interface activated by default. The room lit up from an array of shots firing back at one another. If it weren't for the Cho'Zai dressed in nothing but their uniforms against those in the QS-25s, I wouldn't know where to start.

I stumbled forward, stopping myself from joining the skirmish when I remembered there were two entrances to the hangar. Noting how I was the only one who stood before the south entrance, I looked across the way to the eastern entrance. No one stood there either. Figuring it was smarter to stand back from the battle, I decided I would keep a watchful eye on both doorways and meet with any Cho'Zai that neared them. Thus, keeping the conflict from spreading throughout the base.

(Xaizar)

I was relishing in the bloodshed. To my surprise, however, we were evenly matched. Warv-Alpha and Cho'Zai. Were the Alphas not armored because of their reliance on the QS-25s to alter time, the battle would have been long over with, I'm sure, despite their advancements in hand-to-hand combat.

When I ran out of ammunition for the gun I wretched from that first Alpha's grasp, I came into the possession of a fauchard. I killed four Alphas with it until I stumbled upon Blick. While I couldn't see his face or hear his voice, there was no mistaking his figure. I'd learned to know it so well, in all my years of service to the Diramal. Our skirmish was kept brief before I finally parted from him. It was also through my years of service to the Diramal that I knew better than to even smack Blick's cheek. Within a minute of our conflict, Blick managed to break the shaft of the fauchard and hit me with such a strike it sent me flying more than twenty feet from where I stood. I paused before finding my feet. The young man's gaze and mine were locked as he approached me, but his approach was halted when another Varx stepped in to face him.

I continued to face and kill… dozens of Alphas, each in fewer moves than the one before and more vigorously. Many a weapon crossed my path, many an opening I saw to disarm my foes, but I chose to fight each with my bare fists. Were it not for my limber tentacle appendages beneath my skinsuit, I'm sure my hands would have been on the brink of breaking; fists bashing against hardened steel. Claws tearing apart sections at suits'

17

arms and chests. The faint physical pain, dulled by vigor and the pleasure I took, in making each of my opponents *suffer*. Seven moves, six moves, five, four, three—Voruke pulled on my shoulder and dragged me somewhere isolated within the hangar. Once pressed against the wall, he struck me and pushed me back once again. Voruke spoke, outraged, while we were still in altered time; frequency stabilizers planted in our cochlea allowed us to communicate fluently without delay in the auditory rendition of our shared words.

"What have you done?! We were told to *comply* with Blick—"

"On what grounds do you accuse me of insubordination, Voruke?!" I growled back. "Did I cry out commands among our ranks to retaliate? Surely, you can't think we were the only ones left to be content with today's events—"

"You unveiled your arm and chanted for the death of—"

"That was after the conflict broke out."

"*Regardless* of who started this skirmish, it was *your* responsibility to keep the others in line. You failed, and now every remnant of power and influence left to us will be wiped off the map."

"As was inevitable, ever since the Diramal lost his seat here in Utopion. At least now, if we act quickly, we can escape through the launch bay, warn our assets around the globe, and give them a chance to regroup and join us in the waste," I argued.

Voruke scoffed and shook his head. He raised his finger to me.

"Time and time again, Xaizar, you forget yourself. Always failing to see the bigger picture. It doesn't matter how little we've worn down their numbers over the countless millennia. So long as Amat lives, without our influence among the humans, he diminishes our odds of winning this war dangerously," Voruke said.

My attention was intuitively led elsewhere, toward the south entrance of the base. A lone Alpha stood. It was strange how I suddenly felt drawn to him through some unseen connection. And there it was, that feeling I had felt from the moment he left that interrogation room.

"Are you dozing off?" asked Voruke, sternly.

I shifted my attention back to Voruke.

"As if your bickering couldn't do anything else for me. Shall we find a means of opening the launch bay doors?" I asked.

Voruke growled.

"Start redirecting the troops immediately toward the exit, and I'll open it," said Voruke.

I nodded and as we went our separate ways, I headed straight for Log.

(Log)

In the little time I was there, I only faced two Cho'Zai, who stumbled their way toward the south entrance. Considering I didn't see any near the east, it kept me from moving across the hangar, making the battle feel a lot longer than it was, since I was just standing by. Feeling both restless and afraid, waiting and hoping that *one* particular Cho'Zai would find me, unsure if I would have the same vigor when and if he did.

When at last he made himself known, walking through the skirmish, unchallenged, I stiffened as we locked eyes. Xaizar wore a knowing smile on his face, as if he could see through my armor. He stopped just on the edge of the raging chaos behind him, a good ten paces between us. I shifted my leg back and held a wide stance; Xaizar did the same. Flicking the claws of my suit out, I rushed toward the Cho'Zai, and our conflict finally ensued.

Xaizar fought with less honor than a wild child as he dodged my first punch, grabbed my arm, and gnawed on it. I locked our legs together, placed my hand on top of his head, and jumped back. Crashing against the ground, I was able to free my arm, hardly injured thanks to my armor. I pounded my elbow against the Cho'Zai's chest, once, twice. He halted the third with his hand and pushed my arm with all his strength, forcing us to roll over one another. Pinning my limbs down, he lay atop me and bit into my shoulder.

I growled as some of his teeth had found their way through the seeps of the suit. Jolting my head back, I knocked the steel point of my armored ear into the side of the Cho'Zai's snout. It hardly seemed to faze him, no matter how many times I did it. His teeth dug deeper. I howled and maneuvered subconsciously, thrusting my hips back against the Cho'Zai; knocking the air out of him until he finally rolled off. Slowly pushing myself off the ground, I caught the Cho'Zai's foot just before it would have hit my chin and twisted it. The Cho'Zai jumped in the air, contorting

19

his body so that I would not break his leg. Falling to the ground, he kicked his heel against my shoulder. I, in return, scraped my claws deep against Xaizar's calf. The Cho'Zai stiffened, as we both stumbled back to the ground. Xaizar, and I shared grimacing stares as we found our feet. The Cho'Zai bent and raised his legs, pressed his hands against the ground, stood on them, arched his legs back off the ground, and pushed off with his hands, into an upright position. All done with a swift and *inhuman* flexibility.

Once again, we stood across from one another. The Cho'Zai licked my blood from his teeth and lips as he grinned sinisterly at me. I rushed up, jumped, and kicked at his jaw, twice; the second one landed. As he stumbled back, I pressed forward and scratched my claws across his chest. He threw an eager punch at me as I twisted out of its path and whipped my fist across his snout. The Cho'Zai stumbled back further.

Xaizar widened his stance as I continued pressing on him. He threw another punch, and I caught it. Using my grasp against me, he pulled me in close as he spun around and wrapped his arms around my chest, locking my own there. I hit the back of my head against his snout. His grasp lessened enough for me to duck down, and with his arm still in my grasp, I spun behind Xaizar and curled his arm back. Holding him there, I scraped and tore at the flesh of his scalp as he flailed his free hand at me.

Having torn through enough flesh, I saw how something at his scalp squirmed and stretched out toward me. My grip on him abruptly loosened as that painful sensation returned to my ear. The Cho'Zai twisted and hit me to the floor with his elbow. I froze there, as I witnessed Xaizar reach back behind his scalp and tear away his own skin from the top of his head over his face. He turned to me and revealed his true image. Tentacles squirming out from the gaping holes that encompassed his face.

Lights flickered around us. I looked back to find the launch bay doors opening and all the Cho'Zai rushing to it. Xaizar grabbed me by the seeps in my chest armor and raised me high over himself. His tentacles squirmed and vibrated like quaking water. Once again, I was overcome with the most extreme sense of fear I had ever encountered, rendering me helpless. Xaizar proceeded to crouch down and remove something from beneath his boot. A small knife, triangular in shape, with a thin, curved handle to lock his inner fingers around. My breath caught as Xaizar aimed between the seeps of my armor and jabbed the blade into my gut. The cold sensation of warm blood gushing out of my intestines stirred up tremors throughout my bones. All fell silent as the shocking thought of my imminent passing flooded my mind. I couldn't stop gasping, with my jaw hanging wide, staring into those quivering tentacles of the Cho'Zai. *Oh no. Why? I could have done something. This is what I wanted. I've failed Warter. I can't stop shaking. I'll be sent to the shadow! I'll see my parents soon... my parents...*

Pow! The abrupt impact of my body on the ground put a halt to my train of thought. Before me was a titan of an armored soldier, pinning Xaizar against the wall. Each blow carried such ferocity that the wall at the Cho'Zai's back cracked and crumbled. To my amazement, while I saw several openings for Xaizar to return a blow, he merely parried one or two against my rescuer. The lone soldier had beaten Xaizar until the Cho'Zai was limp and could hardly stand on his own two feet. He raised his fist for one final blow that would have likely been the end of Xaizar but paused himself. He looked back at me, then at the Cho'Zai, and dropped him.

Retracting his helm as he approached me, I recognized him just before I blacked out.

"Blick..." I uttered. "*Huh*, I'm going home..."

***

I found myself lying in a dark place, darker than the hangar. Still burdened by my wound. Aside from the thin layer of water I rested in, the particle sensors on my visor could not detect any definitive objects or life forms in sight. It didn't feel like death. In fact, I had the strangest sense that despite my circumstance, I was going to live.

"You *are* going to be alright," a woman's voice said.

I knew that voice. I turned my head toward where it came from. My breath escaped me, and instantly my eyes filled with tears. I retracted my helm to see her with my own eyes in case my vision was deceiving me. Yet, there she was still, with such a peaceful and proud smile on her face.

"Mom," I gasped.

She nodded in reply. I felt a strong hand clasp over my wound. I looked up and followed its arm, to see my dad squatting beside me with the same expression on her face as my mother. The tears finally fell from my eyes.

There were so many things I wanted to tell them but couldn't put into words at that moment. Yet at the same time, I had the sense I didn't need to and that they already knew everything I would have said.

"How?" I asked, my lips trembling.

"We've always been right here," said my father.

"And we've been so proud of everything you've done," said my mother. "Looking after Warter, taking responsibility, facing your fears."

"Can I… am I going with you?" I asked.

"Now's not your time, son," said my father. "But we will stay with you until all is well."

"And after that?" I asked.

"We'll still be where we are now. At your side."

"For now, just rest," said my mother, as she stroked her fingers through my hair.

I eased my head onto the wet ground, but fought to keep my eyes open. Just to embrace their faces as long as I could. Until finally my mother trailed her fingers over my eyelids and weighed them down.

II
The Seven Crescents of Giclon
(Amat)

Giclon: a city covered by some of the most ancient ruins on Galiza. The Solixa Monuments, as M.I.S.T. had labeled them. Across the globe of Galiza rested many varying ruins, among which M.I.S.T. categorized them all into three different classes, as there were correlating features among several of these ancient mechanics. But the Solixa Monuments, while they were the oldest of the three classes, they were eerily the most active.

The Monuments that lingered over Giclon were that of seven pointed mechanisms arcing over the city. Their highest points reached anywhere between twenty-five to thirty miles up, sprouting from a small hill that stretched around the rear of the city. Even in the light of day, a shadow lingered over the city of Giclon, engulfed in a signature green shine from the Solixa Monuments, no brighter than twilight.

The culture that thrived here before the war was not a pleasant one. This city had the highest rates of crime, suicide, corruption, and conspiracy. It was the *stench* of Utopion, a conspicuous flaw in what our country stood for.

Many who lived there claimed they saw peculiar spirits and unnatural entities in isolated alleyways and on lonely streets, which some of the locals attributed to the crescent structures. No thorough investigation was ever conducted on them, at least, none the general public was aware of.

The structures themselves were metallic, rusted, with tiny glimmers of eerie green lights emanating from within them. In dust storms, the light could be seen stretching down to the surface in full beams. During such instances, the city would quarantine and all activity within the city would cease. It was in these storms that the locals reported having seen the illusive entities at their clearest. Standing idle within the beams, seemingly staring into various homes.

Since the dawn of the city's foundation, the lore that surrounded it had not only the locals, but other parts of the country spooked as well. To put the concerns of the good Utopian people to rest, M.I.S.T. conducted a hands-off investigation in the Galizian year 2289. It was a group of four physicists who didn't go anywhere near the structures themselves. But they did attribute most of the local brutish activities and behavior to a lack of sunlight. They also credited the light emanating from within the structures as having solid photonic matter or "solid light." Light that has such a high volume of photons that it becomes solid, to a degree. And the figures people had sometimes seen were justified in that they were outlines of individuals who had knowingly or unknowingly walked through one of the beams emanating from the structures. Distorted over time as the photons worked to re-solidify the beam once again, justifying their inhuman appearances.

While most outside the city were satisfied with this explanation, others within, were not. According to the majority of the sightings, there was more to the mysterious shapes than mere disfigured outlines. As no investigation had been committed to the structures themselves… the structures and the figures were considered *alien* in nature by the Giclonians.

***

I stood at the south end of the city, atop a building, helm retracted as I gazed up at the seven structures arced over the city. The light they emanated was more visible to the naked eye in pitch-black darkness compared to any natural cover of nightfall. Illuminating the city as if it were alive; otherworldly, but alive. Then again, I had only seen recordings of the city and the strange lights the structures emanated from when I was a boy, with a much more open mind before my installment in Alpha training.

"Sir," Shím spoke over comms, "the troops await your command on the south border of the city."

I took in one final sight of the city in its entirety, enveloped my helm over my head, and joined my troops. Zothra turned to notice me, just as I walked up from behind, as if he sensed I was near. He acknowledged me with a salute. Mae raised her head to me. Quim maintained a hard gaze at the structures, as if she suspected something about them. Walking past her, I heard her whisper: "What unfamiliar things linger here…"

Shím came to my side and acknowledged me. I trailed my gaze along the line of my troops, looked back at the city, and back at them. I retracted my helm, taking advantage of the lighting that engulfed the city and felt the breeze. Not to mention the strength it likely demonstrated to the men and women under my command.

"Giclon city," I said. "A place of mystery in plain sight, yet so poorly understood. Do not take the myths that surround this place lightly. The people who lived here had reason to suspect its strangeness *long* after M.I.S.T.'s halfhearted investigation of it. For that, we should be mindful of its contents. Now, the city is small enough for us to cover as a single unit of our numbers. We will create a column and take a straight shot through the streets. Search through buildings as you come across them. Always move in pairs, if nothing else."

"Yes, sir," said the troops in unison.

"Form a line, let's move in," I said.

I turned to lead the march but was halted by Quim, who stood as still as a statue, looking down at me. I gazed up at her.

"Do you wish to speak with me, Pac-Qua Quim?" I asked.

She nodded.

"You are right to make us mindful of the hidden things that linger here," Quim said. I tilted my head in reply. "I sense them, sir. Tethers of ones lost. The crescents serve as their puppeteers."

I paused, trying to understand what Quim was saying.

"Are you saying that the figures standing in the lights, emanating from those Solixa Monuents are a threat?" I asked.

Quim nodded.

"They may be, sir," Quim said.

"I imagine, then, it would be wise to avoid them," I said.

Quim nodded.

"Thank you, Quim, for your counsel," I said, as Quim saluted me. "I'll relay it to the others."

After having stressed to the troops across a channel not to engage with the lights or anything appearing within them, we proceeded into the city.

***

25

The figures were more defined than I'd anticipated. From a distance, each might have seemed very human, but each one we passed couldn't be further from a true human outline. Many were identical to one another, though there were varying changes in overall size. They all had dimensions to them, but, even when I dared myself closer examinations, they had no clear characteristics beyond their outlines. Most had five very long, pointed fingers. Head-on, these outlines appeared to stand tall with their chests out, though at their rears, their spines curved out like shells. And again, at front glance, their heads appeared round and normal in shape, but from a side view, their skulls or perhaps extensions of their skulls sprouted straight out of their occipital lobes. There were perhaps other peculiar characteristics to be noted about these figures that I failed to observe. Except that on occasion, I'd notice one turn, tracking me as I walked by.

"Do they frighten you, sir?" Zothra asked, coming to my side as I locked eyes with one of the figures.

"There's very little that frightens me, Zothra," I said, continuing to walk. "The unknown is not among those things. One who seeks to expand their knowledge cannot fear what they do not understand, even if they fear what they might discover. Rather the foreseeable known, the possible known but not in certainty."

"An intriguing answer, sir. To that I would continue to ask, does this place, these figures, arouse your search for knowledge?"

"They might, if I was driven enough to enlighten myself on the secrets they hold," I replied.

"Say you did have the necessary drive and the means to uncover the secrets of these shapes and those structures." Zothra and I gazed up at the seven crescents. "You would know as well as anyone with half a brain, let alone a scientific expert, that these Solixa Monuments and their projections are not of human origin. Would that not strike the fear of Anua's Shadow into your heart?"

"It may, but with all those things at my disposal, a thirsty curiosity and tools to quench it in this hypothetical scenario, my pursuit of knowledge would outweigh my fear of its mysteries," I replied.

"Even if by the end of it you might regret the uncovered fact, as your findings would come with a heavy dread?" asked Zothra.

I paused and looked at Zothra.

"You're suggesting the secrets one would unveil about this place would be detrimental to one's own understanding of the world around them and perhaps even of themselves," I said.

"Precisely, Diramal."

"Were that the case, in my position, I would try to focus on the brighter side of the scenario. To find a silver lining in the discovery and take pride in my actions," I said.

Zothra chuckled as he turned and continued to walk.

"I suppose we'll never know for certain. But with that in mind, perhaps you should tread carefully in your newfound interest of understanding the invaders and why they are here. You and the rest of us may live to regret it," said Zothra.

"Let me be the judge of what I may live to regret, *Cho 'Zai*," I replied.

I took my leave of Zothra and found Shím walking alongside Quim. Shím observed a trooper fixated on one of the figures in the green light. Standing just before it, leaning close, the figure moved subtly, with a similar intrigue about the trooper. Shím noticed the interaction and just as the trooper started to stretch his hands closer to the light, Shím yanked on the trooper's shoulder and forced him to proceed onward, barking at the trooper's idiocy. I snickered at Shím's handling of the situation and met with Quim.

"Pac-Qua," I said.

"Sir."

"Have your senses alerted you to any further warnings about the city?" I inquired.

"This city reeks of death, old and new," Quim replied.

"It does have a rather messy reputation, as I understand it. How new?" I asked.

"Within the last two days, a brutish battle ensued," Quim replied.

"Were the shapes in the light involved?" I asked.

"For that, I would have to inspect a body, one that was present. At the north end of the city."

"This battle you speak of was carried out there?" I asked.

Quim nodded.

"Very well, I shall keep that in mind. When you've located a body from the battle, call for me," I said.

Quim nodded once again.

(Mae)

I did my best to keep my focus from the shapes. While they seemed harmless, the aura they amplified sent chills down my spine. I almost screamed when I caught one following my movements as I walked past it. After a time, I thought it best to keep to the buildings and when outside, to keep my eyes down. Glancing up often enough to avoid the shapes in the light.

I stepped over a limp body but paused as I noted a gentle wave of light brush just beside my shoulder. I turned around, hesitantly, and noted a beam of green light shining down from one of the crescents overhead. At its center stood a shape facing me. It tilted its head and gracefully lifted its arm, offering an open hand to me. My heart skipped a beat as I frowned and turned my gaze away. Scanning the ground, I noticed the body's face. It was… disfigured.

I kneeled to get a closer look. The body itself was certainly human, female, middle-aged, but somehow her face had reshaped itself. Her nose and mouth were flat, jaw gaping and stretched grotesquely. The eyes were smaller than they should have been; her mane was limited to her scalp and her ears were curved.

I looked back at the shape in the light, its hand still stretched out to me. With such a proximity to that figure, I assumed that the woman's misfortunes were the shape's doing and steadily backed away. Only to stop once again as I noticed a face within the head space of the figure. Had I not known better, I might have been convinced the shape was revealing its true features. But I recognized that face all too well. I held my gun tightly as I shifted to the side, trying to catch a better view of its body.

"Mae?" a voice came from behind me.

I stood, spun around, and aimed my gun dead ahead of me as Amat flung his arms up.

"Whoa, hey!" Amat blurted. "It's just me."

I looked back up to the building I saw the Shadow Scar attach itself to. I held my fire when I realized it was gone.

"Does this thing have you spooked?" Amat asked as he walked closer to the shape in the light.

I crossed my arm over Amat's chest and held him in place.

"Don't get any closer to it," I told Amat. We shared a glance and I showed him the woman's body just outside the light's edge. "See this woman?" Amat nodded. "I think the light did this to her face." I pointed at the woman's disfigurement.

Amat hovered his hand over her jaw as he studied the body.

"I suppose this answers the question as to just how dangerous these things really are." Amat opened a channel to the troops. "Squadron, this is Criptous, further suspicion of the lights' lethality has been confirmed. As a strong reminder to all of you, do not engage—"

"Amat," I said, cutting him short. Amat dropped the signal and focused on me. "There's more. The Shadow Scar, the one that killed my sister, it's here."

Amat took my hand and lifted us off the ground.

"Then we'll see it dead before the end of this. If it's here, others are likely with it, and if one was dull enough to reveal itself to you, it just means they're going to play games until we least expect them to attack. But we'll be ready, and we'll be safe, together," Amat said.

(Olson)

I looked down at my fizer and read aloud the printed message that appeared: "Reassignment for Rika Rogen. Prioritize sustenance interfaces within submerged ships. By order of Diramal Criptous." Followed by the final note of the messenger's ID signature: "Reikag Vykin."

As I registered the orders, I gave a heavy sigh. *Rogen's not going to take this well.*

I marched my way up to the ship's main deck, expecting to find Rogen. Instead, I was met with a pair of Dukas and three M.I.S.T. personnel. The Dukas presented me with the front and backs of their hands as they turned to face me. The Doctors present in the room did not address me until after I attracted the attention of one.

29

"Doctor Niker," I began. The doctor shifted her attention to me the moment I spoke her name. "Where's Rogen?" I asked.

Doctor Niker collected herself.

"She's in the core; went there shortly after we retrieved and patched up the last of the ship's data logs. Said the final key to making the ship fly was in engineering."

I nodded.

"Ever since we've arrived on this vessel, you've acted as Rogen's second. Is that correct, Doctor Niker?" I asked.

"In a sense, yes, sir," replied Niker.

"I'm designating you as the new lead on repairing the ship's systems. Rogen will be indisposed for some time," I said.

Niker held a contemplative pout and nodded her head. She was a brilliant physicist, Niker, and was crucial to the back-engineering of the ancient craft. But compared to Rogan's genius, Niker was a mere pupil and not the most specialized in the revitalization of the vessels.

"Understood, sir."

"As you were," I said, turning to exit the room.

I always enjoyed entering the core engine of the submerged ships. Something about their cool radiance in a world that had been so cruelly robbed of light felt like the most refreshing thing to embrace. Rogen stood just under the small, blue star, heavily concentrating on the interface set before her. I took my time, coming to her side to gently redirect her attention. I found it was often the best way since I'd been alone in a room with her before, calling to her by name, and still she could not be distracted.

Even then, Rogen hardly noticed me before I cleared my throat. She turned to me and her face lit up.

"Io-Pac Criptous, a pleasant surprise to see you here," said Rika.

"Pleasant as it always is to see you as well, Doctor," I replied.

Rika's smile gleamed even brighter, as if to say "thank you."

"We're very close, Io-Pac. A few more weeks—maybe fewer—on this stellar engine, and I'll have the ship up and running. From there, I can take the programming and adapt it to the others. We'll have an entire fleet of ships worthy of the invader craft themselves in less than two months."

I allowed myself a smile as I felt Rika's enthusiasm. It quickly faded from my face.

"Not if we starve before then," I said bluntly.

Rika's expression swiftly shifted to uncertainty.

"Rika, in the time I've gotten to know you, I've come to learn and respect how much this means to you, so trust that I regret having to relay orders of reassignment by the Diramal's decree. Rations are in short supply with all the Skivs and Warvs we've been raking in. We need you to find a way to reverse-engineer the sustenance interfaces in the ship's mess hall. Make it replicable and more user-friendly for the masses," I said.

Rika's excitement had completely been erased from her expression as she stiffened. She glanced at the interface she'd been previously occupied with and sighed.

"I understand, Io-Pac Criptous," Rika said. "Should I start immediately?"

"Yes," I replied.

"I'll make my way to the mess hall promptly then," said Rika, a crack in her voice.

She walked past me. *Idiot,* I thought to myself. *At least give her some reassurance.*

"I should think it would be more than reasonable, however," I said aloud, stopping Rika, "that when your colleagues have finished your work, I shall call upon you to execute the final piece of the puzzle and fully restore the ship in due course."

Rika's passionate smile returned once more, but not with the same splendidness.

"If that is the least you could guarantee me, Io-Pac Criptous, it would be more than appreciated," said Rika.

With that, Rika and I acknowledged one another with a gesture of the back and fronts of our hands and carried on with our duties.

(Zothra)

By the end of the first day, we'd covered half the city and collected a handful of Skivs, but no Warvs. We took refuge in nearby buildings and my troops were given strict orders not to rest anywhere outside the buildings for their own safety. Amat didn't want to risk a shape beaming down upon someone in their sleep.

I lay on my back, wide awake. Sleep was not as great a necessity for my species, compared to the humans. Above me were small ruptures in the roof, wide enough to see the green lights streaking down. I stood, having grown restless, carefully stepping over the slumbering humans on the ground, until I reached the opening of the building. I gazed up at the crescents and realized how little was known about the Solixa. Ironic as it was that they did not join our cause, yet remnants of their technology and tethers of their existence remained. For as young a species as they were, they achieved so much in so little time. After their unfortunate refusal of our offer for a union with Drakkar, resulting in their own demise by our hand, the Zeltons had claimed this planet as a base of operation, as they'd done with so many others. The remnants of their existence on Galiza, still indirectly evident in the Latrodect Monuments. But, of course, we ensured the human scientists within M.I.S.T. never made that connection.

Before the humans came to this planet, we'd been studying the Zeltons' activity on Galiza. Prior to our own installations, the Zeltons had all seven crescents well-guarded under particle shields. To this day, we do not know why. I fear I may yet discover it firsthand in the progression of this mission.

Suddenly, I received an incoming message on my fizer. I retracted the armor around my forearm and studied the ID code. *Voruke?* I altered time and found some place isolated to receive the call.

"Voruke—"

"Zothra!" Voruke blurted. "I have to report… inspection failed… Xaizar…"

I frowned at Voruke's impatience and even more so at the mention of Xaizar.

"Voruke, slow down, your signal is cutting out. Restate your report," I said.

"The inspection failed," Voruke stressed. "Members of… retaliated against Blick and the Alphas, waging a battle inside the… Xaizar has been captured and Quavek stayed back to… The Diramal has ordered you to leave Criptous' command and rendezvous at…"

"Voruke? Voruke, rendezvous where?!" I asked.

The signal was lost in that instant. I sat alone for a moment and contemplated my options. Giclon was a city in the middle of nowhere. If I fled, it would be days—even while moving in altered time—before I'd reach the next town. From the sound of Voruke's message, it seemed like the others were left with no choice but to flee the base, which meant we'd lost all access to any means of military transportation. Even if we hadn't, long-range comm signals were distorted in the desert. But then there was one possibility that dawned on me. If there were other Varx here, I could integrate myself among them as they would surely have access to a transport to get here in the first place. Not knowing who would be leading a local operation, I couldn't reach out to them at that very moment. But as I made my way back to the humans, I knew that if any Varx dwelled in Giclon, they would reveal themselves before Criptous's work was done here.

III
Runaway Child
(Amat)

They did not hold a solid perimeter around the building. It was a tight formation, however, along the outside edges of our shelters—a broken line of the shapes in the green light, staring blankly into the buildings. Quim had woken me after sensing the gathering of these peculiar entities and showed them to me.

"Have any of the troops neared them?" I asked.

"None that I know of, sir," said Quim.

"Good," I replied, stepping forward to inspect the line of lights stretched out along the buildings. "Well, at least there are some gaps here and there in their formation. And it doesn't seem like they're moving at all. We can make our way out, there and there." I pointed at two gaps in the formation of the shapes. In that moment, a beam of green light shone over us through ruptures in the broken roof. The light hovered over me, but before I was engulfed by it, Quim pulled me aside and the light shone over a resting man's legs.

The man tensed his brows but did not wake as his legs twitched. Jerking more violently, he recoiled his head. Howling a cry as his legs stiffened and cracked; his knees bending back the other way. Quim and I came around to his side, avoiding the light as we pulled him away. His cries startled most of the troops awake, who scurried to their feet in near hysteria when they caught sight of the surrounding shapes.

"Don't panic," I barked, trying to hold people back from the light that persisted in shining overhead. "Everyone steady yourselves—"

"Amat!" I heard Mae's voice cry out.

Still, their fear could not be soothed. I stood and raised my pistol above my head as I opened a channel to all of those under my command. I fired twice and they finally calmed.

"Listen," I barked over the channel. "We are currently surrounded. Pac-Qua Quim and I have just witnessed how severe contact with one of

34

those things is." I gestured to the shapes outside. "And there is one, right there. We are all going to calmly make our way out toward those gaps in their formations. If you are in a neighboring building and do not see any gaps in their formation, stand by and I will guide you through an alternative route myself. Now, proceed *cautiously*," I said.

As the troops started moving past me, I kneeled back down beside the man with the broken legs and Quim with me.

"Do we have a medic here? A medic?!" I blurted.

"One here," a woman's voice replied in the back.

"Come near the light in the center of the room. We have a man down here," I commanded.

I looked back and examined the man's legs. The seeps in his armor looked forcibly clenched and stuck in place. I looked around at the underside of the soldier's legs and saw they were bleeding.

Quim, at my side, hovered her hand hesitantly over the soldier's leg nearest to her, before finally touching it. After barely poking the bleeding flesh that puffed out of the soldier's armor, Quim gave a startled gasp and quickly retracted her hand. I looked at her, curious, as I tried to hold pressure on the wound.

"What is it?" I asked.

Quim looked at me with her expressionless helm as her shoulders rose high and low. She managed a shake of her head and said: "Not here, sir."

"What?" I asked.

Finally, the medic arrived. She made her own assessment of the wound and promptly said: "The injury seems to pertain only to the leg region. I assume the light shined on them?"

I gave Quim one final, confused glance.

"Precisely," I replied to the medic.

The medic shook her head as she examined his legs further.

"What's your name, trooper?" I asked.

"Jippif, Duka Vlirg Jippif, sir," Vlirg replied.

"Duka Jippif, can you remove your armor—"

"Actually, Doctor, I don't think that's such a good idea," I cut in. "See how his legs are bleeding? My guess is: however the light managed it, some force strained his legs so far back the armor cut into his flesh."

"Be that as it may, I can't do anything for him unless the armor is removed," said the medic.

"Be that as it may, removing him from the armor without immediate access to a regenerator or the proper medical equipment could rupture his wound further and kill him instantly. Now the seeps at the back of his legs seem expanded enough that we might be able to see his flesh if we flip him around. If we can, do you have something that could stop the bleeding?" I asked.

"I should," the medic said as she searched her bag. "Ah, this should do. It'll temporarily slow his heart rate."

"I'll call in a Fade and arrange troops to see him safely to it," I said.

"I'd ask to go with him, to ensure he makes it through," said the medic.

"Granted," I said.

After I sent the medic off with Jippif, seven other Dukas, and the Skivs we'd found, I helped assist the rest of my troops safely out of the buildings the shapes had almost utterly encircled. From there, we proceeded deeper into the city.

The journey onward was fruitless in our efforts to find more Skivs and Warvs, providing only the sights and silent company of the shapes standing in the green light. That is, until we reached the north end of the city, where we stood in the armpit of the slope that held up the seven crescents. As it neared the end of the day, we stayed a while to thoroughly inspect the area and ensure we weren't missing anything, per my orders.

"I don't think we'll find any additional souls in this city, *laddin*. Other than the ones that crowd our march," said Shím.

I stood staring at the center of the slope as a bright strike of green current randomly sizzled out from one of the crescents overhead. My attention remained unbroken as the brief flash provided enough light to catch a glimpse of the hole in the hill's side. I turned.

"Quim, come to my side," I said.

Quim joined me as we proceeded to investigate the hole together.

"Watch my back," I said.

Quim remained silent as she stopped in her tracks and turned her gaze to the buildings at our rear. I reached the hole, recently dug, big enough for a person of the average height to walk through. A figure was just barely within range of my particle sensors, but I saw it, sitting there, no more than nine hundred meters deep within the cave. A human. I stepped in to call out to them, but just as I unveiled my helm, I saw another figure come into view, scaling the roof of the tunnel as their horned head came closer. An invader… a Zelton.

"Sir," Quim called out, calm but strong.

I stepped back out from the tunnel and gazed up. Along the slope and even on the third crescent from the middle, of which we stood under, a sizable force of the invaders revealed themselves. Quim raised and primed her gun to them. I raised my hand.

"Stand down, Pac-Qua, I should like to see how this plays out," I said.

I told the same to the troops at my back, when they too noticed the arrival of the invader force. It was almost grotesque, watching each of their hairy, plump bodies squirm out of the hole, with no break between their exits, swarming the slope. They did not demonstrate so much as a hiss in their gathering.

Finally, they settled and looked at me with much intrigue.

Odd, how they react to us. By our armor, it should be clear that we are a potential threat to them, yet they look at me with curiosity in their eyes.

"Hello." My voice carried across the open land. "As the leader of humanity, it gladdens me to bear witness to such a historic event between our species. If possible, I should like to open a dialogue with you, preferably with a leader among your ranks, to further our understanding of one another."

Saying this was a little strange, seeing as I still had some hate for these beings. Though, it was not enough to cloud my interest in our apparently long-standing relationship with them, from what I remember hearing in the Dûlabega Quadrant Incident recording.

(Mae)

I made my way to the front of the line and beheld, in awe, the number of forces that had swelled around Amat and Quim's positions. Right then, I was nearly overwhelmed by my emotions; I wanted to rush out there and be by Amat's side, but instinct held me back, as I knew he wouldn't want me to interfere with what he'd been granted. An audience with the invader forces.

"I couldn't help but notice you have a few of our kinsmen within that hole there," I could hear Amat say. "This is something I've seen you do before, and I'd like to know what you do with them."

A hissing uproar developed among the aliens, in the same precise pitch, as if they were answering Amat's question in unison. Amat sat with that reply as he tried to contemplate his next words carefully.

Instinct drew my attention elsewhere. Further down the line, in the opposite direction, stood the Cho'Zai Zothra. A sort of spokesman to Amat, who seemed to be the only thing binding the allegiance of the Cho'Zai as a whole to Amat's command as the Diramal. His anxious glancing in every which direction suggested he didn't seem the least bit concerned with the events that were unfolding. *Is he searching for something?*

His attention finally homed in, though it was for too brief a moment for me to locate what he'd set his eyes on. The Cho'Zai immediately blended into the crowd, and I followed him, pushing people aside to keep Zothra in my sight. I couldn't stay on his trail for long as the nearby forces blocked out his figure. The troops stood still; no sign of the Cho'Zai for me to follow.

The silence left me with nothing but my thoughts to go on. I looked to the hill and high atop the crescents. There, my particle sensors had picked up hundreds of signatures crawling, scaling up the structures, and creeping just behind the slope's horizon. Signatures of various shapes and sizes, among which, one caught my eye. Using my Hud, I homed in on the entity and observed it holding a large weapon over its shoulder, aimed at the crowd of alien forces. I cried out as I recognized it, but my cries were dulled under the fleeting wave of fire projected both at the invaders and our own ranks.

(Amat)

The blast was powerful enough to obliterate dozens of the aliens and send some more into the air. They shrieked and widened their stances, drawing weapons; some stood ready to attack me and Quim. A moment passed and they rushed toward the crescents. I sent out a surge signal and opened a channel to my troops.

"Hold your fire, do not shoot any of the invaders—"

I shielded my eyes from another blast that landed at the center of my lines.

"Avoid contact with the alien presence! Take cover in the west side buildings, return suppressing fire to the crescents! Let's move!" I barked over comms.

I altered time and dashed for the ruins. As we ran, lightning struck from a crescent, coursing along and spiking from the inner arc toward my troops. Those close enough to the strike were flung in the air, twirling. The shapes within the lights also beamed in the way of our path; deliberately it seemed. As Quim and I neared the buildings, along with my troops, I witnessed several beams of light shine down upon them and watched as their bodies stiffened and contorted violently. Jaws stretched unnaturally low, knees inverted, spines hunched, and flesh surpassed the durability of the QS-25 suits that gushed blood spewing from their interior.

As their lifeless bodies fell to the ground, I caught glimpses of defined features about the shapes. Not enough to make out their true appearance, but particular characteristics. Such as jaws with severe underbites, long saber teeth, shell-covered shins…

I had no idea what it meant or what the shapes hoped to achieve. It was merely clear that their lethality and intelligence had surpassed my former understanding of them.

What remained of my numbers safely secured themselves within the various buildings to the west of our position, and the shapes started closing in once again, trapping us. Before I'd allow us to be completely closed off from the fight, I sent out another surge signal and called out a quarter of the troops under my command to follow me back out and reach the rear of the crescents to flank the enemy. With Quim still at my side, we raced back out across that open stretch before the slope, dodging around every light that intersected our path.

Don't stop moving!

At the rear of the crescents, I paused to account for how many troops I'd lost in the stretch. Dozens of crooked bodies lay across the open field. I almost cursed myself for the command, having caused the loss of dozens of men and women. I looked past the bodies and my fear became reality: every light the three central crescents could shine engulfed the buildings my troops had taken refuge in. An army of ghosts.

"Diramal." Shím reached out over comms.

"Krollgrum MgKonnol," I replied.

"Praise to the Goddess you're alive, sir. I assume you're among the men I can barely perceive through my Hud, on the top of the slope?"

"Unless there's another group of soldiers between the central crescents, your observation is correct, MgKonnol," I replied.

"You can see what the rest of us are confronted with, then?"

"I can. I foresaw that tactic by the lights and felt it wise to reserve most of you from the updated rally point. But while you might be pinned down, at least you're all safe from the crescents."

"We do have troops armed with pulse cannons, sir. Perhaps in obstructing the crescents, we can eliminate these... spirits from the equation," said Shím.

I peered up at the crescents and witnessed the battle waging between Shadow Scar and invader.

"Delay that order, Shím, we've got invader and Shadow Scar forces on the crescents, lording the lights above your position. We also have Skivs located in a small tunnel just below our position. If we tear down these structures, it could cave in on our kinsmen. And I want to see if we can ally ourselves with the invaders against the Shadow Scar," I said.

"We are to hold our positions then, sir?"

"And have the pulse cannons in position, yes. I'll send out a surge if I decide we need them," I replied.

"Very good, sir," said Shím.

"Criptous out."

I huddled my troops together and devised a plan. I emphasized that they were not to attack any of the invaders unless their own lives were at stake. If there was still an opportunity to establish a dialogue after this battle had ended, I didn't want anything burning that bridge.

I divided my troops into three groups. We altered time and scaled up the crescents. As we reached the top of the crescent, I dodged around an occupied invader and swiped at the ankle of the Shadow Scar that confronted it. The Shadow Scar landed flat on its chest and as it motioned to push itself off the surface, I buried my claws into its back, keeping the Shadow Scar down. Before I could kill it, the alien reached one of its arms down, a blade in hand, and created a river of blood from the Shadow Scar's throat.

I looked up to acknowledge the alien, but by then it had fled. My troops had moved in to join the fight, keeping their aggression reserved for the Shadow Scar.

I locked eyes with a Shadow Scar who had just killed a Zelton. I stood and armed myself with a knife as it pushed the limp Zelton over the edge of the crescent. Dashing toward the Shadow Scar, I zig-zagged my approach and dove toward the thing, thrusting my blade at its abdomen. It caught my arm and, without hesitation, I whipped my claws across the Shadow Scar's face. The shock was enough for it to let go of my arm, but it swiftly gathered itself, faced me once again, and flexed its bicep. For a fleeting moment, I took in its appearance as I backed away from whatever sprung out of the barnacle-like protrusions all along its bulging muscles. A few landed on my armor, splattering acid that burned through it.

Distracted, the Shadow Scar landed a blow. I stumbled, but kept myself from falling. I had just enough time to respond to its next attack after I saw that the liquid had not eaten through my flesh. As it swung its blade down at me, I contorted my body and raised my own, piercing the creature's forearm. Beyond the stiff clenching of its body, the Shadow Scar seemed hardly bothered by the blood-gushing wound it had just received. In a quick follow-up, I swung my leg out and around, smacking against the Shadow Scar's gut. It sailed back, far enough to fall past the crescent's edge.

I gazed down past the crescent's edge to make sure I had killed the foe. The next moment, a blade pierced through the seep of my helm. Angled just right before my eye to see its point, but not deep enough to feel its sting. My interface had been mostly shattered and my vision badly distorted.

Wasting no time, I took hold of the Shadow Scar's arm with both hands and twisted it. As I squeezed and twisted, I prayed to Anua the Shadow Scar would not overwhelm me. Before I could snap the ligament, the Shadow Scar hit me. Whilst I couldn't make out what it had hit me with, the blade had been retracted and I'd lost my grip. I quickly motioned to retract my helm and allow my natural illuminating eyesight to take over. As the pieces split apart, I failed to anticipate the Shadow Scar's next blow, and it landed across my jaw. The impact knocked me down. So close to the edge, I felt myself slip down the side of the crescent. I pierced my knife into the worn metal as my helm fully retracted.

I looked up and a foot landed on my chest, sending me down further. Fortunately, along the underbelly of each crescent, sprouted long, icicle-shaped rods. Large and durable enough for me to latch onto, numerous enough for me to maneuver around. A strong wind, caught by the crescents, blew past my hair as I looked around for the attacking Shadow Scar.

Once again, it had fallen toward me, weapon held high above its head. I swung myself forward and latched onto another rod before the Shadow Scar could land its strike, with another below me to set my feet against. I twisted back to face the Shadow Scar and took in its appearance, as it moved furiously to catch up with me. Its figure, dressed in a spiked armor, was peculiar. Though I wondered if the spikes at the back of its head were mere extensions of the armor or jagged bones sprouting from its scalp. Its eyes were wide and triangular, its mouth gaping.

It swung forth, this ferocious thing, latching on to another extension of the crescent, and kicked me in the face. As it raised its knee for another strike, I swung forward and kicked both my legs into the Shadow Scar's chest. It fell a short distance before catching itself and swiftly made its way back up to me. Perched atop a spike stretching out from the crescent, I looked back and started to bound and maneuver my way underneath the structure. Mid bound, the Shadow Scar latched itself onto my ankle and pulled me down. We fell toward a spike that curved up *wickedly*. With a swift movement, I kicked the Shadow Scar in the face and twirled us toward the crevice of the spike. The back of my armor scraped against the inner edge of the spike as I started to fall past it. Extending my arm quickly, I halted my fall on the same spike.

I looked down at the Shadow Scar and clasped the seeps at my leg shut before it could dig its claws into my flesh. Its face was illuminated from above. A strong wind blew past, and I gazed up, noting the bolts of electricity coursing up the crescent in a thunderous display, much like a plasma ball. In that moment, I knew how to end this chase.

The Shadow Scar continued in its attempts to climb up my body. I swung the toe and then the heel of my boot across the Shadow Scar's face. Still, he clung tightly. I lifted my knee and stomped his face. Finally free of his grasp, I swung myself within the crevice of the spike and began scaling the crescent, carefully avoiding the projectors that emanated the green lights down on the surface. Bashing and smashing a few that crossed my path. Before long, some of the projectors started shifting toward me, as if they were trying to shine their light directly on me.

Finally, there sat a rod sparking at its tip with electricity, not thirty meters before me. I glanced down and observed several others, with bolts of lightning curving out and connecting between various rods. Again, the rod before me sparked, exerting a more powerful shock wave than before. The green rays of light pressed closer as the Shadow Scar barely scratched against the back of my armor. I swung past the sparking rod. In the air, I contorted my body toward the Shadow Scar, who remained ever so close to me. It twisted and stretched its arm forward, bearing its blade. The blow would have cut across my shin if I hadn't raised my palm to him at that precise moment. Rotating my wrist, I 'versed the Shadow Scar back to the rod. *Strike!* The green sparks lashed up along the left side of the Shadow Scar's abdomen, chest, and helmet. I latched onto a passing rod and stopped my fall. A few moments later, I observed the Shadow Scar, its flesh burning, throwing one arm out after the other as it fell... down... down... down. My eyes felt deceived, however, noting that at the last moment, before he fell below the shades amongst the green lights, the Shadow Scar held his arms at his sides and notably *flew* across the air.

That's a first.

The winds were at their strongest by the time I neared the top of the crescent. Dust clouds kicked in as tiny grains of sand crashed against the corners of my eyes and blinded me. The sounds of war beckoned above me still, hardly audible over the storm's woe. Surely the battle had to be nearing its end. It was only a question of who was winning. And I would not send out a surge signal before finding out.

With a final pull on the ledge to the top of the crescent, I looked around and noted that despite the many losses, those that remained, on all sides of the battle, continued to maintain a spirited vigor. With the help of the Zeltons, our forces were almost evenly matched against the Shadow Scar. But an evenly matched fight did not guarantee victory, and even if it did, a slaughter on all sides was guaranteed. It took me back to a luminous place, slowly falling under shadow. I could feel her soft powdery surface beneath my feet again, running in every which direction as I tried to protect as many of those men and women under my command as I could. Only to find all but one, dead, in the aftermath of the incursion that started all of this.

My head was jerked back as thick fingers engulfed my neck. I was lifted off the ground and brought eye to eye with a six-peg-legged Shadow Scar. A ball and socket joint in the middle of each leg, ending in a point. Its lipless, bloody grin was enough to bring my attention back to the present. As it reached behind to pry out a large scythe-like weapon from its back, I took a deep breath, raised my arms, and sent out a surge signal. The Shadow Scar tilted its head.

I flicked out the claws of my suit and scraped them against the Shadow Scar's arm. The Shadow Scar bellowed a strange noise as I dropped to the ground, jumped, and twirled over the Shadow Scar's weapon as it swung. Swiping at its rib cage as it brought its weapon back overhead, but I rolled out of the way of the blow. The Shadow Scar forcefully pried its weapon from the metal I had been standing on moments before and that's when we felt it: the pulse. Everyone paused what they were doing. I watched, barely able to see the transparent blue waves expand and surpass the crescents. I yelled in hopes that my troops would join me in lying flat against the crescent, as the wave came crashing down, splitting the crescent in three.

The surface trembled, and those who stood were pulled down against the metal so hard their bodies were broken while others who remained close to the edge were flung from the falling structure.

The moment the pulse hit, the points of the ball-socket-legged Shadow Scar forcefully dug into the metal and it bent its upper body down.

Our faces were inches away from one another as we did our best not to drift from the structure's surface.

Shifting slightly, it threw an open hand at me. With my claws out, I swung my arm and dug into the palm of the Shadow Scar. The thing let out a strange roar and pulled me over itself. My claws left deep gashes as I flew toward the edge of the surface, hovering for a time after my momentum ceased.

I dove slightly to latch back onto the falling piece of the crescent. Using its large, scythe-like weapon, the Shadow Scar swung out and around toward me. Its legs were curled in, still launching toward me. Just before we would have collided, it flicked out its legs and pushed me down to the side of the broken crescent. The structure was more rigid along its sides and was easier to grab onto. I scaled my way around, glanced up, and twisted back as the Shadow Scar swung its scythe down at me. Sparks flaring out of broken mechanisms forced me to look away, and I gazed back just as the Shadow Scar pried its weapon from the structure. Moving quickly to grab onto the weapon's shaft, I found our strengths to be equally matched until I raised my palm and twisted it back. My arm holding the weapon crashed against the metal as the Shadow Scar reversed its movement, bashing its weapon into the side of the structure. Still twisting my hand back, the Shadow Scar raised its weapon and me over its head. I stopped and the added weight of my body overwhelmed the strength of its swinging arm. Falling on the rear extension of the Shadow Scar's body, I pulled back against the shaft of the weapon, pressing it to the creature's neck.

Once again, we were in a battle of push and shove. I looked out beyond the point of the crescent. The impact was coming; I knew it was seconds away. Tugging tighter with my arms, I jumped, tucked my knees, and kicked the Shadow Scar in the back, just as the structure hit the ground. The shaft broke in two and the Shadow Scar lost its grip on the half that mattered. As I took hold of the top half of the scythe, I twisted and planted it into the structure. Looking back, I saw the Shadow Scar tumble through the air as the structure slid and came to a gradual stop after demolishing much of the city.

I gathered the troops that remained on the structure after dealing with a few Shadow Scars who'd also survived the crash. The Zeltons had fled just as the structure slid to a halt, heading back the other way, likely to my kinsmen in that tunnel.

With my troops together, I opened a channel to everyone under my command, via my fizer.

"Kalbrook, MgKonnol, Zothra, Quim, report in," I said.

Some time passed.

"Right behind you, sir," said Quim.

I spun to see Quim limp toward me, her chest rising and falling.

"Are you well enough to continue the mission, Pac-Qua?" I asked.

She sighed heavily, as she lowered herself to a knee for a moment's rest.

"Don't worry about me, sir. I'm far from my return to death's embrace. I'll live to see today's end." Her expression altered as she noted my lack of a helm.

"It was damaged in battle," I said promptly. "But my eyes will manage well enough without it."

Quim nodded, respectfully not inquiring further.

I returned my gaze to the city, still awaiting word from Mae and the others. Raising my fizer, I displayed a digital map of the area to home in on the locations of my troops that were unaccounted for. Oddly, the map was distorted, though there was no sign of damage to my fizer. I didn't pay too much mind to the digital grid before closing it entirely.

"Should we call in the others?" asked Quim.

"Come again, Pac-Qua?" I said.

"Given our circumstances, Diramal, should we not regroup and try to collect our kinsmen at the slope?"

"I had, just as you approached me, Pac-Qua. You heard me over comms," I replied.

Quim turned to face me; her head tilted curiously.

"I'm afraid not, sir, I merely heard you call out my name…" Quim's tone drifted.

"Well, how does that—"

"Pardon my interruption, sir," said Quim, as she stood, staring past me to the sky above. "But I believe I may know the question you'll ask, and the answer lies there."

I twitched my head back and gazed up at the sky as Quim pointed to it and joined my side. A large shifting cloud with dull, green flashes in its smokey shadow hovered above. I noted how the edge of the cloud had just stretched over and beyond our position, which meant its formation was recent and must have originated from somewhere nearby. I looked back to the slope where three of the central pillars had been torn down and from their remaining bases, thick, glowing clouds levitated into the air.

"It must be an electromagnetic cloud, a black zone. So long as it's overhead, our comms are useless," I said.

"How should we proceed then, sir?"

I took a moment to gaze back at the impact trail of the crescent piece we stood on. *Mae is out there, somewhere.*

"Let's rally what we can of the nearby troops. Then take half the forces we find back to the tunnel that hid the Skivs. I'll take the other half and continue to search for the remaining forces," I said.

"Yes, sir," Quim replied.

IV
Blood and Lust
(Log)

The sound of the steady beeps of my life support echoed within the small room I'd been confined to. The bright lights reflected off the white walls. A sudden ache surged across the left side of my scalp. I squeezed my eyes shut and moved to raise my hand over my eyes. My arm jerked back at a burning sensation on my wrist after I'd twisted my body too far to one side. I felt two hands gently push me back, followed by a voice that seemed to come from far away. Still, the lights were blinding. A few moments later, the lights shut off and I blinked my eyes open.

"Log. Log, Log, Log, it's alright. You're alright, they restrained you because you're still decommissioned," said Blick.

I cursed silently as I threw up my arms against the plasma restraints for spite, their color changing from a purple to a deep red. Growling at the dulled, burning pain they left my wrists marked with.

Blick frowned at my self-infliction, placing a gentle hand on my shoulder.

"I don't think you did anything wrong; the restraints are merely a precaution. I'll remove them after security reports back on your actions from the launch bay footage," Blick continued.

Hardly able to hold back the resentment in my tone, I asked Blick: "Are Warter and Kita alright?"

Blick took a moment to register the names, as he was not entirely familiar with them.

"They are. As I understand it, Krollgrum Kita is something of a... caretaker to you. She checks in on you from time to time, yes?"

"She comes to check in on the kid. *I'm* the caretaker," I replied.

Blick nodded as his gaze trailed down. I followed his stare—he held a knife between his hands, lightly spinning the point against his index finger.

"That the one?" I asked.

Blick glanced at me, down at the blade, and at me again, raising it. "This? Yeah. I was going to give it to you once I received the report on your activity during the battle. Unfortunately, I've had to confiscate the suit along with your weapons for the time being. You can discuss their return with the Diramal. I assume he is the reason you had them in the first place," said Blick.

I raised my eyebrows and jerked my head noncommittally.

"On the upside of things, I'm sure you'd be happy to know I've incarcerated Xaizar," said Blick as I turned my head back to him. "If I'm satisfied with the report my people bring me, you'll have the blade and the Cho'Zai all to yourself."

I eyed Blick for a long moment.

"Why?" I asked.

Blick looked puzzled.

"Why, what?"

"Why involve yourself in my personal affairs?" I asked. Blick opened his mouth to speak, but I kept on. "His very existence is what has haunted me, but that doesn't mean I need to kill him myself. I just want him gone; I don't care how or who does it," I said.

A moment passed, and a soldier walked through the door. He addressed Blick, then paused when he noted the tension between us. He readjusted his stance and saluted Blick.

"Yes, Duka?" Blick asked.

"Pardon me, sir. We've fully inspected the footage of Io-Pac Log's actions in the launch bay. The only bodies he engaged with were among the ranks of the Cho'Zai," said the Duka.

"Thank you," Blick said, shifting his attention back to me, silently dismissing the Duka.

"Sir," the Duka replied, and turned promptly to the exit.

Blick raised his arm to me with the blade in hand.

"It seems the opportunity has presented itself," Blick said. "I only offer it to you because, for many years, I was the former Diramal's subject. And, at times, was included among his highest-ranking officers."

I contemplated the action as I took the blade in my hand.

"You're not the only one marked with haunted memories," Blick continued, as he deactivated the plasma restraints.

(Quavek)

At the climax of the battle, that idiot Xaizar shed the blood of Log Criptous, as if starting the riot wasn't bad enough. Then again, we'd all probably be on death row if it weren't for Xaizar's rashness. Not that I had much faith in Vykin to spare some of us; he chose his side a long time ago after what transpired between him and the Diramal. In a way, they'd both been looking for Amat, one almost as long as the other, yet for entirely different reasons.

After witnessing Vykin's conflict with Xaizar, I'd moved within the air ducts in the event that Vykin left Xaizar with a scrap of his life intact. Unsurprisingly, he had. At his heart, Vykin always had a certain empathy, though he would scarcely show it. It was the only thing that separated him from the rest of us.

Sure enough, Xaizar had been moved to the brigs of Y'Gǔtsa, in the highest level of the base. A reasonable but extensive venture from the launch bay, just four levels above. Some passageways felt as tight and discomforting as my own skinsuit, but I managed. I found Xaizar in a small room illuminated by blue light. They rested him awkwardly on the bed there. With that in mind, I moved on throughout the airways, seeking an exit strategy. We couldn't exactly just walk right back down to the launch bay. And while Xaizar's kin were considerably nimble, he would not fit through the air ducts as I had. Instead, I sought out the emergency exit; every base had one located at the upmost and bottommost levels.

I maneuvered around the corridor that stretched along each of the cells and I counted seven guards before finding the exit, two of them Alphas just outside Xaizar's cell.

Though I did not check from the very beginning of the corridor, so there may be others.

I doubled back to make sure—another two standard guards stood at the main entrance, making it a total of nine armed enemies we'd have to deal with. I searched myself and found six micro-bots along with their programmer. With them, I could prime the guards' weapons to burst, dispersing shrapnel everywhere. Leaving Xaizar and me with a reasonable three guards to handle ourselves.

I sent out the bots, designating a pair to the two Alphas that guarded Xaizar's door. I studied my fizer until it acknowledged that each of the bots was primed to set off the weapons the moment the guards squeezed their triggers. Returning to Xaizar's room, I silently lowered myself in. As I extended each of my six limbs down, elegantly; touched down on the ground and retracted my smaller arms into my chest. I twitched my head as I slithered in a knuckle walk toward Xaizar and removed the bag from over his head. The head of his skinsuit loosely latched to his face. I grazed my hand across his cheek in an attempt to wake him subtly. Still, his tentacles and body remained limp. I placed my hand over his face and brought out one of my retracted ligaments, extending its finger in Xaizar's ear. Mucus seeped into the Qi-Varian's ear canal. I gave it time before enough would have surely reached his cochlea. With my finger still in Xaizar's ear canal, I pulsed a neural energy through the mucus and awoke him. Jolting up from his prone position, he gasped and gurgled. If it weren't for the confines of the room, he would have likely given away our position.

I belittled him for his moronic, primitive reaction. It took him longer than anticipated to ease his rage, even after he'd set his eyes on me. I pushed off him and inspected the shadows of the Alphas that remained calmly dormant outside the cell.

"You came back?" I heard Xaizar whisper.

I twisted back, scowling at the little fish.

"Don't flatter yourself; you're too great a liability to leave in Vykin's care," I hissed.

I kneeled before the door, opened one of my chest appendages, and shifted its fingers through the keyhole, ever so slightly, to make the *snap* of the lock's unfastening as soft as possible. I tucked my arm through a seep in a shelled layer of skin that guarded my hip. Past it were my ovaries. I clicked my pincers and murmured a deep chirp as I guided my hand and latched onto what I was searching for. I turned back to Xaizar.

"Ready?" I hissed.

"For what exactly?" Xaizar spoke in a lecherous tone, with a sick expression of intrigue on his face, knowing what part of my anatomy I was prying.

I flicked my head and hissed in annoyance.

With a wicked thrust, I pulled out a young nymph, half the size of my hand, and before it had time to shriek in its waking, I altered time, whipped the door open, and thrust the youngling out into the corridor. The moment I closed the door, the guards outside squeezed their triggers and six small yet booming explosions sounded. Regulating time, I turned back to Xaizar.

"There are three more guards to our left; I'll take two. Focus on the one that rushes closest to us," I told Xaizar.

Xaizar nodded, a riled expression mixed with bloodlust and arousal filled his face. We altered time as I whipped the door back open. The nymph was still alive, despite being surrounded by the broken shrapnel of the guards' weapons. I rushed out and dove toward the nymph; it had grown to almost the size of my arm by this point. Xaizar rushed forward to the nearest guard of the three that remained, a female human. The one behind her, a male human, stopped to take aim and shoot Xaizar. Before he could fire, I raced up and flung the growing nymph at the guard's helm. The nymph pierced its pointed legs into the guard's eyes and swiftly entered his mouth. The third guard, another male, took aim at me and managed to fire, but I rammed into the second and used him as a body shield, pressing forward. The final guard aimed low and landed a shot on my shin. As I stumbled over the body, out of the second's back sprung the nymph, almost as long as a human spine, coated in blood. The third guard fumbled in his aim as he tried to gun down the nymph. Unsuccessful, the nymph landed and enveloped itself around the guard's waist, rapidly tearing through the armor and into the guard's flesh. The guard panicked as he pounded at the nymph with his fist and then grabbed at it to pry the thing off, but the nymph only tore deeper and closer to the guard's waistline. Finally, the guard aimed his gun awkwardly at the nymph; however, it was too late, and blood gushed out from the guard's gut as the nymph tucked itself into a ball and tore deeper and deeper to the center of the guard's body. He'd split in half by the time he hit the ground.

The nymph flipped itself over and crawled over its last kill as it scurried back to me, still on the ground. I shoved the corpse of the second guard away from me and opened up my chest to the nymph. As it burrowed its way in, I embraced it with my chest ligaments and closed my chest once again, crushing the nymph to death. Yet the remains would find their way back to my ovaries and the nymph would be reborn when next I'd find myself in need of it.

Sleep now, child, I thought, as I felt the nymph squirm against the crushing pressure I imposed on it.

I pushed myself up to a knee with my wounded leg back, catching Xaizar's deviously aroused expression. I twitched my head and took out a brilzer, placing it over my wound. The exposed flesh and blood boiled into a foam as the wound steamed and a new layer of skin grew.

Just as I shifted to stand up straight, I felt Xaizar reach a helpful hand under my arm, staring at me, still, with those lewd eyes. I pulled my arm away and marched forward for the exit.

"*Move*, Xaizar," I said.

"I never knew you to be so... barbaric," Xaizar said, as he followed behind.

I opened the passage that led out of the base and heard slime shifting and thick liquid splatter on the ground.

"The excruciating pain you put yourself through..." Xaizar continued, slipping his squirming tentacles into the seep of my hip, as he closed the door behind us. "It's an attractive quality among my kin—"

Swiftly, I took Xaizar's arm, pried it from me, bolted around him holding his arm tight behind his back, and pressed him to the wall. Xaizar exclaimed a pleasured gurgle.

"Touch me again, Xaizar, and I'll not hesitate to release my second nymph that rests dormant, just beneath the shelling of my other hip," I said.

Like water, Xaizar maneuvered in such a way that if he were human, would have broken his own collarbone. He'd managed to twist and contort his body out of my pin and succeeded in pressing my back against the wall instead, pinning my hands above my head. I hissed and extended my neck at Xaizar, snapping my pincers at him, but he stood too far out of reach. Xaizar gasped with exhilaration at my discomfort.

"I've heard you Korthodon can procreate without the need for a male. I wonder what else that implies," he said.

"Go any further with this, Xaizar, and I'll devour your face," I hissed.

"Ooh, don't tempt me, Quavek," Xaizar replied, as he shifted his tentacle hand through and around my long, bony fingers. The eyes of his skinsuit face ran over me, stopping at my chest.

"Why not stretch out your thorax ligaments? Surely, they're long enough to reach and subdue me?" said Xaizar.

I said nothing in reply.

"Ah, is it your nymph? Is that why you hold back? It's still revitalizing, is it?" Xaizar continued.

Indeed it was, and how Xaizar knew that was beyond me. Inside my chest, my arms there were still breaking down the nymph for its rebirth process. If I lashed them out in that instance, the nymph would be forever dead.

"You know, not only do we Qi-Vari find pleasure in self-imposed pain, but most especially when it's inflicted by others." Still pressing my hands against the wall, Xaizar arched his back and tensed his shoulder blades. His uniform ripped, exposing his extensive cartilage that served as his spine, bulging, and tearing through the skinsuit. Using the tentacles on his true face, he squirmed and wriggled the entire head of his skinsuit off. Features about the human mask budged and shifted as it slipped away. Xaizar sighed with relief as he bent over, lowering his head toward my chest, sniffing, then rising slowly, leaving hardly any room between our faces. He extended the small tentacles that resided within the holes of his face toward me.

"Go ahead, have a nibble," Xaizar gurgled.

I held a stern expression and turned my face away. Xaizar chortled.

"You change your mind, you let me know." Xaizar took one final daring inhale at my scalp and whispered: "Thanks for the rescue. 'Was *exhilarating*, to say the least.'"

Xaizar gripped his tentacle hand and his skinsuit hand tightly around my own as he flung me toward the wall behind him. I let out an ear-bleeding shriek as a shock wave surged through my skeleton. Fortunately, the remains of my nymph were still safe inside my chest. As the dust settled, I heard Xaizar shrivel out of his skinsuit entirely as his feet slapped against the ground with every step in his approach toward me.

"Nothing personal, Quavek, I just figure I should give you some time to think on what I've said. Knowing you and your anatomy, you'll be on your feet long before anyone else shows up on the other side of that door. And, *uh*, unfortunately, with how heated things have become between us, I just can't trust myself to be alone with you at present. I'll see you with the others."

Xaizar chuckled deviously as he walked away. Despite my urges, I knew I had to remain still and rest for a time, lest I risk fatally harming my nymph. I had no choice but to allow my vision to fade into darkness and could only comfort myself with the thought that one day, I would see Xaizar dead. Whether it be by my hand, or another's.

(Log)

The stench of the nine bloody bodies on the ground seeped beyond the entrance of the detention center. Before entering, I knew Xaizar had escaped. Blick's subtle shift in pace as he approached the door suggested he smelled it too. His boulder shoulders cut off my sight, though the rich scent of rust flared my nostrils.

A slaughter.

Blick entered slowly with his head weighed down. Six of the guards' weapons had been detonated somehow, bursting into hundreds of tiny pieces, flying at just the right speeds to pierce through the seeps of the QS-25s that dressed the fallen Alphas. A little further, toward the end of the hall, another soldier, female, with her Hud bashed into her face. The other two, male, something had… exited out of one's back and severed the other in half.

Blick examined the wounds of the last two with an enigmatic familiarity. Hovering his finger over the waist of the severed soldier as he studied the wound more closely.

"Something cut him. A splice maybe?" I asked.

Blick delayed his answer.

"It's hard to imagine… but I can scarcely think of anything else that might have caused such a wound," Blick replied. His words were peculiarly swift.

Blick raised his attention to me and marched to Xaizar's cell. Unsurprisingly, the Cho'Zai was not there. Blick growled low as he slammed the door shut.

"I'm sorry, Log, I thought maybe—"

"It only means we live on to see one fall before the other," I interrupted Blick. "Whether that be myself or Xaizar, it will come one day. I know I'll find comfort in either. Is there anything else you'd require of me, Reikag Vykin?"

Blick looked deep into my eyes. It seemed he noted something about me, almost a change of which I was not aware.

"You seem distant, Log. No offense, but I've often seen you to be a rather passionate and in certain respects, reactive individual. Yet here we stand, robbed of the chance to rid the world of a man whose very memory has tormented you for months and you don't seem the least bit upset," said Blick.

There it was, not in its entirety, but at the surface level… my nonreactive response. It wasn't until Blick's mention of it that I noticed I was a Dövar. One who had ventured into the realm of death and, with only a spark of life tethered to their body, had been revived. My perception of reality turned into a focal point; every moment passed in an abnormal flow. I didn't know how much time had gone by before I finally noted Blick standing puzzled, motioning to say something more.

"You need not be concerned about me, Blick. I'll take my leave now," I said, twisting away into a swift march back to my quarters. With my feet on autopilot, my thoughts were focused only on my next move. Nothing distracted me as I took no cognizance of my surroundings. My concentration lay solely on completing the next task and then the next; my body would fill in the gaps. Before I knew it, I'd opened the door to my quarters, to be met with an abrupt gasp from Kita, who stood there in the doorway.

V
Too Easy
(Mae)

When Amat ordered the pulse cannons to take down three of the seven crescents of Giclon, everyone on the ground fled the moment the lights dissipated. There was no order to our flight, and we didn't have much time to avoid the six falling pieces. Each crescent had been torn into thirds, with the base still connected to the top of the slope.

I found refuge in a building that sat between two of the falling pieces. Along its eastern corner, most of the walls had been torn down from previous conflicts in the area. I tucked myself away there, just as one of the central pieces landed, the spikes along the structure's underbelly flung everywhere. Several collided through and within the building that concealed me, caving in the ceiling above.

Tucked away at the innermost corner of the room, I was spared the worst part of the cave-in and my suit absorbed the impact of what little debris did manage to hit me. When the collapse settled, I was left with nothing more than a bruise on my forearm. Yet the ground still rumbled in the distance from the sliding crescent pieces and I waited until the ground was quiet.

Easing my way through the cluster at my feet, I searched for the opening from which I entered. Unfortunately, tall spikes obstructed it, with narrow gaps hardly wide enough to squeeze my fingers through. Yet while the spikes were sharp around the edges, they were also very flat from front to back. I turned around, carefully moved around some debris, and created a narrow runway. Starting from as far back as I could fit, I altered time and bolted toward one of the spikes. On the final step, I dove forward and contorted my body, hitting one of the spikes head-on with my shoulder. It broke at the base and flipped back, piercing into the next building over.

Stumbling, as I regulated time, I glanced to my right and followed the trail of the central crescent pieces. The closer piece got as far out as to what looked like the center of the city, an approximate five miles away from where I stood.

I pray, oh Goddess, that you kept Amat and the others safe.

My eyes trailed to the sky, noting the dark cloud, emanating green sparks. I followed the trail back to the three severed structures and brought up my fizer to locate Amat via its tracker. But the hologram came up all distorted.

Electromagnetic interference.

I glanced back and forth to either side of me. I was conflicted between regrouping with Amat or doubling back to search for survivors. A moment's hesitation and I thought to myself: *Amat will be alright with the others. He'll likely prioritize the Skivs back at the hill. As his second, I should gather what remains of his forces.*

I altered time and dashed in the opposite direction of the torn crescent and began my search.

The city was somehow quieter than when we first arrived and met with the shadows of the crescents. It felt less lively, perhaps due to the lack of radiance the lights provided, perhaps due to the fresh scent of death in the air, or perhaps for the deafening silence. At least when we were faced with the shadows in the light, their presence called for a certain... caution that filled the tranquil atmosphere.

While running through the remnants of the city, searching for survivors, I wondered what else might be lurking in the dark. I stopped at times, standing as still as any other piece of rubble on the ground. Listening to the most subtle ambient ringing, undisturbed by the most elusive breeze. There was someone near and they were being all too careful to keep their existence hidden.

I continued to run through and across the various buildings as the *drum* of my every step thundered through the air. Launching from one broken rooftop to another, I glanced down and thought I saw someone sitting behind a crumbled wall atop the next building over. I barrel-rolled and turned swiftly with my gun in hand. The armored body was still and limp from the gaping hole in its chest. But there was something less obvious. On the ground where I'd landed, tiny pieces of rubble floated— at least it seemed that way. Rather, I was seeing the impact of relativity;

the correspondence between my movements in a quantum field and the world around me. The rubble was not floating, but rising, ever so steadily. Watching long enough to see the shift in its descent back onto the ground. I was about to turn away when I noticed again just a very slight wobble about the rubble as it fell, as if something else had rushed by or climbed along the wall.

I'd let my guard down as my eyes went wide with the thought: *That's a pressure flux!*

I turned and rushed off the roof, rolling onto the ground, and proceeded to run a few paces forward. I stopped and walked back, kneeling close beside one of the rising clusters of rubble I ran past. While examining it closely, I thought to myself: *If it wobbles again, I can use that to find whoever's tracking me.*

My focus narrowed as I watched for the most subtle change. Apart from the rise and fall, the rubble was almost completely still. But then, in its downward motion, just before it hit the ground, I saw it. A unison bank to the left and a change in their trajectory, falling at an angle off to the right.

I whipped my head up to the right and caught it, with the suit's particle sensors barely able to pick up its outline, tucked high on the side of the building above me. Without hesitation, I reached for my gun to take aim, but the thing had pounced down, surging a shock wave so powerful and near to me, I flew several feet across the plaza. I rose slowly, examining my gun; the muzzle had been damaged, rendering it useless. I noted the Shadow Scar panting eagerly, yet waiting ever so patiently with its wide, jaw-stretching grin gleaming at me. I tossed the gun aside, took hold of my splice's hilt and flicked it as the nano-blade formed itself.

The Shadow Scar shifted its six pegged legs as it let out a laugh that echoed out to me, followed by a repeating message: "Time to join your sister." The Shadow Scar unsheathed a wide blade from its lower back that stretched almost as tall as it did.

We charged one another, and the Shadow Scar swung the blade into the ground as I slid beneath it and cut across its right hind leg. It let out a horrific cry as it swiftly turned and flicked one of its middle legs into my back, sending me flying once again. I bared the suit's claws and managed to scrape myself onto my toes. Glancing up, the Shadow Scar threw another swing of its grand blade at me as I leaned out of its path and sliced across the Shadow Scar's waist. We swung our blades around and the clash unleashed another shock wave, one that shattered the nano-metals of my splice and quaked the bones in my palm and arm. Hesitating, I extended my claws out at the Shadow Scar, but it caught my wrist and threw me against a wall.

It rushed to me and raised one of its conjoined, pointed legs, aimed at my heart. A blink of an eye away from the leg's sharp point piercing through my chest, I called out the only name I knew could help: "Amat!!!!"

The Shadow Scar reeled its leg in for the kill… *slice!* It gurgled a cry as it pulled away from me with a quarter of its leg having been severed. A human figure stood with his broad back to me, pushing the Shadow Scar back further while wielding a splice, his helm retracted. Ignoring the pain, I found my feet and rushed out to reclaim my own splice. Examining it briefly, I noted that the nano-metals had retreated into the hilt, so I flicked it and forged the blade once again.

The Shadow Scar stood unsteady, and its movements were slowed, but it was no less feisty against its newfound combatant who met the blows of the Shadow Scar using the flat sides of his splice, so as to better parry the larger weapon. I rushed beside the Shadow Scar, stopping abruptly when it caught sight of me. The Shadow Scar managed a fluid movement that forced the man to stumble back and threw its large blade back toward me. Overextending its arm behind it, I rushed forward and stabbed my splice *deep* into the Shadow Scar's rib cage. The Shadow Scar let out a loud gurgle as I tore my blade out, twisting away from its follow-up blow. It met with the man's splice, which pierced all the way to the other side of the Shadow Scar's wrist, forcing it to drop the blade.

The man and I shared a distracted glance and, in that instant, I recognized Amat. He nodded at me as if to say: "Finish it!" A fist to the head knocked Amat to the ground. I threw myself between Amat and the Shadow Scar, swinging my splice through a few fingers of the Shadow Scar's wounded wrist hand. The Shadow Scar curled in on itself, reeled back and cried out a wail that was ear piercing. It turned to scurry away, but Amat chased after it, diving for its hind legs. The Shadow Scar fell over as Amat quickly crawled on the Shadow Scar's back and locked his arms around its neck.

"Finish it... finish it... finish it, Mae!" Amat's voice pulled me out of my trance.

I looked down at my splice. *It will take too long to kill the Shadow Scar with this.* I turned to the Shadow Scar's wide blade that it dropped.

"Mae... Mae... Mae," Amat's voice echoed once again.

I took up the weapon, watched as the creature fell to its side, rolling over Amat, repelling back onto its legs, and kicking its shelled ball-socket joints as high back as they could toward Amat, barely scraping his armor. Dragging the blade behind me, I dashed toward the Shadow Scar. On the last step, I leaped forward, swinging the blade into the Shadow Scar's gut. It stiffened and then shivered as I nudged it deeper.

Staring up into those lifeless black eyes, I growled: "For Reia."

Amat hopped off the back of the Shadow Scar as it plopped on its side. We all regulated time, watching as it choked on its own blood, still grinning wide, still gurgling. Taking its final breaths, the Shadow Scar let out a broken laugh, said: "Too... easy..."

Amat came to my side as we both stared down at the Shadow Scar in silence.

"You wouldn't kill it," I said.

"No," Amat replied.

"Why?" I asked, turning to Amat. "You had the opportunity several times; you could have shot its face a new one right when you dropped in."

Amat remained collected as he slowly looked from the Shadow Scar to me.

"Many times, you've told me the story of how your sister passed," Amat replied. "I've heard the vivid details about the Shadow Scar who did it over and over. My priority in this conflict was to protect you; I would have given my own life to ensure that. But, knowing the scar that this shadow left on you, it was not my place to take its life. It was yours."

I was neither flattered nor upset by his words, as I didn't know how to feel in that moment. I hadn't gone out of my way to find the Shadow Scar that rested before us there, having never expected the opportunity to avenge Reia. But I felt no relief nor sensed any in her spirit. It was simply done and the chaos of the world continued to ensue around us.

But then, something finally caught on to me.

"Amat... how is it that you're able to alter time without your helm being sealed?" I asked.

Amat's reaction suggested he'd been oblivious to the fact and hesitated before answering.

"Ah... well... I can't answer that question completely, as even I don't truly know the answer. But I will tell you what I can," Amat replied.

(Amat)

Reuniting with Quim, Mae and I arrived to the news that the Skivs who had once occupied the small tunnel in the side of the hill, had been moved... lost.

And so, this mission and all who gave their lives for it were in vain.

Filled with derision, I scorned myself for having failed them all—my troops and those I should have saved.

"Should we tear down the remaining crescents, sir?" asked Shím.

I turned from the tunnel and furrowed my brows at the four crescents that remained over the east and west sides of the city.

"No." Quim spoke low but sternly as she came forward.

"But, they're dangerous. We've seen firsthand what they do to people who come into contact with them," Shím said.

"You don't know what you'd be robbing, my friend." Quim turned to me. "Sir, do you remember when I touched the wound of the first soldier who made contact with one of the lights?"

I briefly flicked through my memories to the precise moment Quim was referring to.

I nodded and replied, "I do."

Quim gestured for a private audience with me. I moved to her side, and I followed after her feather-light steps. Far enough from everyone else's earshot, Quim spoke.

"Few outside of us Dövar know that when we interact with the dead or, in this instance, one who has been... marked by a spirit, we can see into the lives of those who passed through their eyes."

I shifted and raised an eyebrow as I considered Quim's words.

"And what did you see when you touched Jippif's leg?" I asked.

"I cannot tell you in great detail what I saw, sir. To do so would cost us the rest of the time we are due to spend in this life."

"What can you tell me then?" I asked.

"The figures are dying memories of a species who once occupied Galiza before humanity. Preservations of a greatly self-oppressed civilization, who pray to be made whole one day."

"If their means in becoming whole is to rob others of their lives and defile their bodies, why then should I allow them to live?"

"Because they're all they have left of themselves... if you give the command to tear down those last remaining crescents, sir, it would be an order of genocide. And believe me when I say, sir, that the place beyond this life is far colder and darker."

I stood silently in contemplation. I was struck by the fact that out of all my interactions with her, this was the most I'd seen Quim display a sense of feeling, of concern.

As I made my decision, I sighed.

"This world will be a barren rock before the year is out. At the very least, the figures will pose no threat to us by that point. The crescents shall remain intact and there will be no further missions sent to this city for any reason whatsoever."

Quim gave a gratified nod.

The winds picked up and the sands blew. Several dim lights shone down upon us; the Fades had come to take us back to Y'Gŭtsa.

VI
Blessing
(Amat)

It's been many months since I listened to the Důlabega Quadrant Incident recording, and in that time, there's still much I haven't been able to piece together. What it suggests, however; that the Zeltons weren't always our enemies, drives me still, to establish a dialogue between ourselves and the invaders. While prioritizing a few of M.I.S.T.'s scientists to fully decode and compute the alien language would speed this process, many of their personnel have been stretched thin with the research and understanding of the submerged starships. And at the end of the day, perhaps the Zeltons see that both sides have cut too deep into the bloodshed of this war for there to ever be any reconciliation of it. Thus, I've judged it to be in the best interest of humanity if we prioritize a way off this world, where we can collect ourselves and start anew… for a time, at least.

When the opportunity arises, I still attempt civil contact with the Zeltons. Each encounter is soured, however, by the uproar of the ever-pressing Shadow Scar. Some of whom may very well have been human, once… among other things. What's become apparent to me is that the Cho'Zai and the Shadow Scar are one and the same. It's only one example, but Log's vivid recollection of his interrogation with Xaizar and the Cho'Zai's peculiar transformation is enough to make the connection.

It's been six months since I took the Diramal's seat and roughly three of those months since I assigned Rika Rogen to reverse-engineer the starship's sustenance interfaces. We've only just started adapting the technology and installing it throughout our bases. It's a curious sensation, but it leaves no one hungry and buys us more time to collect what remains of the Skivs and Warvs. Questions remain why the Zeltons take such an interest in those two factions. There's been no evidence to suggest the invaders do anything with them, beyond what we've observed; they just offer a curious protection. To put my mind at ease, Lara suggested asking Skivs to volunteer themselves and be released back out to the waste, where they would be tracked and set to engage the invaders. But even if they agreed, I would never allow it. Too much had been put on the line to bring them to the bases and preserve their lives. I wouldn't take the risk, despite whatever fate awaited them in the invaders' care, even if they were once our allies. They aren't now.

In the midst of all this, Log impressed me: taking the boy he'd orphaned, Warter, under his own wing, with Krollgrum Kita at his side. I haven't concerned myself with their relationship as much as I have Log's with Warter. I can't help but note Log's boost in maturity, almost to such an extreme it makes him seem unrecognizable. And though it's very subtle, I can sense, for the first time in a long time, he's happy, or at least content. I don't want to take that from him, but I will soon ask him to fight at my side once again. If he refuses, I will respect his decision.

Mae has been more troubled with the origin of the Shadow Scar of late. Ever since we killed the Shadow Scar that murdered her sister, she's been trying to solve a riddle in her mind. What are the Shadow Scar? I've given her access to all Blick could find on project Dark Wave. A vague explanation for why humans have been involved with it, but not the others with various anatomies and attributes. That aside, we've grown much closer; in her spare time, Mae has taken a liking to visiting with my mother and sisters. Slowly becoming a part of my family.

Blick remains a loyal ally and friend to me. He earned that much and the privilege of someone I would count as family, when Log recounted Blick's intervention between himself and Xaizar in the launch bay. I wasn't pleased to hear of Log's violation to his disciplinary action. But provided Blick's report, stated that Log had engaged minimal Cho'Zai targets and no friendlies, I was neither displeased. It was around the time of that incident that Log's shift in character began. And I suspect a correlation. Log won't talk about it, and I can't quite begin to suspect what troubles him. Maybe he knows something I don't, something he may be afraid to share with anyone, including me.

The only other thing that concerns me is the Diramal himself. In all this time, there have been no leads to his whereabouts. Whether he has fled to the waste with his cursed Cho'Zai creatures, or remains somewhere hidden within the walls of Y'Gǔtsa, I can't be sure. What I can be sure of, is if the truth is the ladder, I can't see him coming out into the open anytime soon. The Warv-turned-Alphas roam around the halls of Y'Gûtsa day and night. Even if they couldn't kill the Diramal, I trust they would put up a fight *vigorous* enough that the encounter would spread alarm. Despite the turnouts of my personal conflicts with him, I almost wish the Diramal would show his face so that I wouldn't have so many restless nights, wondering when he'll strike at me. When he does, he'll go straight for my family and if I'm anything short of ready for that… *I don't want to think about what'll happen if I'm not.*

Only two countries remain that haven't yet been fully liberated from the Zeltons' dominant hold over our world. Those being the Dronomen Isles and Druteika. I've relayed orders out to our allies to encourage additional aid be sent to these countries. But they are all too eager to leave the planet, now that word of the submerged starships has spread. Everyone feels they have sacrificed enough, knowing there's a planet within reach that could give us a new start as a species. I've made it clear, however, that the starships will not launch until all active countries around Galiza have been liberated. With the loyal Warvs at my back, we will ensure that day comes, and we will make our final stand *together.*

***

Shím stood tall and silent as I looked over digital mappings of the Dronomen Isles that had been formed from recent reconnaissance over the areas. There were four in total: Welshmire to the east, Scoat'tír to the north, Anglik to the south, and Irenole lay to the west. Anglik looked to be in the worst shape of the four and if they didn't get help soon, it would surely go dark.

"I'm surprised at how such small pieces of land have remained active in this war after so long and yet countries of much larger scales have fallen in much less time," I said.

"I can't say much for the other Isles, sir, but we Irens are a spirited folk. We'd band together no matter our age or physical strength to keep safe what is ours," said Shím.

"When was the last time you were in Irenole, Shím?" I asked.

"Nearly seven years, sir."

"How old were you then?"

"Oh, a little less than fourteen."

"I take it your memory of the landscape is a little hazy at this point then?"

"Ah, perhaps a little, sir, but no, I've a photographic memory and I can tell you almost every detail of my home Isle, like I'd only just left it."

I nodded my head.

"How confident would you be then in leading a team through the streets of your home island?" I asked.

Shím seemed taken aback for a moment.

"I'm confused, sir, I thought you were leading the operation to aid the Dronomen Isles."

"I am leading the operation, but a man who is familiar with the land at my side is therefore more knowledgeable than me in terms of how we can play out our strategy and reach out to the people there. I'll ask you one more time, how confident are you in taking the lead on this mission?"

Shím walked up to the grid that displayed the digital maps, pulled up Irenole, scrolling over the 3D landscape until he came to a wide stretch of an open field.

"Still empty as ever," Shím mumbled. "Can I ask how recent the reconnaissance that gathered this grid was, sir?"

"I received it this morning," I replied.

"*Mm*, this field stretches for miles. If you don't know your way around, you could wander in the middle of nowhere for days on end till you starve or die of thirst. But if we land there, it'd be a good startin' place for us to gather ourselves and divide our forces, considerin' the invaders mainly keep to the cities and anywhere there's people."

I nodded.

"Good to know. Say we land there, where do you suggest we move next?"

"The largest town is…" Shím said, scrolling across the map, "…due south, Claumidin, it's close to where I grew up. If there was anywhere the Warvs and Skivs of my people'd be takin' refuge on the Isle, it'd be there. At least for a time, it has the largest Kaw department and armory on the Isle, not to mention food'd be much less scarce in this town; it's where we got all our imports. Of course, I'd encourage us to divide our forces across the rest of the Isle, but this spot right here is surely where the majority of the Irens are making their final stand."

"How long would you suspect it would take to sufficiently cover the whole island?" I asked.

"Well, I'd ask how many troops we have for each Isle?" asked Shím.

"Nearly twelve thousand in total," I said.

Shím raised an eyebrow. "Almost a thousand for each corner of every Isle."

"If that is what you feel would be the best course of action, to save what remains of humanity in the Waste of Galiza," I replied.

"As a precaution and to avoid a guilty conscience of having left anyone behind, I'd ask said course of action be taken."

"Then it shall be done. We will leave tomorrow and together, my friend, you and I will lead this final front."

Shím stomped his feet together and saluted me.

"Yessir."

I'd selected several members among the Alpha Warvs to lead the other band of platoons that would be entering the other countries. Among them was Pac-Qua Quim, who would be leading one of four groups, aiding Anglik. Olson and Mae would be partaking in the front on Irenole, while Blick remained in Y'Gûtsa to govern the forces we'd be leaving behind. Yet there was one other, whose presence I'd require in this great escapade.

After I've had my say, I will allow Log his own.

***

I knocked on the door to his quarters, and my younger cousin answered promptly. He seemed caught off guard by my arrival; I couldn't tell if he was pleasantly surprised or dismayed.

"Diramal, sir."

I nodded my head.

"Log," I replied, addressing him by name rather than rank to set the tone of our exchange.

Warter walked into my view, stretching his body past Log to catch a glimpse of me. I'd hardly seen the boy myself. He looked well, stronger than when I'd first seen him. I could sense there was a certain discipline to the boy; I could see it in his eyes. I wondered whether the child's innocence would have been better lost via the hardships of the Alpha program as opposed to the chaos of the war. As so many children, younger than Warter, had undertaken and earned a *strong* sense of confidence and maturity for their age. After a few moments passed, I observed Krollgrum Yatů step in beside the boy, wrapping one arm across his chest while her other held his shoulder. The Krollgrum gazed at me and spoke something to Warter that was just out of earshot. Suggesting maybe she knew what I had come for. Kita and Warter then walked out of view.

"We need to talk," I said.

"Come in," said Log, as he moved aside for me to enter.

I entered and took in the sight of his quarters as I made myself comfortable.

"Looks cleaner from last I was here," I said.

"Ah, that would be Kita's doing."

"She's been staying here with you?" I asked.

"Days at a time. Though I'm still the one who does most of the cleaning. She holds me accountable to it," said Log.

I almost wondered if there was more to that explanation, but I wouldn't bring up personal matters that weren't mine to know. Especially with Kita just in the other room.

I cleared my throat.

"If the living situation becomes more permanent, would you be sure to inform me? There are many other Skivs and Warvs without quarters still," I said.

Log nodded.

"So, what brings you here today?" he asked.

I glanced down at my boots as I gathered my thoughts.

"Before I answer that question, Log, know that I come before you not as the Diramal, but as family, and regardless of your answer, it doesn't change anything between us."

Log only gave a simple nod as his gaze dashed awkwardly about the room.

"In the past few months, I've taken note of the progress in your recovery and maturity. In part with that, our conflict with the invaders is nearing a foreseeable end, at least for a time. And if you would honor me, I would like to have you return to my command."

Log's stare was plain, yet I sensed something deep in his stare. An uncomfortable shift in his character. Beyond that, I couldn't say for certain what it related to. Log took his time responding.

"I…" his attention drifted momentarily. "I do have some fight left in me, Amat. I haven't grown soft, but in the time I've spent with Warter, I can't help but feel an obligation to ensure he's looked after."

I tilted my head.

"Be direct, Log," I said.

"I'd prefer not to risk losing my life and leaving the boy on his own once again."

I sighed as I considered Log's words.

"Kita seems to care for the boy as much as you do and you both seem close enough that if you were to fall, Anua forbid, Kita would look after the boy in your stead—"

"He's my responsibility; no one else's," Log cut in.

"And if I demanded it of you?" I asked.

Log squinted his eyes and leaned back in his seat, his jaw hanging slightly.

"I'd find it contradictory to demands you weighed on me, when I was hardly in a proper condition to fulfill them," said Log.

"And you have done better than I ever could have hoped you would, in your execution of those demands. But the time is coming, Log, when we will make our final push against the invaders and even if you do not accept these demands I give you now, you will need to comply with the ones that'll be relayed to you in due course," I said.

"And if I refuse those orders? Will you activate my neuro-chip, or worse yet, will you place a code nine inside my—"

"That's enough." I spoke sternly. "Never in a thousand lifetimes would I condemn a member of my family to such a horrid scenario." Log lowered his eyes and shifted in his seat. "If you do not comply with these orders and have no interest in contributing to the final days of the war, I will retire you. You'll be permanently stripped of your rank and you'll have no further engagement with militia operations," I said. I relaxed my shoulders and leaned in close to Log as I cooled my temper. "I did not come here to argue with you, nor force you into doing anything, Log. I'm merely reaching out because I need your help, and judging by your attitude at the idea of getting back out there, a question stirs in my mind. Do you fear you'll see his face again?"

Log slowly shifted his eyes up at me. His blank expression exuded a strange coolness.

"Xaizar's?" Log asked; his voice rasped the name. I nodded. "My counselor has helped me face the trauma he left me with. But I have not been on the field since and while we both know what happened was due to a mix between my encounter with Xaizar and the Diazep, I can't help but wonder if something out there would trigger my rabid behavior once again."

"I understand your unwillingness to take that risk, I do. The last thing I would want is for you to lash out, the same way that you did at Atheika. But I would ask that you give it a night's rest before you make your decision final. You would have my assurance, as your cousin, that if you did feel the slightest bit alienated out there, I would arrange for your immediate return to Y'Gûtsa."

Log took a moment before replying.

"Is there anything else you wish to discuss with me, Diramal Criptous?"

That almost felt like a subtle slight to my face, given that Log and most everyone else knew how much I despised being referred to as the Diramal. I stood, looking down at Log, who continued to avoid my gaze.

"The fleet leaves at 8 a.m. tomorrow morning. If your position remains as it is, you need not attend the take-off. But if it changes, you'll find me in the launch bay." I started walking toward the door and stopped before exiting. I turned my head slightly. "Even if this war ends, Log, I fear there may be another on the horizon if, Anua forbid, the Diramal and his Cho'Zai find their own way off this planet with us. If that happens, I sense the ferocity they'll unleash upon us will be far crueler than the wrath of the invaders. Should that day ever come, I may truly need every able man and woman available to me to defend what remains of our race. Which includes Warter," I said.

After Log said nothing, I turned forward and exited the room.

71

(The Diramal)

The outside air was thick with the stench of death and burning rubble. A much more satisfying fragrance than the clean, bland air from within Y'Gûtsa. I listened carefully to Quavek's words, who had also remained hidden within the base, operating as my viperous watchman in burrowed holes.

"So, Amat means to liberate both the Dronomen Isles and Druteika at the same time, with his legion of waste *Shrak,* taking the lead on the front, heading to Irenole?" I asked.

"Yes, Diramal," replied Quavek, with a bow. "His growing band of friends and family will be accompanying him as well. Except for Blick and perhaps even Log Criptous. That one seems plagued still by the workings of you, *Xaizar.*"

Quavek hissed Xaizar's name and gestured to him scornfully. She'd been acting strangely toward the Qi-Varian in the past few months, for reasons I couldn't speculate.

"How fares Drakkar on the matter of moving the humans off this rock?" butted in Voruke.

"On that matter, his patience exceeds my own. He won't have any one of us move on Amat or his family until the boy has gathered humanity for the launch to Serakis. I sense that time is near. But then, I don't see why we can't beat Amat to the chase," I said.

"Sir?" asked Voruke.

"All the humans Amat has gathered for us would meet with the same fate as those we were to capture on our own. And it seems the boy could use a challenge after having consecutive victories in recovering the waste filth. Zothra…" I said, turning to him. "I want you to go to base Bōkwart and reach out to Ho-Jinn Clōv'ket; he'll arrange a transport for you to arrive in Irenole. The rest of you will be going as well. Your mission will be to take any Skivs you can find into custody, as much as it will be to toy with Amat and his allies. If Log goes, Xaizar, your focus will be on him. Reveal yourself to him, subtly at first, but when the time is right, face him and remind him of the fear you scarred on his mind. Do try to restrain yourself from killing the young Criptous. If the worst unfolds, however, our plans will not falter. I'll not allow any fatal harm to befall Amat, however, I… Drakkar wants him alive long enough to rally the humans against the Zeltons." My three Qi'val and lone Vorüm'Qij nodded their heads. "Voruke, your target will be Olson Criptous. If he and Log are together, isolate Olson from his brother. Zothra, your priority will be Amat. Again, you are not to kill him, but you may push him to his limit, exhaust him, bring him close to death, but do not have him meet with it. And, Quavek, do you think you could handle Amat's woman?" I queried.

Quavek's mandibles clicked and twitched ecstatically.

"Oh, it would be my pleasure, Diramal," replied Quavek, and her appendages twirled with excitement.

"Though not all of them will fall victim to your treacheries at first, as one will surely, the others will follow," I said.

"By your wish, Diramal," said Zothra, hunched in his stance.

(Amat)

I'd been standing in the launch bay for about an hour before Olson's Fade arrived. I'd sent another commander to oversee his work with the starships in Aubwen, Afeikita. Obviously, I wouldn't have pulled him away from that post if I didn't have a stirring suspicion about the dangers that awaited me in Irenole. Somehow, I felt I'd need all those closest to me at my side to survive it. At first sight, Olson's expression seemed to suggest he preferred to have remained in Aubwen, though he was no less happy to see me, as we greeted one another warmly.

"Io-Pac Olson Criptous," I said, with a smile.

"Amat, sir," replied Olson.

"How fares the condition of the ship in Aubwen?" I asked.

"With Doctor Rogen back in the ship's engineering, we should have them all up and running in no time."

Olson and I walked beside one another.

"Considering that I've never seen one of these ships for myself and that this one now makes the count over eleven hundred, do you think there will be adequate space to take all our kin away, aboard these craft?" I asked.

"Without a doubt, sir. I'd say we have more than enough space and as we continue to make new discoveries about each of their engineering and interfaces; by the time you are ready to strike, we should have enough knowledge about the ancient crafts to strike."

"And are we actively training our men and women to operate these craft?" I asked.

"We are, indeed, sir."

I patted Olson on the shoulder.

"Well done. Has there been much else you've been able to find out from the ships' logs: where they came from, what started the war that Galican showed you?"

Olson sighed.

"I'm afraid not. Many of the ships seem to show me much of the same battle from various perspectives, and not all are as clearly conveyed as the other."

"And at the end, that final transmission seems to cut out in the same areas as before?" I asked.

"Yes, though, I think it may be safe to say—if it's what their race is truly called—when the audio cuts out at '…ons' it may have been this commander, Stordar Glīzen, calling the Zeltons by name."

I calmly gestured for Olson to lower his voice when he mentioned the name of the invaders. This information was not widely known. Though I had made it my priority to establish a dialogue between humans and the invaders, my reasons for doing so had remained a secret. I was under the impression that people would either care too little about the subject, as it wouldn't make sense to them, or it would result in chaos. I didn't like having to conceal such information from my kin and I promised myself that if the opportune moment presented itself, I would openly disclose that Human and Zelton were somehow connected through an alliance long forgotten.

"I'd consider that a probable assumption," I replied. "On the subject of Commander Stordar Glīzen, presumably the leader of humanity at the time, have you been able to recover much intel about him?"

"Unfortunately, not, sir," replied Olson.

I nodded.

"That is alright, we've already learned quite a lot as it is. And in time, I'm sure all the pieces will come together. Perhaps once we reach an understanding of what's really been going on over the past two decades, a truce can finally be made."

After escorting Olson to his quarters, I'd taken care of my daily responsibilities as Diramal and made sure all was ready for the launch the following day. After which I visited my family's quarters, being greeted by Mae. Everyone's faces brightened as I entered. Mae enveloped me with her arms and kissed me passionately.

"How did it go with Log today?" asked Mae.

I grumbled as I rubbed Mae's shoulders.

"Not as well as I expected. He grew agitated with me after I'd only just mentioned the idea of him falling back under my command. He said his obligations were tied to Warter."

"Well, at least that's honorable; it could be worse," said Mae.

"I know, but I think he's suppressing something deep within himself and he's using the boy as an excuse not to rejoin the war rather than address his unresolved fears."

"Well, he is younger and more sensitive than you. I know you may think you endured more than he has when you were his age, when this all started. But Log is like a younger brother to you, and Olson, an older one. Give him time and be open to what Log needs; he'll come around."

"I should hope so." I sighed.

"Have you spoken with Blick recently, Amat?" asked my mother from the living room.

"Only for brief instances, in my office," I said.

"You should pull him aside when you have a chance. He comes by from time to time, since the Cho'Zai left the base, just to check on us. Each time he comes, his eyes seem sadder."

"I've noticed, in the small exchanges I've had with him. I didn't know he still came by to check in on you all," I replied.

"Oh yes, at least a few times a week," my mother said.

"If the mood is right, I'll try to speak with him next chance I get," I said.

(Log)

I spent much of the rest of the day sitting in isolation, my mind busy with Amat's proposition, watching as Kita and Warter played together. I wouldn't go so far as to say she was like a mother figure to the boy, but she seemed to do well enough in keeping him happy, and it pleased me to see the kid better off than when I found him.

Since day one, I'd made it my priority to rebuild Warter's life, his world, after I shattered his old one. *If I was to go back out there and fight alongside my cousin and my brother, I don't sense it would mean my death. But on the faint chance it did, I would not risk losing my life and leaving Warter on his own once again.*

And it is not my own death I fear or even encountering my own trauma again, as Amat would believe. My sense of self has nearly all but fled, ever since that last encounter with Xaizar. In taking care of Warter, I've almost been reborn and in the grand scheme of things, he's taught me more about myself than I have on my own. Amat would have me throw all that away; for what? The reassurance my presence gives him in his sense of confidence, just so he can feel in control of the chaos that rests in the waste. No, the man will do just fine on his own; he always has.

"Log? *Log?*" blurted Kita.

I snapped out of my train of thought as my attention came back to the present.

"Hm?" I asked.

"You seem distant today. I wanted to make sure there wasn't anything troubling you," said Kita.

"Oh, no, I'm fine, Kita, thank you," I replied.

Kita nodded.

"I think I'll stay here with you again tonight; would that be alright?" asked Kita, placing her hand over mine, as if to say she knew what was going on in my mind and wanted to talk about it later.

I looked down at my hand, her thumb trailing back and forth along its side.

"Of course you can stay," I replied, looking up at her.

I never understood entirely what Kita saw in me, and I never asked. But I was no less grateful for the comfort she provided in my life. Perhaps she had some way of seeing past the broken man that I was and acknowledged only the spirited qualities of my character. Though I could scarcely recall what those qualities might have been, provided my state of mind.

Night came and I saw Warter to bed. I always did it myself, sharing long conversations with the boy, sometimes amusing him with stories about myself and poor made-up tales that he often found amusing for their roughness. But that night's conversation would be different from all the rest.

I pulled up a chair after seeing Warter under the sheets and sat back in a lounging position. We stared at each other in silence, as we sometimes did, to start. Before long, Warter noted my thumbs nervously rubbing against one another.

"Something's on your mind."

"Mm-hm," I mumbled, while nodding.

Warter took that as a sign that I wasn't ready to talk about it just yet and remained quiet until I spoke up.

I took a deep breath.

"You know, in the time we've been living together, I've done my best to prioritize my responsibility to you and I can only hope you feel I've done right by you," I said.

"You have. You're not my father and Kita is not my mother, but I deeply appreciate what you both have done for me."

I exhaled as I rubbed my thighs.

"And I should hope that we only continue to do right by you," I said. "Do you know the man who walked into our quarters today?"

"I've recalled seeing his face before and his voice sounded familiar," said Warter.

"But you don't know him?" Warter shook his head. "His name is Amat Luciph Criptous; he's my cousin and the Diramal of the militia. He's the reason you and I are where we are today, and this afternoon he asked something of me. Something I'm not sure you're ready for."

Warter stared at me in silence for a moment.

"He wants you to return to the war."

I nodded.

"I would rather avoid my reentry into the war. Not out of fear, but simply due to my obligation to you. I can't imagine the thought of leaving you deprived of another… without a caretaker, should something terrible happen to me."

I was going to say "family" but I wasn't sure how Warter would respond to so bold a suggestion.

Warter gave an understanding nod.

"I've almost always appreciated what you've tried to do for me. And while you did take the lives of my parents, you should not give the remainder of your own to me. For the Goddess has blessed you with your own destiny to fulfill, as she has us all. My mother always said, in case anything ever happened to her, 'it's up to us to do right by ourselves and earn our embrace from Anua,'" said Warter.

I gave a half-smile and nodded.

"Off to sleep with you," I said.

Warter nodded and gently closed his eyes. I watched as his face relaxed and his jaw slackened. Only until I was sure that he was fast asleep did I stand, brush my fingers across his fur, and leave him to rest.

I still wasn't entirely convinced that I should leave Warter behind, but perhaps my next conversation with Kita would persuade me so.

Lying there in bed together underneath the sheets, our legs and arms were interwoven around one another. So strange as it was, being unable to *feel* love. I had been severed from the emotion, among others, since the incident with Xaizar. Even stranger that while I didn't want to admit it to myself, I didn't *love* Kita. Despite wanting to, my heart had lost its ability to channel the emotion. Made me wonder how we found ourselves consistently enveloped in each other's company. But then, maybe it was just that, my lack of emotion. Wouldn't have made any difference to me, either way. There was something soothing, however, in the beating of her heart, pulsing against my chest. It was in those moments, where I was able to channel at least a faint sense of empathy and open up, slightly.

"I heard what he told you, your cousin," Kita said.

I sighed and frowned.

"It's not something I'm in the position to undertake," I replied.

"Because of Warter?"

I looked over to Kita, as if she'd forgotten something.

78

"And you as well," I replied.

Kita was taken off guard by my words, as if I'd offended her.

"You say that as if I couldn't look after Warter myself. Need I remind you, Log Criptous, I am a Krollgrum who fought at your side and saved *your* life more than once." Kita gave a mocking grin.

"That's not what I was saying, Kita. The boy is my responsibility. If something were to happen to him, anything, even if he was under your watch, I'd blame myself. Or worse, if I find, *Xaizar*"—I spoke the name, as if it were a curse—"out there and he causes me to sabotage the mission, end my life, Amat's, or my brother's…" I shook my head. "No, I'm too great a liability to let back on the field."

Kita gave a look of sympathy as she pressed her hand over my heart.

"I think, if I may speak candidly, Io-Pac Criptous?" Kita asked.

Kita looked up at me with a gleam in her eyes.

I chortled for spite, with no exhilaration in my heart and quickly, my smirk faded.

"Of course," I replied.

"I think you are stronger than you know. Even if you don't, I do. I've seen you at your worst, to where you are now, and even at your lowest point, I saw strength and sense in you. On those final two days that we were in Atheika, you were so weak, yet you had the strength to admit you were unfit. You handed the command over to someone you trusted to ensure the mission's success and see most of those Skivs safely to the base. When you were given the responsibility of taking Warter under your wing, though you were frightened, you faced that challenge willingly, knowing it would be hard. Now you are confronted with another great trial that will test your strength and I believe no matter what you face, you will find a way to come home safely."

I took a deep breath, processing Kita's words, and I had to admit she had a point. Where I had my flaws, there were things I could have done in addition to make them worse, yet I found a way to maintain my composure and see that they weren't as bad as they could have been.

"Have I granted you some clarity?" asked Kita.

"By the morning I'll have my decision made," I said, even though I'd already made up my mind.

(Amat)

My eyes slowly opened, revealing my dimly lit bedroom. The lighting was so graceful, and my muscles were nearly lulled back to rest by the soft cushion of my bed that I had sunken into. I turned my head over to Mae, still deep in her slumber, breathing soundly. I gently brushed my fingers across her face, careful not to wake her. *Her beauty is monumentally greater when she's asleep.*

I turned to the clock; it would be at least another three hours before the launch. The alarm would wake Mae in an hour—that would have been hardly enough time for me to fall back into a deep slumber. *I might grow even more groggy by then.* I stood from the bed and dressed myself in uniform after freshening up.

As I wandered the halls of Y'Gůtsa, I crossed the paths of many patrolling Alphas who paused and saluted me in unison. I replied with the same gesture as I strode past. Before reaching the launch bay, a figure walking in the same direction as me, further down the hall, emerged. It was too hard to tell at first, but as I gained ground on him, I could see he was slightly shorter than me. A little closer and I'd recognized his ruffled fur—not too many others like it.

"Couldn't sleep?" I asked.

The figure paused and turned toward me, drowsy.

"Not after the food for thought you gave me yesterday," replied Log, monotone.

"So, you are coming then?" I asked, as I stood before my younger cousin.

"Under a few conditions." Log nodded.

I crossed my arms.

"I'll hear them," I said.

"Kita remains here with Warter," said Log.

"Of course," I replied.

"And if anything happens to me, you look after them both. I wouldn't force Kita to look after Warter, but I trust that she would if I encountered the worst. If I'm lost, make sure they don't lose each other," Log said.

"They won't," I replied. I shook my head. "Sixteen years, Log, you've come a long way."

Log's expression said that he wasn't.

"Shall we?" Log asked, continuing his way.

Many of the Warvs were already at the launch bay loading the Fades with supplies by the time we arrived. Not a single one of them lacked in discipline or urgency.

"It's a reassuring sight, to see the Alpha insignia returned and admirable warriors worthy of the rank," said Log.

"*Mm.* Are you saying you never felt worthy of it?" I asked.

Log passed his eyes over me, shyly.

"Sometimes I think so. I certainly wasn't worthy of the Io-Pac rank."

"Perhaps you were not ready to receive the promotion when you did. But I stand by my judgement, in the potential and strength your character holds, Log. That, in itself, made you worthy of it. I only hoped the shift in responsibility would accelerate the maturity of your character. I was not wrong in my decision any more than you are not feeble at your core. But I was blind in my timing and I apologize for that."

Log nodded silently.

"Will you try your luck at another dialogue with the invaders before we leave Galiza?" Log asked, trying to change the subject.

I sighed.

"I would, if the Jinns weren't so pressed on leaving. There are a few among them that have threatened to disobey my command and hijack the various starships beneath the ground so that they may leave early."

"They think they'd really stand a chance without the full force of humanity at their backs, when even that may not be enough to blow a hole through the invaders' blockade over our skies?"

"With the way they think, probably," I said.

Log and I walked in silence for a moment. I sensed my cousin was finding a way to bring up a sensitive matter.

"I assume you've heard from the battle that unfolded here that the Shadow Scar and the Cho'Zai are one and the same," said Log.

"Since their exile, they've grown to be a more persistent nuisance in the waste," I replied.

"If that's true, I take it they are a major factor in why your attempts at negotiation with the invaders have failed, time and time again."

"You would be correct in your assumption, yes." I shook my head, frustrated at the thought of the Shadow Scar. "It's as if they know my every move before I make it, trailing my every location when I take a new squadron of Alphas out there."

"Have you or any of your troops made attempts at capturing one and interrogating it?"

"We have. In fact, there were a few we managed to apprehend. Each one had a unique anatomy from the last, bearing little if any resemblances to one another. Shortly after each capture, however, these creatures demonstrated a formidable ferocity and broke free of our grasp, killing themselves before we could initiate our interrogations. One of them mauled the face off a fellow Alpha, just to grab his gun and aim it at the Shadow Scar's own head." Log and I paused; he seemed taken aback by my words. "I've examined many of their anatomies amongst their fallen brethren..." I said, continuing to walk forward. "And I still can't say for sure how, or why, there were many that resembled humans." Log looked over to me, an expression of discomfort on his face, the first emotion I'd seen him display in a while. "To this day, I'm not sure why the invaders came here to begin with, but if there is one thing I sense and fear will come to pass, Log, it is that our next war, after this one, will be with the Shadow Scar and what we might discover from it."

Log's discomfort faded, and his plain stare returned.

"It seems unlike you, avoiding your curiosity about all the secrets surrounding this war; the invaders, the Shadow Scar, Uncle Bod's and the Diramal's knowledge of these things before the war broke out," observed Log.

"Some secrets are best left hidden, I should think. Until a time comes when not just one man seeks to reveal them and bear the weight of their reality," I said.

(Mae)

I woke up to the loud beeping of Amat's alarm and moved slowly, reaching my arm over the device to shut it off. Sighing as I brushed my hands over my eyes and pulled myself out of bed, stretching my back before setting my feet on the cold metal floor. A cramping pain surged inside me, and I gasped as I placed my hand over my lower abdomen. I took a deep breath as the pain passed and felt oddly fatigued as I made my way to the bathroom, my stride unbalanced.

How can I be so weary? I slept well and long enough through the night.

As I entered the doorway to the bathroom, my movements triggered the lights. My head instantly ached with nausea at their radiance, and I was blinded as my throat tightened. Stumbling toward the toilet as vomit spewed over my tongue and past my lips. I coughed and spat out the residue, rinsing my mouth after. My heart still raced from the adrenaline as I placed my hand over my stomach. There were no physical signs of it yet, but I could sense the child growing inside me—Amat's child. Though I noticed shifts about my body in the weeks prior, I couldn't be so sure until that moment. I'd never been pregnant before. All the same, you might call it a mother's intuition.

Goddess, bless us, a baby! I... I haven't the slightest clue how to feel about it. Of course, I'm overjoyed about what it'll mean for our future, mine and Amat's. But, the war, humanity in its current state ... is this the time or environment to have a child? I shook my head. *Should I tell Amat? No, no he's already got enough on his mind. What about the med bay, should I have them check it out?* I wondered, looking back at the clock. *No, there's no time for that and if I'm going to keep it a secret for a time, I'll need to avoid raising Amat's suspicions. After this mission, then. Yes, when we return from wherever it is we go next, I'll tell... wait, no, that won't work either. Amat will still be confronted with the issue of moving humanity off planet. After that then, yes, once we've left all this behind, surely, we'll have some time to discuss it then.*

With that, I promptly got dressed and headed for the launch bay to meet with Amat and the others.

VII
Irenole
(Λmat)

A couple of hours had passed before Shím, Olson, Lara, and Mae all joined me and Log in the launch bay. Shím filled the others in on the details of the plan.

"So, who will lead the groups to the northern, eastern, and western towns?" asked Mae.

"There aren't any towns to the east," replied Shím. "It's mostly just farmin' land out that way and the rest is free-range country. There are, however, several small towns to the north and west ends of the Isle."

"Well then, who will go and scout *them* out?" asked Mae.

A moment of silence passed over the group. I had the intention of bringing each one of those people in that circle into Claumidin with me. If it had persisted much longer, I would have swallowed my pride and decided but—

"I'll do it," said Olson. We all looked at him. "Just give me the coordinates, Shím, for the major towns in those areas and I'll search them."

"I'll go too," blurted Log, almost hesitantly.

I looked at my younger cousin, surprised.

"Are you sure?" I asked him.

"I am." Log nodded.

"I'll join them," said Lara.

I looked over to Lara and nodded.

"Very well. While I know it will take more time, I'll only allow this if you all stay together. You can start with the towns to the west, work your way up north, and if you take longer than us in Claumidin, I'll rendezvous with you," I said.

Log, Olson, and Lara nodded.

"Yes, sir," they replied in unison.

"Is there anything else we should be informed of, Shím?" I asked.

84

"No, sir."
"Then let's take these Fades to the skies," I said.

I sat beside my friends. Not hearing very much of what they discussed, it sounded like Olson was excited to have the opportunity to speak with Log again. The last time they'd seen each other, Log was still sick in the med bay. Wasn't too long after I became Diramal that I sent Olson away to investigate the starships further, with Rika. I imagined they had a lot to catch up on. Though, I noted that Log remained oddly quiet, and his words were kept very brief. Shím and Lara—sitting just on the other side of Mae—spoke passionately with one another, with hardly any notable gap in their conversation. But aside from comprehending their tones, it was all background noise to me, being so focused on my own thoughts. A great many things preoccupied my mind: the Shadow Scar, the whereabouts of the Diramal, the purpose of the invaders, if it was wise to let Log free from my side, even if he was aided by my sister and his brother—

Suddenly, I felt someone touch my hand and pull me out of my head. Looking down, I saw her fingers intertwining with my own. Meeting with the smile that reached Mae's eyes, I could sense the unspoken question that stirred in her mind. I gave a half-smile and a nod, somewhat distracted still. She could sense it. At the same time, however, I briefly noted the subtle ecstasy in her expression. The radiant joy that filled her face seemed to suggest she was happy about something. Something I couldn't begin to ponder at that moment.

The Fade rumbled beneath our feet and deep thunderous booms echoed outside as a thousand drops of Galiza's purple rain fell from the sky and harsh winds whirled around the Fade's plating.

"Ah, we must be getting close," said Shím. "Hardly matters what time of year it is, even in the warmer seasons, there are light drizzles that fall on my Isle."

"You say 'warmer' as if it's almost always cold in Irenole," Lara replied.

"Ryne, it is. Though if you were born there, you'd grow accustomed to it, obviously," replied Shím.

"I'll inform Sarak to be on her guard. No doubt there'll be an aerial force awaiting our arrival," I said, standing slowly.

I walked up to the cockpit, treading so lightly, Sarak hardly noticed me.

"Sarak." She whipped her head in my direction, not frightened, just surprised. "Shím tells me the rain means we are nearing our destination. Does your navigation confirm that?" I asked.

"As a matter of fact, we are less than seventy minutes out, sir," replied Sarak.

"Good, I want weapons charged then. I think it's safe to assume we'll encounter some conflict as we get closer. Have the Fades from the other bases fallen in with us as well?" I asked.

"Yes, sir, they have," said Sarak.

"Open a channel, tell their troops onboard to armor up, if they haven't already," I said.

A great big flash of red lightning cracked the sky, not too far from our position.

"Will our Fades survive a strike from one of those?" I asked.

"It certainly wouldn't be good, but if you're asking whether a single strike would decommission a Fade, the answer is 'no,' sir," said Sarak.

"Good to know; be sharp as we continue," I said.

"Yes, sir."

I proceeded to inform my own troops on board the Fade that the time had come to armor and gear up. As my QS-25 sealed itself around me, the Fade rocked again, this time with the sounds of gunfire and *whooshing* alien fighters dancing in the skies. I rushed back up to Sarak.

"Sarak, how far out are we?" I asked.

"It'll be another fifteen minutes before we get over the target area, sir. We're still over fifty miles out."

"That's too soon to receive contact; we're still over open waters," I said. "What gave us away?"

"I don't know, sir. The invader forces just arrived on top of us. The storm dulled my scanners, and I couldn't detect them in time to maneuver out of their course trajectory."

Another red flash momentarily lit up the sky and burst one of the alien craft into tens of pieces. Then a second sounded and illuminated from behind us.

"Don't worry about that, just stay on course. I want all the Fades in altered time, and I want guns shooting down surrounding enemy targets. All Fades are to fly at full speed to reach the target area, ASAP," I said.

"Yes, sir."

After retrieving my weapons of choice, I ordered every one of my troops to stand in line, ready to jump when the time was right. Mae walked at the front of the formation to join me.

"Amat, what's wrong? Why aren't we deploying?"

"It's gonna be some time before we can," I said. "The invaders met us too far out from the target area. The storm interfered with our scanners, and the enemy couldn't be detected in time to avoid detection."

Another strike sounded, followed by a loud metallic moan. *I hope that wasn't a Fade going down!* Many more clashes and chaotic noises echoed outside the ship as we drew closer and closer to Irenole. Before long, the Fade started to quake, seemingly without end. I rushed back to the cockpit.

"Sarak, what's the problem?" I shouted.

"I've got to push her harder, sir. We all do; we've lost three Fades. We'll be over the target area in one minute."

"How long can you maintain this speed?" I asked. "The Fade sounds like it's about to tear apart."

Sarak looked over at me.

"Long enough, sir," she replied.

There was a look in Sarak's eyes that told me she was confident she would be able to get me and all my troops out of this scenario, but perhaps not herself. An abstract red line in the distance *slowly* zig-zagged its way down to the land from the sky above. I shook my head.

"Sarak, if she's going down, I can't let you stay here," I said.

"I'll remain here and see to my duties, sir," replied Sarak.

"It's a ship, Sarak."

She nodded.

"Someone needs to see she stays airborne so that you can go down there and save those last surviving members of our kin."

"This isn't open for debate, Sarak," I said.

Sarak turned forward.

"ETA is thirty seconds, sir," Sarak said.

"Sarak—"

87

"Rest assured, I don't doubt my ability to keep her airborne, sir. I never said she was going down and I'm confident she won't. I promise you, my friend, this will not be the final day you see me."

I would have made my request of Sarak an official order. But something in her eyes, and her calm, confident tone stilled my tongue. I trusted her and, in that moment, I could sense, in my heart, I would see her again.

"Helms on, be ready for deployment!" I shouted, rushing back to my troops.

By the time I returned to the head of the formation, Sarak had turned off the lights and opened the hatch. The rumbling stopped momentarily, then a swift clash of fire and buzzing filled the air from the aerial enemies.

"Go!" I shouted. I looked over to Mae, Lara, Shím, Olson, and Log as I ran toward them, reaching my arm out as if to say, "Follow me," and down we fell. The sky was full of alien vessels, like a hive of bees surrounding their nest. I opened a channel and quickly blurted: "Activate your suits!"

Altering time, everything around me slowed down, and a vessel swept under me a few feet away from my body. The seeps on my suit flexed as I rolled rapidly and carried enough air under me to arch over an alien vessel that swooped under me. Promptly, another came head-on toward me. I dove straight down and expanded my body horizontally once again. Looking at either side of me, observing hundreds of Alphas falling with me. In one glance, an Alpha got hit by a swooping vessel; in another, two Alphas collided with each other, both avoiding impact with vessels. Another vessel curved up toward me so swiftly that I had to arch my fall in a way that had me in an upright position, and my body was inches away from hitting the craft. From above, a thick arched branch of red lighting crashed toward the ground, slower than a flash but still quicker than me. Another alien vessel rose toward me at an angle, forcing me to dive down and spiral past it.

On and on that went, until finally, I landed in the open field Shím spoke of. I retracted my helm and looked to the sky with my own eyes, illuminated in my ultra-violet-esque vision. I didn't see how many more Fades had fallen out of the sky, but there were still a number passing over the island and many more of my troops had yet to find their way down to the surface. Gave me hope that Sarak was still alive. I opened a channel, desperate to find out what had become of my friends, but then I thought not to. If they were still alive, they would need every ounce of concentration to find their way down safely. And it was only a matter of time before members of my squadron would start opening channels of their own. Waiting for that felt longer than it was. Desperately, helplessly, looking up at all that chaos. There was no doubt a few Alphas had likely been hit by one of the vessels so harshly that they were either knocked out or killed on impact. I witnessed a few land on the ground without having deployed their chute. *Goddess, I hope that wasn't Shím, Lara, Log, Olson, or Mae.* I would pray in silence every time I'd witness another limp body splatter somewhere in the distance.

Finally, the last of the Fades passed over the Isle and the field was full of troops who had successfully touched down without having been injured or killed. Sure the last of them were with me, I opened a channel to my surviving troops. Nervously gulping before I spoke, almost choking on my own breath, anxious to hear the response I'd receive, if any.

"Mae Kalbrook, Shím MgKonnol, Lara, Log, and Olson Criptous… come in," I said.

"This is Log, I read you, sir."

My eyebrows rose.

"This is Olson, I read you loud and clear, sir."

I let out a sigh of relief.

"This is Shím, I'm still here, sir."

"This is Lara, I read you, sir."

I held my breath for the final confirmation.

"This is Mae, I'm okay, Amat."

I took a moment to collect myself.

"I'm glad to hear…" My voice cracked with eagerness. I cleared my throat. "From all of you." I looked around and spotted a tree with a skinny trunk. "There's a small tree twenty yards out to the east. We'll meet and formulate our plans there," I said.

"Yes, sir," came the response in chorus.

VIII
First Handshake
(Zothru)

After having arrived on the shores of Irenole via an Aquamerion, a military-grade water vessel, we were met with a considerable, but unmatched, force of Zeltons on the beach. Effortlessly, we swept the land from under their feet in a dominating victory. We held our positions until the skies grew heavy with rain, spitting red sparks of lightning and engulfed with Zeltonian sphikes, battling human Fades. As the fight waged on, Quavek prepared a homing device to track the comm signal shared between Amat and his allies, monitoring what they spoke of.

"Alright, Lara, Olson, Log, I believe you all volunteered to take the towns to the west and north, so Shím, where should they start?" Amat asked.

"There's a town twenty miles northwest of here—Niskle. It should be the closest one harboring my home kin; likely so, anyway. From there, travel further north to Galledon, a militia base. I imagine it's abandoned but it'd serve as a good refuge. Then there's two more towns northeast of that: Kettelen and Beldalk," said Shím.

"Could take us more than a week to cover all that," said Lara.

"Not if we split our forces," said Log.

"That will *not* be happening," Amat butted in. A moment of silence passed. "You will stay together, always. As much as I trust you, Log, I do not want you commanding on your own, should something trigger you. When you've cleared each town, contact me and I'll arrange a Fade to come and pick up those you find."

"Yes, sir," replied Olson, Log, and Lara.

"As soon as we're done in Claumidin, I'll join you all," said Amat.

I dropped the signal and looked to my fellow Qi'val: Xaizar, Voruke, and Quavek.

"Well, it seems we all know where we're going. Quavek, you're with me, Xaizar and Voruke, take half our forces up the coast and meet the brothers and the Criptous sister at Niskle. But remember, we are here to intimidate, not to kill Amat and his allies," I said.

"Ah, but with Log being the exception. Remember, Zothra?" asked Xaizar.

"Not if it can be *helped*, Xaizar. Bear in mind that while the Diramal has little regard for Log, he'd prefer it if you restrained your bloodlust and be worthy of the rank Qi'val... for once," I replied.

Xaizar's tentacles shriveled into the holes of his face as he turned away from me.

"Quavek, shall we?" I asked.

"Indeed, we shall," replied Quavek, twitching her pincers at Xaizar.

(Amat)

Shím led us to the outskirts of Claumidin, where we regulated our quantum fields and held our positions, taking in the sight of distant bursts of light and the deep rumbles of gunfire that filled the atmosphere. I looked over to Shím.

"What do you think all that is? Militia? Warvs? Shadow Scar?" I asked.

"I should think the latter two are more likely, sir. Last I heard the militia of my Isle were defeated before the end of the war's second year," he replied.

I nodded.

"Whoever it is, I'd say invader forces are almost certainly involved as well. Likely due to our arrival. But it's hard to determine, from where we stand, the origin of the near conflict, let alone who's on either side," I said.

"It could very well be chaos all around," said Mae.

"We won't know for sure until we get closer." I opened a channel to all the Alphas under my command. "Alphas, we are about to enter the city. If possible, do not engage outright. Scatter yourselves and keep your distance from the conflict until we know what's going on. Now, let's disperse," I said.

Everyone under my command altered time and flooded the edges of the city. Many of the buildings were made of stones and had either domed or towering, narrow triangular shapes about them, with spikes reaching out of the top edges. This didn't give me and or my troops very much cover throughout the city. In fact, the piles of rubble, spread out across the streets, were likely better sources of shelter to take to, as we moved deeper into the city. When the raging explosions and gunfire sounded nearer, I climbed one of the towering buildings and observed what I could from its peak. I sent out a surge and opened a channel.

"Alphas, come in, this is Diramal Criptous." The rank was still bitter in my mouth when spoken aloud.

From within my helm, I enhanced my vision, zooming in on the conflict, to discern who was involved. With this, I was able to identify several live invaders, fighting what could only be Warvs, judging by the conditions of their QS-25s.

"I've confirmed the parties involved within the conflict; they seem to be Warvs battling a front of the invaders, whose forces seem to be emanating from further south. The Warvs are holding from the west. Keep a lock on my position. We'll make our way east and cut around, flanking the invader forces. When we meet with the Irens, Shím, you'll take the lead," I said.

"Ryne, sir," replied Shím.

"Fall out," I commanded.

We raced through the streets, heading east, and maintained our distance to keep from catching the eyes of the nearby enemies. When sightings of the invaders dissipated, I led my troops to cut south beside the alien forces. The layout of the land had changed, as we found ourselves just outside the city. Parts of it were rubble, but much of it was like a large plaza with stone fences reaching shoulder height, forming a maze of routes. My troops vaulted over each blockade, taking cover at times as we pressed closer and closer to the invader forces. The land sloped down slightly, into an array of trenches, where we caught the invading forces off guard. Despite our unsuspected arrival, more and more of the Zeltons seemed to pour in around us from the south and had become aware of our presence.

One jumped down at me from above, performing a series of fluid movements with its arms and legs, twisting and arching its spine. By the time it landed on the ground, both pairs of its small hands at either side of its body held long-shafted weapons that seemed to manifest themselves out of thin air. They were green in color, and vibrant. Bewildered by what I had witnessed, the Zelton launched forth, flailing its weapons with such elegance, leaving me hardly any time to process the action. Halting myself as I raised my gun to shoot, as the time for that had passed—our bodies too close to line up a good shot. Left with no other choice, I stepped back and dodged its every swing. The invader swiped one of its weapons at my chest, to which I leaned back. It swiped again at my waist with its second weapon, and I ducked forward. The invader raised its first weapon high above its head and tried to dig its blade into my back, but I rolled out of the way and the weapon pierced the ground.

Without effort, the invader pried its weapon free and rushed toward me again. I aimed my E.S.P. 101 and fired several shots, to which the invader blocked every round with its weapons. Even if a round landed on the shaft of the weapons, the energy from which they were made seemed to absorb every shot. I chucked my gun aside, deeming it useless, launched myself back off the ground, and pulled out my knives. One combined clash of our weapons was enough for the invader's vibrant blade to cut through the steel of my knife like melted butter. In addition, the blow had sliced against the armor at my forearm, wounding me mildly. I stumbled back with my arm raised to examine the wound. The armor had a steaming cut on it, but my flesh was unharmed. I didn't know what else to do, yet at the same time, my will wouldn't allow me to yield without giving this fight my all. The invader lunged forward, thrusting one of its weapons straight toward me, and I twisted my body sideways. The alien swung the same arms toward me, but I arched backwards and pierced my second blade through the alien's rib cages. The alien let out a screech as I tried retracting my blade, yet with its other arms, it crossed over the other weapon and cut along the top of my shoulder. A surge of energy shot through my arm, rendering it infirm. Losing my grip on the blade, I fell back. Clasping my newly branded wound, I tirelessly pushed myself back with my heels. The invader pressed forward without hesitation, but not menacingly this time. It slowly flexed its pincers and hissed gently.

My attention was drawn to its eight eyes, when it subtly brought one of its sparkling green blades up to my face. I didn't know why, but the invader seemed somehow curious about me, as if it were looking through me. This too, I had never seen before. Granted, when I'd tried communicating with them in the recent past, they seemed attentive, but never like this, I gasped.

Perhaps this is it! My chance—our chance at establishing a dialogue between our two species.

I dropped my blade and slowly raised my hand in a welcoming gesture. *Bang! Bang!* Two holes through the Zelton's head brought it down, before it could even notice my gesture. Startled by the intervention, I was swiftly overcome with disappointment in the failed exchange. I lifted my head to my savior as she reached her hand down to me.

"Amat! Are you alright?" asked Mae.

I glanced down at the Zelton's weapons. They'd vanished as quickly as they'd manifested. I sighed as Mae gasped, noting my wound.

"You're injured." Mae reached toward my shoulder, but I stopped her.

"I'll be alright," I said. A moment of silence passed between us. I wasn't irritated with Mae, at least I tried not to be. I simply couldn't help but wonder how that interaction might have played out if Mae hadn't intervened. All the same, I swallowed my pride and thanked her.

"What were those weapons this one bore? I've never seen any like them before and yet somehow, they've vanished," said Mae.

"I don't know and now's not the time to find out. We need—"

A sudden blur fell from above close to Mae's position, bearing bladed weapons that I'd seen their kind armed with before. Altering time, I saw that the invader had leaped toward Mae with arched claws. I unholstered my pistol, shot the alien, and cradled Mae away from underneath the limp invader. I regulated time to see that Mae was alright.

"Well, I suppose that makes us even," she said. I could see her smile behind her helmet, by the sound of her tone. I couldn't help but smirk in reply.

One, two, three, four invaders fell in to either side of us. Without hesitation, Mae and I altered time, rolled off one another, and defended ourselves. I was about to face my two head-on, when I looked back at my one blade completely intact on the ground a few feet behind me. Quickly, a strategy formed in my mind. Rushing back to retrieve the weapon as one of the two Zeltons chased after me, I slid across the mud and grabbed the knife; the alien was right there. With a strong *push* off the ground, I lifted my blade up and sliced the invader up its gut and neck. Its own momentum brought it crashing down behind me. The second one and I charged one another. It swiped at me with one of its jagged half-swords in hand; when it missed, it launched a punch at my armor, which caused me to keel over but hardly deterred me. With another swipe from its other hand, I spun out of the way and punched it in the face. The Zelton thrust its blade at my gut, but I parried and pinned it down with my own. Our faces were inches away from one another, as I swung my blade up, slicing the Zelton's shoulder and in a fluid movement, into the side of its neck.

I looked over at Mae finishing off the second invader who confronted her. She glanced at me and we shared a nod. We carried on with the battle, staying as close as we could to one another. The Zeltons were relentless in their fight, and it waged on for *hours*. There came a point where the trenches were so crowded with limp bodies in the mud that you could easily stumble if you didn't mind your steps. I noted several who lost their lives just to that alone, falling vulnerable on the ground, followed by a mighty, lethal strike from a Zelton.

In the dawn of the fourth hour, what remained of my troops rallied to the Warv front at our backs, standing against the seemingly endless horde of invaders. Holding our ground, a sizeable gap was maintained between our forces as the invaders screeched and displayed wild frenzies. I could have ordered my troops to charge, but I kept them in line and ensured they did not spur the invaders into further conflict. In a peculiarly humble spectacle, the invaders had all regulated time, and as we noted it persist, I too allowed my troops to regulate time and catch their breaths.

In an unexpected instance, a singular, incoherent screech rose over all the others combined. The invaders calmed their feral mannerisms, and, in their place, the invaders got on all eight of their limbs in unison. Slowly rocking their bodies back and forth, as they chanted a graceful clicking sound. I maintained an unblinking stare at each of the invaders, ready for whatever came next. Contemplating whether I should have stepped forward and reached out to communicate. But my weary mind felt too intimidated and paranoid by the ominous behavior of the invaders.

After a time, I could see in the distance the crowd of invaders started making way for one of their own. This Zelton was a strange one, in the sense that it seemed to command a certain respect from the others. Another odd occurrence—I had never observed any kind of leadership displayed amongst their kin. The superior Zelton came all the way to the forefront of their numbers and paused across from me. Its gaze was unbreaking. It looked at no one else but me, as if I was the reason why it had decided to show itself.

"He seems focused on you, laddin," said Shím.

"Perhaps he's come to talk, assuming it is a '*he,*'" said Mae, glancing at Shím. "Amat." My attention was broken from the lead Zelton and diverted to Mae. "Go speak with it. This could be the moment you've been searching for."

I looked back to the lead Zelton and took a deep breath. The first step was the hardest. Just the thought that lifting my knee to get my foot off the ground alone would be enough to restart our conflict frightened me. I got as close as I cared to the lead Zelton, and tensed slightly when it confidently approached me the rest of the way. We reached a point where only a few steps divided us, and once the leader stood its ground, the horde of Zeltons silenced their chants.

I swallowed as I retracted my helm and passed on the blessing of Anua to the lead alien. Promptly second-guessing the gesture, as the Zeltons were the sole reason for which Anua was destroyed.

Not true, I corrected myself, *even when I'd annihilated the entire first vessel's worth of ships, the body of Anua was still intact. It was the collective decision of the Diramal and several of the Jinns to obliterate the alien craft and the embodiment of our Goddess with it.*

"Greetings, I am Amat Luciph Criptous, leader of my kin... humanity. I understand you are called the Zeltons. Are you the leader of your kin?" I asked.

The lead Zelton did not respond immediately, but it did seem to have a similar curious look in its eyes, as the one before did. As if it was studying me and again, seeing through me. Finally, the alien spoke, but in its own native tongue, which I could not comprehend. I shook my head.

"I'm sorry, I don't understand," I replied.

The alien nodded and lowered its head in disappointment, or maybe contemplation? It looked back up at me and reached out its hand. I tilted my head and my heart raced with exhilaration. Cautiously, I reached out my own hand and when they joined, the alien spoke again. Though the language sounded harsh, with a mixture of vibrating frequencies, its tone sounded pleasant and reassuring. The Zelton then calmly pulled away and turned back toward its kin, as they all fled together.

"Well," said Shím. "It seems negotiations are finally getting somewhere. Well done, laddin."

"If negotiations were what you hoped to achieve here…" said a woman's voice behind us, followed by the sound of over a hundred guns being cocked. "You'll find we're not interested, Utopian *scum*."

Shím and I, along with everyone else under my command, turned around to find the entire Iren Warv front aiming their guns at us. Several under my command were ready to aim back, but I stayed their hands. Shím pointed at the woman who stood at the top of a small hill above her kin.

"I do believe I recognize that voice there," said Shím, loud enough for the woman to hear.

The woman scoffed.

"And how might you know me?" she asked.

"I'd recognize the sweet sound of your voice anywhere. Granted, it's grown a bit deeper. But after hardly escapin' it for over twelve years, as we chased one another up and down these streets 'most every day. You and I were hardly separable, Aod," said Shím, speaking with gestures to make himself stand out more.

The lead female Warv tilted her head. She dropped down among her numbers and made her way down to us. Not a single member among her forces was distracted by her passing presence and nor were any of mine intimidated by the Irens' upper hand on us. Finally standing before Shím, the woman retracted her helm. The glow of nearby fires revealed her mild burns, stretching from her left cheekbone down to her neck, perhaps even further. Her expression was hard, yet her eyes were hopeful.

"Remove your helm, Utopian," said Aod.

Shím snorted.

"Before my family made a life for me in Utopion…" said Shím, as he retracted his helm, "I was an Iren."

97

Aod raised her eyebrows; she didn't seem to fully recognize Shím, but she did seem to have a sense of confirmation about her.

"Oh, my guess was correct. You've the same silver eyes."

"Goddess! Shím?" asked Aod.

"Ryne, in the flesh, lassa," Shím replied with a smirk.

Aod and Shím shared smiles and embraced one another. Mae walked up beside me, inviting herself to the interaction.

"Not that I want to ruin the moment, but since it seems we have an understanding now—"

"I've known Shím since birth," Aod interrupted Mae. "Our two families were practically one; he's Iren. I don't believe anyone said anythin' about the rest of you."

Mae took a step forward; her body language suggested she was about to say something rash.

"I imagine you haven't heard," I said, stepping in front of Mae. "Having no access to comms and your militia being depleted—"

"Do you know how they were depleted?" Aod asked sternly, cutting me short. Her tone almost suggested the answer.

"I'd be intrigued to find out," I replied.

"If you've noticed, many of our suits and weapons are on the fresher side of what you might have observed the average *Rouvká* wear." While I didn't understand the term, Aod spoke the word like it was a curse.

"Rouvká?" I asked

"The term, put simply, serves the same meaning as 'freedom fighters,' sir, though with a more negative connotation. Like how the Warvs were regarded," said Shím.

"Why a negative connotation?" asked Mae.

"Freedom is not a luxury that sits well beside an autocratic system," said Aod. "It is not meant as a slander toward ourselves; we proudly regard ourselves as Rouvká. It mocks what it means to you tyrannical militia. A kind of waste, a *nuisance*."

"I assume then, you're the reason we lost contact with the Dronomen Isles? You overthrew your own militia," I said.

Aod nodded.

"And we'd do worse to your kind, bein' from that cruel empire of a country," she said.

Aod raised her hand and her Rouvká took aim.

"No!" blurted Shím.

Aod glanced at Shím, confused. Mae marched forward, but I pressed my arm across her chest.

"You tell your kin to fire upon us and you'll be doing more harm than good to your morals," I said. Aod tilted her head. "These men and women that fight beside me were once regarded as a sort of Rouvká, as well. Warvs, as Shím, mentioned. They were discarded among the waste of my country and the man who led it before me would see them all rot before handing them the opportunity I have."

"And what might that be? Have you branded 'em? Brainwashed 'em into spreading your tyranny, even with the world this convoluted?" asked Aod.

"While I did offer them the opportunity to continue their fight against the invaders at my side, that duty was not forced upon any of them," I said. "I exposed the former Diramal for the corrupt man he was." Aod turned to me with intrigue. "He plotted to kill my aunt and uncle for concealing sensitive information, and he broke the mind of my father years before, which resulted in his death and the start of the war we find ourselves in today. Since his exile, I have taken his place and made it my priority to offer sanctuary to all humanity, isolated from the militia's priorities."

Aod smiled mockingly.

"Who is this young laddin, Shím?" she asked.

"He's Amat Luciph Criptous, Aod, Diramal of Utopion. My friend," replied Shím. Aod raised an eyebrow and turned slowly toward him. "And what he says is true, every word of it. We've come with the intention to help."

Aod looked me up and down and then glanced over at Mae. Aod pointed at her.

"Almost had a rise out of you. Thought you could take me, did you?" asked Aod.

"I could have you on the ground before you finish your next sentence," replied Mae.

Aod laughed, amused.

"Well, we might just have to see about that later, won't we? By your earlier notion I think you and I might one day make pleasant friends," Aod said. She gestured to her troops and lowered her hand to them, as they let down their guard. "I'll allow you and your troops to join us at our base of operation; we'll talk more there."

I nodded and Aod fell back toward her kin. I turned toward Mae, who restrained herself. I smiled at her scornful expression to Aod.

"I'm grateful for your efforts Mae to stand in at that one's offenses," I said, gesturing to Aod. "But these are people scarred by passed influences of our country and hardened by the terrors of this war. While they may be strong, their minds are seemingly prone to even the slightest offense. And we must be cautious of our words and actions in their presence."

Mae nodded as her breath steadied.

"I'll follow your lead then," said Mae.

I smiled at Mae through my helm and together we led our troops in behind the Irens.

IX
A Little Nip
(Log)

We reached the first town in under an hour of running in altered time. It was as Shím had described it would be. A certain silence filled the atmosphere, one that told my intuition there were no Skivs to be saved, nor Warvs to be liberated. But then again, there was another subtle feeling that something else, rather, skulked about. Someone familiar to me. Xaizar's scent wasn't heavy in the air, but the stench of his essence was no less potent. My lack of understanding how I could know this, compelled me to push aside my intuition as mere paranoia. *This is not the place or time to fear what I cannot know for certain.*

Olson stayed close at my side while Lara took the lead of the troops. We didn't say much to one another, yet I could almost see through my older brother's eyes, as their distressed gaze pressed on me. Not that it surprised me; even I couldn't deny my shift in character from that last incursion with Xaizar. To some extent, I'm sure everyone noted it, but I can't imagine it threw anyone else off more than it did Olson.

My relief was cut short when, once again, my sixth sense roused my suspicion. Xaizar *was* near and he'd gotten closer. I opened a channel and queried to my cousin: "Jinn-hid, have you seen anything out of the ordinary while we've been out here?"

Lara paused before answering, as she considered the question.

"Nothing that I'd suspect was threatening. The whole town is empty. Why, have you, Io-Pac?"

"*Mm*, no, but I do worry—"

"About what?" butted in Olson.

"Worry, Io-Pac?" asked Lara.

I cleared my throat.

"Nothing." I could hardly whisper the lie out of my mouth. A silence fell between us as I felt Olson's gaze boring into me.

"I think we've lurked here long enough." Lara opened a channel to the troops. "Attention all ranks, this is the Jinn-hid, we're moving out, heading further north. Track the coordinates on each of your fizers to the next point of interest. Over and out."

I glanced down at the confirming "beep" my fizer exclaimed after having received the coordinates.

"Hopefully this next site will have *less* gloom to it," I mumbled, marching forward.

"Log," Olson blurted. I turned around and faced my brother. "Are you feeling alright?"

I only gave my brother an assuring nod and continued to fall in behind Lara.

We carved our own path north, through a thin forest until we reached Galledon. It was barely in view, would likely be invisible without the particle sensors on our visors. The entrance stuck out in the side of a hill.

"It looks dead," I said.

"Doesn't mean we shouldn't investigate it still," Olson said.

"I imagine getting in will be the hardest part," said Lara. "Those should be the hangar doors; without power, they won't open on their own." She opened a channel to the whole squadron.

"It would take some time, but we can probably tear down an opening with the pulse cannons," said Olson.

"That'll work," replied Lara.

I twitched and glanced behind me as I sensed Xaizar once again. Not only did he seem frighteningly closer while still imperceivable, but also with others at his back. How I could know this, I wasn't sure. Perhaps it was a trait that came with being a Dövar.

Ah! Not possible. He is either dead or a quarter of the way around the world, in the waste of Utopion. Now pull yourself together, Log.

"Log!" Lara blurted. I swung my attention to my cousin. "I've given the order, we're falling out."

I nodded my head.

"Right behind you," I said. Both my brother and my cousin gave me lingering stares as I marched past.

A few paces later, Olson halted me.

"Log, we're not blind, you're disturbed. More important than that, you're different. Your entire character is reserved, even on the flight over here."

Staring at my brother I replied: "My mind is sound, Olson."

Olson halted me again as I tried to walk past him.

"There's something you're not telling us, brother," said Olson.

In fact, there was. It was no mystery that I'd a rough encounter with Xaizar that required a trip to the med bay, but the only two people who knew nanites had revived me from the dead were myself and Blick. And therefore, we were the only two people who knew I was a Dövar.

"Now is not the place or time, Olson. I am only distracted by my own superstitions at how quiet this entire run has been thus far. Now, let me have my arm back," I said, in a collected manner.

My brother sighed as he loosened his grip. I patted my brother's shoulder, and together we returned to the squadron.

A line of three Alphas bearing pulse cannons stood a hundred meters from the entrance to the base, with the pulses set to narrow. Everyone else stood a few paces behind them. The first line of fire Lara had ordered, faded past the walls, and retracted five times faster than they seeped through, cracking the wall. Lara ordered a second line of fire; the wall chipped and was coated in cracks. The third, chunks of the wall's center flung out and created a small hole. The fourth, the hole was made wide enough to let us in.

Lara led the troops through the breach after the dust cleared, and Olson and I followed from behind. Silence, dark, cold. A dim fluorescent light illuminated the right side of the hangar, revealing dancing dust that spiraled up to the light. Only two Dailagons were docked, with misaligned ramps scattered all the way down the runway. In the time we took assessing the hangar, I felt a sense of security. Xaizar's essence had fled my conscious. The emptiness of the base left me with a strange feeling of comfort, a sort of exterior reflection of how I'd been perceiving myself the past few months.

The moment passed and my heart skipped a beat at the persistent sense of Xaizar's aura.

"Do we know how far down this base goes?" Lara asked.

Olson activated his fizer, processed a scan of the base, and brought up a hologram of Galledon.

"Fifteen hundred meters," Olson replied.

"That'll likely take the rest of the day, if not some of tomorrow, to cover the ground at each level," said Lara.

"If I may offer some advice on the grouping, Jinn-hid?" I asked.

Lara was briefly thrown off by my suggestion.

"Of course, Io-Pac," Lara replied.

"I suggest we place a sentry of twenty troops to guard the breach in the hangar's entry," I said, gesturing to it.

"Twenty?" asked Lara.

"Or more," I replied.

Lara nodded respectfully as she assigned twenty-five troops to guard the opening via her fizer.

"Your input is well appreciated, Io-Pac," said Lara. She addressed the rest of the squadron. "The rest of you will divide into fifteen groups, one for each level of the base. I've color-coded your fizers at random."

Lara proceeded to call out what level was associated with which color. She assigned the three of us to the deepest level: sixteen.

We had to wait for our engineers to restore power to Galledon, enough to operate the elevators anyway. There was no other way to reach level sixteen. Bypassing the security code, we were on our way down within an hour. As we descended, I sensed more immensely, the emptiness of the base.

Galledon is as devoid of life as Niskle was. Descending further, a beat of numb pain pulsed through my heart. Intuition told me the sensation emanated from deep within the base. A lingering energy of a—no, several human souls.

The elevator came to a halt and the doors opened to a dark room. The four Alphas under Lara's command raised their aim and traced their eyes about the interior.

"Is it just me, or are the rest of you also unable to see the contents of the room?" asked Lara.

"No, you're not alone on that," Olson replied.

"Depth shouldn't impact our particle sensors; whatever's in there, it's causing some kind of interference," said Lara.

I didn't see specific outlines of anything within the room. But there were subtle curvatures spiraling up toward the roof, like smoke puffing from a grand fire. Since neither Olson nor Lara had mentioned it, I thought it best not to share it with them. I felt what I was seeing was a likely extension of my newly gained abilities as a Dövar.

"Press forward," Lara commanded.

The Alphas activated lights at the ends of their guns and moved into the dark room. Lara opened a channel and requested more Alphas find their way down to level sixteen after us. A thin layer of black water covered the ground. I shut my eyes as the sight took me back to my reunion with my parents when I passed on from this world, briefly. I took a deep breath as I looked around and continued to inspect the room.

Every splash of our steps echoed, suggesting the room was quite large and expansive, with very little filling its space. I was drawn deeper and with every step I dragged across the ankle-deep water, that numb pain crept back into my heart. That feeling of death, it was there, in that room. While it did not feel welcoming, I was drawn to it all the same. I could never admit it to myself until that moment, but ever since I found myself in the warm embrace of my parents' souls, all I wanted was to return to that place and time. The… spirit—I'd consider calling it—that drew me to this feeling, was rageful. Worse than that, it was frenzied. It was human, but the remnants of its psyche had been split between itself and something else.

I slowly reached over my heart, as I felt an overwhelming sense of hopelessness befall it. I could not see it in detail but I knew I'd reached the source. Columns of concealed pods suddenly illuminated from within, and I clenched my fist at the sight of the disfigured body resting within one. Her skin had turned as dark as the void that continued to cloud the room and even murk the surrounding lights. Her jaw had been stretched and contorted, her arms were shriveled and broken. The only bit of color that remained about her was her eyes. Yellow, they were.

I growled as I shared in the spirit's anguish and hovered my hand over the glass dome that concealed her. It wasn't words that compelled me, but an instant compulsion to bare my claws and scrape a hole in the glass.

Reaching in, past the hole, I touched the corpse's shoulder. Consciously, I was taken to another time, within the confines of Galledon, through her eyes; Briam, her name was.

She'd been taken against her will, to this place by two, no, three Cho'Zai. She was scared.

I watched through her eyes, felt through her nerves as she squirmed and resisted against their grasp.

They confined her to this pod, sealed it off.

I felt her ears fill with her own screams, as the glass was too thick for them to pass through.

Needles.

Four needles, arching down from biotic arms, injecting something... evil. At either side of her neck, into her heart, and past her third eye. The arms retracted. Still screaming, voice changing. She tore through the restraints as her entire biology started changing. She didn't want it, even as the serum spread through her, influencing her mind and heart, tearing away every connection she'd ever made, every passion that had brightened her life. In spite of all that, she rejected it. She held on to her love. When the evil within Briam sensed it could not break these bonds, it killed her.

"Log?" Olson had patted me on the shoulder and returned my mind to the present.

I jumped back, riled slightly as a residue of Briam's rage stirred within me still. Olson observed my unease and stayed perfectly still with his hands raised.

"It's okay, you're alright. I'm here, your brother's here. You know me," he spoke calmly.

I nodded, as I looked at him up and down and relaxed.

"I know what these are." My voice broke into a whine and too low for Olson to hear.

"What?" Olson whispered.

"This is how they made the Shadow Scar, Olson. This, right here, all of it," I said.

Olson held a perplexed stature.

"How, uh..." Olson cleared his throat. "H-h-how do you know that?" I gestured to Briam.

"Don't you see the correlation?" I asked. "We already knew from the files Blick uncovered that they were products of an experimental program."

"I recall, well, what Blick brought to us a few months ago. My question is, how you can be so certain?" said Olson.

A sudden dread befell my mind: sounds of swift and precise gunfire, flashes of fellow Alphas falling to their deaths, and dark figures creeping over their corpses. The utterance of a man's voice over comms pulled me out of it. My eyes shifted intuitively to Lara, ready to bark a command at her before the speaking Alpha finished his warning.

"Jinn-hid, we need to get back up to the hangar." I beckoned to Lara as I marched to her. "Now!" I howled before Lara or anyone else could object.

I opened a channel to all the Alphas under our command, as we ascended in the elevator. "Attention, all Alphas, this is Io-Pac Log Criptous. We have Shadow Scar hostiles that have breached into Galledon. Be on watch for any suspicious movements. They've already killed our twenty-five watchmen at the gate. Hold firm at your positions."

"How do you know that?" asked Lara, sounding concerned for me.

I hesitated before answering.

"I... I just do, I can't say how," I replied.

Olson began to say something, but he restrained himself. I could sense he wanted to wait and see if what I had said was even fact.

"If you're wrong in this, passage will be arranged for you to be sent back to Y'Gŭtsa," said Lara, in an almost motherly tone.

"I'll take that chance," I replied.

The elevator door opened; I was the first to march out and down the runway to the broken entrance, where twenty-five dead and bloody Alphas lay limp. Each one with a three-inch-wide hole near and or around their chests and rib cages. I cursed to myself, as I felt Xaizar's presence at its closest, while he continued to linger in the shadows.

I heard Olson's footsteps as he came beside me, felt his eyes as he turned them onto me.

"Let us exterminate the pest in the house, brother. Then, I will tell you how I know it's here," I said.

A creak echoed behind us, and we all turned and aimed high. Lara opened a channel to all the Alphas under our command.

"Attention, all Alphas, this is the Jinn-hid. We have signs of unidentified contact, hangar, each of you make your way here as backup. Keep your quantum suits active," Lara said quietly.

Lara closed the channel and another creak sounded off to the right. *Come on, we know you're here. Quit playing games.*

A long moment of silence… the furthest Dailagon activated. In the time we took to shift our attention to it, the engine went from a steady start to a high-pitched *zing!* Bursting off the ground, it swiftly aimed its guns at us. Some of us activated our QS-25s in time to evade the first round of blasts fired by the Dailagon; most did not.

I pulled Olson down and back, far enough to evade the lethal blast. We scurried for the nearest cover, not knowing if Lara was alright. I could only pray that she was. The Dailagon fired again at Alphas who remained out in the open. Blurred shadows in the dark struck others down in one, if not a few, swift movements.

I felt their horror, their pain, their fading grasp to hold on to their lives. It almost compelled me to run out there carelessly, to encounter a conflict of my own and meet with another death. Olson nudged me on the shoulder, keeping my attention on him, and signed that we needed to take out the Dailagon. I looked at the craft, hovering, watching still, processing what my brother had communicated to me. I looked back and nodded. *"I'll take out the pilot, you watch my back,"* I signed. Olson nodded.

We waited as the hovering Dailagon slowly panned over our position and turned back the other way. It was then we moved. I rushed out, heading straight for the enemy Dailagon, hovering close to the inactive Dailagon in the hangar. A ramp sat beside it. *I'll run up and leap off the grounded Dailagon, onto the target.* I dared not look behind myself, so as to not break my focus and trusted that Olson was alright on his own.

Charging up the ramp, I bounded across the grounded Dailagon, leaped off the left wing… *slam!* A Shadow Scar had launched from above and collided with me, a fingertip away from the active Dailagon. We tumbled beneath it. The Shadow Scar managed to seat itself on my back and began raising my arm to break it. I swiftly tugged my arm back and hit the Shadow Scar in the side of the head with my opposite elbow. We rolled back the other way, twice, until we both ended up on our backs. Glancing at one another, before I could register its features, I punched the Shadow Scar in the face. Reeling my arm back for another blow, the creature halted my arm as it enveloped its tentacle hand around my fist. It rolled itself back on top of me and pressed its face close to my helm. The tentacles in his face quivered and squirmed tauntingly. *Xaizar!* I thought, growling. A dashing movement drew my attention past the Shadow Scar's face. With his free hand, Xaizar raised a peculiar weapon to my chest. Before he set the shot, I pushed his elbow up with my own free hand and diverted the shot into the ground. *Boom!* The Dailagon above us burst into a fiery flame. In a frenzy, I tucked my legs underneath Xaizar and kicked him up into the flames. Rolling away, I cleared myself of the fallen debris.

The Alpha who destroyed the Dailagon rolled across the ground, and shifted her attention to me. I couldn't be sure, but her silhouette implied it was Lara. She signaled me to recon around the room. I moved to fall in behind her, but halted after observing something rise from the flames of the burning Dailagon. It rose in an arch of thick, melting, black liquid that resembled ink. As the liquid coursed over the flames, dousing them, it revealed its producer: Xaizar. He was panting, and by his stance, agitated. My attention was drawn away as the rest of the Alphas came rushing into the hangar and then again as my brother came to my left shoulder. As did a tall, slender creature come to Xaizar's side, with several of their Shadow Scar brethren at their backs. I turned my head, one final time, as Lara came to my right shoulder. The mistaken Alpha I presumed to be responsible for the Dailagon's obliteration.

I looked ahead, staring at Xaizar across the way. Lara raised her hand and dropped it as our armies clashed together. The tall, slender Shadow Scar found its way to Olson, just as promptly as Xaizar and I reignited our own conflict. Lara rushed past, leading the charge of our army against the rest of the opposing force.

I armed myself with a splice and flicked the hilt, manifesting the blade, just before Xaizar and I met. Xaizar dodged down and back before unraveling his own weapons at his forearms. Tucked away in dimly illuminated attachments, a pair of long, durable, glowing whips flailed elegantly at me with every twirl and whirl of the Shadow Scar's arms. The whips were fleshy, but strong, as even the mightiest throw of my splice

109

only seemed to chip away at their integrity. In a swift throw of my blade, one of Xaizar's whips latched around my wrist, locking itself in place and squeezing, harder and harder. I growled as I flicked out my claws with my free hand, spun closer into the whip to drag the Shadow Scar to me, and clawed deep across Xaizar's face. Several of the tentacles on it fell and squirmed on the ground. He stumbled back and I advanced, angled the edge of my splice against the mechanism from which one of the whips dangled and cut past it, across the Shadow Scar's forearm as I twirled passed him. Xaizar clutched his arm as I stood behind him and thrust the splice through his shoulder. The Shadow Scar threw its head back as he fell to a knee. I was about to pry the splice from the Shadow Scar and strike the final blow when my intuition drew my attention elsewhere. Not fifteen paces from me, I saw my brother, still fighting with the tall, slender Shadow Scar, and was overwhelmed.

Distracted, I had allowed Xaizar to lash his alternate whip around my neck and pull me over himself, onto the floor. Again, it squeezed tighter and tighter, as the Shadow Scar stood above me. I grabbed onto the whip and pulled Xaizar onto the floor beside me. Landing on his chest, in a swift movement I pried my splice from the Shadow Scar. Xaizar tensed, and as I felt my head begin to swell, I pinned Xaizar's left arm to the ground with the splice. He flailed his whip arm out and released its lock from my neck.

With barely enough breath to stay conscious, I forced myself off the ground but was once again stopped by Xaizar's grasp on my arm.

"Don't be fooled by this game," Xaizar's words echoed in a pant. "The Diramal will reunite us soon enough and I revel at the thoughts of how I will make you suffer further…"

The Shadow Scar's grasp gave out as his head fell limp to the floor. Paying little mind to the Shadow Scar's reverberating message, I sprinted to the tall, slender Shadow Scar who had pinned my brother to the ground. It threw down a long, bladed weapon. In our collision, the weapon had been swung far enough and scraped deep enough into my brother's armor that blood was drawn. The slender Shadow Scar slid back and tossed me aside.

I widened my stance, holding the gap between us, briefly taking in the appearance of the thing. A flat forehead that curved back, narrow, glowing pink eyes, spikes along its jaw and a small wiggling appendage that drooped from where its mouth should have been. Its body was broad, bulging with a peculiar and complex bone structure. Its gut had a layered shell that extended down its center. In a swift movement, a glowing, squirming appendage sprouted from its skull, its tip aimed at me. The creature molded its arms together as its shell-like skin sprouted two sharply edged bones from the ends of its arms.

I flicked my suit's claws out and charged at the creature. Using the Shadow Scar's height against it, I elegantly dodged around its first few swings and thrusts of its spiked arms at me. Though the way it moved was peculiar to me. It was as if, on the attack, its movements were much swifter than even I could keep up with, but as it retracted and readied its next attack, the creature moved more slowly. As if it was somehow speeding up its natural altered time in bursts. Noting this, I became distracted once again and barely managed to avoid a lethal blow, with the creature's arm still piercing across the side of my shoulder.

Refusing to grasp my wound, I devised a plan that would allow me to land my first couple of blows on the Shadow Scar. I ran right up to it, and just before coming face to face with its gut, the Shadow Scar had reeled back one of its arms. I immediately rolled out of the way as it threw its arm down.

Didn't work, I'll have to try again.

Once again, I ran right up to the Shadow Scar, widened my stance, waited a moment after one of its arms came shooting down at me, and dove right between its legs. I looked back and saw that it had worked— the creature planted its spiked arm into the ground so deep it struggled to pry it back out.

Racing back to the creature, I swung my claws and scraped all along its back. Sliding away from it as I turned, the Shadow Scar shrieked at me. Charging once again, while its arm remained stuck in the ground. When within its reach, the Shadow Scar swung its long, free arm at me. I dove over it, grasping the arm as I passed, tucked my legs as I flipped, and slammed the arm over my shoulders, breaking it. The Shadow Scar shrieked once again, with its other arm finally free from the ground. I rolled away and watched as it stood, *snapping* its elbow back into place with a vigorous whip of its arm.

I growled in frustration and dashed at the Shadow Scar once more, this time being more calculated with my moves so as to stay in front of the creature and attack after each thrust of its arms it threw at me. Stabbing down, diagonally, I twisted my body and scraped my claws up its broad chest, long neck, and lower jaw. The Shadow Scar batted its head and the squirming appendage from its scalp flashed a teal light at me. Suddenly, I felt my consciousness drift inward, and I felt the numbing embrace of death return to me. Just out of sight, I could see my parents once again.

This is the past, I told myself, before I allowed consciousness to drift off to that place and time entirely.

I blinked and shook my head as I gazed up at the Shadow Scar swinging another spiked arm down at me. I rolled to the side, clawing at the Shadow Scar's leg as I passed. The Shadow Scar fell to a knee as I rushed from behind for a killing blow, but then again, the wriggling thing at the top of its head flashed its teal light at me.

As I felt my body go limp, I drifted back to that same place with its gracious embrace of alleviation. My parents stood tall, reaching their arms out to me as I hovered to them.

No! I yelled at myself, as my consciousness whipped back to the battle.

My heart skipped a few beats as I panted hard, gazing back at the Shadow Scar lording over me. It arched its head back for another lash of the light antenna at the top of its head… *slice!* The figure dashed behind and around the Shadow Scar, picking me up off the ground. The overlapping echo allowed me to recognize Lara's voice when I finally processed her words. I hardly noticed we were standing beside one another, Lara glancing back and forth from the Shadow Scar to me.

"Are you alright? Can you stand?" Lara asked, over and over and over again.

I nodded and pushed her aside when her attention had stayed on me too long, allowing the Shadow Scar an opening in our defense. Tracking the timing and the motion of the Shadow Scar's arm, I spun and knelt as the spiked arm drifted past me. In almost just as swift a motion, the Shadow Scar retracted its arm, but not before I clapped my hands at the center of the edged bone, squeezing and pushing until it snapped off. The

Shadow Scar reeled back as I spun back around and stabbed it in its side, with its own shell-skin.

The Shadow Scar tensed and shrieked at the highest pitch I'd heard from it. I made to push in deeper when I saw that it still stood tall, but the Shadow Scar struck me aside. Lara rushed to my side, her splice raised at the Shadow Scar, but its focus had turned elsewhere. Its call had gotten everyone's attention, including that of the Alphas. Though the other Shadow Scar seemed to be listening with intrigue, as if the tall creature were broadcasting a message to them. Just as soon as it silenced its shriek, the Shadow Scar fled the base, though the tall one scurried back and rushed past with Xaizar over its shoulder.

Lara and I shared a glance; we stood and stepped out to gaze down the opening. There was no one there. I skimmed over the corpse of a fellow Alpha, picked up his gun, and glanced back at Olson. I promptly signed for Lara to inspect his limp body. Lara nodded her head in reply and rushed to my brother. I held my aim down as I eased my way to the exit.

Still in altered time, I became enveloped in the sound of my helm filling with oxygen and the breath leaving my nostrils and the clank of my metal boots meeting the ground. It was almost hypnotizing, the intimidation that narrow opening had over me.

"He's alive... he's alive... he's alive!" I heard Lara's words echo.

I spun my head to her when I heard something echo across the floor. A loud *clank!* Without so much as looking at it, I rushed forward and leaped away from the blast caving in the ceiling.

Three Alphas held Olson up on either side of him as we rushed to the elevator. Lara had ordered our science officers to redirect power to the med bay immediately so that we could revive our wounded and potentially, some of our dead. With Olson having priority.

X
Feisty Iren
(Amat)

We followed Aod through an illuminated underground passage; members of her people were paired beside each one of mine. Even though we'd established ourselves as no threat to the Irens, Aod's stubbornness against Utopians was unyielding. As a condition of her hospitality, Aod made my troops and I retract our helms and keep them off while in her presence, knowing a QS-25 could not alter time without it being fully sealed. I didn't mention how our purpose in being there would involve taking them back to Utopion and, with that in mind, I wondered how well it would go over when the time came to discuss it.

Much of the journey was carried out in silence, as Aod explained the passages were not only utilized by the Irens themselves, but the "Skáthovoír," as she described them. Which Shím went on to translate as "Shadow Dwellers."

Our destination was a heavily guarded and large door, stretching at least thirty feet high and across. Fifteen Irens were installed before it, and five of them sat behind shielded plasma turrets. Everyone stopped and Aod went on alone, briefly to address her Rouvkás. They all aimed their guns at her and she stopped immediately after, yet her posture was calm. I frowned and jumped at the action. Processing Aod's cool mood, I stopped myself from carrying out my rash thoughts. Still, I slowly placed my hand behind my back and unstrapped my pistol, ready to fire at any given moment. I felt a gentle hand on my wrist and looked over to my side. Shím shook his head at me, reassuringly.

"Tútha lich úm Anua. Túcha ech coffál muad Drú Amúna?" called one of the women that stood guard.

"Ech Rálta Aod Mag Bettle, úm Dia Anua. Ma lach ásig orm rís, cathas íertha brí aor," replied Aod.

114

The guard nodded and signaled for the door to be opened, while the others let their guard down. Aod gestured for the rest of us to follow in behind her.

"Shím, what was that they said to one another?" Mae asked.

Shím smiled.

"The guard said, 'Be welcome, child of Anua. What are the words in which we praise her?' Aod replied, 'I am Aod Mag Bettle, of the Goddess Anua. May her body be whole once again, when the skies break free.'"

"Skies break free? I assume that's a reference to the invading presence over our atmosphere," said Mae.

"Ryne, I'd suspect so too," said Shím.

"May both be so, by the end of all this," I added.

Entering the wide chamber, I saw many of Shím's people, most of whom looked weak and starved. I saw what the Irens were living off, and it wasn't much. In fact, it was barely something that you could consider a snack.

"It appears you're running low on supplies," observed Mae.

"Ryne, dangerously. Though we've been low on supplies for at least a year now. Since then, we started gettin' monthly shipments from Scoat'tír. But the payloads have been intercepted twice the past couple of months, thanks to the Skátho-voír. As a result, we've had to ration what we can from three months ago," replied Aod.

"We have carriers that can fly here and back within an hour, bearing... sustenance." Pausing at the thought that the Irens were likely unfamiliar with the concept of the sustenance interfaces we'd adopted from the submerged starships. "It would be an unusual nutriment, but your people would be well-nourished," I said.

Aod stopped and turned toward me slowly, with a quizzical expression on her face.

"You seem hesitant to receive a gift that your people so desperately need. Seeing as how you care for them so much; I would have thought—"

"Do not presume to understand me, *Utopian*," blurted Aod, over me. "Ryne, I love my people dearly. My heart doesn't break any less after one of them follows the other to the Luminous Paradise. But we are a strong

115

people, who have endured much since the Scorching Cleanse of our Mother. My kin will endure much more before we perish."

"Should your endurance be stretched so thin?" asked Mae.

Aod shifted her attention to Mae; her eyes were cold as she replied: "Without question, it should. For there will come a time to rejoice and rebuild our numbers and pass down our hardened souls to our future generations."

"Not that you must accept the aid I offer, but if you do, it will require that we move all these people across a considerable distance to an area where we can land our Fades and load them aboard. If these people are too weak to run, should we encounter any hostiles, let alone walk the required range, they might as well be left here to rot," I said.

Aod pulled out a knife and swiftly moved up to me. She paused, holding the edge of her blade against my neck. Mae had taken out her own weapon, pressing it against Aod's side, just as swiftly. The surrounding Iren and Utopian forces had taken note of the event and, just as swiftly, aimed their guns at one another. Some even got a quick enough jump on the other that they disarmed them. Shím had backed away slightly with his brows furrowed. He motioned forward to speak to Aod, but a Rouvká came to his side, grabbing him by the arm with one hand and pressing a pistol into Shím's back. I stood calm, meeting Aod's fiery eyes. Her shoulders rose and fell with every breath.

"You'd be wise to choose your next move carefully, Aod Mag Bettle," I said.

"You'd be wise to choose your next words carefully, Diramal," replied Aod, pressing the edge of her blade more tightly against my skin.

I frowned at Aod's response. Mae pulled back the hammer of her gun.

"I see one drop of blood roll down his neck and I'll blow out your hip," said Mae.

I glanced over at Mae and silently commanded her to stand down, with my gaze. She lowered her eyes and held her ground.

"On what you said a moment ago, Aod, I merely spoke an observation of a very possible outcome for your kin. Sometimes facts are hard to face, but they are no less a part of the reality we find ourselves in. And I've come to tell you of the fact that the Irens will, in all likeness, perish regardless of whether you start getting shipments from Scoat'tir again. In just a few weeks, many of the surviving members of our kin will be leaving Galiza, in ships we've located beneath the planet," I said. Aod tilted her head, not with intrigue. She almost looked offended, but it wasn't quite that either. "Now, with Shím having grown to be a good friend of mine, I would rather not see his people be left behind for dead, nor any other surviving culture of our kin. But if you will not take my help, then I will, regrettably, take my forces and leave you all in peace."

Aod didn't retract her weapon right away, but I did feel her slowly ease her pressure from my flesh. Before long, Aod had fully removed herself from me and our opposing forces let down their arms.

"So, Aod, what is your answer?" I asked.

"Send in your supplies, Utopian. Then we'll discuss how you intend to move us… *unharmed.* For if even one of the infirm are slaughtered out there, a life from one of your own ranks will be cut down in kind," she said.

XI
Squeezed Thin
(Amat)

I was relieved to hear that Koyůt Sarak had managed to make it safely back to base when I reached out and asked her to return over Irenole, bearing supplies for the Irens. Within an hour, the supplies had been dropped and delivered to Aod's people, as promised. I demonstrated and stressed its jolting effects before handing them out. While there were many startled reactions to the energy interfaces that we'd grown accustomed to in Utopion, in the end, none were dissatisfied with the nourishment medium. It was the young who had the hardest time adjusting to the interfaces. In observing their frustrations, I noticed just how few of the children were under the age of ten. Anyone older than that was either too old to fight or fitted with a QS-25. The youngest soldier I noted couldn't have been older than twelve. Not that it shocked me; the concept of a child soldier was an ordinary sight to see in my country. Only then, it struck me differently. Having seen so much war and endured so much struggle, even in my training, made me realize what a great loss much of my species had been subject to. An early loss of innocence, of unconditional joy and love that we are all so blessed to have when we are born into this world, trained out of us until we grow hard and numb.

It made me think back to my observation of Mae a few nights past. Watching her lie so tranquilly at my side. I wondered: *could the entire world ever know such peace, all at once? After all that's happened?*

As I continued to wander around the sealed base, I unintentionally caught sight of Shím and Aod speaking together. They didn't seem to be arguing, but even from a distance, I could sense tension between them. It was the way Aod looked at Shím. They seemed to be in a respectful disagreement about something; I could only imagine what it concerned. Perhaps Shím was confronting Aod's distrust of me or maybe a personal matter. I did not feel it wise to get involved, regardless, so I kept my distance and before turning away from them, I noted Shím place something small into Aod's hand. It was some sort of object, perhaps some kind of jewelry or memento, I couldn't be sure. But I might say it had sentimental value to the both of them, noting how Aod's expression had shifted to awe and joy after she'd received the totem. The two embraced one another and I left.

After the Irens had been fed, Aod called a meeting with me, Shím, and Mae to discuss a plan that would see us safely to an extraction point where the Irens could be transported from.

"I think it goes without saying that you'd prefer we don't bring your kin back to Utopion?" I asked Aod.

"You'd be correct, Diramal Criptous," Aod replied.

I nodded.

"I understand and that's not a problem. If you'd prefer it, one of my cousins has located several of these buried starships across Galiza. From what I understand, with all the people that we'd be moving, there should be adequate space for your people on the ships beneath Utopion, Afeikita, and Zeta," I said.

"Afeikita is a Utopian-conquered country. Zeta, on the other hand, will do just fine," said Aod.

"Simply stating the name of the country itself, would have sufficed," butted in Mae.

Aod glared at Mae, and an awkward silence fell over the group. Shím cleared his throat as he walked up to Aod's side.

"Great, now we know where our people are goin', which is perhaps the most barren piece of land on the planet, occupied by one of the most territorial cultures in the world. I'm sure they have a lot to be grateful for, given these hard times and surely wouldn't be hardened further by them. If anything, we should assume they might be a cozier people, having been unified by this global threat. Where should we establish our evac point?" Shím said, speaking with a sense of sarcasm throughout.

Aod seemed unamused.

"Not that I've been keeping myself up to date on Zetian mannerisms, but Shím is right. Judging by their brutish history, the way your kin would be treated among theirs is unpredictable and it's possible that they'd be in even greater danger in their custody than anyone else's," I said.

"I'd take my chances with the Zetians over the Utopians," said Aod.

"*You* would, but what of your kin? You speak on their behalf; do you think they desire to endure more pain and suffering? You're allowing your emotions to dictate a crucial decision for the well-being of *all* Irens. And don't forget, Zeta is its own empire. It has conquered several countries for itself whose cultures have long been wiped out, like the Gihids, Fagorins, and Kyphids," Mae said.

"Don't lecture me on historic feuds to make your autocracy seem all the more glamorous," barked Aod.

"On the contrary…" I said, speaking up. "You mentioned that Afeikita is a Utopian-dominated country and while there was a war between our two countries years ago, since the start of this one, we have abandoned much of our dominion and influence in countries like Afeikita. Aside from the hovering invader presence, you'll find no Utopian forces lingering in the governments there. And the Afeikitas are a much more considerate kin than the Zetians," I said.

Aod stared at me, squinting, and let out a sigh.

"Very well, take us to Afeikita."

I nodded.

"We shall," I replied. "Now, getting back to what Shím said earlier, where should we establish our evac point?"

Aod shook her head, irritated.

"Much of the Isle is an open field and the few cities and towns it divides are filled with either invading forces or Skátho-voír."

"Which doesn't seem to leave us much choice for a good place to settle down with hundreds of your kin, while we wait for our Fades to come pick us up, I'd imagine," said Mae.

"No, it doesn't. However, there's the Commathor Bridge ninety miles north of here that connects Irenole to Scoat'tír. The bridge is a considerably longer stretch, but it's shielded and well intact. On the other side, there's a small Scoat' haven, where your Fades can easily land and my kin will be safe," continued Aod.

"Sounds like we have an arrangement then," I said.

"There is one risk we run in takin' this path. On this route…" Aod said, tracing her finger along the digital map we all surrounded, "…we'll have to pass through Dunlark, a city that sits about halfway through our route."

"And what's so concerning about Dunlark, Aod?" asked Shím, his arms crossed, and his expression puzzled.

"It's a Shí city; we haven't gone there in a long time."

"Shí city?" I asked.

"Ryne, a ghost town, laddin," said Shím.

"Well…" I said, thinking back to Giclon, "…we've certainly had some experience with that of late."

"It's where the Skátho-voír, on this Isle, have made their home," Aod said harshly.

We all glanced at one another. I crossed my arms and sighed, covering my mouth.

"What about the land surrounding the city?" asked Mae.

"Nothin' but open fields, as I said, which I won't drag my kin across. And we don't have enough food and drink to get us through the journey it would take to make the longer routes across the smaller towns," said Aod. I felt Aod's gaze pressing on me, almost deviously, as I stared down at the route Aod had displayed for us. "You're sure you wanna take this risk, Diramal? Mind you what I said earlier. For every one of my kin that's slaughtered out there, by this scenario you've dragged us in, I shall return onto your own troops in kind."

I stared back confidently, unfazed by Aod's demeanor as I leaned over the table.

"*None* of your people will see death on this mission," I replied.

"You seem so sure, when time after time, from what I hear, you've lost squadron after squadron under your command, again and again. On the field, upon Anua. You have a reputation, Amat Luciph Criptous, for losing more people than you likely care to keep track of," mocked Aod.

Aod and I stared in a persistent silence for a moment.

"None of your kin will die on this mission, Aod Mag Bettle. I'll see to that myself," I said.

"Pray that you do. Or I'll see that you are shunned to walk in the shadow of Anua, lost to her void for all eternity," replied Aod.

***

121

We waited until the morn of the following day before moving the Irens out across their country. Aod had done a head count: there were seven hundred among the civilians and more than twice that number among their army.

I still couldn't wrap my head around why Aod could be so stubborn. At the end of our last conversation, it almost seemed to suggest she had a kind of madness about her. As if she would rather see me fail than see her people reach safety. Something I would never willingly embrace—failure—and it only made me more determined to see each of the Irens safely off the Isle. I would achieve this by sending multiple groups of scouts ahead of the group to secure the area thoroughly.

The journey would be a four-day march north, stopping in small towns along the way. The first two were suspiciously empty. We covered forty miles of land and saw no sign of an alien threat, let alone Shadow Scar.

Perhaps that last interaction on the battlefield truly did spark a sort of temporary armistice. Though I'm not quite sure what I did, if anything, to encourage such an act from the Zeltons. Still, it feels like someone's watching us. Someone waiting for the most opportune time to reveal themselves. That time may yet be when we reach Dunlark.

By the third day, we would reach it.

(Zothra)

Since the day of our arrival, Quavek and I have commanded a force of Varx to trail Amat's movements across Irenol. For the past two days, we've been carefully following him and his troops north. Tonight, we discovered that he is leading a pack of his kin into a city flooded with Varx. The night before Amat and his troops would reach Dunlark, Quavek and I traveled ahead of them into the city.

We were promptly greeted after we set foot on the main streets. Distant chatters of various languages and calls echoed throughout the spire-shaped buildings. They could tell who we were, as could we, them. The taint of Drakkar's power resting within each of us unified our intellect like a hive. I smiled at the restlessness I sensed within each of them, their fervor for bloodshed, as was their rabid nature, among these breeds of Varx.

Proceeding further along the street, we noted the whispers turned into pleased chants of our names. "Zothra" and "Quavek" they roared. I glanced up and witnessed a broad figure plummeting down onto the street. The ground cracked at her landing. She rose slowly from her squat and approached us. She was… a Mydiagorn. Her neck was thin, long, scaled, strands of hair stretched back behind her scalp as if something pulled them that way. Cheekbones broad and wide, her sunken eyes rested at their high corners. Two arms rested from her shoulders; talons dangled from her hands. Her back was arched but guarded by a layered shell. The last notable characteristic was her tail, prickly and capable of shooting out hallucinogenic spikes.

The chanting stopped completely once we met face to face.

"Welcome, Qi'val Quavek and… Vorüm'Qij Zothra?" The Mydiagorn paused when she noticed me.

I raised an eyebrow.

"Something off, Vormaul?" I asked.

"No, it's just your…" The Vormaul stopped when I tilted my head, warning her not to express what I knew distracted her about me. "Eh, never mind, it's not important. I am Kaiphor Huvara, I command the legion of Varx that occupy the north of Irenole. We are most intrigued by your arrival. What brings you out our way; how may we serve two of the strongest select members of the Varx?" said Vormaul Huvara.

"We come seeking your aid. The human known as Amat Luciph Criptous will arrive here with hundreds of armored and meek members of his kin by midday tomorrow," Quavek said.

"Ah, Criptous, the Diramal's—"

"Yes, that one," I butted in.

Huvara nodded.

"I trust this means a fight is on its way. The others will be most pleased. They're eager for one, as I'm sure you sensed," said Huvara.

"I did indeed. Our priority, however, is not to kill Criptous, or any of the members of his company. Drakkar won't have it done until Amat has retrieved all the surviving members of his kin into the sanctuary of operational military bases and launched them off this planet, using their ancient, buried vessels," I replied.

"With all due respect, Vorüm'Qij Zothra, this domain is under *my* command and in the weeks my legion has gone without a quarrel, they've grown restless. Fights have broken out among themselves; I've hardly managed to keep them in line as it is. And if human bloodshed is what will settle their frenzy, I will grant them it."

I stepped up to Vormaul Huvara and brushed my fingers through her thick scaled hair, squeezing the strands between the interdigits of my fingers. I yanked my arm vigorously, jerking Huvara's neck. She ground her teeth while baring them. I started to walk around her.

"Tell me, Vormaul Huvara, how many Varx occupy this city?" I asked.

"Well over seven hundred, Vorüm'Qij Zothra," replied Vormaul Huvara.

"*Mm*, that'll do nicely, combined with our own numbers. Don't you think, Quavek?" I asked.

"It'll be more than enough to overwhelm Criptous, yes," replied Quavek.

"And his kin—"

"No, you *shkorzia,*" I cursed, reaching my hand up one of the lower crevices of the Mydiagorn's shelled back, squeezing firmly at the most sensitive point in her body. The Mydiagorn clicked her mouth rapidly as she rasped. The Varx in the vicinity gave an uproar as they witnessed and sensed our interaction.

"Don't you listen?" I continued. "We are not to kill Amat, nor will you allow *any* of your numbers to assault his kin. As they will be future candidates to add to our army before this minor conflict with the Zeltons has ended. Instead, *this,* is what we will do," I said, crushing an organ inside the Mydiagorn. "We will *squeeze* Amat to the edge of insanity, drain him of all his will, and leave him infirm. That is all you and your numbers shall do, no more, no less."

Finally, I retracted my arm from the Mydiagorn's back, having had no intention of debilitating her in the first place. Huvara stumbled away, panting, reaching behind her. The Mydiagorn bowed and lowered her gaze from me in shame.

"I understand well what you would have us do, Vorüm'Qij. I shall arrange a sentry to await Criptous's arrival," said Huvara.

"My troops will handle that. Amat's been sending scouts ahead of the main group. If your troops are as bloodthirsty as you say, I won't trust them to keep their composure the moment they set eyes on a few straggling human foot soldiers. Our focus will be Amat himself," I commanded.

"Understood," replied Vormaul Huvara begrudgingly.

"Quavek, Kalbrook will likely stay close to the group while we chase down Amat. Have you thought of some way you could separate her from the others?"

"I have more than one scheme in mind for her, yes," Quavek hissed.

"*Mm*, good," I replied. "When we see Amat's forces nearing the city, our kin will hold positions within the buildings. I understand this is a city you've held for quite some time."

"Over a Galizian year, yes," replied Huvara.

"Amat will likely know of its reputation, as I'm sure the Irens would have informed him of it. Knowing him, he'll venture into the city alone; if not, with maybe a handful of his kin to survey the city. That is when we will strike…" I raised my finger to the Mydiagorn before her expression could grow too enthusiastic. "But at the right time."

Suddenly, the air filled with screeches emanating from the north. Flying low in the sky, small formations of sphikes dashed overhead of us. I chuckled at the irony.

"It seems your numbers may just get their thirsts quenched after all, Vormaul Huvara," I said.

XII
Undying Love
(Amat)

As Dunlark came into view around midday, we held our positions a good five miles out, on a hillside, at the edge of a forest. To either side of the city rested barren, open fields that would otherwise leave us exposed to the enemy. At least the city would provide us cover from the eyes of the invaders. Couldn't say the same for whatever Shadow Scar forces that dwelled *within* Dunlark, however.

"So, you're sure you want to lead your people through there?" I asked, as I came to Aod's side.

She glanced my way before looking back toward the city.

"Without question."

I shook my head.

"I do not doubt my ability to keep your people safe once we are in the confines of Dunlark, but I would strongly suggest you reconsider your options here. We've found cover within these thin woods that have served us well. We could remain here and arrange for the Fades to pick us up in the field."

"Where my people and your ships will be left vulnerable to the invader forces instead? No," replied Aod. "We will either go through Dunlark or turn back and you'll leave, Utopian."

"We've not seen sight of the invaders in two days. I strongly urge you to reconsider, as I suspect, for whatever reason, they are no longer troubled by our presence," I said.

"In other words, you have a hunch. I am not one for trusting in such things."

"Yet you trust your people will safely venture through a Shadow Scar-infested city?" I asked.

We stood in silence for a moment.

126

"We will await your orders, Diramal Criptous. When your Alphas report back to you on the condition of Dunlark, I'll hear your decision," Aod said, and began to walk away.

"I won't be sending any of my troops into the city," I said. Aod stopped. "I know all too well the strength and ferocity of the Shadow Scar. I will not risk sending my kin to be slaughtered, to validate information I'm already sure of."

"How selfless of you," said Aod, mockingly.

She continued to walk on her way. I sighed in irritation.

"I see Mag Bettle hasn't gotten any easier to deal with," Mae said.

I looked over to her as she approached me.

"Not in the slightest," I replied.

"Have you asked Shím to speak with her? They seem close," said Mae.

"I don't doubt that's what he's been trying to do. But Aod's too stubborn," I replied.

"You both are," said Mae.

I snorted.

"Should I take that as a compliment?" I asked.

Mae shrugged.

"If you consider it a compliment to your leadership, yes." Mae paused a moment. "I heard you say you weren't going to send any of the troops ahead into Dunlark. Will you scout the city on your own?"

"Yes," I replied.

"You sure you won't need someone to watch your back?"

"There are many times when I have. But I don't feel this will be one of them," I said.

"Do you really feel that way, or are you only saying it to keep the rest of us out of harm's way?"

"Both," I replied.

"You're lying," said Mae.

"I'm not," I replied.

"Amat, there's more than likely an entire army of Shadow Scar within that city, one that may outnumber our numbers here—"

"All the more reason that I should go in alone," I said.

"When they make themselves known to you, you won't survive," said Mae.

"Do you really feel that way, or are you only saying it to keep me out of harm's way?"

Mae paused and sighed heavily.

"Just… don't put yourself in any greater jeopardy than you already have," said Mae.

I shook my head.

"That I can't promise…" I took Mae's hand. "But what I can, is that no matter what happens over there, I'll find my way back to you."

"You'd better."

After notifying Aod that I'd be making my way into Dunlark, I altered time and headed straight for it. I paused to let them know I'd reached the main streets.

"Roger that, Diramal," replied Aod. "I'll start marching my kin that way. Update us with any concerning finds."

"I shall. Io-Pac Kalbrook, you'll have command over our troops, in my stead," I said.

"No, I won't," a voice said, panting behind me.

I turned around to find Mae jogging toward me.

I tightened my grip on my E.S.P. 101 and grimaced at the sight of her.

"What are you doing? I told you to stay back with the group," I said.

"You never said anything like that. You merely stated you'd be going into the city alone," said Mae.

"And so I will, with no contradictions. Which is why *you* will go back and join the others," I said.

Mae pulled her head back, offended.

"Have you forgotten our days in training when I stayed on your heels every step of the way through our drills and even bested you at some of them?"

"This is not about you being able to keep up with me in a drill, Mae. This is an almost guaranteed suicide run that will certainly cost dozens, if not hundreds, of lives, if nothing but the utmost cautious. With any luck, by venturing alone, I'll catch sight of the threat before that can happen," I said.

"And in exchange, make it a cost for one life, your own? You have no right to decide that—"

"My life is my own to command, Mae, mine, my decision!" I barked. "And if I am to die today at the expense of saving others, then so be it."

"Then as is my life to do with as I will, as there is only *one* commander of it, and it is not you," said Mae.

She marched past me and made her way into the city.

I shook my head and growled as I opened the channel back up.

"Shím, the command of our troops will be placed under your responsibility in my absence," I said.

"Understood, sir," said Shím.

"Mae," I called, marching after her. She didn't hesitate. "Mae!" I grabbed her arm and turned her toward me.

"Let go of me, Amat!" growled Mae.

I held firm, but not tightly enough to hurt her.

"Only if you'll listen when I do." I spoke sternly.

Mae stopped her squirming and looked up at me. As Mae calmed her breath, I loosened my grip before she finally pulled away.

"I'm not asking you to stay back because I think you're incompetent at handling yourself. Knowing you, I'd think twice before making that judgement," I said.

"Then what is it about? Why are you afraid? And don't say you're not; I've known you long enough to see past your confidence," said Mae.

I sighed.

"In Giclon, after we killed that Shadow Scar together, I told you about something the invaders and I have in common. To this day I can't explain it, but I know I can count on it to get me through whatever I'll face in this city. And even with the help of the ingenuity of the quantum suits granted to our kin, I hold a much larger upper hand in being able to alter time naturally. The luxury of which no one else has been granted, including you. I made a vow to myself when my father died that I would never let anyone I loved die before their time. I failed that vow twice over, when my aunt and uncle died, and I won't allow myself to do so again, not with you," I said.

Mae remained silent, processing all I'd said. She retracted her helmet. I glanced around to make sure there were no hostiles while she had her guard down. Mae slowly placed her hand on my jaw to focus my attention.

"That's a clever way of you answering my question without actually answering it. It's also a clever way of you saying you love me. It's for that reason, I won't go back to the others. For what would it say about the love I bear for you, if I were to let you face this on your own?" asked Mae.

I placed my hand over Mae's.

"If we're going to do this, you stay by my side. *Every* step of the way. You don't leave my sight. Do you understand?" I asked.

"I do," replied Mae.

"Let's move then, we've got a lot of ground to cover," I said.

Over the course of the next few hours, Mae and I ran up and down the streets of Dunlark, through the tall spire buildings and dome-shaped houses. The most suspicious activity we caught sight of was debris tumbling down from ceilings, but we never saw any indication of an invader or Shadow Scar presence.

Finally, Aod opened a channel and sent out a surge.

"Diramal, we've reached the southern outskirts of the city; am I clear to move my people through?" asked Aod.

I sighed before replying.

"It almost seems too good to be true when I say we haven't found any sign of the invaders or the Shadow Scar here. Still, Io-Pac Kalbrook and I will stay ahead of the group, and I'd advise you and your troops to be alert while passing through," I said.

"Of course, see ya on the other side, Diramal," replied Aod.

"Should we double back?" asked Mae after I closed the channel.

"That's a good question, but we've still got much of the city ahead to explore. It would help if one of us were to go back to keep close to the squadrons, while the other remained here to clear a more direct path based on their course," I said.

"I assume you'd expect me to be the one who'd go back," said Mae.

"No specific name came out of my mouth," I said.

"But that would be your preference."

I paused before answering.

"It would," I said.

Mae shook her head.

"Something is out of place here, Mae. The day is not yet over; this city, apparently, has a reputation for being the most treacherous to venture into on the Isle, yet it's barren, silent. It's been two days since we've caught sight of either of our enemies and that concerns me. I have a good feeling we won't go a third with the same outcome, not in this place," I said.

Mae nodded.

"Thank you," I said.

I went on to scope out further into the city, securing a path for the Irens.

"Amat, I've regrouped with the others, and we're at the southeast end of the city," said Mae.

"Good, keep to the east as you make your way north. We'll make that our path, as it'll be less ground to cover that way," I said.

"Roger that," she said.

I'd made it all the way to the northern border of the city when I found bodies; fresh invader bodies, lying limp throughout the buildings and in the streets. I could tell by the steaming, gaping wounds and the ripe blue blood draining from their corpses. Not to mention the teal blazing fires in the plowed paths their crashed ships left behind.

There were almost no signs of any opposing force that had fallen among the alien carcasses except… one sliver of flesh that appeared so obviously out of place. In all my years of fighting the invaders, I had never noted any features about them that resembled triangular ears. I briefly examined the small hairy flesh, squishy, yet at the same time, sturdy to the touch. I walked a little further and found another strange ligament: a long and bony finger with a teardrop nail stretching from it. Too small to resemble any kind of invader claw. These discoveries lead me to only one conclusion.

Shadow Scar. Curious, how they're so persistent at hiding the existence of their kin, even now.

"In any case, if the rest of their bodies are missing, that means that there must have been others left alive after the battle, to remove the dead. Most of them anyway," I said.

I had to get back to the others. They had ventured halfway across the city without having encountered any trouble. I observed them from several stories above, keeping to the buildings to ensure no threats lingered from within. Having scouted the area, I opened a channel to Mae, Aod, and Shím.

"Commanders, this is Criptous. I've got intel on the route ahead. Though the city appears empty, at the northern borders there are clear indications that a recent battle took place. Numerous invader bodies, and vessels, and signs of a Shadow Scar presence, hiding their tracks," I said.

"So, the city isn't so empty as it appears," said Shím.

"I suspect not," I replied.

"But you still haven't seen any signs of a live threat, have you?" asked Aod.

"No, but I'll keep surveilling the area until that changes, or we escape the city," I replied.

"Roger that," replied Aod.

I stayed close to the rest of the pack, never letting any of them escape my sight, trailing up, down and around within the length of the crowd. Still, there were no signs of Shadow Scar, or the Zeltons. I didn't know whether to feel at ease or anxious. More than half of the way through Dunlark, I finally heard something. Some rubble, falling out of a broken screen window in the next building ahead of me. I stopped and opened a channel to Mae.

"Mae, I've just detected a sign of a potential enemy presence. Stand by for combat," I said.

"Roger that, be careful," Mae replied.

I paused before dropping the signal, hesitant to say anything at all.

I altered time, gave myself a running start, and leaped the gap between the two buildings, the seeps of my armor carrying me across before I finally crashed into one of the screen windows. I rolled across the ground and whipped my pistol out, ready to aim by the time I was upright. Scanning my surroundings, I heard nothing but the sound of my own breath filling the interior of my helm. It was a strange external silence, one that felt purposeful. I didn't need to see my enemies to know that they were there.

I stood and cautiously moved across the room, lightly crushing the broken glass scattered out across the floor. I felt their eyes on me, waiting to spring a trap for the prey they patiently awaited. I could have certainly stepped away, called for backup, but I worried that would have put the Irens at risk.

A subtle thud sounded from the ceiling above me. I aimed up, only to witness some dust fall from a rigid crack. It sounded again, a little further ahead from the last one. I took a deep breath and followed it. The further I walked, other creaks and thuds joined the first, in various sections of the ceiling.

There's more than one.

I followed the sounds to a blockade of desks and chairs. Locating a small gap in the formation, I crawled through it. It was a tight squeeze, but I managed. Once I had my head through, I panned my eyes one way and then the other... nothing. Still, the noises overhead sounded off.

Not much further was a large opening in the ceiling that had caved in. Without hesitation, I made my way toward it, pulling the hammer back on my pistol. Another fall of rubble from the ceiling sounded behind me. I stopped, waited, and turned around briskly to look at whatever might be hanging there... nothing. Though a faint pulse of wind sounded once I'd made my move.

I stepped back toward the opening, taking in my surroundings. I hadn't seen the left side of the room when something rose slowly from behind a small blockade. It didn't look sentient, though its appearance was no less disturbing. A twisted thing with a broad, molten face. Empty eye sockets the size of fists. A drooping, broken jawline. One shoulder hung lower than the other. It did not speak, it did not acknowledge me, it was only there, and I had witnessed it move. If it was not alive, something in this room was, to put it there. I shuffled back a few more steps and felt my feet meet with the rubble that had fallen from the ceiling. Turning around, I found a way up... *scream!* I stumbled back onto the ground, lorded over by a creature with a V-shaped head. Tens of small eyes filled its face, over its forehead and where its nose should have been. Two tall and narrow

133

horns stretched from the angled sprouts of its head. Long squirming tentacles sprung up from the back of its head. Sharp, bone-like features sprouted from its shoulders. It screamed again from its wide, lipless mouth. I needed the noise to stop, *needed* it to. Despite my shock, I raised my gun and shot aimlessly at the thing. It vanished the moment before I squeezed the trigger.

Panting, I altered time as I found my feet. I couldn't look in two directions before I met with the same creature, once again pouncing on me. I fell back to the ground. The creature slowly cracked its mouth open in a disturbing smile as it leaned in toward me. It screeched again as I punched it in the face and kicked it off me. Launching myself off the ground, I ran again, as other, numerous screeches followed. Not getting far, the Shadow Scar grabbed me by the ankles and mounted itself on my back. With one throw after the other of its arms, it started to tear vigorously at my armor, until its long nails dug into my skin. I howled in pain, trying to wiggle free of its hold on me, before the creature itself turned me around, punching me in the face and then enveloping both its hands around my neck, pressing down hard. With one hand, I tried pulling away at one of the creature's arms and with the other I pressed the barrel of my pistol into the creature's rib cage and fired repeatedly until I could break free of its grasp.

Tossing the corpse aside, I rushed up to my feet one final time, pausing only momentarily to witness the horde of more creatures in various twisted and demented forms chasing and rushing toward me. Slowly, deep, overlapping voices sounded over comms. I could hardly make sense of what the word or words were. Either way, it meant a channel was open, which was a good thing. I briskly turned around and rushed toward the nearest window. When I finally leaped through it, I briefly exited out of my altered time state, only to shout: "Run!" Over comms. Several windows shattered behind me as various screeches and horrible cries followed. By the time I had tumbled into the next building, I had altered time once again.

(Mae)

I glanced up quickly as I heard Amat crash through a glass window, watching as he sailed through the air into the next building before him. Moments later, hundreds, if not thousands, of bodies that my molecular sensors vaguely picked up, crashed through the glass building as well, chasing after Amat. Several let out terrible cries and screeches, and not one sounded identical to the other.

"Move!" yelled Aod from up the line.

I couldn't bring myself to rush with the crowd, seeing that flow of vicious outlines continue to leap from various levels of the first building and dash on in the same direction as Amat. Not until someone bumped into me. Stumbling forward, I finally began pacing with the crowd. Still, my eyes glanced to the buildings ahead, trying to get a peek at Amat to make sure he was okay. Seemingly out of thin air, he arrived before us, falling out of the sky, enveloped around one of the Shadow Scar. The crowd came to a stop once the bodies of Amat and the creature quaked the ground beneath them. I could hardly see Amat as he pried his blade from the creature's chest, slowly finding his feet. He looked back up at the screeching creatures as they started to follow his trail down.

"Go!" Amat blurted with a flail of his arm. "I'll lure them away."

"Down this way!" Aod shouted, as she led the group down a street heading west. I was about to chase after Amat to give him support, when Aod continued: "Kalbrook, MgKonnol, have your troops give us cover fire as we come around!"

I paused, hesitating as I watched Amat's body vanish down the street in a blur, emitting light blue, electric rounds from his E.S.P. 101 up at the buildings as he ran. I sighed and pulled myself together, ordering those under my command to fire away at the buildings to our right as we herded the Skivs away from Amat and the Shadow Scar that pursued him. Oddly, there wasn't a single Shadow Scar that made a direct attempt to launch itself at us. A thought raced through my mind that I couldn't quite make sense of.

Why are they only going after Amat?

We ran down four blocks before Aod decided it was safe for us to slow our pace and allow everyone a brief break. Out in the distance, we could faintly hear the Shadow Scar cries and Amat's E.S.P. firing back at them. I marched up to the front of the line to speak with Aod.

"I'm going back," I said promptly.

Aod acknowledged me, ignoring my sense of urgency.

"For what, your pretty commanding Diramal?" Aod scoffed. "He made his sacrifice so that we could make the rest of our way through this city as safely as possible. And when the use of his distraction runs out... I'll need you and Shím here to command our numbers, should the Skátho-voír return and they surely will."

I brought my face to Aod's.

"You think I need your permission?" I growled.

"Clearly," Aod replied, unfazed. "Or you'd have already fled to him by now."

I curled my fingers into fists. I was about to argue further, when I realized I was only wasting time I could have already spent helping Amat. I sighed with a nod.

"Don't be surprised if I'm gone when next you call for me," I said.

I turned briskly and started walking away from the Iren.

"I'd expect nothin' less from a Utopian," replied Aod.

I paused momentarily, shook my head, and continued to the back of the group where I found Shím.

"Shím," I said.

"Ah, Mae, are yeh—"

"I need you to select a member among our ranks to lead in my stead," I said, cutting Shím short. "Even I know Amat won't survive taking on all those Shadow Scar. He'll need help if he's going to see it safely back to the group," I said.

Shím nodded.

"Ryne, I'll take care of it. May the Goddess seep her light onto both of ya," he replied.

I altered time and headed in the direction of the screeches and gunfire.

(Amat)

Leaping past piles of rubble, vaulting over keeled desks and torn furniture, the Shadow Scars stayed on my heels. They seemed to be trying to pass me up, cut me off, and overwhelm me. But they remained just tightly enough on my trail not to come into contact with me. I pushed the limits of my time-altering ability both through the QS-25 and my natural ability for it. My heart palpitated, my lungs tensed up and grew sore; I hadn't felt so worn out in altered time since the early days of this war.

After crashing through the fourth building, the Shadow Scar started making moves on me. The first spurred itself behind me as I turned a corner. In of the nook of my eye, I caught sight of a fleeting figure; unable to process much of its features, only the outline of its broad shoulders and its long head. With a quick swipe of my knife, I cut at the creature's throat as it reached out toward me. The blow caused the creature to whirl around as I left it behind me… only to meet with it again moments later. The Shadow Scar had come around and cut me off. I stumbled as I came to an abrupt stop. Though its neck oozed with shiny dark blood, it seemed as feisty as ever. I only had a moment to take in the features of its face, mouth split apart like an inverted "V," a flat nose just above three eyes and branching bones stretching at either side of its tall rectangular forehead. It momentarily caught me off gaurd; colliding into one another, I raised my blade to the creature's heart. The Shadow Scar vigorously squirmed with the last of its strength as I pried the blade from its chest and bolted off the ground.

Kicking my feet harder across the ground, I pumped my arms more swiftly back and forth, one, two, three, four, five, six, seven, eight, nine, CRASH! The roof above me collapsed and a larger Shadow Scar dropped on top of me. I arched my body and raised my arm above my head as it plummeted down on me; my legs never stopped running. The Shadow Scar landed hard against my forearm, and the contact briefly made all time and movement stop for me. The world seemed to tremble, and all sound *pulsed* into utter silence. I hardly noticed it at the time, but with every bit of sheer will and strength I could muster, I pushed my arm up against the colossal figure and struck it aside. All time and movement picked up slightly, still altered, as I raced on.

Pushing further beyond the limits of my power as my vision became tunneled and the terrain in front of me seemed to stretch and twist upside down. Quantum Fade dawned on my conscience. *I can't do this much longer.* A deep gurgle sounded beside me as I slowly turned my head to the left and saw the hands of another Shadow Scar reaching out toward me in a pounce. Fatigue had finally caught up with me, as a tear of exhaustion rolled down from my eyelid. Just as the creature's disfigured face came into view, its long, narrow tongue squirmed out of its mouth; I knew it was going to collide with me. Another brawl that I scarcely felt the tenacity for. There would be no way of escaping the closing Shadow Scar. They would overwhelm me, surround me. I took one final deep breath to prepare for the fight… STAB! An armored hand bearing a knife *jabbed* its way underneath the creature's chin, while the arm of my protector swiped it aside. A few paces further, she caught up to my side. I didn't need to see her face to know that it was Mae. My heart filled with adrenaline and my vision broadened. Growling as I suppressed my fury, I took Mae by the arm and willed myself to run even faster, harder. The floor cracked and quaked at my every step. Mae fought to keep up with me, but she didn't let up in the slightest. It was then I noticed that a chunk of the level we were on had been blown out and many of the pillars that held up the roof were either severely damaged or torn apart.

Not much is holding this place up.

I had no idea if it would work, but if it did, at the very least it would buy us some time to strategize a plan of escape. As we ran to the other side of the building—where we would have to jump once again, out in the street likely as there wasn't an immediate building in sight—I pulled the pins from grenades at my belt and started chucking them at nearby pillars. The impact was enough to detonate them instantly. Seven pillars had been blown out before the building started to moan and the ceiling started to crack. Three more and the building began tilting back slightly.

Come. On!

I threw one final grenade steps before Mae and I would have to make our exit. Obliterating one last pillar, the ceiling finally caved in behind us as Mae and I raced out, tumbling onto the street. My momentum dragged me further than Mae. Though the Shadow Scar did not follow us down, our struggle was not over.

Shards of glass fell from above as I struggled to push myself off the ground and gazed up at three-quarters of the four-hundred-story building gradually tilting over. Time was now flowing naturally for me. I quickly found Mae, stumbled to her motionless body, and took her into my arms.

Limping forth, down the street, with heavy chunks of debris falling from above, I tried desperately to alter time once again. Yet each time I made an attempt, it was as if the very cells of my body churned; the fabric of my biology was resisting the activation of my power.

"Come on, what's happening?!" I growled.

More chunks of debris fell from above, each one falling closer than the last as the building tipped further. Picking up my pace, I continued trying to alter time, managing to use it in extremely short bursts. Not enough to reach any great distance, stumbling each time I was forced to snap out of it. The pain was much like an overwhelming queasy sensation shooting throughout my body. The building crashed onto a much smaller one on the other side of the street.

"Come ooon!" I howled.

The middle of the tipped structure split in half and hurled a great chunk of its contents onto the street, like loose intestines dropping out of a gaping wound. Just before reaching the edge of the building's shadow, time finally altered once again. It was torture to hold onto it, but I would not let go this time. As the blanket of debris was stopped just above my head, I had to crouch slightly to run under it. I felt my strength fading; my arms and legs nearly gave out as I took one final leap out of harm's way. I howled with relief as I rolled across the ground with Mae, freeing myself of the altered flow of time. A loud crumble sounded behind us. I coddled Mae's body as best I could from any rubble that might have rolled its way into us. None did, only a thick dust cloud that sheltered us… for a time.

XIII
Innocents
(Zothra)

We'd lost a considerable number of forces from Amat's clever stunt. Quavek, Huvara, and I watched Amat and his aider from the roof of a nearby building. It was certainly within our ability to kill them both where they rested, down in the street there. But that is not what the Diramal asked of us. I almost rejected my sense of obligation to him in that moment. No matter, the boy would meet his end soon enough. *I only hope to be the Diramal's choice when he gives the order.*

"Your troops performed well, Vormaul Huvara," I said. "While there were some who struggled to keep in line and refrain from attacking Amat or the Skiv party, they did well."

"I am proud to please thee, Vorüm'Qij Zothra," replied Vormaul Huvara.

"I'm not *pleased*; you should have held a tighter grip around those who disobeyed my orders. But it matters not, at this rate. The mission has been a success, thus far. See that it stays that way when Amat and his ally awaken," I said.

"Yes, Vorüm'Qij Zothra. Promptly so," replied Vormaul Huvara.

When Huvara had left earshot, Quavek stepped closer beside me as we both looked down at the two pesky humans.

"Do you think it's her?" I asked.

"Without a doubt," replied Quavek.

"Then you know what to do. When Criptous and Kalbrook awaken, we will work to separate the two. Once that happens, the Io-Pac will be yours to have your way with," I said.

"I look forward to it," Quavek hissed.

(Amat)

I don't imagine much time had gone by when I awoke, as there were no signs of the Shadow Scar nearby, except for faint shrieks and chatters out in the distance. Mae rested just a few meters behind me, her body twisted awkwardly. Crawling toward her, I winced at the ill pain that still lingered in my body from before. I wasn't trying to alter time; all the same it was there, and I wondered: *What does this mean?*

I crawled stiffly up to Mae's body, suppressing growls of discomfort as I made my way to her. Pulling on her shoulder, I rolled her flat on the ground. Her body moved limply. Desperate, I retracted my helm and rested my head over her chest, trying to locate her heartbeat. I couldn't hear anything through her armor. I sat up, lifted Mae into my arms and retracted her helm, raising my finger to her snout. A soft, warm exhale blew past. I sighed with relief as I rested my head on her chest.

"Thank the Goddess," I whispered.

I raised my head and glanced around; still the cries carried across the air from a few blocks down the way.

We need to move.

I took a deep breath and rose with Mae in my arms. My body ached all around; however, the stiffness lessened the further I marched. We reached the end of a block down the street, in the normal flow of time, not seeking to reacquaint myself with the strange biological pain I felt, when last I tried to alter it.

I found refuge in a small, ruined home and found a bed to set Mae down on. I collapsed beside her, sighing one final time as I took in her slumbering beauty.

"What am I gonna do with you"—I stroked some strands of hair back that covered her eyelids—"if you won't listen to me?"

If it meant you would be kept safe from the dangers that surround me, I would cast you out of my life and have you live your own, I thought, daring not to speak it aloud.

I wondered then, also, how someone could fall in love with another so broken as I, to the point that Mae would be willing to aid me in the face of death, time and time again? It was a type of love I could not comprehend, being so used to putting *myself* before others. I would not say I had any less love for Mae, but I would sooner see her turned away from the high stakes of my life, rather than willingly drag her into it alongside me.

Some time passed, and I hadn't heard another screech from the Shadow Scars since. I allowed my eyes to rest. *Just a short rest. Hopefully Mae will awake before I drift.* Yet it wasn't a few moments after I had shut my eyes that my conscious escaped into the deepest recess of my mind.

Once again, I found myself in the black void, staring down at the ripples of the water that enveloped my boots. It seemed so peaceful; I could almost hear the water quaking. *Water.* My ears filled with the sound of it as my mind started to feel entranced. The sound was not very clear at first, but it was deep and low. Still, I stared at the ripples, continually stretching out from my ankles, yet I hadn't even flinched since my arrival. The sound became louder... *waves, rolling waves. Breaking against the shore.* I closed my eyes and took in the first deep, genuine sense of peace I had felt since I was very young, since before my time in the militia. I curled my lips into a smile. Out in the distance, a loud, deep chirping echoed across the air. At first, I frowned, then I heard...

"Open your eyes, Amat," said my father.

I opened my eyes. My father and I were on a beach, the sun shone bright, the sands were a faint blue, and the seas were a gem green. Out in the distance, I saw several Zaiwarks. A very long and broad aquatic creature, stretching up to a hundred seventy-five meters across. Their skins are scaled and smooth. At their head is a large, gaping mouth as wide and long as the circumference of its own body. The females have short, broad tusks at either side of their mouths, with long tentacles stretching a quarter of their body length from their jawline. Just behind their heads, at the bottoms of their bodies, they have two sets of fins. The front ones are longer than the ones at the rear. The males have two short horns at the tops of their heads. At either side of their mouths stretch fleshy pincers. Two short fins sit close to their heads and a larger one, closer to the center of their bodies. Rigid bones stretch from the center of their lower backs. And at the ends of their bodies, both sexes have powerful flapping tails to push them across the waves.

My father and I observed as the Zaiwarks arched their bodies, in a school, up over the ocean surface and back down again. We didn't need to say anything between ourselves to know that we were both having a good time. A child's laugh sounded in the distance, breaking my focus. I shifted my eyes onto the giggling boy, who was kicking swiftly across the sands and into the edges of the water. He jumped with an ecstatic sense of enthusiasm as he pointed to the Zaiwarks.

"Daddy, look it's the 'Gaiwards!'" the boy exclaimed.

Gaiwards? That sounds familiar.

The boy's father slowly walked up to the child, amused by his son's mispronunciation. He squatted down at his son's side and pointed with him.

"Yeah, there they are, your 'Gaiwards,'" said the father, playing along with his child. They looked at one another and the father presented the boy with something in his hand. "Are you ready?"

"Yeah!" cheered the boy.

The father and the son were dressed in sift suits; they were equipped with a form of current propulsion technology, allowing the user to move over forty miles per hour. This is achieved in the suit's ability to amplify a field around itself; utilizing the surrounding water to create a contained current and propell them in any direction. The father and son put on their final attachment, a rubber helm with an opening around the face. They both pressed against a button behind their ears and a transparent yellow shield filled the opening.

The father took the boy's hand as they ran and dove into the ocean together, springing in and out of the water as they trailed behind the Zaiwarks.

"Do you remember this day?" my father asked.

"I remember this place and fragments of the things we'd do here together. Aside from the last five or six years, I've lost many of my distant memories; an adverse effect of the code nine neuro-chip," I said.

"Perhaps you can find comfort in knowing they are still here, despite being suppressed," my father said.

I turned to my father with a curious look on my face.

"Why are we here? We've never had a meeting like this before," I asked.

"To show and remind you of something," he replied.

"Of what?" I asked.

"Your innocence. You'll need it for what comes next."

"What's coming?" I asked.

My father took a moment before replying.

"You need to fight, Amat," my father replied.

I was thrown off by my father's words.

"Fight? But I have been, for almost four years now, that's all I've done."

"No, you need to *fight*. Look down at your boots again, Amat," said my father.

I did as my father instructed and saw that they were covered in water again. The ripples had stopped, and I returned to the void. I looked up and before me was a Zelton. My stance shifted as the invader tilted its head at me. We stood in silence, until finally, the invader began approaching me, calmly. I couldn't quite read its expression, but its presence suggested it meant me no harm. Its movements were graceful, stepping lightly on its feet, letting its arms sway loosely. Its shoulders were relaxed, its breathing tranquil.

Finally, we met face to face, and the Zelton glanced down at my waist. After a moment, my gaze followed. The invader had offered me one of its hands. I looked back up into its eight eyes and it subtly inclined its head toward me. Slowly, I joined my hand with the Zelton's, and we shared a nod. The creature expressed a noise that almost seemed pleased. *BANG!* The alien stumbled into me as its legs gave out, clutching at me. I gasped as I observed the Zelton gaze up at me, helplessly. Though I might not have been able to see what it felt in its eyes, I could see life fade from them as the being gave one final hiss of a breath. Its grip slowly gave out and I helped rest the Zelton on the ground.

The water was disturbed, as the shooter began his approach. Lifting my head toward him, it didn't take me long to recognize his broad figure. The Diramal chuckled, as he lorded over me.

"Pitiful," the Diramal said, as he aimed his pistol at me.

Amat, fight... I heard my father's voice in my head, faintly.

The Diramal chuckled sinisterly as he pulled back on the hammer of his weapon. In a fluid movement I pushed off the ground and reached for the pistol to disarm the Diramal, only to stumble forth, past his vanishing body. I looked all around; the man was nowhere to be found. My gaze returned to the dead Zelton, who had also gone missing.

"*Tsk, tsk, tsk...*" I spiraled up to my feet swiftly and faced the speaker behind me. Only... he wasn't who I expected. I lowered my aim, dumbfounded by his appearance. "You've no idea how greatly this desperate dream of negotiation and unlikely peace dulls our mind."

He was me, but not in nature. This mirrored version of myself had an almost unfiltered deviousness to him that needed neither words nor action to show it was there. His skin was somehow paler; perhaps it was in part due to the strained black veins that bulged from the exposed skin at his neck and hands. His eyes were a deeper blue that almost seemed to transcend a dark purple as the dim light shifted about his irises. And that hidden smile, formed by the effortless, subtle curvature of his lips. Not only a mere expression of confidence, but also sly and deceitful. He walked up to me this... reflection. Taking his time with every step.

"At last, we meet, face to face," he said.

"Funny you say that. There's a guy, identical to yourself that I see 'most every day when I come across a mirror. Though he's much better looking than you," I replied.

The other me snorted.

"I'm no reflection. If you truly knew who I was, you'd find that we're not so different from one another," he said.

I shifted, pondering the hidden message to this... opposite.

"A moment ago, you rejoiced in the fact that we've finally met, one on one with each other. But in what context have we encountered one another before?" I asked.

"We have been in contact almost every day since you enlisted in the Alpha program. Back then, we formulated a deeper synergy, and there wasn't much that divided our two characters. Ah, but when your father pulled you back under his wing, he polluted your mind with a certain rebelliousness that parted our connection." The other me started to circle myself as he spoke. "Your father implemented ideals that allowed you to consider possibilities outside the boundaries of our moral compass, to *spit* upon our duty to our country and question the authority... of the Diramal—"

"Do not lecture me on how I have performed my duties to my country, nor my unruly behavior to the *former* Diramal. My actions there are justified in the immeasurable corruption he enacted during his reign," I barked.

"Perhaps." The other me swiftly leaned in beside my ear as he uttered the word. "But that still doesn't change the fact that we are one and the same."

The reflection stood before me and reached his arm out. In his palm rested a pistol.

You must fight, Amat... I heard my father's voice cry out dimly in the back of my mind.

Before I felt my arm move, I had reached for the gun and enveloped my fingers around the grip. The other me gestured off to the side with his arm, bearing that same smile on his face. I turned my head in the direction his hand pointed and witnessed an invader... a child, standing idle, staring blankly at the both of us.

"Kill it," said the other me.

Once again, hardly noticing that my body had made the adjustments, I found myself aiming down the pistol's sight at the child's head. My index finger twitched at the trigger, squeezing it subconsciously, not hard enough to fire. And in this daze of movements, I might have gone through with it. If it wasn't for the innocence I saw hidden behind the child's eyes.

Fight it, Amat, fight... my father said distantly in my head.

A child, I thought.

Even at the end of a barrel, the youngling seemed as clueless and unthreatened from the moment it first appeared. Though my intent was good, my arm trembled at the effort to lower my guard. Even retracting my index finger from the trigger palpitated my heart.

"Kill it, this is the *spawn* of your enemy!" the other me barked. It was then I noticed his body was pressed to the back of mine, his arm guiding my aim down at the child Zelton.

"No," I growled, tensing my neck. "Not my enemy."

With a tense stretch of my hand, I released the gun and let it drop to the floor. My dark reflection fled to the shadows as I gasped for breath. Only a few moments passed before he returned.

"*Tsk, tsk, tsk*, you're sick. These creatures have slaughtered millions of innocents, no doubt many among them were children no older than this *pest* that stands before you and you'd let it live?!" My reflection shook his head. "Disgusting."

In the blink of an eye, I saw fast ripples trail out from where the pistol rested. The other me had altered time to retrieve it. I widened my eyes.

Amat, fight! My father's voice was clearer than ever.

I jolted into altered time, kicking one, two steps toward my dark reflection, his gun already aimed at the child. I reached my arm out to push him aside. My ability to move as quickly as I hoped was delayed as I witnessed the reflection turn his head toward me. Inches away from his body as he curled his lips up to his eyes and pulled the trigger.

"No!" I yelled, as I stumbled to the ground, having been somehow forced out of my altered time state. I shook the water off my face as I pushed myself off the ground and turned back toward the child. The sight before me forced my legs to quiver and stumble back onto my knees. A slaughter. Endless it was, and for the first time in all my experiences in this void, the water was accompanied by a color that seemed to seep naturally with the scenery of the area. The blue blood that drained from countless young bodies of the Zeltons.

Words couldn't fully form themselves from my mouth, and my muscles were weighed down by the overwhelming shame I felt. Though I had not done this, a part of me had and from that I felt unworthy to touch even a single body that surrounded me. Then came the pain, the mourning pain of a million mothers, the raging fury of a million fathers. But what was worse was the result of the remorseless action I had undertaken. My sight was abruptly internalized as I was shown what could have been out of every life I had robbed. That was almost enough to kill my very spirit.

In my unimaginable sorrow, I felt a hand rest itself on my shoulder. I was still too weak to even look up.

"Amat, look at me, son," my father said.

It was an effort, but my eyes met with his.

"Dad... did I do this? Did I slaughter innocents when the code nine neuro-chip dominated my conscience?" I asked.

"No. But this may yet be a possible future that you will unfold. Should you allow that double of yourself to overtake your character," replied my father.

"What is he?" I asked.

"He's you, Amat. A trait born within yourself, birthed with his own scar of evil. And he is *very* strong. What you just went through was your first victory against him."

"You'd call this victory? This?!" I blurted.

"In this void, as you observed, your traits are separated, your bodies discerned. Thus, your actions are your own in this context. You didn't pull the trigger, he did," my father explained.

"I could have done something," I said.

"You did. You chose mercy and you wept for the losses of your enemies. You chose love, Amat. That is why you mourn as you do now. And that is more powerful than any cruelty, or dark influence," said my father.

"Love couldn't save any child that died here," I replied.

"Did you see their lives? What they all could have accomplished if this great tragedy hadn't befallen them?"

"I can't remember how they all went," I replied.

"But you did see them?" my father asked.

"Yes."

"Then they are saved. Their bodies may be limp, but you will carry on their lives, in memory." My father placed a firm grip on my shoulder. "The point to all this was to stress you're fighting a war on three fronts. Against the Diramal, the Zeltons, and yourself. And the danger of you losing the third is both highly crucial and pivotal."

"To what?" I asked.

"The fate of the cosmos," said my father.

XIV
Bug-mare

I opened my eyes to Mae's staring back at me, her exposed fizer dimly illuminating her face. I glanced at her hand that had paused short of my helm. I revealed my face to her. We were both relieved to see one another well and safe.

"How long have you been up?" I asked.

"Not long."

I sighed as I arched my back.

"I already know why you came back to help me, so I won't ask. What I'd rather know is why you feel that way in the first place? How can you feel the way you do for me, Mae, even after three years apart from each other?"

Mae seemed almost offended by the question, briefly. Then she placed her hand over my chest, looking down toward my heart.

"There are lots of reasons for it. Some, perhaps most rather, are a mystery to me. But the most outstanding reason, is this, your heart. You're very selective about who you show its qualities to. But when you do, I can see how deeply it loves and cares despite your brittle persona that you often take on. Where others have their feelings, their strengths and weaknesses all over the place, you demonstrate control over yourself. Does that answer your question?" asked Mae as she looked up at me.

I took Mae's hand and brought it up to my lips, pressing them to her cold armored knuckles.

"You see more in me than I do, myself. I can't put into words why I feel for you the way I do. I can only give you assurance that you rest in the place of my heart where I hold my family."

My eyes drifted from our locked gazes, shifting down at our hands. Mae brought hers up to my chin and joined our gazes once again.

"It's enough," Mae replied with a smile.

Mae and I kissed passionately.

"Are you ready to move?" I asked.

Mae nodded.

The outside world was silent and still, but I knew our enemies crept close in the shadows. It would only be a matter of time before they showed themselves again.

"Promise me one thing, Mae," I said, once we scanned the area. "If we're separated or worse, and you find your way back to the others before me, promise you'll go and help my sister and cousins. I don't know how, but I can sense they're in distress."

Mae took my hand.

"We'll go back for them, together."

I shook my head.

"Promise me," I said.

"I promise," Mae replied, tightening her grip on my hand.

We took our time exiting the ruined home we took refuge in, scanning the area for signs of our enemies. Their cries still mockingly within earshot.

"Alright, let's go, or this game will never end," I said, looking over to Mae. "Be ready for them."

Mae nodded and together we dashed out from the ruined building in altered time, heading northwest, hoping to regroup with the others. Though the streets appeared empty, I could feel hidden eyes on us. Thus, I kept my wits about me, glancing around from moment to moment, to ensure none of the eyes watched too closely.

I signaled Mae to pause after we'd been running around for a time, finding no trace of the others. I opened a channel after we'd pulled ourselves out of altered time.

"Shím, Aod, this is Diramal Criptous, come in. Mae and I are on the move, seeking your location; we need coordinates ASAP," I said.

There was no reply. I cursed under my breath at the thought of what that could mean. I paced forward furiously as I sighed.

"Aod, Shím, report—" BOOM! A flash of green light from behind sent me flying several meters across the street. Midair, I altered time and flipped my body around so that my feet would grind across the pavement. My armor steamed as I panted, flicking my glance up toward Mae. I was relieved to see the blast had not reached her. She stood tall, looking around in every direction for our enemies, weapon in hand. I let out a heavy exhale as I found the strength in me to fight again. I was about to join her side, as I took up arms and glanced up at the building to my left. Saw the dim outlines of the Shadow Scar leaping out from the high stories in a seemingly endless flood. Before I could take two steps, a dozen of the disfigured creatures had set themselves between myself and Mae as more followed. I saw her raise her gun to them, but I shook my head. Despite its uselessness in the space of altered time, I flailed my arm to Mae and yelled: "Run!"

I did not turn my back to her until she'd left my sight. Interestingly, none of the Shadow Scar chased after her, at least none that I could clearly see. I fired my E.S.P. 101 at the growing formation of Shadow Scar and finally, another chase began.

(Zothra)

My hand was raised high as I stood beside a fellow Varx, armed with a plasma canon. Her name was Skítha, and she exclaimed an eager phrase in her native tongue as she knelt there, holding Amat in her sight. I swiftly took note of her finger pressing on the trigger.

"You will refrain from pressing any further or you will lose that finger," I said.

Skítha glanced up at me.

"Watch him," I commanded.

The Varx shrugged her sight back to her aim. With my sharp eyes, I observed Amat take a few brisk steps away from the human, Mae Kalbrook. I clenched my fist as I gave the order.

"Fire," I said.

I watched as the red ball of light hurled its way down to the Criptous boy, landing inches away from his back. The force of the blast sent him flying several meters. His *concubine*, Mae, took notice of the incoming blast and rolled out of its way. I smiled balefully, sighing with a cruel satisfaction. A confident smirk on my face with one hand held high, I kept the ravenous Varx at bay. Then unclenched my fist and gracefully whipped my open hand forth. The Varx at my back streamed out of the building that concealed us, while Quavek strode to my side.

"And so, the chase goes on. I'll see to it that the Varx stay on Amat, so that you'll have Mae to yourself. Though she will surely try to help him," I said.

"No doubt she will, but it will not prove to be problematic. I shall find my opening to take her," replied Quavek.

"Then let us delay our tasks no further. Proceed Qi'val."

(Mae)

Amat's pursuers stuck to him hard and ruthlessly. Though he urged me to flee, I could not, in good conscience, leave the father of my child to fend for himself. I chased from afar, eyeing those that snatched at Amat's heels. Any that came too close to him met with my keen aim before they could reach their various appendages toward Amat. I chose my shots sparingly, so as not to attract the Shadow Scar to me, nor Amat, who would surely act rashly if he knew I was near. I felt Quantum Fade casting over my heart and consciousness after having kept up with Amat for a time. But I pushed through, determined to buy Amat the necessary time to devise an escape strategy.

In my struggle, I briefly developed a sort of sixth sense. My intuition spiked in its sensitivity. Somehow, I knew I was being followed. Despite this, I could not take my focus from Amat in my drowsy rush of adrenaline.

As my vision blurred, I could hardly see, yet still perceived a lone Shadow Scar cutting in ahead of Amat. The creature no doubt wanted to catch Amat off guard. I shook my head as I raised my aim, taking deep breaths as I tracked the lone Shadow Scar's movements. My heart palpitated in my ears as I squeezed the trigger with what seemed my final flare of strength. My body fell limp to the ground and my breath rushed out of my lungs.

(Quavek)

I maintained my distance from Kalbrook as I sensed her strength fading. Only after I saw that she had fatigued herself and her body had fallen flat on the ground, did I get closer. I retracted her helm, observed her nostrils flaring with every quick breath she took and felt her pulse.

Quantum Fade.

I reached into my uniform and pulled out a sedative, which I used to stabilize Mae's systems. Even if I wanted her dead, those were not our orders from the Diramal. The sedative would be enough to stabilize Mae's breathing and spare her from the more adverse effects of Quantum Fade, but not enough to fully stimulate her consciousness.

Next, I pulled out a device of my own making that I called the hippo-mite. Imperceivable to the naked eye, this tiny bot was designed specifically for finding its way into the human brain, via the ear canal, latching itself onto the hippocampus and returning to a panel device, where all of the subject's memories and thoughts are displayed.

My eyes, capable of homing in on a speck of dust, observed the hippo-mite crawl out from its compartment after I'd opened it. When the hippo-mite activated, I sprouted one of my limbs from my chest and extended one of my long fingers to it. The minute bot hopped onto my flesh, and I eased my reach toward Mae's ear, to which the hippo-mite swiftly entered. All I could do then was wait and observe for its exit. An early sign of this is a drop of blood leaking from the ear. It is caused by added stress to the eardrum contributed by the hippo-mite's second pass through it. But, overall, it is quite harmless to the subject.

As soon as I saw the blood oozing, I reached my finger back out for the hippo-mite's departure and returned it back to the panel. I activated the screen and two columns appeared: one for internal dialogue and another for memories, separated into hundreds of thousands of files with vague descriptions beside each of what their content entailed, from what the hippo-mite could process and distinguish. I sat back and altered time, to an almost complete stop, giving me plenty of time to look over what rested inside Mae's head.

Fortunately for Mae, there didn't seem too much I could use against her, in my contribution to the mission. Many of the one-liner descriptions about the files came off as lighthearted as I passed my glance over them all. She was very close to her family. But then, on that subject, I finally found something of use. A fire that had tragically taken away her parents when she was hardly ten years old. After having opened the file, I saw that it was her older sister, Reia, who led Mae out of the flames. As I listened to the voice inside her head throughout the traumatic experience, she

153

seemed to have since grown fearful or at least disturbed by the sight of fire.

Certainly could be useful, I thought, flexing my pincers.

A little further down the line, I learned of Reia's recent passing and how Mae had avenged her death by killing the Varx that murdered her.

Might be wise to steer clear of this. Regardless of its virtues, it may prove to be too surreal for Mae. Which might cause her to snap out more easily of the little game I have planned.

Finally, I reached the more recent days and came across something that surpassed all of Mae's other traumas and the potential leverage they held over her.

So, you're pregnant, hm? I thought with a chuckle. *That'll do just fine.*

(Mae)

In the surrounding darkness that we are all met with before we enter the world of our dreams, I heard a steady heartbeat. It sounded faint at first, as if I were somehow hearing it through a thin wall. The beat grew louder and with every thud, I saw a dim light ignite, like it was shining through something. The light hovered closer, and I started to perceive an outline of an infant. The beat continued in its *thud-thud, thud-thud, thud-thud…*

I reached my arms out to embrace the child. A subtle breeze blew past my fur. I could see its resting eyes, so peaceful as it hovered over my hands. *Snap!* A large, hairy figure, with drooping limbs and a wide gurgling mouth chomped into the upper half of the child. It stared at me with those numerous black, empty eyes as it continued to slowly devour the infant. I screamed in horror, not only at what I saw, but at the sincere sense of loss I felt. Loss of what, I couldn't say in that instance, but it was an immense fear that I dared not investigate.

I found myself alone in a dark room… a bedroom. A place that was neither familiar nor unfamiliar. I'd never seen any of the surroundings before, but there was some hint that suggested a day may come when I might. I reached my hand over to the other side of the bed as my eyes adjusted to the darkness. I was faintly surprised to see that no one was there. I took in the rest of the room, where some pictures hung; their glass covers reflected glints of a moon that was not Anua's light. Four faces were visible, and two figures stood shorter than the ones that stood behind them. I had barely started to process their features when I heard a cry, a babe's cry. Instinct took over as I whipped the sheets aside and stormed out of the room. I followed the dire wails up a flight of stairs to a smaller room. I kicked the door open after having been confronted with its lock. There I saw my son, soiling his sheets with his tears. Before I could move to claim him, in the blink of an eye, the room was enveloped in flames. I raised my arms defensively but not long enough to be distracted from the danger that surrounded my child. I whipped my head back in his direction and I was relieved to see that the flames had not touched him. Wasting no time, I ran across the flames, barefoot. The adrenaline in my veins numbed the pain as I grabbed him and looked him up and down to ensure he had not been injured. He hadn't.

Just as I thought to turn the other way and escape the flames, the window that sat high on the wall, letting in cool moonlight, twisted into a black, empty void. I crept back as I heard horrid screeches. The babe's screams escalated in his terror with every screech that followed. I pressed the child's precious head into my breast as I twisted it away from the spontaneous manifestation. Which, in that moment, sprouted a shelled head with hundreds of wriggling teeth, and below it perched two spiked, grasping forelegs. The head jerked and twitched its way out of the portal as the rest of its monstrous, mucous-covered body followed. I still hadn't seen the full extent of it when the creature finally stopped to notice me. It hissed a phrase that I couldn't fully comprehend. Regardless, I was hardly concerned with the thing emerging into my child's room as I observed the flames stretch higher. I turned briskly and zipped through the blazing waves, shielding my son with my arms and face.

The creature let out a retched *squeal* as I marched down the steps. Before I reached halfway, something fat and wet smacked itself against my back and knocked me down to the ground. Still, my tight, protective hold on my child held firm. But then, again, the fat body trampled itself over me, crushing me. The babe screamed its cries of terror still, muffled in my clothes. When the creature's body finally passed over me entirely, much of my strength had left me and the child rolled just out of my reach

155

as my arm plopped flat. Soaking in the mucus that filled my mouth and nostrils, I stretched my fingertips toward my son. Steadily closing the gap, centimeters away from his wrappings… a long, bony leg smashed itself on my hand. I *howled* at the shattering of my bones. The leg slid itself over my broken fingers and against my child, dragging him closer to the hideous thing. I pushed myself off the ground despite my pain, but before I could rise to meet the creature face to face, the dream had ended… only to begin another.

With the imagery of the former events still fresh in my mind, I found myself somewhere else. In another black void that had no connection to where I was before. I could hear my own heart, raging, feel the anxious sweat rolling down the side of my face. It was almost enough to wake me.

Wait… wake me?

Slowly, something came into view, a crystalized substance, yellow in color, glowing in the dark. Like the first… dream… it hovered toward me. I realized the child was frozen inside it; solidified in a frightened pose. Its arms and legs stretched out with its face stuck in a wrinkled cry. I could still hear the infant's screams, somehow, echoing in the darkness. The closer it got, the outline of the crystal would flash a different appearance, greeting me with a long, terrifying face. Two large, lifeless eyes, a fine jawline with no obvious sign of a mouth, a bulging forehead with a short antenna at either side. The face continued to flash in and out of my perception as the crystallized infant drew closer. With every flash, the face looked more horrid. My chest rose and fell heavily with the anticipation of what would happen once our faces met. But then I swiftly recalled the notion I had earlier.

Hold on, this can't be real, and it isn't. The child hasn't been born yet.

Blue tentacles squirmed out of the place its mouth should have been as the face inched closer.

I'm dreaming and I need to wake up.

Bushy hairs sprouted from the holes that were its ears.

Come on, Mae, wake up.

Melting galaxies poured out of its nostrils, inches away from me.

Wake me up! The words were in my head, yet I heard myself cry them out as clearly as if I had screamed them aloud.

My eyelids whipped open, and I sprung up just as quickly, gasping and panting for breath. I couldn't see much at first, as my helm had been retracted somehow. Something rustled within the room. I swiveled my head in its direction, only to witness the tumbling rocks that it pushed back in its scurry. I did not remove my gaze from that dark void where no light reached, across the room, as I reached my hand around in search of my fallen weapon. At last, my fingertips found the barrel and I inched it closer into my palm. Armed, I enveloped my helm around my head. There was a delay in the activation of the molecular sensor. Finally, they bolted, the room lit up in a blue hue and a *face*... a wide, flat, walnut-shaped face, with small antennae stretching from the tip of its head, bladed bones extended from its cheeks and narrow drooping mouth, with eyes the size of fists, stared back at me. It did not move, this bug thing, but we were both well aware of one another. And it bore its stare even harder at me, if only to intimidate.

Without altering time, I primed my weapon and fired at the creature. Whether any of my shots landed, I couldn't say; the thing had vanished before I took my finger off the trigger.

I glanced around, frantically searching to see if the creature was still nearby. I found no sign of it. I allowed myself a sigh as I leaned over the ground, feeling my abdomen. The knowledge that the soul of my unborn son was safe and sound gave me comfort.

If it is to be a boy.

A great crash sounded in the distance, followed by distinct faint screeches and cries. I rushed to my feet and looked out of an opening of the building. I couldn't see anything, so I climbed higher, to the roof. There I saw a cloud of dust rolling over the streets and past some of the buildings to the west.

Amat!

XV
Slip
(Amat)

Running down the street from my pursuers, I sensed their speed clutching at my heels, and I saw a line of ammunition spew across my way from above at a Shadow Scar that nearly collided with me. I looked back in the direction the fire had come from.

Mae… please, Goddess, keep her out of this.

I leaned forward and arched my head down, taking short, quick strides as I prepared myself to move faster.

Perhaps if I can outrun Mae and force the Shadow Scar to move faster with me, it will keep her out of trouble.

I picked up my pace, shifting the movement of my legs to such an extreme it felt like they'd gone numb. A sonic outline warped at my back as I sprung forward, quaking the ground, shattering nearby glass. I had never gone so fast, but this hardly distracted me. All I cared about was getting Mae safely out of harm's way.

Unable to hear my own heartbeat; hardly able to perceive my surroundings, my vision shifted inward. The steady breath of air entering my nostrils and leaving my mouth filled my ears as the world ahead twirled and spun upside down. Was I entering another dimension, another reality? Some splice between the physical world and time itself? *If such things were possible, what marvels would await me there,* I wondered. And it was then, I drifted between space and time for what seemed like eons.

My very essence had split, stretching across countless dimensions. Each one showed something different from the last. There was no place my spirit had ventured that I could not see, somehow witnessing them all in the same moment. It would be impossible to recount all the places I saw, yet some looked bright and happy; some looked bright, yet set back a few generations in their technological advancements; some looked as dark and gloomy as the world I had come to know; some looked grimmer, encapsulated by evil. Some even looked like a world I had never seen before. It was still Galiza, but not the one I'd been brought up in. Whether these perceptions were simply of another plane of existence or time itself, I didn't know.

My consciousness was not of my mind, body, or soul. It was immense, beyond what we could comprehend in our perception of everyday life. Not only did I see these places, but I was somehow connected to each of them, in every way that they existed. Did that make their existence any more real? If I kept on in my race against my enemies, would my mind and soul pass over into one of these neighboring realities of my world?

Numb, of my own self-awareness, I couldn't even feel my arms pumping, my body trembling with every step of my sprint. I could hardly hear my own breath. Had I slipped too far into the reaches of altered time?! No, I'd gotten myself into this, and I could pull myself out. I focused all my attention back onto my physical body. I breathed harder, thinking it would disrupt the flow of the time warp. The aching pain and fatigue slowly caught up to me as I hoped it would. A ghosted flame felt as if it were burning in my lungs, legs, and shoulders. My attention narrowed back into my body. My sight was fogged, however, and my entire body was encompassed by a thin misty shield that guarded me from walls and barriers in my path.

Gradually bringing myself to a halt, as the blurring shield faded, I was able to take in my surroundings of a ruined building. Focusing on what rested dead ahead of me: a clutter of sharp, rusted debris. I tried to stop myself, but my body was too heavy to halt my own momentum. Diving to the ground, the rigid scraping of my armor eased my impetus… but not enough to avoid the large gaping hole, set a few feet before the debris. With haste, I reached for the knife at my waist to stab into the ground, knowing that the force may yet have been enough to dislocate my shoulder. Unsheathing my blade, the ground fell away from below my chest, and I plummeted a good seven feet deep into a pit, landing on one of the scattered, sharp metal rods sticking out of the ground. Air left my mouth in a gasp as the jagged point pierced through the right side of my abdomen. The pain was brief thanks to the shock that forced my eyelids closed. Bleeding, alone, with not enough time to know if I had escaped my enemies or if they would soon catch up to me.

James Alan McG

(Zothra)

My fellow Varx and I stood astounded at what we had witnessed. I pushed past my troops to witness Amat's remarkable stunt.

"No one, not even the Diramal himself, has moved so fast within the constructs of altered time," I said.

I didn't know whether to be intimidated or impressed.

"Should we follow his trail?" asked Vormaul Huvara, as clashes of Amat's body pounding through rubble constructs echoed across the air.

"No, I think not. For now, we will regroup and head for the Commathor Bridge. That is where the main party of humans have surely fled and where Amat will be headed as well," I replied.

"So, this isn't over?" asked Vormaul Huvara.

A great wave pulsed across the land and a building in the far distance moaned as it came crashing down against another.

"This is all far from over, Vormaul Huvara. And Galiza will not be the place it all concludes. But it may just be Amat Luciph Criptous's final resting place, soon enough."

(Amat)

I woke up to the sound of… some kind of gel being laced onto my wound. There was a cold burn sizzling over my flesh. Looking to my side, I jerked at the sight of one of the invaders standing beside me. My spasm choked my cry and only added to the pain in my side.

The alien scurried away, but only so far as to be out of sight. It stood at the rim of the pit above me. Grasping tightly onto the sharp rod that had nearly impaled me, I lightly placed my fingertips on the gel. It was boiling and it had stopped the bleeding. I growled as I lifted my head up, trying to spot the invader. With it nowhere in sight, I grasped the rod with both hands, breathed quickly, and lifted myself from it. My strength invigorating and fading simultaneously as my arms trembled with every inch of progress that came in prying my body from the rod. My insides sliming and grinding against the rugged edges of the rod. Fortunately, the rusted metal sprout was not that long, and hadn't protruded too high behind my back. Still, I whined as I cleared myself from it. A flood of cold

160

washed over my gut and I quickly entered a state of shock as I fell back onto the ground. I knew I was bleeding internally, likely in my colon, where the rod struck. I pressed my hands firmly over the wound as my teeth chattered and my chest rose and fell vigorously.

So, this is how I leave the world.

A dark figure arched itself over me. Its movements were so quick I couldn't make out its form. The figure had moved my arms aside, holding them firmly but not violently above my head. Not that there was much I could do about it anyway, since much of my strength had fled. Next, I felt another hot chill fill the gap in my wound; swift it came, like the figure's movements. I had hardly any time to process it before I was turned over, with my front on the ground and the same was done to the rear of my wound. The figure let out a quick hiss and moved away from me. With my vigor somewhat restored, I reached a hand over my wound. It had been completely covered with the gel and a comforting warmth substituted my harsh internal cold.

I flipped myself over, catching my breath, and saw it again—the Zelton, standing at the high rim of the pit. There was a faint sense of familiarity I sensed about the alien, like our paths had crossed before.

"Ah, you look like the same Zelton that came before me at Claumidin. I guess negotiations turned out better than I imagined." I chuckled at myself, feeling like the fool in this scenario. I don't know why, but it suddenly just came over me how pointless negotiations with the invaders seemed, given how the language barrier proved, time and time again, to be one of the biggest faults in this endeavor.

Moments after my silent remark, the invader did reply, however, in its own native tongue, of course. Yet its tone sounded reassuring somehow, in its intent. As if it had made an agreeable gesture at my comment on the negotiations. As if *it* understood *me*. I struggled for a moment, trying to find the right words to say next.

"Curious, your tone suggested you understood my words just a moment ago… though I wouldn't know for certain except maybe through this. If you could do me the gesture of a head nod, to show that you understand what I say now, I'd be very—"

Before I could finish my words, the invader had nodded. My mind filled with ecstasy at the profound discovery I had just made. The expression on the Zelton's face seemed the same, yet I sensed amusement and equal excitement within its attitude.

"So, you do understand us," I said.

The Zelton nodded once more. I laughed. Something caught the Zelton's attention, luring its attention elsewhere and compelling it to dash off as a light shone its way.

"No, wait! Come back," I called.

"Amat?" a woman's voice sounded.

"Mae? Is that you? Ahhh!" I asked.

"Yes… are you hurt?" Mae asked, as she came to the edge of the pit, shining her light down on me.

"I was injured…" I said, grunting as I pushed my back against the wall to find my feet, hugging my wound. "But I'm… I'll be alright."

"Goddess!" Mae gasped. Mae extended her hand down to me. "Can you reach up?"

"I think so, here, lend me your other arm, I don't want to risk straining anything internally on my right side," I replied.

Mae switched her arms. I took one deep breath, followed by a sequence of quick ones, kicked up the wall and reached for Mae. The wound in my side hurt, but not as much as it likely would have if I were hanging by my right arm. Mae strived to pull me up with all her might and didn't waste time in prying my dead weight out of the pit. As she arched her arm up high, she rolled back and used her own weight to bring me to the edge. Mae pulled me over her and rested. We took a long moment to catch our breath, looking at one another through the dark HUDs of our helms.

"Are you alright?" I asked.

Mae gave a light chuckle and shook her head at my concern for her instead of myself.

"Are you?" The question caught me off guard. I had to stop and think before replying.

"I am," I replied.

Mae nodded.

"Let me have a look at the wound."

I exhaled.

"Alright." I crawled back and sat up against some nearby rubble as Mae shone her light down at my injury. She tilted her head at the strange red-brown, smooth texture that filled the hole in my flesh. Even I was a little taken aback to see its content, yet not as much, knowing something had been done to seal the wound.

"One of the invaders applied some kind of healing agent to keep me from bleeding out while I was alone," I said.

"You... felt them do this?"

"I was conscious." I nodded.

"Does it hurt?" asked Mae, as she felt around the edges.

"Not as much as it did when I removed the rusted rod from my flesh. Little did I know that it kept me from bleeding out. I spent a few seconds on my back, going into shock, and then this happened. The invader remained close by until you showed up. Still, it was astonishing behavior to observe—an invader demonstrating concern for a human life, a soldier's life more specifically."

"It is astonishing," replied Mae, not sounding as enthusiastic as myself.

I started to push myself off the ground, shifting my weight to the left side. Mae raised her arms out to me when she saw that I'd nearly stumbled but I raised a hand to her, assuring her that I was alright and found my feet. I took one step, followed by a heavy breath. The vibration that shot through my body irritated my wound, but I managed to stand upright beside Mae. She helped to wrap my arm around her shoulder with our eyes locked.

"Think I'll need help with this one," I said.

I could sense the smile behind Mae's helm and in her words: "I've been waiting to hear that one."

We'd wandered up around two blocks, heading dead north.

Surely by this time the Irens have cleared the city... I hope. It does concern me that I didn't receive any reply from anyone over comms.

Fortunately, in all that time, neither Mae nor I were alarmed by any shriek or swift movements in the rubble.

What I did in our last encounter with the Shadow Scar must have made them cautious to follow us further. That or they have other things in store for us.

What had the world become? No, not the world, what had come to it? What long line of misfortunes were laid in fate to lead us all down this path of wanton death? What future, what past even, might have played out so differently, had the universe not allowed such cataclysms to pass? Surely, as beings that exist within its constructs, share its ancient manifestation and wide space, it must have a will, a tolerance for what games we play throughout its anatomy.

Funny how we should worship Goddesses and objects that we associate them with. Would it not make more sense to worship the universe itself, as it was the bringer of all things present and past? Not as a thing, a physical place or concept of how it all came to be, but as a fused entity that we ourselves are a part of. With such a perspective in mind, could it be so much more difficult to think such tragedies to fruition?

But this war was not a thought. No one saw it coming, except, perhaps a select few. The former Diramal among them.

What a beauty death must be to witness for oneself, a peace to experience, in a place so chaotic. If not a place to be, as no one can say for sure a Luminous Paradise or even an eternal walk across shadow could await us after we pass. But if it was not a place that awaited me, surely a person. Yes, what exhilaration would await me when, at last, I am joined with my father, on whatever plane he continues to exist. What adventures we should have together, there. Why then should I stop myself from going now?

As the muffled sound of the Iren accent breached its way into my comms, I felt my legs give out after two more steps. My eyes rolled back into my head, and I fell limp to the ground. The last I heard was the sound of Mae's screams as she fell with me. All sound faded into silence before I lost total awareness of my surroundings. I felt my body fill with a new awareness I had never been so conscious of. In my final moment of conscious feeling, I had the sense that I could either shut down for a time… or ascend from my fleshy conduit. It was then I slipped away, like some great force had pulled my fingers free of their grasp around a deep edge. Was this death, or another slip between spaces?

XVI
Run for the Commathor Bridge
(Amat)

It felt like a deep, unbreakable rest, dying. I was beginning to understand what dawned on me, despite my stubborn grit to stay grounded within the constructs of my body. At the dawn, there is not a place to arrive, nor an almighty entity put forth to judge you. There is nothing, no guide to sway your choice to go on further, no gate you are met with, not even a void. You are suspended, physically and consciously. Left with a choice, an intuition that something awaits you beyond the dawn, or a fight to remain tied to your life in the mortal world until your body is healed well enough for you to return. And it is a fierce battle of wills indeed, to maintain a sense of physical life, mental and emotional ties. Everything that binds your experience to reality against the fleeting temptation to let go, to unveil the curiosity of witnessing what awaits you on the other side. But I would not go there, not out of fear nor pride, but duty. Never before had I received a sense that I had a greater purpose left unfulfilled and I would hold on as long as I could until my friends—

A gentle, admiring chuckle interrupted my will was. Golden streaks stretched into view, from the corner of my perception, tied to a radiant figure who gracefully stepped before me. Hundreds of little lights composed and twirled about his figure. Though I'd never seen this entity, something about him was faintly familiar. Some suppressed nostalgia had been awakened by the mere presence of this being. He did not come as a judge and I sensed deeply that he was not meant to be there at all. Yet there he was.

"How I pride myself in you, Reinosso. Call it stubbornness, call it will, call it destiny…" The being slowly shook his head, his hands wrapped around his back. "You are different from the others, no doubt."

I couldn't speak the words, but the intent was there; my curiosity to know who this being was and he sensed it, acknowledged it with a nod but did not answer. Only looked away, briefly. When he turned back to me, I observed in awe, as his appearance had changed abruptly. Where once he looked to be a gold, radiant being with human features, he now stood taller, his body was hard and shelled, engulfed in a red light. His head had three points, two extending from either side, and a third at the top. His mouth was a wide mandible, his nose flat and eyes thin. The legs were pegged, as were the arms, yet some sort of squirming appendages that might have served as fingers wiggled gently just outside the tips.

"The first has corrupted you and your kin so harshly that your very physical appearance has been altered. The presence of Drakkar within the Vix has affected you all in some way, dulling each of your powers."

Drakkar? Vix? What were these names the being had mentioned? The being looked away and once again his form changed, this time into a long creature with wiggling appendages and pink skin engulfed in a blue light. There wasn't a sign of a single bone in its anatomy, except for the numerous concentric rings of spiked teeth in its wide, round mouth, below its five orange eyes.

"You won't remember this interaction after you've returned, and you will return. I know that you would hold onto this place for an eternity before you allow yourself to move on from it." The being walked up to me, inches away from my vision. "I am sorry I'm not there to guide you, like I was for the others. I have seen, however, that you won't need me, for you are Reinosso, mightiest of the Hanu, the greatest leader of the Cosmos."

Once again, his form changed. In the blink of an eye, I didn't understand how, he had taken on the form of an invader, a Zelton engulfed in a green light.

"I say with confidence that you will be the one to set everything right again. The others, when you meet them, they may have their doubts, but you will see balance restored. You must, as there shan't be another."

Their voices called to me, sounding first as echoes from deep inside a tunnel. Creeping closer until they sounded like they were just beside me. I felt the warmth of two hands tightly grasped around one of my own. Warm tears falling on and trickling down my arm. As my fingers were reinvigorated with their own strength and life, I grasped back at the hands. Heard a gasp as she called my name once again.

"Amat?" Mae asked.

I sighed my first breath and promptly took in a deep inhale. I had never stopped breathing, but it had been slowed, severely. My eyes opened; their vision was blurred and irritated by the surrounding light, as if I had never used them before.

"Oh, thank the Goddess!" Mae cried as she leaned over me, hugging my shoulder.

It felt like little time had passed. I had no recollection of my interaction with the bright being from the dawn. It was as if Mae and I had been alone, walking the streets of Dunlark one minute, the next I was on that table, with everyone at my side.

"What happened?" I asked; my voice was weak and cracked easily.

"You nearly died, laddin. While the wound at your side had been sealed from bleedin' out, there was still much internal bleedin' that nearly took your life." Shím rubbed some of the fleshy, rubber-like residue that had sealed off my wound, between his fingers. "Curious, this stuff. How'd it get on ya?"

I took my time, proceeding to tell Shím and the others how the substance ended up on my wound.

"An invader?" replied Aod, sounding surprised.

"The same one that came forward to us at Claumidin, I suspect," I said.

"If it was, truly, it's curious enough that it would have tracked you all that way. But also to intervene in a time of need and keep you alive; it's unheard of among the invaders," said Mae.

"Not for their own kin, I'd imagine," I said. "Doesn't matter why it helped. What does, is how it will impact our future relationship with them. I have seen evidence that the invaders are harboring Skivs as much as we are. Protecting them from the presence of the militia. One can speculate as to what that means," I said.

Silence fell over the group. I finally broke it by asking: "Ah, where are we, anyway?"

"This is an old base of operation, just half a mile before the Commathor Bridge, beneath the surface," said Aod.

"I imagine it took some time to escort me here. And that my survival was in question," I said.

"We certainly had our doubts, laddin," said Shím.
"Aod, all of your people made it safely this far?" I asked.
Aod nodded her head. "They have."
I sighed with relief. "Ah, I did say that they'd all reach safety, didn't I?" I allowed a small, proud smile to grow on my face, briefly. "How soon then, can we expect to cross the bridge?"
"As soon as you're well—"
"Promptly," blurted Aod, over Mae.
Another silence fell over the group, and I could sense the tension between Aod and Mae. With a heavy sigh, I pushed myself off the table, gradually, to an upright position.
"Amat, no, don't push yourself. You need to restore your strength," said Mae.
When I was upright, I glanced into Mae's eyes, still holding her hand and once again I tightened my grasp on hers.
"Do you feel that? Your strength seeping into me? I do. We need to move, Mae; it sickens my heart to think of Galiza as a wasteland, a death sentence, but that is what it has become. And if we do not leave it soon, it will be a grave, shared by us all." I took my first couple of steps on the ground, standing straight. "I am well enough to proceed. Gather your people and prepare to lead the way," I said, staring deep into Aod's eyes.

As I restocked my suit with invader blood, I observed the state of my wound. I pressed and trailed my fingertips over the bandages. To my surprise, there was hardly any pain despite my fatigue. I lifted my bandages and studied the scar that couldn't have been more than a day old. While the bandages were stained with blood and the stitches were freshly woven into my skin, the wound was flat, not swollen. In fact, if the stitches had not been there, one might have assumed I never had a gaping wound at my abdomen to begin with.

Could this be an effect of the gel that the Zelton sprayed onto the wound? No, it was removed when the others tended to me. But, there's not even a rough scar. How can this be?

"Do you need help with your armor?" Mae's voice sounded behind me. My neck stiffened slightly as she caught me off guard. I let the bandages lay flat on my skin once again and turned toward her.

"No, thank you, my love," I said. Mae's jaw dropped. It was the first time I had addressed her so.

"Your love?" replied Mae with a smile.

"Yes," I said, walking up to her. I took Mae's hands with my own. "You are my love. I love you, Mae Kalbrook."

Mae blushed as she answered.

"I love you too, very much, Amat."

"I know you do. If this mission has taught me anything, it's that much. And while I couldn't always admit it, from our first getting to know each other, I have always held a place for you in my heart. I hope you can forgive me for the times I haven't been totally honest with you or neglected you," I said.

"Amat, where is all this coming from?" Mae asked.

I left her grasp, turning my back to her, stopping before my armor in its worn shape.

"I cannot recall where I went after having almost slipped out of the grasp of this world, but I cannot deny that my spirit fled somewhere else. I could have died, Mae, I may have even, for a time. That thought alone has simply made me more grateful for the blessings of my life, is all."

Mae walked to my side, turned my head toward her.

"You speak as if your time is so limited still," said Mae.

"Time is limited to us all. But mine is far from its end," I said reassuringly, despite it not feeling that way in my heart. I could not deny the fatigue that burdened me at that moment. This mission had worn through me; body and spirit. But so long as I breathed, even the dimmest spark of will would shine within me. It was what I was trained for.

"Diramal Criptous," said Aod. "Are you ready?"

I took a deep breath, stepped into my armor as it enveloped around me, turned toward Aod, and replied, "I am."

By the time we reached the bridge, most of my fatigue had faded away. Still, I prayed for an easy path to the base in Scoat'tir.

"I will take the rear," I announced to Aod. "I don't foresee us being confronted with our enemies ahead, but I do sense that they still linger on this side of the bridge somewhere."

"How can you be so sure?" Aod asked.

169

I ignored her question and scanned the area ahead.

"Mae, Shím, take command of our troops at either wing of the group, the water beneath the bridge is just as good a hiding place as any. I'll let you know when I'm in position," I said. I turned my back and headed to the tail of the crowd.

We took our time crossing the bridge; all militant eyes panned over their surroundings to keep the pack of helpless Skivs safe from any nearby threats. Once again, it seemed too quiet by the time we reached the halfway point across the bridge. A deliberate silence was held in the air, in the background of marching boots and skidding bare feet. It was the type of silence that you make while breathing, ever so subtly, to keep your presence unknown.

"Mae, Shím, send a few of your troops to the edge of the bridge, I want eyes on the water," I ordered.

"Understood, sir," replied Mae.

"Right away, laddin," said Shím.

We continued to press forward, with still no sign or report of anything off. Was I just being paranoid, or was there something to my intuition?

"Criptous." Aod's voice sounded over comms.

"Aod, what is it?" I replied.

"With the other end of the bridge comin' into view, as has something else. A large welcomin' party of invader forces."

"Do they appear hostile?" I asked.

"No, they're quite calm actually."

"Stand by to alter time, Aod, we're going to switch places in the pack on my mark," I said.

"Copy."

"In three, two, one, mark," I said.

I altered time and started to walk around the crowd of people on the right side. Sound in altered time is a lot like sound in space—you don't really hear it. Except, unlike space, here and there, deep rumbles sound, and if someone speaks or screams over comms, you can hear a delayed reverberation of their voice. But something seemed different this time around for me. I could almost hear more, as opposed to when I'd been moving in the normal flow of time. I found a certain clarity in my hearing that I'd not had a few moments prior.

Before I'd walked halfway past the group, I heard a sharp trickle that sounded like something had rippled over the water. I directed my attention to the noise instantly and stopped a moment to observe the troops walking past the edge to see if they'd noticed it. Their focus remained unaltered. I unholstered my pistol and slowly walked toward the edge of the bridge.

My own intuition was so vitalized; I didn't even consider thinking the words "I know you're there."

Standing right beside the passing troops, I witnessed a small metallic ball sail overhead and land inches away from the pack. *Bolting* and then sliding toward the grenade, I arched my body the moment my fingers clasped around it and launched the explosive into the air. I regulated time to warn my allies, my voice muffled slightly by the sound of the detonation.

"Grenade!" I yelled.

The troops all flinched at the sound of it going off and aimed all around as they tried to identify the attack's point of origin. At the same time, at the end of the bridge, the Zeltons let out their hissing screeches and started to disperse beneath the bridge and toward us.

"Everyone, hold your ground, get the Skivs across the bridge ASAP! Eyes on the lookout, suits active!" I yelled.

There was rustling in the waters below. Taking a closer look, I peered over the edge of the bridge and saw how the water boiled with frenzied movements between the Zeltons and the attackers. Before I could look too long, a dark blur leaped up in front of me. I raised my aim to shoot as I altered time instinctively. A second blur passed between us and struck the creature down before either one of us could harm the other. Just as I settled into my altered time state once again, my eyes trailed after the second figure. Before it stopped, I identified it—a Zelton, slowly turning back toward me as if it felt my eyes on its back. The Zelton nodded to me and swiftly made its way onward to continue its fight against the creatures.

An enemy in common, but it feels like more than that. Things are changing too rapidly between us.

I sent out a surge, regulated time, and relayed more orders to my troops.

"This is Criptous, speaking to all troops present. Do not fire upon any of the invader forces present. I repeat, do *not* fire on any of the invader forces present," I said.

"By the shadow of Anua, why shouldn't we?!" Aod broke in.

"That's the second time one of them saved my life. And most of their numbers appear to be in skirmishes with the other life forms beneath the bridge, the Shadow Scar," I said.

"Skátho-voír," Aod growled.

"Yes, judging from that, I think the invaders are trying to buy us some time to make it across the bridge fully," I said.

"Then let's not waste a moment of their sacrifice. All of you pick up the pace, move forward, don't stop. If you have children with you, beside you, pick 'em up and move faster. We need to get off the bridge," said Aod.

Aod and I returned to our positions at the front and rear of the pack, our eyes keen on the ensuing battle taking place. The Zeltons continued to fight *fiercely* in the waters, as there was hardly any sign of a Shadow Scar breaching from the water below. Though, when there was, a passing Zelton made short work of their presence. Striking it down and dragging it back into the river. We humans spent hardly any of our ammunition.

About ten feet away from the end of the bridge, a large bomb landed close to me while I was in regulated time. It detonated as I became aware of it. Instinctively, my body altered time on its own. The raw form of altered time felt so amplified and I used it to create a rupture in the ground, pounding the street with a stomp of my leg, shooting a force that sent several of the troops close by me out of harm's way. Just as quickly, my back leg was lifted from underneath me by the shock wave that launched me into the air. I could feel the growing temperatures scorching my flesh as portions of my armor tore free from their place. The burning pain eventually snapped me out of the altered time state and in an instant, I felt the full ferocity of the explosion, twirling and shooting my body into the air. *Howling* in my ascent, losing consciousness as I arched my way back down into the water. The impact woke me up before I could drift away. I shook my head, glancing all around me, witnessing the various blurs shifting in entangled movements with one another. With my raw, enhanced vision, bright blue bodies coiled against dim, purple bodies with distinct outlines across each one.

As water seeped into my helm, I took a quick breath of air that was steadily flowing out of my suit and started to swim up to the surface. Just before emerging, a large purple body collided with me, far more muscular and larger than myself. It dragged me back down with it, staring at me with narrow, depthless eyes. I almost recognized it. Its face scarred and its armor mutilated by a long-past strike of lightning. A crown of spikes trailed atop and along the back of its scalp. With as much strength as I could muster, I struggled against the Shadow Scar's grip to no avail, until a Zelton clashed into the Shadow Scar's side, digging its top and bottom claws into the creature's body. Its grasp loosened enough for me to escape. With my consciousness fading, I swam spastically to the surface. Knowing that the water in my helm wouldn't leak right away, I retracted it from my head. With a heavy gasp of relief, I filled my lungs with fresh air, only pausing a moment before swimming, in altered time, toward one of the pillars that held up the bridge. After having reached a pillar, I flicked out my claws and started to vigorously scale its side. Reaching the edge of the bridge, my fatigue finally caught up to me. My lungs burned from exhaustion and as I rested on my stomach, with my legs dangling, something heavy latched its claws into my calf.

The Shadow Scar had nearly dragged me back down to the water with it. If I didn't drag my claws deep into the sidewalk, the Shadow Scar may have done just that. Having halted our descent, I looked back to see the same Shadow Scar from the river hanging off my leg and a Zelton, hanging off the Shadow Scar's waist.

Growling as my leg throbbed, I used the other to kick the Shadow Scar repeatedly in the face. One, two, three, four, five, six times and with a little help from the Zelton, who dug its own claws into the Shadow Scar's lower back, they fell free from me, back into the water.

Sighing with relief, I made my way back onto the bridge. Rolling onto my stomach, I noted the surrounding bright blue double-paired legs standing around me. I took a few more breaths before I dared to look up at them. Zeltons, seven in total. The one whom I focused on tilted its head at me, curiously. There wasn't a notion that they meant me any harm. Still, I kept my wits sharp.

Grunting as I stood to meet their gaze, they all held indescribably curious expressions on their faces. Some might have even expressed concern. One glanced down at my leg, then back up at me. It slowly grabbed at something from its waist and raised all its arms as it glanced at what it held and gestured back at my leg. I shook my head, confused. "What?" I sighed. The slightest shift in my stance shot pain through my wound and forced me to a knee. Whining as I fell; the aliens chattered amongst themselves in a seemingly anxious manner. The Zelton that held the device in its hand, slowly kneeled beside me, reached around my leg, and sprayed something onto my wound. I was still drained but monumentally relieved of my pain. The Zelton and I looked at one another; it offered one of its right hands to me to help me back up. My fogged psyche couldn't fully comprehend the gravity of how extraordinary this interaction really was. As if it were one of my own, I took the Zelton's hand and together we rose to our feet. The alien rested its other right hand on my shoulder, reassuringly. I managed a light laugh at the events unfolding before me.

The ground trembled slightly. The aliens motioned toward something at my back, forcing me behind them before I could take a good look at the Shadow Scar behind me. Turning around, the spike-scalped Shadow Scar towered over the Zeltons. The creature suddenly revolted in a series of blurred movements, tearing apart two of the Zeltons in the blink of an eye. One of them motioned toward me, pushed me back as if to ward me off. Stumbling away as my mind started to catch on with the imminent danger of the highly skilled threat at large. I alter time and bolted off with a slight limp in my step.

I ran, breathing harder than normal, glancing back behind me. The skirmish between the Shadow Scar and Zeltons had already ended, or perhaps was taken elsewhere. Just before reaching the end of the bridge, I was tackled to the ground, growling as the pain in my leg surged once again. Tumbling across the ground, my hand felt desperately for one of my knives. The Shadow Scar rested on top of me; its disfigured face was coated in either water or Zeltonian blood. Staring down at me with a devious, mocking grin. I launched my blade into its back, beneath its shoulder, and the creature let out an odd, chirped squeal as it whipped its heavy fist across my face, knocking my arm limp. I spat and coughed out some blood as the Shadow Scar yelled in pain, retracting my blade from its flesh. It growled as it inspected the bloodied blade, returning its gaze to me.

"The true Diramal sends his regards, Criptous," the Shadow Scar said, as it lifted the blade over its head.

I gasped, not at the blade, but the voice. I knew it. It had been almost too long to recognize it; his face just barely escaping my recollection. But when it clicked, there was no mistaking him.

"Zothra—"

Just as the Shadow Scar motioned to strike me, a lone Zelton rammed its horns into Zothra's side, and he tumbled some distance from me. The Zelton stood its ground within a closer distance to me, defending me. The Zelton made a series of movements with its arms and forged a weapon composed of pure energy, green in color. It took on the form of a large, canon-like gun, with a large blade that arched over the barrel. Zothra returned with his own weapon composed of energy, black in color. The two clashed without the use of altered time. Zothra whirled his shafted weapon at the Zelton, to which it parried the blow with the blade at the barrel of the weapon and then again, swinging inward. The Zelton locked Zothra's weapon down with its own and the two exchanged *wrathful* noises. The Zelton spun back, twirling its weapon up, cutting across Zothra's arm. Distracting him long enough to get a lop-sided shot off in Zothra's direction. No matter the fact it didn't hit Zothra directly, the blast sent him back who knows how far.

The alien stood still to catch its breath, calming down. Then, like a wild primitive, it pounded its two left fists across its body, gurgling and arching back in a jerk, letting out a loud clicking screech. The Zelton continued to catch its breath and shrugged its shoulder, as the energy weapon gradually dissipated. It turned, walked up to me, and knelt at my side. The Zelton did not speak. Perhaps it contemplated what to make of me. Its indecisiveness was cut short when human voices sounded in the distance, coming our way. The Zelton made a noise, only this time it didn't sound like gibberish, it sounded like a language. Before I could think about it further, the alien gently placed the back of its claws against my eyelids and shut them.

Faintly conscious, I could hear voices echoing around me once again; among the chatter, I recognized Mae's. In that moment, I could recall that Olson, Log, and Lara were likely still in Irenole and that in my condition, I would be prioritized to send back home. Thus, in my final moments of strength, I uttered the words: "Olson... Log... Lara... don't forget Olson, Log, and Lara," to Mae.

XVII
Wish You Were Almost Dead
(Zothra)

As Quavek and I rushed back to our rendezvous point, I went over what had happened on the bridge.

Stupid idiot! I mocked myself. *After so many megannums of loyal service to the Diramal, how could I allow my emotions to get the best of me back there? Nearly killing Amat in the Diramal's name after I'd been told to show restraint. Never thought I'd consider it good fortune to cross blades with a Zelton, let alone their leader, Fargon. It seems she's finally found him, Amat, the one we'd all been searching for. Shame she couldn't get to the boy before we did and an even greater shame that all Fargon's efforts here on Galiza will be for naught when Criptous meets his end.*

Quavek and I rendezvoused with our numbers at the beach, where we initially arrived. Voruke awaited us there, with Xaizar resting on the ground. By the look of him, Xaizar seemed to be recovering from the edge of death.

"You two are late," Xaizar wheezed, struggling to raise his own head at us.

I cast a hard stare at Xaizar. Crippled to the point of being infirm and yet still filled with audacity.

"Amat's course forced us to be patient. We couldn't reach him until tonight. Not that I need to answer to *you*, Xaizar and you'd do well to remember your place before gurgling such words to me again. Understood?"

Xaizar's face vibrated, irritated as he rested his head back.

"Yes, Vorüm'Qij."

I turned my attention to Voruke, who I sensed would be more cooperative.

"How long have you been waiting?" I asked.

177

"A few days. We would have tracked Olson and Log for a longer period of time, but Log… he fought with such vigor. He's the reason Xaizar's on the ground and why we retreated early."

Xaizar quivered his tentacles in his temper. I turned my head back to Xaizar, who couldn't meet my gaze.

"Did the young Criptous brother catch you off guard?" I asked Xaizar.

Xaizar remained stubbornly silent. I chuckled, mockingly, and turned away.

(Log)

We made our way into the final town; it shared the same state as all the other sites before it. Silent, dead, and dried of all its resources. The shops were empty, a few scarce corpses of human and invader among the ruins, but no live Warvs or Skivs.

"I hope Amat's had better luck on his run. It would be a shame if the Irens were all lost to this war," said Olson.

"They wouldn't be the only culture to have suffered annihilation from it," I replied.

"Still, I hope Amat's found some of Shím's people," said Olson.

"No doubt he's found someone, with all that rumbling we heard the other day," said Lara.

Olson shook his head.

"It just surprises me that we haven't found anyone since the first day we arrived. Goes to show how devoid of life Galiza's become," Olson said.

"We found the Shadow Scar," I said.

"That's not funny," said Olson.

"Wasn't trying to be," I replied.

"How've you been feeling since that day, Olson?" asked Lara.

Olson shrugged before answering.

He didn't die, so he can't feel too bad. Not like me.

"I can't complain; you got me to a regenerator fast enough to patch me up," Olson replied.

For a moment, I almost wished my brother had died and had been revived. If he had, I might have felt… less alone with myself. I might have been able to compel myself to talk with Olson about how I'd become a Dövar, fleeing and returning to life.

"I'm glad we still have you here, brother," I said, trying my best to sound genuine. While not all my emotions had been severed from my heart, some, deep joy among them, had been walled off somehow.

Olson turned his head to me.

"As am I, brother." His tone sounded pleasant, and it expressed an unspoken "thank you" for protecting him against that one taller Shadow Scar. But the remark swiftly escaped my mind before I could render enough compassion to appreciate it.

"It's getting late," I said.

"Should we make camp at the next town, Jinn-hid?" Olson asked.

Lara shook her head.

"We'll search it tomorrow and make our way back to the rendezvous, after—"

The wind picked up at our backs, roaring over Lara's voice. A vessel hovered overhead. Lara, Olson, and I froze as we observed the hatch crack open.

"It's a Fade," Lara said. "Amat didn't wait for the rendezvous, something's wrong." She marched ahead of us as a figure came walking down the opening. Lara raised her hand to the bright light emanating from within the craft as the figure became clear.

"Olson, Lara, Log!" Mae yelled. "Get on board the Fade, Amat is in critical condition!"

Aboard the Fade, Mae led us promptly to Amat, where his body lay limp across several seats, freed from his armor. Something with sharp claws had dug deeply into his left calf, as it gushed blood from three long scratches. Burn marks covered the tops of his shoulders and around his back. A freshly stitched scar trailed up the right side of his abdomen, though, it was strange how little the wound swelled.

Burns look bad.

"Is he stable?" asked Lara.

"For now. But he's lost a lot of blood in the last twelve hours. We can only pray he'll remain this way until we reach Y'Gûtsa," replied Mae.

I moved to his side and eased my fingers into his palm. His flesh burned with a feverish heat, palms sweating. I didn't share it and no one else saw, but moments after I touched Amat, I felt his grip tug slightly at my fingers.

"He'll make it," I said. They all looked at me with their helpless expressions. I held a strong, confident manner on my face. "He'll make it," I repeated. I looked back down at Amat; only then did I allow my own worry to fill my eyes as I tugged back at Amat's faint grip. *He must. He might be the only one at this rate who can understand me.*

XVIII
The Shadows That Leave the Scars
(Amat)

I found myself in a dark place, with a thin layer of water covering the surface and a radiant being approaching me. Hovering above my palm was a small, rigid, crystalized orb. It was hard to perceive, but at its very center, the orb held a tiny spark. I looked back at the radiant being, its rays of light dimmed as he got closer, and I recognized him to be my father.

"Dad?" I asked.

"Amat," my father replied with a smile. "You see that orb in your hand?"

"Yes," I replied, glancing back down at the crystal globe

"Lift your other hand over it and close your eyes." I did as my father instructed. "Move your hand around a little bit." I curled my fingers and twisted my wrist a few times. "Now open your eyes and look down at the orb."

I slowly opened my eyes, looked down at the globe and saw what appeared to be a vast universe inside. Filled with vast nebulas, stars, galaxies, and planets, and the closer I looked into the crystal orb, the more I saw. A vibrancy stretched in every direction of the orb, pulsating with the sound of a beating heart.

"Did I do that?" I asked.

My father chuckled.

"Not exactly. What you hold in your possession there, Amat, it's an ancient artifact from the dawn of our kin. But we have been stripped of its ownership for quite some time now."

My mind drew a blank as I contemplated the gravity of my father's words.

"I'm sorry, Father, I don't understand. What significance does this artifact hold for our kin? And who stripped it from us in the real world?"

"Should you make the right decisions, all will be revealed to you, in time."

181

"What decisions? What choices will I be faced with?" I asked.

My father held a plain look as he traced his eyes up and down my figure. With a sigh, he paced before me.

"Amat, by this time I'm sure you've learned a lot about the invaders, via the transcript Blick brought to you after you overthrew the Diramal. You've learned that they have a certain openness with the members of our kin counted as Skivs and perhaps even the Warvs. You've learned of a mysterious force, outside the invaders, that's been at large since and maybe even prior to the time frame of this war."

"What are you suggesting?" I asked.

My father paused before continuing.

"When you were on that bridge, was there not something that seemed peculiar in the way the invaders responded to you?"

I frowned and nodded my head, reflecting on the incident.

"There was something about their attitude that seemed… civil, non-threatening to me. In fact, one of them saved me from… a Shadow Scar. There was something familiar about him though… his voice, it was Zothra's, but I already knew the Shadow Scar and the Cho'Zai were one and the same." I said, taking a moment to reflect. "But what was more noteworthy was how an invader put its life before mine to fend off Zothra. Which means… perhaps our ties with the Zeltons haven't totally faded!"

"Tread carefully with that one, Amat. Zothra is the Diramal's most superior warrior. When faced with him, you must consider your *every* defense and attack. There is also much that you and our kin's eyes have been blinded to, Amat. Including our bonds that are still thinly preserved with the Zeltons," my father said.

"If you knew this much about the Zeltons, why wouldn't you have made that clear to me sooner?" I asked.

"It is not my place to provide you with answers to the questions that stir your mind. I can only provide you with visions and allow you to make your own conclusions."

I glanced back down at the crystal orb that held a universe.

"I suppose you can't tell me much more about this then?" I asked.

"I can only tell you that in the real world, this artifact does not shine nearly as bright as you see it now. An ancient darkness has cursed it and our ties to it."

"Would it be wise to find and reclaim it into our possession?" I asked.

"Your mind asks this question, but what does your heart tell you?"

Reflecting on that; I interpreted what my intuition told me to be true. Finally, I sighed and nodded.

"That is your answer," my father said with a smile. "Be mindful of what you see and feel here, Amat. For it is not the future or the past that you see; one who bears such gifts as those only bears the gift of seeing the inevitable. What you see here is the truth, and one can do many a great or terrible thing with that. For you can choose to accept it and free yourself of your internal conflict. Or you can deny it and continue waging a war on three fronts. With the invaders, the Diramal, and yourself. I must go now, Amat, but before I do, know this. It is the only direct source of information I have been allowed to grant you. In time, very soon, you will meet someone who bears a connection with you, not in appearance, tongue, or culture, but blood. When you are met with this individual, you must embrace her into your trust, do you understand?"

I sat with that for a moment.

"Not yet, but when the time comes and I'm faced with what you speak of, I will do as you say," I said.

"Good. I'll leave you now. Farewell, my son," said my father.

"Wait, you said you'd been allowed to grant me this message. By whom?" I replied.

My father only replied with a warm smile.

"Goodbye, Amat," my father said.

"No, tell me—"

My eyes whipped open to the blinding white lights overhead, stinging my mind as I shot upright in the nano-regenerator. It took me a moment to register the blurry, gasping figures that stood before me as my vision refocused itself. A soft hand placed itself over my own.

"Amat?" Mae asked, as I turned my head toward her.

"Mae?" I asked, as I beheld her illuminated face.

Mae nodded.

"We're all here, your family and I are here," said Mae.

"My family?" I asked, as I passed my gaze back to the figures that stood before me. "It is all of you. But, why? What's happened?" I asked.

183

"You were caught in the path of an explosive and a Shadow Scar nearly dug out your calf on the Commathor Bridge," said Mae.

The bridge... I recalled.

"Thank the Goddess for sparing you, this day," my mother gasped as she rushed into me with her embrace. My sisters followed behind her. I slowly reached my arms around them, still dazed in trying to recount my memories.

Zothra was on the bridge. I was saved by an invader.

"Your lifelines had almost flatlined by the time you returned to the base—"

"Zothra was on the bridge," I mumbled, and my mother's words trailed off as she heard me speak. She leaned back and gave me a querying look.

"Zothra? The Cho'Zai?" my mother asked.

"What about him?" asked Olson.

"Amat said he was there, at the bridge," my mother replied.

Mae shook her head.

"There were several Shadow Scar on the bridge, was he among them?" asked Mae.

"He was the one who nearly clawed out my leg, who held a blade high above his head before that invader came to my aid to halt his blow. I heard his voice. '... the true Diramal sends his regards, Criptous,' he told me."

Everyone took a moment to process what I'd said.

"If that's so," Lara said, "that means the former Diramal still lives."

"That much was never in question. But think of what this means when we launch our escape off this world. The Diramal and his army will surely try to infiltrate the submerged starships across the globe and if that happens—" I said.

"We're only escaping one war to fight another," said Lara.

I opened my mouth to speak but—

"I fought Xaizar out there, as well," butted in Log, as he revealed a fresh wound at his shoulder. "And he said the Diramal would reunite us, that there was much he had in store for me. The confidence behind his words... he sounded so sure of himself. It couldn't have been an idle threat."

"I can attest to that," Olson blurted, before anyone else could object, revealing his own sizeable gash along his lower back. "Within an hour of infiltrating Galledon, Log, Lara, and I were attacked. I'll admit Log and Lara can recall much more of it than I can. But I have no reason to doubt their credibility - even in spite of Log's past hardships - and neither should any of you." Olson paused to turn to Log for what he would say next. "He's my brother."

I tightened my fist at the sight of their wounds, my cousins.

Log gave a slow, appreciative nod to Olson, though there was no obvious emotion to read on his face.

"I don't," I replied. "I think it's safe to say that we all endured some form of treachery from the former Diramal's army of Cho'Zai. We should rejoice in the reality that we are all still here amongst one another, despite the challenges we faced. That no doubt could have ended far worse than they did, by the sound of it. Nevertheless, the time has come to leave all our enemies behind and board the submerged star vessels. But with Xaizar's threat in mind... Mae, I want you to set up patrols throughout the exterior of the star vessels. They are to have routine check-ins over comms; updating each other on their status should any of them encounter an attack from the Shadow Scar. Olson, I charge you with the responsibility of overseeing everyone safely from this base to the nearest submerged vessel. Log, you'll be taking charge of cargo; make sure we load all our weapons, ammunition and whatever ration interfaces we have left, aboard the Fades. Limit civilians to three bags per family and consider the weight capacity of the Fades. Lara, I want you to relay a message to the other Jinns that we are to depart within the next twenty-four hours. In the meantime, I'll rebuild what strength I can for the final stand against the invaders. They may have shown some sense of understanding toward us, but not at any rate that we can afford to develop further. And we'll have to assume they won't allow us to simply ascend past their defenses. Dismissed."

"Sir," Log, Olson, Lara, and Mae said in unison.

I motioned to stand, but a firm hand stilled me. I looked back at Mae; her eyes heavy with concern.

"Take your time," Mae said.

"Yes," my mother butted in. "Take your recovery slowly while you can, Amat."

I sighed and nodded.

"I will."

My mother and younger sister Lia remained at my side, long enough for Lara to return with the Jinns' responses. Lara arrived with Blick, who I'd called to counsel not too long before, into my room. Lara stood straight, while Blick clicked his heels together and both presented the fronts and backs of their hands to me. I noted that my mother did not scowl at Blick when he entered but acknowledged him plainly.

"Sir," Lara said.

"Jinn-hid, report," I replied.

"Sir, the Jinns have the civilians under their jurisdiction safely tucked within the confines of the submerged ships and are raring to go at your command."

I smiled, proud.

"Wonderful, tell them that as soon as we have our people loaded on a few ships of our own, we'll all be underway. But they are to refrain from firing upon any of the invader vessels until I say otherwise," I said.

"Yes, sir," said Lara.

Lara motioned to leave but I raised my hand to her.

"Hold yourself, Jinn-hid. Where you're going, Reikag Vykin and these two will be accompanying you." I gestured to my mother and little sister. "When you've finished your duties, see them safely to a Fade, Reikag," I said.

Blick nodded.

"Understood, sir," said Lara.

My mother turned to me; a puzzled expression filled her face.

"Are you sure you're alright? I'd much rather stay in the base until you're ready to come with us," my mother said.

"I'll be better when I know you're all safe and tucked away in one of those starships," I said.

Blick glanced around awkwardly at that, an expression that suggested he didn't know how to feel about the notion.

"Alright then…" my mother said, standing up. "Lead the way, Reikag Vykin and Jinn-hid Criptous."

"Mrs. Criptous. Sir," said Blick.

"Sir," Lara said.

Blick and Lara presented the front and backs of their hands to me once again

I waited for my family to leave my sight before attempting to stand. The last I saw of them in that moment was Lia, who turned back as the door proceeded to shut behind her. Smiling in all her natural young spirit as she waved at me. I allowed myself a gentle smile in return and raised my hand to her.

(The Diramal)

One moment I stood among the waste, my hand hovering over the shell fragment, the next I'd slipped out of the constructs of our central reality and fallen into the void of Drakkar once again. Just as quickly, meeting my gaze as I opened my eyes, the shadowed entity leaned its large shifting face into mine. Dwarfing me in a form that was many times my size, moving on ten narrow legs that bent out in their support. He stomped his front right leg, quaking the water that covered up to my ankles soon after our eyes met. His head twitched with irritation as he spoke my rank.

"Diramal. The Qi'val known as Xaizar, intrigues me of late. I admire his bloodlust for the half-dead Log Criptous. Not to mention, the impropriety he committed against Qi'val Quavek is most… noteworthy. How the Qi-Varian thrives off pain and suffering; he is a model mortal of my ancient designs."

I tilted my head at what Drakkar was referring to in his last statement. "Impropriety?"

"It matters not." Drakkar's tone had turned vexed. His ten legs scurried him about my stance. "In spite of control *fumbling* out of your grasp, here on Galiza, I am *exuberant* about what is being developed off world. A new weapon that I am fervent to witness the display of."

I blinked a few times before replying, needing a moment to process what the dark entity had said.

"And what has you so raptured about this weapon, ancient one?" I asked.

"It is Rausjğa, derived from my very essence. It will tear apart the fronts in Ji'qui'yt and *pulverize* what remains of the Hanu. Fortunate you are, that I find solace in the sheer upper hand Rausjğa shall grant me, Diramal."

"It prides each of your servants—and me, greatest of all—to bring you glory and further dominion, Drakkar."

Drakkar hissed and clicked his mouth as his body shifted in and out of form, molding for moments at a time into various grotesque appearances. The shadow then faded past me, flowing back into the surrounding darkness.

"You speak of glory, Diramal, but it can't be assured so long as one remains at large. If you wish to solidify our victory in this great war, Diramal, a long overdue task must be carried out."

"And what might that be?" I asked, hesitantly.

Drakkar presented himself to me once again, but his figure had shifted and grown much larger in proportion. His empty eyes glittered in a gloomy light as he stared down at me.

"Take Amat's family from him, everyone he holds most dear, rob him of the world he has built around them, and tear his heart from beneath his *bone*. When he is faced with the Zelton armies, allow Zothra to intervene and blow Amat out of the sky."

I swallowed at the long-awaited command I feared Drakkar would one day decree.

"I will go back and inform Quavek and the others—"

"No!" Drakkar broke in as he swiftly slithered his monstrous face into mine, slowly opening his jaws as if to sink his many layered, jagged teeth into my flesh. "Do not send your preferred grunts for this errand."

"You're suggesting I should use one of my lesser troops to carry out this errand?" I asked.

"Yes, and I shall tell you why…" said Drakkar, as I proceeded to listen intently to his next words.

***

I strolled, with my head low, my thoughts convoluted with the commands I had just received from Drakkar. Part of me didn't want to carry them out, another knew there was no other choice; confronted with the burdensome consequence I would have to face should I fail. But first, I would discover what was implied by the ancient one's mention of Xaizar's 'Impropriety.' And in doing so, I sought an audience with Quavek. Where insubordination sat well with Drakkar, it would not in the slightest with me. Especially in regards to the Qi-Varian. Quavek's arrival was not subtle, clicking and chirping as she galloped on all six of her limbs over the terrain before coming to an abrupt halt and perching on a mound of debris. I hardly noticed her presence, still heavily occupied with the raging thoughts within my mind.

"You called for me, Diramal?" Quavek finally asked.

"Yes..." I whispered, continuing to stare blankly into the distant shadows. "It's come to my attention, Quavek, that Xaizar has been rather, *radical*. And not just on his own"—I finally turned toward Quavek—"but with you specifically."

Quavek tucked her pincers and stiffened as she hissed.

"Quavek, what happened between you and Xaizar?" I asked, somewhat tenderly.

Quavek proceeded to shyly explain what had transpired between her and Xaizar after she made efforts to remove him from human imprisonment. And I was moved with woe for Quavek. I walked up to her, took her hands into my own, and gazed deeply into her eyes.

"I don't feel it's my place to carry out his needed disciplinary action myself..." Quavek's head perked up. "I'd offer that responsibility to you, if you'll accept?"

Quavek rapidly clicked and twitched her pincers.

"Yes," Quavek hissed.

Quavek readied a device of her own making while Xaizar made his way to me after I'd requested his presence. He arrived in a great *whoosh!* As he stopped abruptly from exiting his altered time state, a small dust cloud drifted past me.

"Diramal," Xaizar gurgled.

I remained silent, waiting for Quavek's signal, and stared deeply into the gaping holes about Xaizar's face. It was a stare meant to intimidate the Qi-Varian. I almost allowed myself a moment's pleasure when I saw the uneasy ripples he demonstrated about the edges of his face. In the near distance, Quavek crept silently.

"Consider this a warning, Xaizar," I said.

Xaizar tilted his head.

"Sir—"

Quavek altered time and pinned Xaizar to the ground. The Qi-Varian squirmed as he re-entered his own altered time state, trying to resist Quavek's strength. I altered time and stomped the ground just beside Xaizar's head, halting his resistance.

"You would be wise not to withstand her. She won't kill you, but I've charged Quavek with ensuring you never fall out of line again, using whatever means she deems necessary."

Xaizar gurgled in rage as Quavek cut deeply into the back of his head and placed something in the opening. Sealing the cut, she shoved herself off the Qi-Varian and we all exited our altered time states.

Xaizar pushed himself to his feet and reached behind his head.

"What did you do to me?" Xaizar asked.

"As a Qi-Varian, you can endure much that others would consider physically devastating and, in some scenarios, convert it into pleasure. Except in two circumstances, when a sharp blade flays at the top layer of your skin, little by little *and* when your statocysts are disrupted by electrical signals. And seeing as how I can't kill you, well..." Quavek activated the device she planted within the Qi-Varian's mind and Xaizar promptly lost his balance as he began to rapidly shed moisture from his body and ink flooded from the sockets of his face. Xaizar trembled and convulsed violently, gurgling as he collapsed to his knees.

When Quavek deactivated her mechanism and allowed Xaizar to recover, I grabbed Xaizar by the neck, lifted and threw him in a lake that ran just beside us, so that Xaizar could recover the lost moisture in his body and wouldn't die from dehydration. His body promptly absorbed and swelled up from the running water as he recovered his strength.

The Qi-Varian attempted to alter time and rush into Quavek, but Quavek had activated her device once again. Xaizar stumbled out of his altered time state and gurgled in inking convulsions once again.

"I think you can handle things well enough from here, Quavek," I said.

"Oh yes, Diramal, Xaizar and I will be just fine on our own," Quavek said.

"Just see to it you both reach one of the Stellavars before the humans launch them."

"Of course, sir."

I made my own way to one of the human Stellavars and made further arrangements to see Drakkar's wishes come to fruition, while Quavek stayed back with Xaizar… to set his mind straight.

(Amat)

After dressing myself in uniform, I decided to pay my quarters a final visit before heading to the hangar. A few treasured possessions of mine rested there that I would never again see, except one that could be salvaged. A photograph of my father that I could tuck into the confines of my coat.

I reached the door; the hall was empty, and all the occupants of the base level would have arrived at the hangar by then. The door slid open after I'd pressed my hand on the ID interface. I looked down at my feet, dreading the realization that this was the final piece of home that I'd made for myself on Galiza and would have to leave behind. My eyes raised to the sight of a pistol aimed directly between my eyes. I focused my vision past the weapon and noted the Cho'Zai who held it.

"No sudden moves, Criptous," someone from within my quarters said. "He's already altered time, that one; motion to disarm him and he'll shoot. Step inside."

I did as the individual commanded. Coming through the doorway, the Cho'Zai's movements blurred as he transitioned beside me. I heard the hammer of a second pistol click back to my right, as another female Cho'Zai followed beside me.

"Stand here," said the Cho'Zai sitting on my furniture, a confident grin spread across his face.

The thought crossed my mind to ask them how they got inside the base. But it was a pointless question. They'd gotten in somehow and were holding me at gunpoint.

"I know what you are, all of you," I said.

The Cho'Zai on my couch was unmoved by this notion.

"Doesn't matter to us what you think you know. Because the truth is, despite what you may have discovered about us, you can't know the half of it."

"I know enough," I said.

The Cho'Zai chuckled.

"No, you don't. In any case, it doesn't matter as we've come to make short work of you. Rahvor. Verka," said the Cho'Zai, motioning to his comrades.

In the same instance, I altered time and raised my hand to Verka's weapon as I leaned back to avoid Rahvor's shot, which penetrated Verka's shoulder. In a quick motion, I twisted my palm forward into Verka's face, knocking her back, immediately ducking down as I kicked my leg out and slid it across Rahvor's ankles. I looked up to address the Cho'Zai that had been sitting on my couch next, but his heavy fist whipped across the side of my scalp and hit me like a ton of metal. I proceeded to drift out of consciousness.

My eyes hesitated to open, sealed together by the gunk in their corners and around their rims. The thick cloth placed over my body distorted my sight of the base. I felt myself being pulled by the forward motion of a gurney. Noting the plasma restraints enveloped around my wrists, I was careful not to spasm or move too rashly and kept my arms close to the rails on either side of the gurney. I took a deep breath as I considered the purpose of all of this.

They're obviously not here to kill me. They had ample opportunity for that between the time I'd been knocked out and now. Perhaps it is another one of the Diramal's games, perhaps they are bringing me to him now. Still doesn't answer the question as to how they got back inside the base in the first place—

"So how long do you suppose it'll be before the others are done?" asked one of the Cho'Zai. It must have been Rahvor, as it was certainly a man's voice, but not that of the initial Cho'Zai I had interacted with.

"No doubt they've already finished," Verka replied.

"If they have, then why not just leave this one here and regroup?" asked Rahvor.

"We could, if we'd already heard back from the others; until then, we stick with the kid to make sure he stays out of the way. The infirmary is coming up; we can hold him there until we're in the clear," said the third Cho'Zai.

Keep me out of the way for what?! I asked myself, as I dug my claws into the palms of my hands. I took a deep breath and collected myself. If I wanted to know what was happening, I couldn't let them know I was awake.

The gurney came to a pause as a door slid open and the Cho'Zai escorted me inside.

"Hey there, Doc," Rahvor said, followed by a woman gasping. A swift wind carried through the air as papers dispersed up in it. Muffled cries and moans sounded over steel piercing flesh. "Your shift's over." The body thudded to the ground, followed by the sound of splattered blood. I sent a silent prayer of mercy and safe passage for the soul of the doctor who had been murdered in my presence.

While prayers to Anua must surely be useless at this point, I pray that there is a place and perhaps a spirit that can guide this woman's poor essence into an illuminated paradise. And whatever forces govern this world and our lives, I hope they can forgive my meek state for being unable to protect her.

"What did you kill that one for?" asked Verka. "She could have been added to our ranks."

"The humans are a dying breed and in case you forgot, they nearly shifted the tide of the war against us, Vix and Varx alike. They're a greater liability than they are a potential asset," replied Rahvor.

"Enough of that. Verka, help me move Criptous over there. Rahvor, clean up your mess," said the third Cho'Zai.

A few moments later, the gurney was moved once again, this time beside a table that was just slightly lower than the gurney. The gurney was set, and the shadow of a hand loomed to the cloth over my face. Before the Cho'Zai could pull it back, I shut my eyes and acted as though I was still resting.

"*Eh*, just as I thought," said Verka.

I listened patiently for the paired footsteps to walk away just far enough for me to crack my eyes open again. As the three Cho'Zai mumbled amongst themselves, I took in my surroundings, eventually trailing my gaze down to the table to my left. There sat a thin, hooked surgical tool.

The generator for the plasma restraints was a small dodecahedron-shaped device suspended between the interwoven energized entanglements. The tool was small and arched enough that if I could reach it, I could disable the restraints like one would pick a lock. My head was still reclined, I'd only managed to observe the tool from the corner of my eye. Blinking several times, the position of the surgical tool was instilled in my mind. This way, I could keep my eyes on the Cho'Zai as I reached for the utensil.

I lifted my head, just enough to see the Cho'Zai past my chest, as I stretched my arm out to my side. I was careful not to overtravel, gently guiding my fingertips over the edge of the table and beyond. Sliding across the surface until I reached the butt of the tool. It was there, however, that the restraints worked their true function. The color had shifted from purple to red and the shield envelopment tugged tightly at my wrist, burning my flesh. I held back a growl as I strained my neck and burst with a heavy sigh, pulling my arm back slightly. The Cho'Zai remained occupied with themselves. The thought crossed my mind to lie back down and collect myself.

But what if they decide to come this way and move me again in the time it would take me to recover?

Thus, I reached once again, inching closer and closer to the tool. Finding its end once again, the restraints surged with flaming energy that stung my wrist severely. I worked my fingers as they crawled further around the tool's body. Trembled gasps seeped through my gnarling fangs as my arm spasmed from *surging* pain. Deep breaths helped, long enough for me to slowly retract my arm with the tool in hand. By that time, it felt as though hardly any strength was left within it.

Setting my arm down at my side, I sighed with relief. Proceeding to position the tool into the generator of the restraints, I had to feel it out, as I couldn't risk raising my head, so high as it was, to see the generator. The first was the tip of the point, pressing against the top of the generator. I angled the tool with my fingers to arch it over the side of the device. The point scraped along, just loud enough for me to hear. The Cho'Zai remained distracted by their own rambling. The tip had reached the end of the side, which meant the point of entry was down a separate side. Carefully, I positioned the tip of the tool back on the side of the dodecahedron-shaped generator, turned it, and trailed the pick on the next side over. The tip met with the end of the third side, tucked closely into my fist. And a good thing too, for one of the Cho'Zai had casually turned her head in my direction, just as a passing glance. To which I shut my eyes and held still for a time, until I heard all three of their voices mingling with one another once again. Taking a deep breath, I twirled the generator onto its fourth side, this time a little more quickly, and met with the edge. I shook my head in frustration, turned the device for a fourth time, collected myself, and gently traced the tip up the side until it clicked down into the generator's plasma core. The swift movement made the restraints tighter and hotter for a moment, until I retracted the tip. Slowly moving it back in, the core dispersed like shattered glass, the restraints faded, and the device fell onto the bedding.

One... down.

I passed my eyes over the Cho'Zai; they didn't seem like they'd be moving from their position any time soon. I took a deep breath as I altered time. My surroundings blurred and all distant sounds muffled. I slid my free arm across my body with the tool in hand and passed it over, into my right grasp. Returning my left arm back to my side, I managed to disable the second generator after two quick turns. That very same moment, one of the Cho'Zai's fizers beeped and lit up on his forearm. He motioned to bring it up to his face and answered the call as I regulated time.

A screen illuminated from the fizer and the Cho'Zai was met with a dark face.

195

"Hrün-grík," said the figure. It took me but a moment to recognize it was the Diramal.

"Sir," Hrün-grík replied.

"The others have finished their duties within Y'Gûtsa. You may proceed in moving Criptous into position," said the Diramal.

Hrün-grík nodded.

"Understood, sir, we'll rendezvous with you once we're done."

The transmission cut and the display narrowed into a thin line that shrunk back into the fizer.

"We're moving?" asked Rahvor.

"We are," Hrün-grík replied.

I shut my eyes and relaxed my body as the Cho'Zai looked my way.

"You think he'll stay out long enough for us to get him to the quarters?" asked Rahvor.

"Maybe…" Verka said, as boots clicked across the room. "But perhaps we should administer a little something extra, just in case he doesn't."

"Wouldn't hurt. Go ahead, we'll make sure the area outside is secure," said Hrün-grík.

I listened intently for the pair of boots that clicked closer and closer to me: Verka's steps. I could almost see her as my mind processed the sound closing in on me. When she stopped, I could feel her standing there, sense her quizzical expression as she noted my restraints had been deactivated. Altering time, I sprung up in my gurney, swinging the small surgical tool as she motioned to stick a needle filled with serum into my body. But the tip of my tool had jabbed its way into her neck before she could administer the serum and I tore the hook through the side of her neck. She squealed, after having finally entered her own altered time, still standing. The other two Cho'Zai turned their heads to me. Fluidly, I reached for Verka's pistol at her side, shooting in their direction as I didn't have enough time to take precise aim at the two armed Cho'Zai.

Verka grabbed my arm firmly with her free hand. I looked in her direction to witness the grotesque sight of her removing what could only be described as a skinsuit, unveiling her true appearance. I was too overwhelmed with shock to respond immediately. Her head was cone shaped, a long narrow beak extended from where her mouth should have been, the top seemed cut in half, as it didn't fully overlap the bottom. Her skin was scaled, with long drooping eyelids beneath even smaller eyeballs. Two layers of wide, flapping gills extended from the back of her jaw and from behind her head, leading down the back of her spine stretched bony spikes. The Cho'Zai roared in my face as the rest of her true appearance tore through the skin of her body suit. Before more could be uncovered, I pressed the barrel of the pistol against her rib cage and fired. She let out a yell and let go of my arm. Spinning off the gurney, I took cover as I witnessed Verka grow four feet taller than she stood before, a tail dropped from her lower back and six muscular limbs with sharp bones arching out from them unfurled. Verka rushed toward me, thumping the ground with every step. I unloaded everything I had left in the magazine. One, two, three, four shots in her upper body and her pace didn't give in the slightest. I aimed more carefully with my final shot and sent the bullet through her scalp. The tall reptilian Cho'Zai crashed limply on the ground beside me.

Still overwhelmed with the Cho'Zai's unveiling of herself, the concept did not come as a surprise to me. But even Log's telling of his first encounter with Xaizar could not prepare me for witnessing such a daunting transformation. Collecting myself, I realized I required a weapon. Footsteps rushed across the room from behind me.

The others are moving into position for an assault.

My gaze darted around different sections of the infirmary, until I homed in on the remains of Verka's skinsuit. The section of her waist rested no more than a few paces out of reach. And on it, a belt, holstering a splice.

Plotting what to do next, I peeked around the corner of my cover to make sure no one waited for me there and refocused on the splice. Bolting for the weapon, staying low, one of the Cho'Zai cut the lights before I could reach it. Darkness clouded my stride for two swift steps before my eyes adjusted. Just faintly, the grip of the splice came into view as I slid across the floor and the Cho'Zai jumped out of hiding, twisting and shifting their arms in abstract motions as peculiar energy weapons formed into their grips out of thin air. Taking the splice in hand, I moved onto my knee and flicked the blade out into formation.

I was almost intimidated, noting how the invader's energy weapon had cut right through the steel of my blade in Irenole. But then I recalled

197

how on recent occasions I'd been able to move faster than even the Cho'Zai or Shadow Scar or whatever their true collective name was. All I needed to know was that if I pushed myself hard enough in the next few moments, I could beat these two, despite the upper hand they held over me.

With the deep inhale of my breath, their movements seemed to slow as I entered an intense altered time state. Exhale and their charge at me quickened. Dashing forward, I moved for the narrow gap between them. A baited tactic on my part. At the last second, I pushed harder into the realm of altered time and bounded to the left as the Cho'Zai swung their weapons at me. Sliding passed Hrün-grík, I skid the edge of my splice against the side of his abdomen. It was a flesh wound, but one that would certainly slow him down as the fight proceeded.

I eased off the depth at which I pushed my altered time as I twisted up and around to face the Cho'Zai once again. Hrün-grík pressed one of his hands against his fresh wound as he looked down at it and then at me, with an amused, sinister grin on his face. Hrün-grík signaled Rahvor to move around me while he went the other way. I took my time stepping to the center of the room, where the Cho'Zai stood at equal distances to either side of me. Glancing at both, I widened my stance, and together they charged me once again. Breathing deep, even with my eyes shut, I could sense how their movements were inferior to my own. Hrün-grík was the first to reach me, swinging down at me with one of his dual-energy weapons. Whipping my eyes open, I halted his blow, raising his arm, so as to place the edge of my splice against Hrün-grík's armpit. Rahvor was a step away as I vigorously spun passed Hrün-grík, spilling his dark blood. Rahvor closed in with his own blow that cut through Hrün-grík's arm. Spinning back toward Rahvor, I swung the splice deep across the Cho'Zai's thigh, causing him to stumble to the ground. Positioned behind Hrün-grík, I stabbed the top edge of my splice into the Cho'Zai's heart for good measure, or at least, where I thought it was. Regardless, it was enough to unite Hrün-grík with his death.

I watched Rahvor as he found his feet a little more swiftly than I would have anticipated. Still set deep in my own altered time space, I rushed toward the Cho'Zai, jumped over him, and swung my splice through Rahvor's wrist. In that instant, he moved far slower than me, almost not at all, signifying that he had more than likely been pulled out of his altered time state. I regulated time, ready to alter it once again, however. His brief shout filled the infirmary. The Cho'Zai sat on his knees, panting heavily, transitioning his vision from his stump onto me. In his other hand, the energy weapon still blazed bright. The Cho'Zai leaned forward, but I swiftly brought the angled point of my splice to his chin as a warning.

"Try anything else and I won't hesitate to remove the other one," I said.

Rahvor continued to pant heavily, staring at me unblinkingly as he thought it over. He finally leaned back, and the energy weapon faded from existence. A voice sounded in my head, speaking to me suddenly. It made its presence known with a sinister laugh.

Well, well, well, you have really outdone yourself here. Massacring the sacred children of Anua, the voice in my head said.

Shut up, I replied.

You know, it's a little self-loathing, to tell another version of yourself to 'shut up.'

I am not you and you certainly, *are not me,* I replied.

The statements we barked at one another, this alternate version of myself and I, were not so complicatedly spoken. But rather an exchange of harsh sensations, sent back and forth, which computed into words in my head; fading quicker than one might read or hear them.

Oh, you wound me, can't you feel it? When I didn't reply the voice continued, *Clearly, you have a dulled memory. Don't you recall our father himself saying we are one and the same?*

Only a few moments had passed in this exchange, when slowly the Cho'Zai seemed to stretch far from my sight and a dark void took my consciousness from the scenario. I was still looking down, where the Cho'Zai would have sat, by the time I noticed I was somewhere else. Looking up, I took in the void that had hosted many a dream of mine, of late. A few meters before me, stood a figure so dark he nearly blended in with the empty background he faced.

One instance he looked to be facing the void, the next his body inverted, muscles, bones, flesh, and all, and faced me. I clenched my fist, ready for whatever came next, as the sinister, illusive opposite approached me.

"I suppose you could have done this at any time," I said.

"What? This?" The Opposite glanced his head up and spun around, stopping when he faced me once again. "No, but circumstances have changed."

"In what sense?" I asked.

The Opposite sighed, then laughed, and held a mocking grin on his face.

"Oh, let's not play games with ourselves, you may not have fully pieced the puzzle together, but deep in our subconscious mind, we know what's coming. The Cho'Zai holding you under restraint, keeping you away from your friends… the call they received from the Diramal saying that the *others'* duties had been fulfilled?"

I started to comprehend what the dark reflection was getting at, but I couldn't see it fully for myself, wouldn't. I took a step forward, meekly raising my finger to the reflection, and my jaw dropped.

"What does that mean?" I asked.

"Fighting on the wrong side of wars have consequences, as we well know."

"What do you know?!" I growled.

"In a few moments, you'll see the resemblance between us," said the Opposite.

I was immersed back into my body, with seemingly no time at all having passed. Rahvor still sat there, panting, my hold on the splice still firmly in place, only now my hand trembled with what I would soon find out. My mind drew a blank, as if it didn't want me to know.

Ask him, said the Opposite.

Ask him what? I replied.

The question, sitting in the back of our mind.

Slowly my mouth opened. I didn't think about the words, they just flowed out.

"The Diramal contacted you while I was on the gurney. He said the others had done something. *What* something?" I growled the question.

The Cho'Zai curled his lips.

Here it comes, said the Opposite, with excitement.

"Before I say, Criptous, know that it has already been done… and there is nothing left for you to do about—"

"Tell me!" I barked, pressing the edge of the splice against the bottom of the Cho'Zai's chin.

With no break in his sly smile, the Cho'Zai answered: "Io-Pac Mae Kalbrook, born Dember seventeenth in the Galizian year twenty-five-thirty-four. Judi Criptous, maiden name Griktin, born Septica eighth in the Galizian year twenty-five-oh-nine. Lara Criptous—"

"What is this?" I asked.

"—born Novica fourteenth, in the Galizian year twenty-five-thirty-six," the Cho'Zai continued, his focus didn't break in the slightest when I spoke over him.

"Tell me what is going on!" I yelled.

"Lia Criptous, born Maugra fourth, in the Galizian year twenty-five-forty. Olson Criptous, born Jornull sixth, twenty-five-thirty-three. And Log Criptous, born Septica fifth, in the Galizian year twenty-five-thirty-seven. All dead, today, Tuthgra eighteenth, twenty-five-fifty-three, at approximately two p.m."

There it is! exclaimed the voice in my head.

I stumbled back as my heart sank, falling nearly flat on my back. I had no words to express; my face and my emotions shifted from depthless sorrow to heated rage. No thoughts filled my mind except the word "dead" echoing in my mind, as I recalled each of their faces. The Cho'Zai stood, clutching his stump as he lorded over me.

"Compliments of the Diramal—"

I altered time, and sliced through the wrist of Rahvor's second hand. I spun around, kicking my leg out. Rahvor fell to the ground, slowly matching my speeds as I mounted him. Strangling the Shadow Scar with no remorse while his stumps whipped against my arms. I pressed long enough to knock him out. Forcing him to fall out of his altered time, as I fell out of mine. I stood, marched to the gurney, and found the two plasma restraint generators. I recovered Verka's gun and loaded it with ammunition I located on her corpse. I then hauled two heavy rolling cabinets beside Rahvor's ankles and intertwined the restraints from his ankles to the legs of the counters.

This should be interesting, said the dark reflection, in the back of my mind. I hardly noticed it, however.

Feeling around my uniform, I found my pouch filled with E.S.P. ammunition, and took out two cubes. Once again sitting atop the Cho'Zai, I laid out his stumps, armed myself with my splice and cut deep across his forearm. The blow woke the Cho'Zai abruptly, as he squirmed and howled. I was hardly thwarted by his cries to do what I would next. So deep in my own darkness, my own pain, I was intent on ensuring Rahvor suffered.

Unable to lift his split right arm, I pressed down on his left and did the same. He tensed so hard that the flesh surrounding his face on his skinsuit tore, revealing part of his true face. Which I had very little interest in noting.

I launched a hard fist across Rahvor's face to shut him up and raised my finger above his head. My eyes must have looked soulless to him. For once he met them, a fear the Cho'Zai had never known was plainly expressed on his face. I took my E.S.P. ammunition.

"These are E.S.P. crystals of my own making. The charge is much more substantial than that of an ordinary E.S.P. crystal. But, like its predecessors, when broken, it releases an intensive shock wave, spazzing anything within its surge radius. Now, against bare skin"—I proceeded to roll my sleeve up and hovered one of the crystals above my arm, making the hairs stand up—"it's bound to cause some static and neural damage. But against"—I pressed the crystals into the gashes at Rahvor's forearms. The Cho'Zai, made a clicking gurgle noise in reply—"raw flesh, well I'll let you experience that for yourself."

"You'll find the bodies in their quarters." Rahvor spat black blood from his mouth.

Rahvor panted heavily as I stood up and took a few steps back. I aimed the pistol and waited. I'd already found my shot, but I wanted—

Ah, keeping him in suspense like he did you, before the big reveal. I'm impressed by how dastardly we've taken this. The voice chuckled. The reflection took in a deep inhale, waited as I did. *Fire.*

Bang! Bang! I set off the ammunition and watched as Rahvor's body spasmed vigorously, as blue electric currents spewed out of his arms. His body lit up a deep orange, revealing sections of his nervous system; burning from the inside out. I watched the whole thing unfold, without any sense of guilt, pleasure, any emotion at all. I couldn't bring myself to feel anything. My world had been shattered. I didn't leave until Rahvor was a stiff burning corpse resting idly on the ground.

So, now you see... the voice in my head said *...we are not so different.*

XIX
Lost in Blood

My footsteps echoed through the empty base as I made my way to Mae's quarters. She was the closest from the med bay. I placed my hand on her ID interface; in the time we'd been together, she'd given me clearance to her place. The door slid open; the main room was a mess.

She was truly a feisty one, Mae. No wonder she put up a good fight, said the voice.

A few steps in and I could see the blood trail, dirtied by the black blood of the Cho'Zai, but no body rested beside hers. They'd beaten, cut, and shot her. Her face was swollen and bruised, uniform bloodied beside her, stripped down almost bare. My trembling hands reached out to cradle her limp body into my arms; pushing aside the thought of every terrible thing they must have done to her.

There was no effort in holding back my tears; I simply could not bring myself to cry. Staring blankly across the room, my unshifting gaze couldn't bear the sight of her lifeless eyes. No matter how tightly I held her, the warmth of my body failed to heat the cold cloak of death that enveloped Mae's corpse. The longer I enveloped her, the more teardrops accumulated at my eyelids. Like rain drops rolling off a stone statue. But I did not weep.

There was a rotting pain in my heart, an ache I could not foresee myself escaping, and, in my mind, formed shadows that made me forget the light of day ever existed. Both called to me, to drag me lower than I already was. But I would not subject myself to the world-shattering pain, nor the thoughts that would surely drive me to madness. I would simply be broken.

How far down we've fallen, how greatly we've shattered. One would scarcely know how to piece our sense of self back together, said the voice.

I set Mae down on her bed, laying her body in a restful position. "Goodbye, my love," I whispered, as I closed her eyes.

I made my way to my mother's quarters, where Lia, Lara, and perhaps even Blick would rest.

Assuming Blick didn't play a part in this. After all, he's betrayed us before, said the voice.

That he has, I replied, passively.

I opened the door to my mother's quarters, sluggishly making my way in. I couldn't bring myself to walk the rest of the way after seeing their bodies, nor could I hold back my guilt any longer. One after the other, my legs gave out, bringing me to my knees as my jaw trembled.

Oh dear, is that little Lia? the voice pondered, not sounding the least bit concerned.

It was Lia's body that lay closest to the door, the first one I noticed. As I crawled to her corpse, I couldn't help but sob and give in to the pain that so desperately needed to be felt.

"Lia..." I wheezed.

I reached my hand toward her, stopping before I could set it down on her broken scalp. I couldn't bring myself to lay hands on them, any of them. Bowing my head as I tensed and filtered my grief with rage.

I howled a curse, loud enough to shatter glass. Gazing back up, I beheld my mother, who had been cut at the throat and then to Lara, who had been beaten. Beside her... rested Blick, shot to death, four bullets in the chest.

"Goddess... Nooo-ho-ho-ho!" I wailed. "No, no, no."

I found it in me to take Lia, Lara, and my mother, all into my arms, resting their heads on my lap.

Yes... yes, this was to be expected. After you removed the Diramal from power. If only you had stayed out of his way—

I barked curses up at the ceiling to silence the voice. Springing up from my seat, clawing at my scalp.

"Do you have any idea how this feels?! How this fucking..."

I dug my nails into my palms as my arms trembled with a tense fury. I whipped around to the countertop in the kitchen and swiped everything off. Altered time and frantically punched through the walls and doors. Kicking furniture over, shattering glass, tossing things all over the place, tearing out drawers from their locked place. I did everything and anything to demolish what I possibly could. Even as my stamina exhausted, falling back onto my knees, howling my cry to Anua, the fire in my heart was hardly doused.

Now that you've settled, what shall we do next? Tear down the rest of the base? the voice asked.

I stared down at the gun I'd retrieved off the Cho'Zai in silence before I answered.

"I'm gonna use you—whatever *you* are—to boil the blood of the Diramal. I am going to amass my darkest depths and I am going to turn them all onto him," I said.

Perhaps we should put a pin in that and see—

"And then… when he's endured everything that I have in store for him, I will destroy you." I trailed my thumb over the side of the pistol before holstering it behind my back. "But not today—"

"Amat?" a familiar voice sounded as the main entrance slid open.

My head swiveled in his direction, watching as he limped into the quarters. I was so overjoyed. Even more so when I saw Log come in beside him, fitted in a QS-25.

"Olson."

My cousins rushed to me. I latched my arms around them so tight, my claws must have dug into the back of Olson's uniform slightly.

"Oh, Oh-ho-ho-ho." I laughed and cried. "You're alive, the Goddess saw you both alive! How? I heard from the Cho'Zai that had taken me, all of you had been killed."

Olson and Log looked at me but before they could answer, their attention was drawn to the others on the ground. Both my cousins approached them slowly. Taking in the remains of our family with heavy eyes. Olson sniffed and wiped his nose as the tears came rolling down his cheek. Log held a stern expression on his face, seemingly holding back his tears effortlessly. He squatted down beside Lia and trailed his fingertips over her eyes, shutting them. Olson shook his head.

"It was the Cho'Zai," said Olson.

"The Diramal." I nodded.

"How could we have let this happen? After all we'd accomplished," asked Olson. He faced me and rested a hand on my shoulder. "I'm so sorry."

I grasped Olson's arm as I looked him in the eye.

"You asked us how we survived," said Olson. I nodded. "They'd overwhelmed us on our way to the hangar and taken us to the armory. It's been cleared, almost entirely, of supplies. There were a few Io-Pacs there, moving some armaments. Our captors killed them both without struggle. Log had found some way out of his restraints first and moved to find a QS-25 while the Cho'Zai hid the bodies of the Io-Pacs. I suspect they weren't planning on keeping us there very long. Shortly after Log found a suit, the Cho'Zai returned. Log had moved to me and started tampering with one of the restraints. Didn't take them long to realize that one of us was missing, so Log moved with haste, as one of them approached me. Log altered time, circled around to the last crate of armaments, grabbed a knife, and dealt with one of them. The second had already reached me by that time and when I heard him unsheathe his own blade, I couldn't play dumb anymore. So, I reached my arm out, slowed the rate at which the blade pierced my flesh"—Olson revealed the bandaged wound—"also dislocating my shoulder from how forcefully the Cho'Zai plunged his blade at me. The next moment, Log came up from behind and dealt with the second Cho'Zai."

I sighed.

"Goddess bless us for what we still have… each other," I said.

Log came up and we all placed our hands on our shoulders, taking a long moment of silence for one another.

"What should we do with Aunt Judi, Lara, Lia, and Blick?" asked Log.

"I left Mae in her quarters."

Olson crossed his arms and rubbed his fingers across his mouth.

"I don't think it would be wise to take them with us. I don't want to upset the civilians. We'll set them in their rooms. Blick can have the couch. After that, we'll go to the hangar, and safely get our people off Galiza."

"What about the invaders? There are ships still closing off our skies," said Log.

I sat with that for a moment. I had to be honest with myself, I'd nearly forgotten all about that barrier in the sky and I hadn't the slightest clue how to overcome it.

"I'll figure that one out when we get to it," I said confidently.

Log nodded, but I could see he sensed my uncertainty, as did Olson. Though they both did me the courtesy of showing faith in my abilities as their leader.

Log and Olson took care of Blick and Lara while I rested Lia and my mother in their rooms. The only thing I could think to say was, "I hope you've all been rejoined with Father and that I may see you all again... in my dreams."

XX
There Is Hope Yet
(The Diramal)

The remnants of my legion, composed of Vix and Varx alike, dwelled deep below the confines of Galiza's soil. Criptous would make his move to leave Galiza soon and we would need a way off the planet ourselves. That is why we've breached the human Stellavars, the collective name of their star vessels. We would come aboard, dull the ships' sensors to track our unique signatures—as it would be programmed to do—and take refuge in the lower levels where we'd be less likely to be discovered.

Zothra walked at my side; he held an atmosphere to him that was much like that of Amat's when the code nine neuro-chip ruled over the boy. I'd had him in my service long enough to know it meant something occupied him.

"What troubles you, Zothra?" I asked.

The Fé'Harkedür twitched his head in my direction.

"Nothing, sir."

"A lie."

Zothra knew I wouldn't admit him silence for too long before pressing him again. He shrugged and stumbled on his words.

"It's Criptous, Sir, many of your followers, myself included, feel it's time we deal with the boy. We worry that if he should live much longer, he will unveil the full truth of the Zeltons and that the only reason you've allowed him to live so long is because of—"

"The only reason he's lived to see today… is because it was Drakkar's bidding, and it must be obeyed if we are to win this war. I know what you would say next, Zothra, but so long as we commit ourselves to the ancient one, victory is assured. No matter what becomes of Criptous at this rate. His species, our most pressing threat, has been taken off the map," I said.

"Of course, Diramal. A great many things occupy my mind at present," said Zothra.

"*Mm*, do tell," I said.

Zothra did not respond immediately. I could sense it in him, a distant memory, one that perhaps led to resentment.

"Nothing worth mentioning, sir," said Zothra.

I sensed he told the truth, in the sense that if he'd said anything it would hardly concern my interest.

"No matter, we've arrived," I said.

Before us rested a smooth, round metallic surface that blocked off an opening in the underground path. I assembled a group of my men to cut out a breach in the plating for us to enter.

"I'll oversee the sensor disarray," said Zothra, as he moved to part from me.

"No, you won't. I've already given that task to Quavek. You'll accompany me further," I said.

Zothra stiffened and nodded.

"Very well, sir," said Zothra.

We took a lift capsule to the ship's docking bay, where the Vourtikahs rested dormant. Man-sized liquid light bubbles, made from the cores of dying stars. The true human cosmo-fighter technology. I paused beside one of them and hovered my hand over its surface, careful not to touch it. Immediately after one initiates contact with these craft, it is activated, whether the pilot is seated or not.

"I saved the final order from Drakkar for this moment exactly," I said.

"Sir?" asked Zothra, puzzled. He sounded almost intimidated; perhaps it was the burden he saw in my eyes.

"You are to kill Amat, via this Vourtikah. Or at the very least, you are to intercept him when he contacts the Zeltons. And if Fargon is here, truly, she will detect him long before he can give the command to open fire. If she succeeds, she'll take Amat under her and then all the work we've done out here over the past several megannums will have little impact on the events to come. Drakkar will not accept this," I said.

Zothra's stance shifted. He'd never seen me so desperate; none had. But in the past year, much had happened and much remained at stake for me. Much that Drakkar sought to take from me, if I did not fulfill this one thing for him. This one simple thing, the death of a very large thorn in my side, a very resilient thorn at that, who also held great value to me. But I stood to lose something greater.

"I understand, sir," said Zothra, trying to hide his enthusiasm.
"I don't need you to, I need Criptous, dead," I persisted.
Zothra nodded.
"I won't fail," said Zothra.
"You never have. That is why I have chosen you. Don't start now," I said.

(Amat)

I inhaled deeply as I took in her cloaked shape—the Peroma. Mended at last by Rika's handiwork. She stood adjacent to me, waiting to pull the drape back.
"Sir?" Rika spoke, taking me out of my fixation. "Shall we?"
I nodded, as I grasped the opposite side of the drapes and together, we pulled them off, revealing the silver painted plating with yellow and blue touches around the curves of the cylindrical wings.
"How does she look, sir?" asked Rika.
I nodded my head, unable to look Rika, or anyone else in the eye at that moment. It served me better to hardly keep track of their presence; she and everyone else that awaited me in the base hangar.
"Launch the Fades, let's load our people into the star vessels," I said.
As I stepped into the Peroma, I overheard Olson speaking with Rika. Perhaps I had upset her, or perhaps she thought she had upset me. It made no difference. I just wanted to be done with the war.

In the hours that followed, I stayed in close contact with the various Jinns overseeing their people safely into the submerged star vessels. Taking brief updates on who was moving to position, who was loading, and who were raring to go. I kept my dialogue short and concise between them, speaking only when I needed to. I had no interest in talking with anyone, just sitting with my own thoughts, wishing I were in isolation to do so.
At last, the time had come; the Jinns had loaded their people onto the submerged craft and the selected, trained pilots were in position to commence. Hovering over the air space of Skergel, a city that laid dormant over one of the star vessels, which Olson and Log had taken refuge within, I ordered the launch. The city crumbled like soft sand seeping out of one's

grasp and the star vessel known as Galican-7429 surpassed the size of the city itself, stretching over five hundred miles. The world rumbled with the domino effect of ship after ship rising in the same instance as each other. The ships held their positions, hovering some several hundred feet off the ground. Each of them glowing in a teal hue that lit up the world in a twilight. I didn't realize how much I longed to see the sunlight until that moment. Something had shifted in me; a slight sense of reinvigoration fueled my spirit, as I took in the gentle glow of the ships.

"Diramal Criptous… sir, the invaders are responding," Ho-Jinn Friker said over comms.

Snapping myself out of a daze, I repositioned the Peroma to face the dark heavens. My eyes adjusted and took in the swarms of their fighter vessels, intertwining with one another in gracefully coordinated movements. The expanse was so great, hardly any outline of the main ships could be seen.

"Diramal, I've just detected an unauthorized launch; it's one of our ship's fighters. It's fled out of our scanners' range."

I wouldn't waste my time with something that seemed so inconsequential, next to what we were faced with.

"Don't mind it, Friker, likely just a deserter," I said.

"Yes, sir," replied Friker.

Still the Zelton forces swarmed each other, steadily.

What do you want?

In a graceful formation, the Zelton fleet of fighters above me formed a gap, as streaks of light stretched down upon the world. I held my breath as I raised my hand to it.

Is that… daylight?!

"Battle stations ready, the invaders are—"

"Everyone hold your positions," I said over Log.

My eyes adjusted as I was finally able to observe the light was not daylight, but emanating from an opening at the heart of one of the larger ships. A few moments later, I noted a small dot lowering itself to me.

A vessel perhaps? Do they send an emissary to me?

The body came lower, a small thing, almost imperceivable if not for the shadow it cast in the light. Finally, its details came into view, and I could see it was a body. A Zelton figure lowering itself down to me, arms stretched out at its side, as if to present a peaceful gesture.

"Goddess!" I gasped.

"Amat, what is it?" asked Log, over comms.

"It's—"

BOOM! The Peroma was hit and thrown to her side by a powerful strike. Dark streaks of light passed in front of my display as I maneuvered down, quickly glancing up to see what had become of the alien figure. But the sky darkened once again, clouded by the ferocity of the alien fighters, raining down upon the world.

"Contact! Open fire," Log ordered.

"No!" I barked. But it was too late. The world thrummed with the pulse of the ancient ships' weaponry. A long, thin golden line streaked across the sky from the Galican, and wider, oval-shaped stretches of light shot across the air, wiping out at least fifty of the alien fighters at a time, before it reached their main vessels. Our Fades and Dailagons joined in as well. The aliens retaliated in full force.

In near hysteria, I opened my mouth to command a cease fire from my fleet. But before I could speak, the Peroma was struck again from behind.

"Amat, a dark vessel trails you," said Olson. "Its appearance is unlike anything we've seen before."

Could it be someone we know, do you think? asked the reflection in my head.

I clenched my fists around the controls as I made it my priority to meet this thing head-on. Forcing the throttle forward as far as it would go, I entered the Peroma into altered time. I pulled up and twirled, as a landslide of invader craft slipped passed, shooting, not at me... but behind me.

Finally, I cut to the left as the storm of Zeltonian crafts continued to make way for me.

Why do they not engage me? I asked myself.

Why do you *not engage them?* asked the reflection.

I glanced to my side at a flash of green light and maneuvered forcefully to the side, as a large streak of green light barely missed kissing the Peroma. Olson let out a grunt as the Galican took the hit, feeling the

213

blast for himself while in command of the ship. Despite the impact, the Galican appeared to take hardly any damage.

"Olson, are you alright?" Log asked.

"I'll be alright. Log, take charge of our lower guns. Find that dark craft and keep it off Amat," said Olson.

"I will," said Log.

"Olson, is the craft not still behind me?" I asked.

"No, the invader crafts shot it away from you when you ascended, but it's still up here," said Olson.

I descended slightly into the chaos of the ensuing battle. Still, no alien craft fired upon me, as if I were somehow cloaked to them or they were deliberately avoiding me. It was a curious thing, sitting idle amongst a raging conflict, watching both sides destroy one another, not being pursued by either, not knowing what to do. I had only one enemy amidst all that chaos.

Black streaks shot from above, obliterating Human and Zeltonian craft. As the shots swiftly grew nearer, I spun and dove.

"Contact, it found me again," I said.

"Roger, sir, where are you located?" asked Log.

"Too far down," I replied, as I pulled up, hovering just a few hundred meters off the ground, heading for the hole in the ground.

My eyes adjusted to the pitch-black pit, illuminating the details within the deep crevice. The unseen, dark vessel behind me, released bursts of selective fire. Nearly every one of them landed, but not directly enough to have a critical impact on the Peroma's systems. Running out of options, I pushed the Peroma full throttle into her descent, and the dark vessel pushed after me. Half a second later, I saw the rubble of Skergel start to surface. My eyes widened as I pulled back on the throttle and briefly shut down the Peroma's systems. The dark craft fell in a free fall, as it launched passed me. My finger, primed on the Peroma's activation button, pressed down, and in just as swift a movement, I activated the ship's altered time.

The dark craft had a short, jagged wing stretching to the left side, while a longer, arched, feather-like wing stretched on the right. A fin stretched down either side of the rear, and at its center was a spherical bubble, with the craft's guns arched to either side of it.

214

By the time I had my own weapons locked on it, the ship had flipped and spurred ahead. I fired regardless and landed a few shots that hardly wobbled it off course. I adjusted my trajectory and together we steadily climbed back up the hole, circling one another, always staying adjacent to the other. I could not see the identity of the pilot, his cockpit clouded by the dark shadows that steamed off it. Abruptly, the dark craft aimed itself at me and sped forward, twirling as it fired. I arched the Peroma over the shots as the dark craft continued dead ahead and into a wide tunnel. I slowly aligned myself with it as I scanned the interior.

Just wide enough for the Peroma to fit, I thought.

But we don't even know if this path leads back up to the surface, said the reflection.

I don't need it to. I just need this thing blown out of the world, I replied.

I pressed the throttle forward and zoomed down the tunnel. The craft was lost but I sensed it had not fled. Reaching the end of the passage, I found a tunneling system, stretching every which way. I didn't like the look of it in the slightest. Holding my position, I tried to decide which path to take, but my attention was suddenly disturbed when a blur moved across the way, down one of the tunnels directly ahead of me. I pressed ahead, cautiously.

Zap-zap-zap-zap! The black streaks blew past me from the right. Without hesitating, I sped forward into the tunnel, not knowing where it would lead me. It curved down sharply, and I had hardly enough time to react as I heard the wing scrape the rock wall. I adjusted course in time for me to follow the path of the next curve upward. I was brought back to the open space and witnessed the dark craft zip across my view. In a delayed reaction, I fired and missed, shaking my head.

It's like my final assessment in the Alpha program all over again, I thought, as I entered the next tunnel across from me.

The next tunnel curved back slightly and looped around. I shot out, high in the spherical space. The dark vessel shot back out at me from almost directly ahead, and we fired upon one another, both landing minor shots to the visors of our cockpits. At the last moment, I twisted the Peroma around and for a fleeting moment, our cockpits passed over one another. I glanced up at the pilot and recognized his faded features.

Ah, the Shadow Scar from the Commathor Bridge and the towers of Giclon. Do you recall who he reminded us of? asked the voice in my head. "Zothra," I growled.

I shifted my focus ahead and pushed the throttle forward as I launched into the next tunnel ahead of me. It was longer in its path, curving way down. As the path flattened, I saw a tunnel up ahead that intertwined with my own. I came up on it, wondering if I should cross over, then shifted my grip on the joystick to its direction. *Whip!* Zothra came shooting down the path faster than a strike of lightning. With my guns just out of alignment, I committed to the turn and sprayed a burst of fire across his vessel, forcing him to adjust his course and aim that did not penetrate the Peroma's plating.

Zothra passed under me swiftly as half of his bladed wing slithered into an upright position and cut across the bottom of the Peroma's left wing. Furious, I pulled back on the throttle as I rotated the Peroma around to chase after the Cho'Zai before drifting much further. Eager to catch up to his tail, I pushed the Peroma to her limit, maneuvering down through the alternative path that crossed over my original one. I got myself in range just before the path curved up. I locked a shot but waited until we curved up the path before firing. The tunnel led back out into the wide spherical space and Zothra continued to fly up. I released fire and landed enough shots to cause a trail of sparkling black dust to leak from the craft's rear. Before I could destroy it, however, the craft's long wing whipped around and faced one side of the blade toward me, to cover the rear end of the bubble.

Still, I pressed on with my fire as Zothra shot up into another tunnel that led straight back toward the surface. Before we reached it, the vessel morphed its second wing into an identical design to its parallel. Only, on its edge were sharp, narrowly spaced rivets. The wing spiraled in front of the cockpit bubble and ate through the solid rock. Chunks of debris clunked against the Peroma as I persisted behind, shattering the glass of my visor, denting the plating. The rear wing continued to take the heat of the Peroma's canons until it split in two. But by then, we had ascended back to the surface. Refusing to hold back, I kept the pressure on Zothra, but before his dark craft had found its limit, the Shadow Scar pulled his ship back, twirled as he fell above me, and cut his riveted wing across my right.

I caught a look at the battle that had continued to wage, and by the looks of things, we were winning. The vessel that must have been the Galican looked slightly gashed and worn throughout its plating, but nothing in comparison to the damage it had delt to the Zeltonian star vessels; refusing to break formation.

Zothra bombarded me with a keen aim, triggering the critical systems. The interior of the Peroma lit up with a blue hue. *Reserve power mode... she doesn't have much fight left in her.* Gazing up to the skies once again, I saw the same ship that had revealed its radiant white light to us; it's plating had remained open. I reminisced over its... colors. It was not just a white light; hints of blue, red, yellow, and other colors were lightly tinted in its shine.

That must be the core of the ship! I thought to myself. *If I remember correctly, the colors that shined within the first Zeltonian ship, on Anua. Assuming it's sensitive, if I can get close enough and lay enough damage onto it, perhaps it would breach a hole in their defenses. Enough to cause a break in their formation, perhaps.*

Seems a risky move, said the reflection in my head.

It's not like I have many options left. If it kills me, at least I'll have done something that would help humanity escape the Zelton's barrier. Besides, what else do I have to live for at this rate? I pondered.

Before the reflection could object further, I bolted the Peroma on a course to meet with the Zeltonian core. Dashing through the skirmish, the alien forces remained passive to me. I heard chatter over the comms, but to my ears they were dulled by my focus. They could have been Olson and Log's voices. Maybe one of them had caught sight of Zothra on my tail and laid down suppressive fire on the Cho'Zai. Nearing the core, I fired everything I had at it. The Peroma rumbled and jerked from an impact to its rear, and I lost speed slightly. Refusing to hesitate, I continued directing fire at the core. The damage seemed to disperse and distort the colors over one another. In the final moments, it was only blinding light that engulfed my unblinking vision. My fingers still pressed tightly against the trigger as I broke through layer after layer of weakened plating. Breaching the back of the ship came at the expense of one of my wings as I escaped the atmosphere. Before me was one brief glimpse of a black, starless void.

Ka-Boom! A wave of light sent me drifting across space, tumbling aimlessly against the Peroma's own momentum. The airlock on the left side of the Peroma was torn apart, along with the wing. All the oxygen had been sucked out into the vacuum in a swift and silent *Whoosh!* Dressed in neither suit nor sealed armament, my eyes swelled and my skin stiffened into place underneath a layer of ice. I exhaled all the air from my lungs and saw my final breath leave my mouth in a frozen fog that crystalized and slowly drifted away from me.

In my final conscious moments, the Peroma rotated me into view of the obliterated body of Anua, past the black void of the universe that I faintly noticed had a lack of stars gleaming in its space and back toward Galiza, where I witnessed the Zeltonian ships had started to disperse and the ancient, submerged ships of my people began their ascent into space with me. My smile froze into place as I took pride in knowing my final act served a purpose greater than myself. My eyes did not close, but my vision ceased… though not before I witnessed another bright, white light shine down upon the Peroma, with various colors inlaid within it. Pulling me up into their vessel.

I gasped with the reinvigoration of life filling my body and something sharp leaving my chest. Still frozen in place and severely blinded, however. My lungs could hardly expand enough to take in the choked gasping breaths of air I managed to take in. Too deep a breath felt as though muscles tore and my lungs might burst. Neither chest nor stomach could expand as I took in breath. I could only gasp. Grateful for the numbness of my nerve endings; sparing me from most of the pain that surely would have been present in my ribs. I could scarcely feel the shift in gravity as my body was raised from my seat and swiftly carried off somewhere. There were voices as well, Zeltonian voices, speaking all around me, muffled from the ice that had frozen over my ears.

Physically, biologically, psychologically, I was in an inescapable fight with myself. Given my severe condition, much of my body wanted to shut down and my consciousness wanted so desperately to fade away. Yet something stirred in me, something the Zeltons had administered, to keep my system stable enough so that I would remain conscious, alive.

Oh please, Anua, whether a Luminous Paradise or eternal shadow be my resting place, take me there now. For either must surely be better than the state my body endures now, I prayed.

I did not feel it when they first lowered me in, but once my head had been fully submerged, I sensed the water fill my gaping mouth and my flaring nostrils. Yet somehow, I could breathe. The tank the Zeltons had moved me into was one of mildly heated liquid. It was not an easy adjustment. The fact that I was crouched there, submerged in a vat, told my mind that I must be on the verge of drowning. My natural reaction was to gasp deeper, faster, surging my ribcage with pain from the stiff frozen layer over my body, as I slowly regained my sense of physical feeling. I tried so desperately to clench my fists, to jerk and move, swim to the surface, assuming they hadn't sealed off the hatch. But I couldn't and despite being able to breathe after being suspended there for minutes on end, my mind still would not allow me to dampen my survival instincts.

I am going to die, I thought repeatedly. *Goddess, I am going to drown!*

But I didn't. That was perhaps the most frightening thing about it—the fact that I couldn't make the connection in the lack of the threat I was under. So many times, I should have passed out in that tank from hypothermia, so many times my heart should have given out from the amount of stress it was under. But whatever it was the Zeltons had revived me with would not allow any of my primary organs to give out in the slightest. I always had just enough strength to stay alive, just enough to be held in a stasis between the physical universe and the doorstep of that void that awaited me in the beyond.

Regaining my vision, it started out blurred but took in enough light to see the blood gushing out of my eyelids after every blink. The carbon bubbles that trailed up from the surface of the tank and the mellow lights installed around the inner rim. What rested outside the tank, I could only imagine. It was at this point that my mind finally started to settle and acknowledged what I was suspended in: oxygenated perfluorocarbon.

Steadily, I regained control over the rest of my body, starting with my toes and fingers, though I dared not move them too much. The bones in my hands and feet were still frozen in place. A while longer and I could move my wrists and ankles, my arms and legs, my neck and finally the tension in my chest and abdomen dissipated.

By then, I felt so accustomed to the liquid that I almost didn't want to leave. And while my breaths had gotten calmer, deeper, my lungs had grown heavy with the oxygenated perfluorocarbon and I would need to remove it from my body before much longer.

Feeling limber, I swam around in the tank. Not thinking of a way out, it hardly seemed likely, anyway. *I do wonder what will become of me once the invaders retrieve me from the tank; that is, if they have any intention of doing so.*

A Zelton's outline approached the glass to the chamber, with its four arms held behind its back. Slowly, I swam to the glass to meet with the being. The glass was so thick it blurred the Zelton's features, but not enough to hide its relaxed shoulders, its easy breathing, and its overall collected demeanor. Neither of us gestured toward the other; we simply acknowledged the presence of one another before, at last, the alien motioned to its side and a loud *clunk!* shifted in the tank. The alien took steps backward. Air seeped in as the glass inched forward slightly, and proceeded to slowly swing open, flooding the oxygenated perfluorocarbon. With much of my strength still depleted, I flowed with the liquid as it dragged me across the cold, metallic floor. I stopped on my chest and felt the back of my throat tense almost immediately, but I couldn't move my arms to push myself off the ground.

Before choking to death on my own vomit, a pair of Zeltons were at my sides, pulling on my arms and holding my chest up. *"Wawwwww!"* I retched, long and hard. My lungs tensed so harshly that a similar pain to that of the frozen stasis surged in my airways. I whined and gasped, catching barely enough air before expelling more excess oxygenated perfluorocarbon out of my lungs. There was still residue of the pasty, sticky liquid trailing down my throat and out of my mouth, as I was able to take a half-decent, gasping, deep breath before hurling once more. Feeling a burst of furious willpower, I kicked my knee up and pressed against the floor with my foot, just before retching up the last of the substance. My body was so shaken that I had to cough the last of it out and I couldn't help but tremble.

The clicking of the Zelton's toe claws echoed through the wide, green-lit room as it slowly approached me. I was able to see somewhat better at this point, but it was still blurred, and my eyes blinked with exhaustion. I looked up at the Zelton who lorded over me. If I had my full strength, I might have said something, but not in this circumstance. I was at their mercy and if they knew any hint of the reputation I held among my people, in our war, I suspected the Zeltons had very little of that in store for me.

The Zelton before me glanced at each of its kin beside me and spoke in their native tongue. The others replied and dragged me away, to another area of the ship, where I was stripped of my clothing and power washed of the oxygenated perfluorocarbon residue along my body. Clean now, the Zeltons dried me with some heavy weighted wrappings that generated their own heat. They then guided me to another room in the ship, smaller, with some sort of sloped table. Fitted for a human, seemingly, with restraints and a long, sharp, arching needle, over the head restraint. I stopped to turn and back away from the device. The Zeltons at my side took my arms firmly, but with only enough force to drag me toward the device. In that regard, they did not seem to want to hurt me, at least not directly.

I meekly waved my arm up to the Zelton on my left, as both proceeded to lock me down in the restraints.

"What are you doing to me? What is this?" I asked slurred.

The Zelton did not answer, and gently took my arm, locking it in place for what would commence next. When all was set, the aliens moved back some paces and stood in place. One hissed some command and the needle above my head proceeded to move into place. I panted helplessly as the device rang with a pitched drilling sound and plunged itself into my skull. It penetrated deep into my cranial cavity, pausing directly behind my third eye. I tensed and growled, digging my nails across the metal surface as the tip of the needle expanded into three thin limbs. They moved swiftly to grasp onto something, something that refused to move from its place. Not some tissue connected to my brain, no, this was something latched to the interior of my skull. The pain urged me to jerk my head back and around, my arms to flail, and my legs to kick, but the restraints held firm. There was a duel commencing in my scalp; the needle was working to detach some kind of parasite there. And as the conflict waged on, I heard the voices of the Zeltons fade in and out from their native tongue to my own language.

"...won't move... he won't... latches onto his frontal lobe," one of the Zeltons said, in a masculine tone.

"Do not retract... it will move to... if we fail... he, above all the others... understand!" said another Zelton, sounding more feminine.

"As you... Fargon," said the former Zelton.

The limbs pulled more vigorously, their sides grinding slightly across my skull as they battled whatever was inside there. My eyes started to roll back as my torso powered free of its restraint and arched high for a moment before two Zeltons came to hold me down. My jaw gaped open as choked breaths entered and escaped it. A final cry, and I howled as the limbs wrenched their target out of my skull, slipping out of the tiny hole it entered from. Only for a moment did I see the black squirming, figureless blob that had been inside my head, before one of the Zeltons zapped it out of existence. They sprayed something promptly on my forehead where the needle had made its entrance and dabbed the sweat off of my face with a warm cloth.

A third Zelton approached me with a steady stride. Her face was slowly revealed from an overcasting light, and she asked me: "What are you called, human?"

I could still hear her native speech, but it was as if my mind had a natural way of translating her speech. Thrown off by the question, I shook my head and replied: "What?"

"Your name, Stargliner. What is it?" asked the Zelton.

"Uuh... Amat... Amat Luciph Criptous," I replied.

"Amat." The Zelton nodded. "A strong name, worthy of your predecessor. I am Fargon, otherwise known as the Mai'Sahara Spica."

"My predecessor? Mai'Sahara? What do these things mean?" I asked, wearily.

Fargon motioned to tell me more but one of the Zeltons at my side cut her short.

"Forgive my disturbance, Mai'Sahara Spica, but is it so wise to assume that this Shadach'mar is truly the Mai'Sahara of the first human Hanu?"

There was no notable shift in Fargon's expression, at least none that I could see.

"You are right to be skeptical in your counsel to me, Gha'Varin. But trust in what I've noted about this one and in my confidence of this decision," replied Fargon.

Gha'Varin bowed his head.

"I do trust thee, Mai'Sahara Spica. Though, perhaps we should keep this one restrained, until what you must tell him settles in," said Gha'Varin.

The Zeltons did not have irises that shifted across their eyes, and Fargon did not even shift her head in my direction from Gha'Varin to me. Still, I felt her stare in that moment.

"I do not fear you." She spoke with such projection. "But what I am to tell you will likely strike you as overwhelming. With that in mind, you shall remain under restraint until we've both reached an understanding with one another."

I would have nodded, but my head was still restrained.

"I will hear you," I replied.

Fargon considered something to herself for a moment.

"Perhaps we should start off with something small. You'd questioned my meaning behind a mention of 'your predecessor' and 'Mai'Sahara.'"

"I did," I replied.

"The term refers to what you might call a reincarnation, but the deeper meaning is far more complicated than that and relates to my mentioning of a predecessor." Fargon paused. "That parasite we removed from your cranial cavity, do you know what it was?"

"I have an idea of the purpose it served," I said.

"It is called an Audicrox, a physically harmless biological weapon. Though, placed precisely before your frontal lobe, favoring the left side of the cranial cavity. The hemisphere of your species' brain that connects to the auditory index, which has developed to serve as an interpreter between our tongues and many others," said Fargon.

"Creating a language barrier," I replied.

Fargon nodded.

"As was its primary function," said Fargon.

I took a moment to let that soak.

"You said it had been placed there, tell me, by who," I demanded.

Fargon took a heavy breath as she paced across the floor and the room lit up with a vibrant hologram of an aquatic setting. Pink isles, covered in a coral-like substance along the shores spaced out over leagues of orange waters. Each isle had tall, smooth, thin, yellow peaks that stretched almost as high as the planet's teal atmosphere. A star hovered just above the horizon; rays of purple nebulas stretched toward the planet like a vortex. Red mists covered the greater stretches of land in the distance. The hologram fell below the ocean's surface before I could take in much more. The hologram proceeded to present me with a large city on the seabed. Red, vibrant domes, systematically connected through an arrangement of blue piped routes and passageways. Tall, organic towers, coursing with plasma energy that seemed to power this great city, stationed on the outer rims.

I was drawn deeper into the red dome at the heart of the city, where several identical figures awaited me. Their heads were outlined in three points, one at either side and a connecting third at the top. They had no lips but intertwining gills at their mouths that could unravel and shift into maxillipeds. Their eyes were two evenly spaced, narrow, and almost flat lines across the lower brows of their heads. They had no nostrils, and their body was rigidly shelled, sharp to the touch. Their dual legs were peg-shaped, as were their arms. Though a soft fleshy extension sprouted from the ends of their arms, with over ten long, thick antennae stretching from them that presumably served as fingers.

"These are called the Vix, keepers of vigor and power" Fargon stated. "And in a time, long before my existence, this was the state of their primary home planet: Kiv'Zjarthin. They are one of the five members of the Hanu, a collection of creator beings that founded the cosmos with all its life and beauty…" As Fargon continued, the hologram of the Vix faded and four other entities came into view as she named them off. "The other four consisted of races known as the Wertles, keepers of intellect and enlightenment…" A pink, glistening, flimsy body, having no sign of a bone in its anatomy, with squirming tentacles stretching from its shoulders and hips. It bore no neck, but a wide, round head, with five eyes all seated right beside one another across its face, above a spherical mouth with layers of drilling, sharp, pick-thin teeth. "…The Hamurak, keepers of matter and structure…" A new figure appeared, with a shorter stature than myself, but extremely lean in muscular mass. It bore a long, wide neck, connected to a droplet-shaped head, though the edge of its mouth was not pointed. It was circular and gaping, with no sign of teeth or tongue. Large walnut-shaped eyes stretched from the center of its face, up and around the back of its scalp. At their rear were two long antennae. An array of four pointed horns sprouted from its jawline. Thin hairs, like that of the Zeltons, covered the Hamurak's body, but not enough to hide its bulging definition. Its arms were long and arched from the elbows down. Three shelled claws sprouted from the end of its wrist, attached to no palm. Its legs were also jagged, and its feet were only as wide as the girth of its legs with three sprouting claws, two in the front and one at the heel. "…my kin, the Zeltons, keepers of the spirit and enlightenment…" Fargon continued as a Zelton figure emerged at her side. "…and yours, human, keepers of guidance and light." The figure that manifested next looked hardly anything like me—its features were barely defined, yet slim in shape, embodied in a glowing light.

I did not respond immediately as I could hardly acknowledge the seriousness in Fargon's voice. I frowned my brows as I struggled to find the words.

You waste our thoughts in considering this creature's *words!* The reflection in my head spoke.

"Uh… how… what—"

"This is surely hard for you to process, I know. But it is the truth of things. Your kin and mine, among these others, built the known universe… as much as we've laid waste to it," interrupted Fargon.

Of course, they laid waste to an entire species; ours. It's only natural that they'ed take their savagery to such a monumental level. The reflection chuckled, sinisterly.

"Laid waste?" I asked, trying to stay focused.

Fargon nodded.

"Countless years ago, beyond any measurement of time you could comprehend, there were the first of the Hanu. Spica was the embodiment of my own kin, Ombeck of the Vix, Shai-Tukar of the Hamurak, Krota of the Wertles, and Reinosso of the humans. All suspended in the isolation of the predated cosmos. It was a reality in which only they occupied… along with a sixth member. Formless, ruthless, and sinister in nature who has

225

been called many names across the different species we'd created. But we Hanu, have always known him as Drakkar," said Fargon.

My hairs pricked up at the name. Yet something in the recess of my mind, felt invigorated by it.

"From what is known about our ancestors' ancient feud against him, the Hanu kept mostly to themselves. Gathering insight, growing their own inner strengths through self-discovery. Divided, however, the Hanu were left vulnerable to the workings of Drakkar and one by one he threatened their existence. But the Hanu, despite their differences, held a connection deeper than any logical comprehension and when one was threatened, they were all made aware. Banding together to fend off this dark entity. Particularly that of Ombeck and Reinosso, strongest of the Hanu, in their own ways. It is believed that, even on their own, Drakkar could not hope to match their strengths.

"At last, a day came when the Hanu reached a collective sense of fulfilled enlightenment. Having a sense that they could serve a greater purpose but also in need of a safer environment, the Hanu gathered and compiled their souls together, colliding faster than the speed of light. The energy their spirits amassed was enough to envelop the universe in a great and *thunderous* flame, lasting eons. Until, finally, patches of renewed space emerged, as did remnants of the Hanu. Scattered into hundreds upon thousands of embodiments that we perceive ourselves in now. Only... the physiology and essence of *your* species have changed over the last four hundred thousand years."

Lies, humanity scarcely existed a few ten thousand years, prior to the great scorching! The reflection spoke defensively.

I blinked.

"Four hundred thousand?" I asked.

Fargon nodded.

"Can you tell me how, or at least, why my kin have changed so much," I replied.

"The answer to that rests within the next segment of our collective history. The connection between the first of the Hanu persisted within us, post the great surging as well as our tendency to do things in isolation from one another. By this time, things had changed, however. We were born into this universe, having five collective minds among our races, knowing what we were now capable of."

Capable of what, the manifestation of life itself? The reflection mocked.

"To create life?" I asked with intrigue.

"Indeed," replied Fargon. "And we promptly began filling the cosmos with planets, species, stars, galaxies, nebulas, and whatever else we dared to construct. When it came to our mortal creations, often one race among the Hanu would start to instigate their teachings at one point of the creation's development and sometime later another among the Hanu would reveal themselves, offering their teachings among the mortals. But there was always a risk that they might be swayed to more sinister values by Drakkar, who had also survived the great surging."

"How?" I asked.

Why do you persist in egging on this pest?! If this is their leader, presumably, we should be strategizing an assassination. The reflection growled.

"When the first of the Hanu initiated the great surging, they merely manifested a transcendence of their immortal forms. While keeping the space around them intact. Which Drakkar is somehow attached to and cannot be broken any more than the fabric of the cosmos itself can. Unless the cosmos itself decided it so," said Fargon.

Aha! A flaw, in this pitiful tale of woe this creature stated the Hanu were the creators of the universe. What power then would the universe have over this, Drakkar..." the reflection's tone took a relishing shift in the mention of 'Drakkar's' name. *"...if the Hanu themselves held no power over him?*

Somewhat swayed by the reflection's words, I voiced the argument: "Earlier you mentioned how *we* supposedly created the universe, yet you speak as if it holds a greater power over ourselves."

"Nature always holds the greater forces at its will over those who roam within it," Fargon replied.

That still doesn't—

"The greatest mechanisms of influence over nature were left us, however, in remnants of the first Hanu's embodiments, one from each. These possessions of the Hanu, as they are called, hold the raw power of

227

our former selves. Radiating with the same light and energy our predecessors once shone with. And as beings gifted with an immortal essence, we are forbidden from any final resting place. But it was discovered that the possessions of the Hanu could facilitate such a place," said Fargon.

When are we finally going to gut this thing? I grow restless of its fanciful rantings, growled the reflection.

"I have reached a place between both life and death..." I argued, losing track of the faded memory just as quickly as it arrived. "I felt... a sort of *dawn* calling to me. Your claim that we are forbidden from a final resting place cannot be true."

"The place you were held, is one that only the Hanu are sent and only members of my kin can guide others out of. If the bodies of the trapped souls are mendable, then the dead are guided back to them. Otherwise, we must find a way to tether their essence to the Hanu's accorded possession. The sensation you felt in being willed toward the dawn is but a limbo of torment that awaits us in mortal death. We all feel compelled to reach out to that graceful beyond, but we will never arrive at it. For it is a place that only our creations can reach.

"This, among many other great discoveries about the Hanu's possessions, drove the Vix to find a way that would restore the virtues of the greater immortality our predecessors were accustomed to. When confronted with this, the other four races would not willingly contribute their possessions to such an endeavor. As the amount of power the combined five possessions held was presumably too great for our lesser forms to attain. For a time, the Vix abandoned the idea, and all resumed their work among the expanding cosmos. Until a day came when the Vix called another meeting of the Hanu and suggested that an individual being be jointly created between all members of the Hanu. A being that would embody all the traits and powers of the Hanu, so that it might serve as a conduit for us to take on the power of the five possessions. This motion was approved, but under the condition that the being produced an heir among the Hanu to serve as the conduit. The idea of giving a mortal creation the amassment of all our abilities access to the most powerful objects in the universe did not sit well with certain members among the Hamurak, Humans, or my own kin."

"And the Wertles?" I asked.

"They acknowledged the calculated probability of the former approach to obtaining the raw power of the possessions and stood unopposed to either. With time, this creation, who granted himself the name of Valzeron, had been nurtured under the care of each of the Hanu at different times. Especially the Vix, who had taken the strongest liking to him.

"When the time was right, the Vix requested that Valzeron take a female partner among the collective Hanu, and produce a child. It wasn't too long after that, the Mai'Sahara of Ombeck was born, bearing the name… Aqil. When Aqil reached the age of a young man among his kin, the Vix called counsel one final time to gather the Hanu, along with their possessions, to make ready the ceremony that would invigorate our eternal lives. But the other members of the Hanu sensed greed in the Vix's eagerness to harness this long-lost power that could easily be steered toward darker motives in the process of the ceremony and refused to hand their possessions over to them.

"Outraged, the Vix sought to steal the possessions of the Wertles, Hamurak, Humans, and my own kin combined, arranging the ceremony in secret. Using Aqil as their conduit. We don't know if the Vix had gotten anywhere near the power they'd hoped to achieve, but in their attempt to grasp it, through corrupt means, they left themselves vulnerable to the influence of Drakkar.

"With the power to each of the possessions left open, the ancient shadow of the universe seeped itself into both the possessions and the Vix. It was… devastating to Aqil; no one can say if he even stood a chance against the very nature of evil itself. Perhaps, on the other hand, Drakkar killed him intentionally, knowing the lengths of the young Vix's power and left nothing to chance.

"When this terrible tragedy unfolded, the other members of the Hanu could not sense it immediately. For Drakkar had severed our unified intuition. That, however, they did sense. The Vix openly revealed what they had become, with a patronizing pride, and the rest of us could hardly begin to formulate what proper action was necessary. As the Vix were warriors, their minds were more fitted to assessing the task we were all confronted with and for a great deal of time, we could not bring ourselves to even consider an all-out cosmic war."

'Cosmic war.' The reflection chuckled. *If such a conflict truly played out, with the involvement of our ancestors, mind you, how do you explain the immense amnesia of such a conflict, across our kin?*

Fargon took a moment to let that sink. My breathing tensed as I was once again weighing the logic of my reflection, counterbalancing the magnitude of Fargon's story.

"By the time we reached the conclusion that retaliation was a necessary and pressing act, the Vix had wiped out and or converted almost half of all our creations into what are collectively called the Varx." Fargon stretched out her words as she slowly came face to face with me. "With Valzeron still on our side, I was the next of his children born into existence. With the purpose of leading the four remaining members of the Hanu against Drakkar and defending our surviving creations from his influence. When I failed to put a stop to Drakkar, the Mai'Sahara of Shai-Tukar was birthed to take my place. And where she failed, the Mai'Sahara Krota was birthed and where he failed, you have now been brought into this existence, as the Mai'Sahara Reinosso. To fight the final hope, where none is left. For at this rate, Drakkar and his servants have wiped out and converted all but *one* mortal creation."

So what, we're a God? The reflection burst into hysteria. *No, we're hardly sensible enough as a nation-wide leader.*

"At last, we arrive at the answer to your question. In the years of this war, our greatest allies and strength rested in your kin, to stand against the Vix and all who follow them. Drakkar acknowledged this early on and focused his forces on your kin. Resulting in the near annihilation of your race. With my kin being the next strongest and most resilient force on the line, we gave what remained of your kin twelve worlds that once belonged to us. Far from the reaches of the war, in the hopes that you might regain your strength and numbers. But in our lack of strategy, many Vix seeped their way into each world, led by the most demented of all their race."

"The Diramal," I growled.

Fargon nodded.

Kill. Her. The reflection urged.

"It is the highest rank within the Vix chain of command. We have not known him by any other reference. Through the Diramal and Drakkar's influence, your species endured psychological, spiritual, and most notably physical deviations to your being," said Fargon.

"Are there any among these other twelve planets that continue to harbor humans?" I asked.

Fargon shook her head. She proceeded to motion toward one of the other Zeltons at my side, who spoke subtly over a comms channel and activated some shift in the ship's plating. As the black, empty space was revealed, many of the other Zelton vessels lowered themselves into view, also revealing some portion of their interiors. As the ships came nearer, I saw what all stood in the foreground of their illuminated interiors. Multitudes of my kin, many of them likely among those I had sought to take back to the various Utopian militia bases.

My breath caught and a tear trickled down my cheek at the horror Fargon's reality had finally disclosed to me.

"What of the other members of my kin in the ships we fought against you with?" I asked.

"Gone, I'm afraid. Despite our best efforts to neutralize the vessels and take the last surviving members of your kin aboard with us, they were of human design. And in their prime state, your engineering is far superior to our own," said Fargon.

Aw, isn't that convenient and not a physical human to be presented right before our eyes. I sense a trick... my reflection hissed.

My breath shivered at the thought of...

Olson and Log... I thought.

"Where did they flee to, the ships of my kin?" I asked.

"The Vix hold the power to move even whole planets into different positions across the cosmos. In the past year, the Vix have been moving one of their planets from their home quadrant in orbit of at a nearby star, with a fitting habitat to your kin's liking. All set in place to lure the remains of your kin into their grasp."

I started to weep.

And so, I have lost them all.

Mm-hm and all thanks to the miscreates that surround us now. Since we seem to be gaining their trust, why not take this opportunity to respond in kind and thank them? The reflection spoke cunningly.

I tensed as I tried ripping through the restraints.

"Let. Me. Out. Of. These," I demanded.

Fargon was unfazed by my tone.

"I know you must have had family that you lost—"

"You have no idea. One of them, *killed* by a member of your kin, in fact. And now the Diramal has taken them all away from me," I rasped, violently.

"Were the possession of your kin under either of our guardianships, I would show you how to present them all here before us. But I sense you've already unlocked your kin's ability to see the truth of things in your dreams, and in those dreams, you are met with the man who fathered you," said Fargon.

"And how could you know that for certain?" I growled the question.

"Being all-wise and knowing is one of my kin's natural attributes. Though, there are reaches that even my sight cannot penetrate," said Fargon

"And among the things you've told and shown me is that you claim we are indirectly related to one another. Sharing the same biological father. Admerion you said his name was?" I asked.

"Valzeron, it is," said Fargon.

"You have saved what can't even be counted as a tenth of Galiza's population. And now, after all you've put us through, you expect us to join forces?" I asked.

Out of the question. The reflection blurted.

"If you would consider having it any other way, you wouldn't get very far. I do acknowledge and see that you *are* the Mai'Sahara, Reinosso. Inside each of us, however, is a tie to the Vix and their taint to Drakkar. If that is the side of you that stirs most dominantly in your mind, I will not hesitate to take extreme measures to see it suppressed. Though my kin may have killed your father figure, the Diramal has stripped you of so much more and caused much of the suffering that has unfolded between us. Which gives us a common enemy. I cannot guarantee the two of us will get along, but you and the remainders of your kin will be guarded most exclusively, if you join our cause," said Fargon, as my restraints came undone.

There is no taint within you, you've seen for yourself, we are one. Said the reflection

My apparent half-Zeltonian sister reached one of her right hands out to me as the restraints retracted. I shifted my gaze immediately onto the blade that rested on the belt of the Zelton standing beside me.

Once we reach for it, we should take care of the guards at either side—

"Make any motion to assault me and I will see you coming before you flinch. Besides, would you seek to kill someone who'd saved your life twice over?" Fargon asked.

I was put off by the question.

"I'm not sure what you mean," I replied.

"The bridge between the Isles and in the pit of that building, a Zelton helped to spare your life. Once from a jagged, rusty rod that had pierced your side and another from the Vorüm'Qij, Zothra, the Diramal's most skilled asset. That Zelton was myself." Fargon paused to let that sink in. "Now, will you take my hand, or will you be met with theirs?" My half sister gestured to the members of her kin at my side.

Considering my circumstance, I sighed, pushing aside my pride and swung my arm into Fargon's as she helped me to my feet; my legs shook, barely holding me up.

"The Diramal killed nearly all the members of my family, except for two, who are now surely at his mercy and will find none. His corruption led to the near extinction of my race. And despite the fact we have been deeply manipulated, you still found it in yourself to save innocent members of my kin. And if what you say is true about Valzeron and myself being the Mai'Sahara of this Reinosso, then that makes us siblings."

Fargon flared her pincers, which gave off a very oddly pleasant expression. It was in this moment *I struck!* In altered time, I launched the palm of my hand forcefully against Fargon's face, knocking her back. Calling upon all my strength, I turned and stomped my foot on the cold stone-like surface, rocking the ground. The pair of Fargon's bodyguards were knocked off balance in their fleeting pursuit toward me, with weapons in hand. Catching the arm of one in its stumble toward me, I disarmed the Zelton and quickly moved to strike at the back of the other. Drawing deeper into the power of altered time, my movements had become far superior to theirs, as I struck the back of my fist against the first Zelton's face, breaking its neck. Turning around to face Fargon, the leader of the Zeltons struck me to the ground, knocking me out.

I awoke, groggy, and with an aching pain on the right side of my head. As I motioned to massage the pain, I halted when noticing the strange string of energy enveloped around my wrists. Similar to that of the plasma restraints, though, its static energy structure gave me the impression that they must have been neutron or proton restraints. I carefully proceeded to raise my hand to my head and aided the pain with the touch of my hand.

I assessed the room that I was in. I'd been moved once again, somewhere much smaller, confined to a flat, hard block. Again, with caution, I dangled my legs over the edge and eased my feet to the ground. I stood tall and observed there were no signs of an entry point anywhere in the room, not even a glass screen or any other indication that someone might be watching me. I took one step forward—

"Careful," Fargon's voice came from within the room. "Venture too far from that table and the restraint at your wrist will induce a small ionization surge throughout your molecular system. Persist against it and your molecules will be met with a collision cascade."

I nodded my head as I hovered my free hand over my restrained wrist.

"I think I'll take a seat then," I replied.

"It's reassuring then, noting that at least *some* of my kin's wisdom resides within you." Fargon waited for me to be seated comfortably. "I must admit, Amat, you are further along in your powers than I initially anticipated. Particularly in your ability to alter time. I trust there's been at least one occasion where it hasn't been as reliable as you're typically used to, jolting in and out of its flow."

"Aside from when I was first learning how to use it, yes. In Irenole, where you and I met for the first time, though, not formally," I replied.

"Yes, it is an event that we call splincing. It is something that occurs from straining your atoms when they split and expand too far apart from one another that they need to function normally for a time. Especially if, for instance, you've witnessed severs in the timeline while in altered time," said Fargon.

"You seem to know a lot about what my limits are with altered time," I replied.

"A lucky guess; it is one of several complexities of the altered time power. Few have been able to master it."

"Like you?" I asked.

"Most certainly." Fargon paused. "I've been informed that in the past Galizian year, you have made attempts to establish a dialogue with my kin, most notably on that Isle you referred to as Irenole. You may recall a Zelton came before you shortly after your initial arrival."

"Let me guess, it was you," I said.

"Yes, and it was my first impression of you. But based on your little outburst a few hours ago that landed you in here, I'm curious as to whether establishing a dialogue remains a priority," replied Fargon.

I took my time before answering, hunching my shoulders forward as I stared down at my feet.

We are one and the same Amat. The reflection stretched his words.

No. I replied with a heavy sigh.

"It does not invigorate my spirit as it once did. What I shared with you, about my family being lost, is true. Now that they're gone, I have nothing left to fight for, nothing to compel me even to seek justice against the Diramal. Vengeance alone, is not enough to go on living for," I said.

"I am deeply sorry for your loss, Amat. I don't lie to you when I say I can sense your sorrow. Empathy on a level of the soul is another attribute of my kin. There're no words to describe how it feels… except that your internal world has shattered," Fargon said.

I did not reply, not out of stubbornness, but because I simply wasn't ready to address the pain Fargon's words had raised.

"I can help to ease that pain, if you'll let me."

I raised my head, slightly.

"How?" I queried.

"I need your expressed permission first. Open yourself to me, create a space for your pain and I shall show you."

I considered a moment and nodded. I let go of my exhausting effort to suppress my pain, allowing it to surface in my heart. Tears started to fill my eyes and my fingers grasped the edge of the block so vigorously that my nails scraped against the stone surface. Just before I felt myself burst into a sorrowful fury, I detected a shift in my heart. Like a spastic nerve movement, I stiffened at the sudden relief I felt. I had not been spared of all of it, but it was enough to lighten my mood. In the same instance, I heard Fargon inhale deeply, squeal, and moan all within moments of each other. The next she started crying, at least I thought she was. Her voice shivered on every exhale and caught on every inhale. Some time passed before I heard Fargon take her first alleviated breaths and settled.

"I have taken on as much as I can bear for now. I sense you feel the relief of it," said Fargon.

I sighed, heavily.

"I must admit, I do," I replied.

A rectangular outline of the wall to my left lowered itself into the ground as Fargon stood there, straight and strong.

"I'm glad," she said.

"Thank you." It was hard for me to put aside my pride, but I couldn't let it go unsaid.

It was then I noticed a long gash at Fargon's chest that wasn't there before, from last I saw her.

"How… did I do that?" I asked

Fargon glanced from the scar back up to me.

"You did, yes, just before I knocked you out," Fargon replied.

"But I don't remember—"

"You wouldn't. I used a variation of altered time called nīving; the ability to actively reverse a person or object's matter and movements as they happened, to a point. In our quarrel your movements were growing increasingly faster, so much that I failed to keep up and should you have landed your follow-up blow after this…" Fargon gestured to her scar, "you would have killed me."

I sighed heavily, holding a silence.

"I am sorry," it took all the sympathy I could muster to speak those words.

Fargon nodded, as she placed her right hands over the center of her chest and gracefully swung them out to me.

"What does that gesture mean?" I asked.

"It means, I willingly pass onto you, the strength of my spirit, in what yours lacks. It is not a gesture that is returned in the same instance it is given, however; to do so would be marked as an offense to the giver," said Fargon.

I nodded.

"I understand," I replied.

"We've moved since last we spoke. I've taken you somewhere I'd like to show you. Somewhere that may reignite your inner will. Would you accompany me in peace, so that I might show you?"

I took a deep breath, suppressing the creeping whispers of my reflection's protest.

"I will," I said.

Fargon waved her hand at the restraints on my wrist as they faded.

"Come, then."

I walked at Fargon's side willingly and at no point did I ever consider raising my fist to her. She sensed this; I could tell by her calm stride. It wasn't a trust so much as it was an unspoken understanding between the two of us, after what she did for me.

But were any among these savages so gracious to the members of our own kin that the Zeltons have supposedly harbored? A whisper of the reflection managed to break through my mental barriers.

"The surviving members of my kin, may I see them?" I asked.

"You will, with time. But they are not who I take you to now," Fargon spoke softly, yet swiftly.

"So, you are taking me to *someone*, then?" I asked.

Fargon shrugged.

"More or less. Where I take you to now is a place that has a sacred bond with your soul as a human. After you have experienced what I've in store for you, however, there will be one whom you'll be met with," said Fargon.

"Who?" I asked.

"You'll see; he has waited lifetimes to meet with you," said Fargon.

I wasn't sure what was meant by that. But I held my tongue from begging further understanding. As it would all surely make sense with time.

We arrived at the main deck of Fargon's ship. She did not enter immediately but turned to me and expressed a reassuring gesture. Raising her left arms to the deck, I took the lead, walking toward the grand glass screen that revealed our current location. I could feel their eyes shifting onto me, as the other Zeltons in the dimly lit room were momentarily distracted from their duties by my presence. Outside the ship was a planet that would have made Galiza seem a small pebble. Judging by the distance we kept from the planet, the Zeltonian ship could hardly be considered a speck of dust next to this colossal body.

In the background, many light years away, rested a stretch of a teal nebula with scattered stars, too few to seem worthy of such a large canvas of space. Though the planet seemed to get sufficient light from its silver star, the planet was clearly desolate. Its surface was a dark gray. It was dead, though somehow, a subconscious connection reached out to me from it. Willing me to step closer until I came before the end of the deck and took this barren world into full perspective.

Abruptly, the Zeltonian ship eased its course toward the planet, but I had hardly noticed at the time. Whatever essence that rested dormant on this planet had become more and more active to my conscience as we drifted closer. It started as whispers, so soft. They did not layer over one another, but they spoke so gently that I couldn't make sense of anything they said, except maybe a phrase here and there.

What came next, were the envelopments of countless arms about my limbs, wrapping and then sliding themselves away. Especially about my shoulders, so much so that the sensation compelled me to reach out in kind. Having opened myself to whatever presence existed here, my fingertips started to feel something brush over them, into them, past my skin and deep into my cells. Slowly, my fingertips glowed a vibrant orange. The light had slowly seeped into my nervous system, spanning over each side of my hands, and continued to pass across my wrists.

It was an energy. At least, that's how it seemed at first. It had brightened my mood; an overwhelming flush of excitement came over me. The light continued to illuminate my arms, radiating through my clothes. On and on the energy seeped into me, facilitating me with the growing strength of a thousand strong men and women every passing moment. The voices at this rate had become somewhat clearer, louder, but their speeches had also started to lap over one another, with a sense of eagerness in their tones. It sounded like they wished to ask something of me, all of them. Each question was identical to the last, though, rephrased in some way or other.

The light continued to reach over my shoulders and just before it crossed my chest, their voices became clear as day, all meshed in unison: *"He shall be mine!"* They spoke, as the light seeped into my heart. I tensed, cursed, and curled my body as I felt the sense of the many souls I had invited onto myself, fighting for dominion over my body. Not to mention each of their burdens, each of their lunacies, each of their torments. I found myself wrenching my body as I stumbled here and there, screaming, laughing, gasping as the Zeltonian ship started to pull away. The further we got from the planet, the less the raging spirits burdened me.

When at last they had left me completely, I fell to a knee and caught my breath. Slowly, Fargon stepped to my side, placing a hand on my shoulder. I shrugged her touch off and sprung to my feet, giving myself some space. Fargon raised her hands, trying to ease me, as I collected myself.

"What was that?" I growled.

"The planet is called Stargline, and you must *never* dare to venture any closer to it than we brought you. It is the home of your kin, the first you had established for yourselves." Fargon paused to let that sink in. "What you felt just now was but a taste of the many souls that couldn't escape the wrath of Drakkar, during your kin's last major conflict with the Vix. In your last stand against them, you were still at the peak of your strength, though not so much in numbers. And while Drakkar could not find a way to convert your kin to his side, he found a way to scar your souls, to dim your light. Leaving those on the planet vulnerable to a mass unfolding of his power. To this day they remain in a state of eternal suffering. The rest of you, who weren't directly impacted by this attack, were changed in a multitude of ways.

"Hence the reason why I brought you here. To show the full extent of what Drakkar has done to your kin and with even greater power at his disposal, it cannot be determined for certain what horrible fates would await the rest of the Hanu and the cosmos combined if we allow him to win. And should you choose to join us, here and now, my kin can shield your presence from Drakkar while you are prepared to face him," said Fargon.

I was about to speak but held my tongue when I heard shy footsteps coming nearer from behind Fargon. My eyes shifted onto a figure dressed in a neon-yellow suit that covered the whole being's body. It bore a pair of heavy boots that clanked against the floor, every step. It was hard to tell on account of the suit being somewhat baggy, but the being appeared to have a very lean physique about himself and something branching at the crown of its head.

"Ah," exclaimed Fargon, as she looked over at the being. "There you are. Amat, you might have remembered I mentioned that the Vix and Varx had either wiped out and or converted all our mortal creations, but one. That *one* stands before you now. His name is—"

"Thrazine," the being broke in. Fargon and Thrazine shared a glance. "My name is Thrazine Kwei." Thrazine walked up to me, awkwardly, stretching down a helpful hand. "I've been waiting a very, *very* long time to see you, Amat."

Something in his voice suggested a strange familiarity, but I couldn't guess how. His voice was aged, and his aura seemed ancient. Taking his hand after a moment's hesitation, Thrazine showed little struggle in lifting me to my feet.

"And what has you so excited for my arrival, Thrazine Kwei?" I asked.

"That all depends on how you answer Fargon's next question," replied Thrazine, turning to Fargon.

"Amat, I have told you things that you are no doubt still processing the weight of. I have exposed you to extensions of your abilities that you may yet be capable of. As well as the conniving schemes your kin has been subject to, by the most formidable force in the cosmos. I kneel before you..." Fargon said, taking a knee. "And I beg you, as the only hope remaining to the Hanu, to the universe, will you stand for us, against Drakkar and his agents?"

I glanced around the room; the other Zeltons had also risen from their seats to kneel before me and await my answer. Thrazine did the same, easing his way to the ground. I stepped slowly up to Fargon. The other Zeltons in the room motioned to place their hands on the weapons at their sides. I reached my hand down to Fargon; she took it and rose to her feet. I looked her dead in the eyes and said: "We must stand together. You should be warned; even now while I have considered all you have told me and acknowledged your integrity, there is an evil that pollutes my mind. A flaw that in my present state makes me unfit for the task you require. And I will need help."

Fargon put a reassuring hand on my shoulder, flexing her pincers in a pleased manner.

"You shall have it," Fargon replied.

"Then it is decided," said Thrazine. "That is, if you have made this decision wholeheartedly?"

"I have," I replied.

"Then I will look forward to guiding you in this path you've laid out. For I have seen what becomes of your actions in the climax of the creation war," said Thrazine.

"How can you know; what past do you have that rests in my future?" I asked.

Thrazine gave a light chuckle.

"You shall have to discover that for yourself, Mai'Sahara Reinosso."

"Mai'Sahara Reinosso," the Zeltons chanted as they placed their right hands over their chests and gently swung them out to me.

Epilogue
(Blick)

I awoke, both my arms tied to separate pillars by plasma restraints. My brow was thick with sweat, as my body leaned forward, with my wrists burning from the strain of the plasma shackles. Pouncing to my feet with a gasp once the pain finally caught on with me. I took in the surroundings of the long chamber I resided in, and before long, I recognized its features.

I'm... I'm in a Stellavar. The plating outside is sound, that must mean we made it off world. But... oh no, Amat's family—

My train of thought was interrupted when a doorway was opened further down the chamber, followed by the sound of women in a struggle. One cried out in pain, asking for her mother.

"Yank my daughter like that again and I will bite your throat out!" an older woman barked, followed by the sound of a slap and a scream.

"Mom!" a young woman howled.

The older woman spat and said: "It's alright, Lia, just try to keep up with them."

"I want Amat!" cried the little girl.

"Leave them be, you ruthless *gumplars*. We're not going anywhere," said Mae.

Mae... Mae! Lara, Lia, Judi. They're alive!

Amat's family was brought before me and thrown down against the wall. Though, to their eyes, the room was too dark, and they were too concerned for the safety of each other to notice me. The Varx shackled the girls in plasma restraints at the wrists and ankles and left the chamber.

"Lia, baby, are you alright?" Judi whispered as Lia cried. Her face was bruised from what might have been several blows to her face in the time it took them to get down here.

"Criptouses!" I called. Only Judi and Lia were startled by my cry. "It's alright, it's Blick. I'm restrained at the other side of the chamber. See the plasma shackles?"

Their eyes battled to locate the shackles' dim lighting.

"Yes, we see you, just barely," said Lara.

"Good," I said, as I took in their features from afar. Aside from Judi's bruised face, Lia was clutching her shoulder, and there was a bit of blood draining from Mae's lip. "How's your shoulder, Lia?" I asked.

"It hurts," she replied.

"Lara, can you check to see if it's dislocated?" I asked.

"How can you see her shoulder is hurting when we can barely see you?" asked Mae.

"That doesn't matter, just, Lara, please, check it," I replied.

Lara, who already sat beside Lia's injured arm, shifted to her side.

"Here, let me see your shoulder, Lia," said Lara, as she removed Lia's hand and felt around her shoulder. "Nothing feels out of place, but... Lia, I'm going to press a little, right here and see if it hurts, okay?"

"No," Lia cried, swiping at Lara's hand.

"Here, wait, I'm not going to press too hard, I just need to see something." As Lara pressed around Lia's shoulder, she hit a point that made her younger sister squeal. "I'm sorry, Lia, it's sensitive there?"

"Yes," Lia cried.

"She may have a sprain, in her shoulder, but it feels fine otherwise," said Lara.

"And what about the rest of you?" I asked.

The girls glanced at one another before answering.

"We're fine. And yourself?" Asked Judi.

"I'll be alright. Just a little worn is all," I replied.

"Where are we?" asked Lara.

"We're in a stell—one of those submerged starships Amat mentioned in the past. Judging by the look of things, somewhere deep in engineering," I replied.

"Do you think he'll be alright? Amat?" asked Lia.

"Lia, your brother is a man of great cunning and strength. Whatever it is he's occupied with now, he will resolve it and find us," replied Judi.

"I meant, do you think he'll be alright after he finds out that we're gone and with the way it was orchestrated, he thinks we're dead?" asked Lia.

Judi sighed, as if she hadn't considered that.

"His will shall drive him through whatever sorrow he's confronted with, until he discovers the truth," she replied.

243

A brief silence fell over the room.

"Your mother's right, Lia," Mae said, as she took Judi's hand. "Amat will find a way to us."

Lia grimaced

"Not after he's lost everything he fought to protect. We were, after all, everything that kept him going, his family," said Lia.

"He still has Log and Olson," said Judi.

Lia glanced in her mother's direction and shrugged.

"Blick, when you mentioned where we were," said Lara, "you were about to refer to the ship as... something. A Stell? Do you know what this thing is called?"

I didn't answer immediately, but I couldn't keep it that way forever, any more than I could lie to them, after having gained their trust.

"I do... what I was about to say initially was the ship model, a Stellavar," I replied.

"A Stellavar. And how would you know that for certain?" Lara persisted.

Again, I hesitated.

"I... I... there's a lot that hardly anyone knows about me—"

I was cut short when the sound of the hatch creaked open, and a set of voices barked down the corridor. Before I processed who they were, Lia said: "Log and Olson."

"Oh, Anua, guide my son," prayed Judi.

"It was you, wasn't it, one of your kind piloting that ship that pushed Amat into the core of that alien craft!" blurted Olson.

His words were followed by a loud punch that echoed in the corridor and the sound of a Varx speaking his native language. *Sounds like Klivon, Olson would be wise to keep his lips sealed around their kin.* Log spat and growled.

"I'll make you bleed for Amat's death, *each* of you," Olson roared, as they came around the corner.

The Klivon socked Olson so hard that his body bent and lifted off the ground slightly, forcing the air out of his lungs.

"Leave my brother alone!" Log barked.

The Klivon swiftly turned, punched Log in the face, and proceeded to push Olson forward, yanking him from the ground and against the wall, beside Mae. Olson was seated at her side and the two Varx placed plasma restraints on both brothers. It was then that *He* arrived.

Even Log and Olson muted their grunting as his footsteps filled the room. Each of the girls held their eyes on him, Judi and Mae with scowls. Lara stiffened and Lia was certainly intimidated in her own way as well.

The fizer at his forearm rang and the Diramal promptly answered it, lifting it to eye level.

"Diramal, sir." I could hear her voice from across the room: Quavek.

"Report," replied the Diramal.

"Per your orders, we've taken Rogen, MgKonnol, and Quim in custody aboard the Ganaborm."

The Diramal nodded.

"Keep them restrained until we reach Serakis," said the Diramal, as he disconnected the feed.

With his back to me, the Diramal spoke in a sound tone to the Criptouses. "Wonderful to be seeing you all again." I could sense the sinister smirk on his face as he turned his attention to Mae. "Though, I don't think you and I have had the pleasure of meeting face to face, Io-Pac Kalbrook—"

"You turn your glance away from her, you bastard. You look at me," said Judi. Slowly the Diramal shifted his attention onto her. "Did you kill my son?"

The Diramal brought his hands together at his front and sighed, leaning his head back. "Not I, no. But he is dead, that much I know," the Diramal said softly.

Lia did her best to hold back the tears, but before long, she broke and wept as Lara hooked her arms around her younger sister. Tears trailed passively down Lara's face. Mae clenched her fists as both she and Judi stared up at the Diramal. Olson motioned his hand over Mae's fists; she flinched her head toward him as he shook his own to her. Log stared blankly at the ground, his body limp with helplessness.

"First my husband…" Judi's voice broke mid-sentence as she tried to collect herself. "Then his brother, Gordon, and his wife, Sally… and now, my only son. What reason do you have to hold such hate against our family?"

245

The Diramal eased his way down to Judi's level. He reached his hand out to her face, gently placing his fingers against her jaw.

"It isn't hate… the reason is no longer relevant now, regarding Amat, who was without doubt *your* son. But Bod, he was just a figure, come to take on a role, for a man who has long since been dead."

Judi grimaced and stiffened.

"What does that—"

"All the more reason to let them go," I broke in, over Lara. "Leave them out of what's to come."

The Diramal turned toward me and stood.

"And take them where?" The Diramal walked steadily toward me, taking his time with every step. "To the Zeltons?" The Diramal chuckled.

"Their family has been through enough. Let them live their last days among the Zeltons; they deserve that much," I replied.

The Diramal shook his head.

"Do you have any idea what Drakkar would do if I allowed that to happen?" the Diramal whispered, low enough for only me to hear.

"I don't care what he'll do to me, so long as these good people get to—"

"*You* don't care…" the Diramal raised his finger to me, whispering harshly. "Do you have any idea what the events of the past few years have all been about? What any of this is all about?!" the Diramal roared, gesturing back to Amat's family.

"You never looked out for me," I said.

"No?!" The Diramal had quieted his voice once again. "Then why have I allowed the purity of your mother that remains dormant inside you to go unscathed by Drakkar's touch?" The Diramal batted his finger at me. "Think about that."

Footsteps echoed from up the corridor of a pair of Varx, each one holding large items, half the size of themselves.

"Ah, perfect timing," said the Diramal, as he met with the Varx and unraveled the possession of the humans and the Vix combined. I pulled against my restraints until they burned my flesh.

"No!" The Diramal flicked his attention to me. "Don't do it," I begged.

The Diramal only grimaced as he took, first the human and then the Vix possessions, placing them before the Criptouses, illuminating the room slightly.

"No!" I barked, as I marched and pulled against the restraints, ignoring the pain of my sizzling flesh.

"What is this?" asked Olson.

"What's happening?" followed Lia.

Smokey shadows started to emerge from the possessions.

"I don't know, just hold onto me," replied Lara.

"Blick?!" blurted Log.

The Shadows started to form a shifting figure that stood tall over the family

"Blick, what is that?!" asked Mae.

"Girls, come here!" shouted Judi, as she arched her body over them.

Their screams and shouts finally started to overlap one another and became too much for me to comprehend what they were saying.

"Stop!" I yelled.

The Diramal's shoulders rose and fell at my scream, refusing to acknowledge me as Drakkar slowly swung an arm over each of the Criptouses. Dark, thin clouds seeped into their eyes, unveiling terrible horrors and unthinkable pain. Illusions that made even Olson and Log give out haunting wails.

"Stop it! Daaaad!" I howled.

Don't judge what you don't understand
Seek to understand what is unknown and misunderstood
Only in understanding can reason be found, and decisions made…

Photo taken by JingJing Huntley

About the Author

James McGettigan is a young, ambitious writer and filmmaker. He started writing this series when he was eleven years old, in early 2012. At the age of twenty-three he's managed to put together three complete books and has dozens of others in the works, in various fictional genres. He's also gaining an immense amount of experience in the domain of filmmaking, working with various artists, like the Trestles, Lyndon-Enow, Goofee Jay; producing his own original content and in the midst of putting together a comedy TV series. He's currently studying at the Academy of Art in San Francisco to get his BA in Video Editing and has intentions of one day converting the Altered Moon series into a film franchise, among other stories he's currently working on.

The Author would also like to express his sincerest thanks to the readers for supporting this series that has been ten-plus years in the making. He would also like to invite the readers to share their thoughts and leave reviews of his books on the online platforms on which they are sold. This would be greatly appreciated and further support the author in his ability to publish the many stories he has in store for the world. Thank you.

Author's Social Media

Instagram: @seamus_eiteagain
Twitter: @james_mcgetti22
TikTok: @james_alan_mcgettigan
LinkedIn: https://www.linkedin.com/in/james-mcgettigan-334140174/
YouTube (Stories of The Dust Cosmos):
https://www.youtube.com/@StoriesofTheDustCosmos/videos

Special Acknowledgements

Judy McGettigan
Anthony McGettigan
Fabiana Lezama Granado
Elias Elmouttaqi
Jason Frank Jr.
Bilal Memon
Jacqui Corn-Uys

Glossary

Aquamerion: A military aquatic vehicle, capable of reaching the deepest depths of Galiza's oceans. A rare model, completely undetectable, highly deadly in sea combat. It utilizes the same technology as a sift suit in that the Aquamerion forms a current around its body to propel it forward across the ocean, through the concentration of bismuth in Galiza's oceans, among other elements that compose a liquid called Rinzen.

Brilzer: an advanced first-aid mechanism, packed full of nano-foam that easily fills and rapidly repairs any critical gashes and gaping wounds in one's anatomy. Predominantly used and manufactured by the Vix and Varx.

Cho'Zai: The most blessed soldiers on Anua's scorched Galiza. Born with natural and rare dark red irises, they are bred for war from the day they are brought into the world. They are sworn to the Diramal before country and civilian. Their obedience lies solely with, he or she who presumes the rank. Complicating their own ranking, they are considered less skilled than an Alpha but fiercer brawlers; they do not answer to any rank that is below the Diramal, but they cannot govern themselves.

Dailagon: Diamond-shaped craft, equipped with anti-gravity technology which can allow the humans to survive an aerial fight with the Zeltons, if they are hyper-aware and extremely tactical. But anti-gravity cannot match the speed of a quantum field and for most humans, aerial combat with the Zeltons is an almost assured death.

Diramal: An autocrat who holds executive authority over the Utopion people and soil. They decide whether or not to declare war, attend foreign meetings, and maintain foreign relations. There is almost no limit to their power and authority, so long as they don't get caught doing the wrong thing. They have final say on what the public is allowed to know and remain oblivious to and thus they keep close relations with members from I.I.D. and M.I.S.T.

Dövar: Someone who has been dead for under an hour (usually a soldier) and been brought back from the dead via the nano-regenerators. They are often very reserved, monotone, and demonstrate a severe lack of emotion and overall feeling. They operate and hold the aura of someone who is only half alive. But there are a few exceptions to this kind of behavior among the Dövar.

Důlabega Quadrant Incident: A documented exchange between the Diramal and the Zeltons dating back to the time of the deep space S.E.F. missions, carried out by Jinn-hid Bod Criptous and the Diramal. Not much can be taken from the content of the exchange but there's a clear indication of a slaughter, somehow carried out by the Diramal himself.

E.S.P. 101 (Electric Shock-put 101): A human weapon that shoots small, concentrated globes of lightning, fired at high speeds and held in three-by-three-inch square quartz crystals. The rounds can and will tear through any material—unless the gun is preset to "stun"—the more dense the material the round hits, however, the more quickly the electric entanglement of the round dissipates.

Fauchard: A shafted weapon, with a long narrow velvet crystal extending up and down the middle of the central blade that exerts a small but effective fatigue against any who disturb it. The blade of this weapon is long, narrow at the bottom half of its extension, broadens slightly at the top half with a sharp crescent top and a thin edge.

Fé'Harkedür: The name of Zothra's species.

Fizer: A multipurpose, tactical device registered to each Utopian militia body—with a few exceptions—embedded in their forearms. Its purposes extend from granting the user grids of their current location, communication, and more.

Hanu: A term that refers to the five creators of the universe as a whole.

Ho-Jinn: A higher-end ranked officer. They can serve on court-martials and hold commands of hundreds of soldiers among the ranks of Gromrolls and Krollgrums.

Io-Pac: A low-level officer rank. They ensure safety and efficiency during missions.

I.I.D. (Information of Interests Department): A Utopion government agency, responsible for tracking and filing all military operations, as well as economic and scientific data.

Jinn: A higher-end ranked officer. They can lead brigades in the thousands, among the Dukas and Alphas. They report directly to the Jinn-hid and they may also serve on a court-martial. Their responsibilities lie mostly in overseeing battle strategy across all brigades outside their own.

Jinn-hid: The second most powerful ranked officer in the Utopion military and the country. Only one may hold the rank at a time. They report directly to the Diramal and it is not normal for the Jinn-hid to command brigades or train soldiers, in addition to their standard duties. Both Amat and Bod Criptous are peculiar in this way. They are the Diramal's spokesman, advisor, and remain in close contact with the Jinns. They hold the power to reserve the Utopion armies to organize brigades overseas. For instance, if the Diramal declares war on another country, the Jinn-hid decides how many soldiers are sent off where and when and how many remain on home soil. In theory, they know everything the Diramal does.

Kaw: Human law enforcement.

Koyůt: Lower air defense rank. They are responsible for piloting and manning the weaponry of the Fades.

Laquar: A durable, liquid shielding used for a variety of purposes. Formed in part by liquid oxygen, plasma, muon particle, and a high enough volume of melted magnetite that it creates a stable force field from liquid and gaseous elements. In addition to its being composed of liquid oxygen and plasma, in the form of a suit or domed shielding at the bottom of the ocean, the two continuously counteract one another, to provide its shelled interior with gaseous oxygen. Metals, or sharp edges will easily break the integrity of the substance. However, the substance is incredibly durable that in the event it's torn or broken, so long as it's not totally obliterated, it will *rapidly* reform itself in a matter of microseconds.

Magplaz: A human weapon that shoots concentrated magma rounds, contact with such a round will pierce and melt through almost any material, with the exception of a few materials and rare metals. Nano-metal specifically—which the quantum suits of the humans are composed of—can offer strong resistance to a single magma round, as the nanites themselves can effectively resist the melting temperatures. Consecutive hits from magma rounds would lead to death if not excruciating injuries of any soldier wearing a quantum suit, let alone anyone who wouldn't be wearing one.

M.I.S.T. (Military Investigative Sciences and Technology): A military corporation, responsible for the investigation and development of advanced technologies and weaponry, much of which is classified. They do, however, contribute to a lot of the progress of the Utopion society as a whole and the Utopion allies, creating cleaner, safer means of transportation, health care and energy usage.

Neuro-chips: A rectangular device that ranges in size, varying on the code; code nine can take up almost a tenth of the brain's anatomy and compensate for the functions in either hemisphere of which it is placed. A standard code one neuro-chip is small and takes on a thin, webbed shape, spanning over the top of the brain. Installed at birth and designed to grow in part with the brain. Any neuro-chip upgrade is used as a means of repercussion in the Utopion society, each one further limiting an individual's freedom and control over their own biology, physiology, thoughts, and emotions.

Pac: A moderate rank for an officer. They hold command over the base armory, and oversee inventory and rations. Their responsibilities extend to ensuring that Fades are loaded with proper equipment and accessories before a launch. They can also serve as training officers among various lower ranks.

Pac-Qua: A moderate rank for an officer rank. They hold the immediate command over base troops when higher-ranking officials are not promptly available.

Qi'val: A rank shared between the Varx: Quavek, Xaizar, and Voruke, among the Diramal's best and Zothra's lieutenants. When they operate outside the immediate command of Zothra and or the Diramal, they can control fleets of Varx at a time, but never Vix.

Quantum Fade: A perilous side effect that can threaten the user of any and all quantum suits. While the suits can facilitate a quantum field for humans in a battle against the Zeltons, their biology is not equipped with the natural and stabilizing Meceuro atoms. Found naturally throughout the anatomy of the Zeltons, the Meceuro atoms split, expand, and bounce off one another at high velocities. Not only does this allow the invaders to alter time at any depth they so desire, it holds their organs, bones, blood vessels, skin, everything in place, so that they may move at great speeds without the risk of harming themselves. The QS-25 allows the humans to match these speeds, most of the time, moving at speeds beyond sound; Amat himself can reach greater. But the difference between the QS-25 and the Meceuro atom itself is that the suit can only protect its users from external threats and if its limits are pushed too far, there's nothing stopping a human heart from imploding or lethal and rapid brain hypoxia.

Reikag: The head of base security. This officer has special clearance and access to various levels of classified information. They enforce laws and can pass judgement among civilians and military personnel until a proper trial can be arranged.

Shadach'mar: A Zeltonian term that has no direct translation to the human language but has a similar meaning to the context of the phrase "Shadow Scar." It pertains to an association to an individual who has a tainted connection to and or a heavy influence under Drakkar and his servants.

Sphike: The name of the smaller Zeltonian combat craft.

Skiv: Human scavengers, the majority of humanity over the course of the war with the Zeltons, abandoned by the various militias of the world. Common people with no tie to military personnel. They spend most of their time starving, huddled away in the ruins of cities and towns, trapped in the crossfire. They're lucky if they can find a few days' worth of food at a time.

Splice: A hilted device that, when flicked, forms a short, nano-metal blade. A weapon that was developed during the rise of regenerative nano-tech, in the first year of the war of the Zelton/Human war.

'Versing/nīving: An ability that allows Amat to reverse the movements of any being he directs his palm toward. Amat is the only individual he is aware of who is capable of this power. Amat refers to the ability as 'versing, up to the point of learning what the power's true term is: nīving from Fargon.

Vi-warmigol: An organic bio-weapon in the form of an insect. They were developed by M.I.S.T. researchers during the time frame of the Utopion/Afeikita War, as a means of infecting open wounds and killing off incapacitated members of the Kintabú alliance. Unfortunately, production of the weapon was discontinued and its use was made illegal when the rotting corpses that had been infected spread a plague that nearly wiped out more than half the Afeikitan continent.

Vorüm'Qij: The true rank of Zothra, the Diramal's second. In lack of the Diramal's physical presence, he holds command of whichever Vix and Varx who accompany him. He is the only bearer of the rank.

Vormaul: A rank among the Varx, commonly associated with hive breed Varx, who operate as "Queen" or "King" figureheads. Telepathically synced and governing over a mass amount of hive Varx—lesser creations that never surpassed primitive psyches prior to their conversion to Drakkar's taint—at one time.

Vourtikah: Shrouds of star cores, man-sized liquid light bubbles, made from the cores of dying stars. When touched by a human—a once luminous race of beings—these oval-shaped objects illuminate with structures that are a unique result of the individual's interaction with it. Those infected with the evil of Drakkar, can impose a similar effect onto these vessels, as evil is its own form of raw power, opposite of light.

Warv: A general Utopion term for Skivs who have scavenged their own means of self-defense, taking up armor and weaponry off dead soldiers. They launch their fronts not only against the invaders but the militia as well. They despise the militia and fear the mysterious Shadow Scar, whom the Warvs have associated with the militia under some kind of twisted, secret genetic modification program. They look out only for themselves and will very rarely take on newcomers. By the third year into the war, they have become formidable in their fighting skill and not a threat to be taken lightly.